"I need to know [...] wife.

"Not just physically, but on every level emotionally, [...] I never want to see loathing in her eyes when she [loo]ks at me, as my mother so often looked at my [fath]er. And I never wish to treat her with disdain the [way] my father treated my mother. I will not have a [ma]rriage like that."

[A] vein pulsed at the side of Thierry's brow and while [his] voice had remained level, Mila could see the [p]ain in his eyes as he turned to face her again.

[I] want you to teach me how to make my wife fall in [lo]ve with me so deeply she will never look to another [m]an for her fulfillment. Can you do this?"

Thierry stared into the glowing amber of his cour[te]san's eyes and willed her to give him the answer he [cr]aved.

"You want me to teach you to seduce your fiancée's [m]ind and her senses, and then her body?"

["I] do."

Her eyes shone brightly as she smiled.

"Your demand is not quite what I expected but I will [d]o what you ask."

* * *

Arranged Marriage, Bedroom Secrets
is part of the Courtesan Brides duet:
Her pleasure is at his command!

ARRANGED MARRIAGE, BEDROOM SECRETS

BY
YVONNE LINDSAY

All rights reserved including the right of reproduction in whole or in part in any form. This edition is published by arrangement with Harlequin Books S.A.

This is a work of fiction. Names, characters, places, locations and incidents are purely fictional and bear no relationship to any real life individuals, living or dead, or to any actual places, business establishments, locations, events or incidents. Any resemblance is entirely coincidental.

This book is sold subject to the condition that it shall not, by way of trade or otherwise, be lent, resold, hired out or otherwise circulated without the prior consent of the publisher in any form of binding or cover other than that in which it is published and without a similar condition including this condition being imposed on the subsequent purchaser.

® and ™ are trademarks owned and used by the trademark owner and/or its licensee. Trademarks marked with ® are registered with the United Kingdom Patent Office and/or the Office for Harmonisation in the Internal Market and in other countries.

First Published in Great Britain 2016
By Mills & Boon, an imprint of HarperCollins*Publishers*
1 London Bridge Street, London, SE1 9GF

© 2016 Dolce Vita Trust

ISBN: 978-0-263-91865-6

51-0616

Our policy is to use papers that are natural, renewable and recyclable products and made from wood grown in sustainable forests. The logging and manufacturing processes conform to the legal environmental regulations of the country of origin.

Printed and bound in Spain
by CPI, Barcelona

ROTHERHAM LIBRARY SERVICE	
B53104027	
Bertrams	20/05/2016
AF	£5.99
BSU	ROM

A typical Piscean, *USA TODAY* bestselling author **Yvonne Lindsay** has always preferred her imagination to the real world. Married to her blind-date hero and with two adult children, she spends her days crafting the stories of her heart, and in her spare time she can be found with her nose in a book reliving the power of love, or knitting socks and daydreaming. Contact her via her website, www.yvonnelindsay.com.

There are so many people who enrich my life but foremost are the members of my incredible family, so I dedicate this book to them.

One

"Isn't that you?"

Mila shoved an unruly lock of her long black hair off her face and looked up in irritation from the notes she'd been making.

"Is what me?" she asked her friend.

"On the TV, now!"

Mila turned her attention to the flat screen currently blaring the latest entertainment news trailers that so captivated her best friend and felt her stomach lurch. There, for all the world to see, were the unspeakably awful official photos taken at her betrothal to Prince Thierry of Sylvain seven years ago. Overweight, with braces still on her teeth and a haircut that had looked so cute on a Paris model and way less cute on an awkward eighteen-year-old princess—especially one who was desperately attempting to look more sophisticated and who had ended up, instead, looking like a sideshow clown. She shuddered.

"I know it doesn't look completely like you, but that *is*

you, isn't it? Princess Mila Angelina of Erminia? Is that really your name?" Sally demanded, one finger pointing at the TV screen while her eyes pinned Mila with a demanding stare.

There was no point in arguing. Hiding a cringe, Mila merely inclined her head. She looked back down at her notes for a thesis she'd likely never be permitted to complete, but her concentration was gone. How would her friend react to this news?

"You're going to marry a prince?"

Mila couldn't be certain if Sally was outraged because Mila was actually engaged to a prince, or because she'd never thought to let her best friend in on the secret of her real identity. She sighed and put her pen down. As an uncelebrated princess from a tiny European kingdom, she'd flown under the radar in the United States since her arrival seven years ago, but now it was clearly time to face the music.

She'd known Sally since their freshman year at MIT and, while her friend had sometimes looked a little surprised that Mila—or Angel as she was known here in the States—had a chaperone, didn't date and had a team of bodyguards whenever she went out, Sally had accepted Angel's quirks without question. After all, Sally herself was heiress to an IT billionaire and lived with similar, if not quite as binding, constraints. The girls had naturally gravitated to one another.

It was time to be honest with her friend. Mila sighed again. "Yes, I am Mila Angelina of Erminia and, yes, I'm engaged to a prince."

"And you're a princess?"

"I'm a princess."

Mila held her breath, waiting for her friend's reaction. Would she be angry with her? Would it ruin the friendship she so treasured?

"I feel like I don't even know you, but seriously, that's so cool!" Sally gushed.

Mila rolled her eyes and laughed in relief. Of all the things she'd anticipated coming from Sally's rather forthright mouth, that hadn't been one of them.

"I always had a feeling there were things you weren't telling me." Sally dropped onto the couch beside Mila, scattering her papers to the floor. "So, what's he like?"

"Who?"

It was Sally's turn to roll her eyes this time. "The prince of course. C'mon, Angel, you can tell me. Your secret's safe with me, although I am kind of pissed at you for not telling me about him, or who you really are, any time in, oh, the last seven years!"

Sally softened her words with a smile, but Mila could see that she was still hurt by the omission.

How did you explain to someone that even though you'd been engaged to a man for years, you barely even knew him? One formal meeting, where she'd been so painfully shy she hadn't even been capable of making eye contact with the guy, followed by sporadic and equally formal letters exchanged by a diplomatic pouch, didn't add up to much in the relationship stakes.

"I…I don't really know what he's like." Mila took in a deep breath. "I have Googled him, though."

Her friend laughed out loud. "You have no idea how crazy that just sounded. You're living a real life fairy tale, y'know? European princess betrothed from childhood—well, okay, the age of eighteen at least—to a reclusive neighboring prince." Sally sighed and clutched at her chest dramatically. "It's so romantic—and all you can say is that you've *Googled* him?"

"Now who sounds crazy? I'm marrying him out of duty to my family and my country. Erminia and Sylvain have hovered on the brink of war for the last decade and a half. My marriage to Prince Thierry is supposed to end all that—unite our nations—if you can believe it could be that simple."

"But don't you want love?"

"Of course I want love."

Her response hung in the air between them. Love. It was all Mila had ever wanted. But it was something she knew better than to expect. Groomed from birth as not much more than a political commodity to be utilized to her country's greatest advantage, she'd realized love didn't feature very strongly alongside duty. When it came to her engagement, her agreement to the union had never been sought. It had been presented to her as her responsibility—and she'd accepted it. What else could she do?

Meeting the prince back then had been terrifying. Six years older than her, well-educated, charismatically gorgeous and oozing confidence, he'd been everything she was not. And she hadn't missed the hastily masked look of dismay on his face when they'd initially been introduced. Granted, she hadn't looked her best, but it had still stung to realize she certainly wasn't the bride he'd hoped for and it wasn't as if he could simply tell everyone he'd changed his mind. He, too, was a pawn in their betrothal—a scheme hatched by their respective governments in an attempt to quell the animosity that continued to simmer between their nations.

Mila rubbed a finger between her eyebrows as if by doing so she could ease the nagging throb that had settled there.

"Of course I want love," she repeated, more softly this time.

She felt Sally's hand on her shoulder. "I'm sorry. I know I shouldn't joke."

"It's okay." Mila reached up and squeezed her friend's hand to reassure her.

"So, how come you came here to study? If peace was the aim, wouldn't they have wanted you two to marry as soon as possible?"

Again Mila pictured the look on Prince Thierry's face when he'd seen her. A look that had made her realize that if she was to be anything to him other than a representation of his duty, she needed to work hard to become his equal. She needed to complete her education and become a worthy companion. Thankfully, her brother, King Rocco of Erminia, had seen the same look on the prince's face and, later that night, when she'd tearfully appealed to him with her plan to better herself, he'd agreed.

"The agreement was that we'd marry on my twenty-fifth birthday."

"But that's at the end of next month!"

"I know."

"But you haven't finished your doctorate."

Mila thought of all the sacrifices she'd made in her life to date. Not completing her PhD would probably be the most painful. While her brother had insisted she at least include some courses in political science, the main focus of her studies had been environmental science—a subject that she'd learned was close to the prince's heart. After years of study, it was close to hers now, too. Not being able to stand before him with her doctorate in hand, so to speak, was a painful thought to consider, but it was something she'd just have to get over. She certainly hadn't planned on things taking this long, but being dyslexic had made her first few years at college harder than she'd anticipated and she'd had to retake a number of courses. As Mila formed her reply to her friend, Sally was suddenly distracted.

"Oh, he's so hot!"

Mila snorted a laugh. "I know what he looks like. I've Googled him, remember."

"No, look, he's on TV, now. He's in New York at that

environmental summit Professor Winslow told us about weeks ago."

Mila looked up so quickly she nearly gave herself whiplash. "Prince Thierry is here? In the US?"

She trained her gaze onto the TV screen and, sure enough, there he was. Older than she remembered him and, if it was humanly possible, even better looking. Her heart tumbled in her chest and she felt her throat constrict on a raft of emotions. Fear, attraction—longing.

"You didn't know he was coming?"

Mila tore her eyes from the screen and fought to inject the right level of nonchalance into her voice. "No, I didn't. But that's okay."

"Okay? You think that's *okay*?" Sally's voice grew shrill. "The guy travels how many thousand miles to the country where you've been living for years now and he can't pick up a phone?"

"He's obviously only in New York for a short while and I'm sure he'll have a strict timetable set in place. I'm over here in Boston—he can't exactly just drop in." She shrugged. "It's not like it matters, anyway. We're getting married in a little over four weeks' time."

Her voice cracked on the words. Even though she played at being offhand, deep down it had come as a shock to see him on the TV. Would it have killed him to have let her know he was coming to America?

"Hmph. I can't believe you're not seeing each other while he's here," Sally continued, clearly not ready to let go of the topic yet. "Don't you even want to see him?"

"He probably doesn't have time," Mila deflected.

She didn't want to go into what she did or didn't want when it came to Prince Thierry. Her feelings on the subject were too confusing, even for her. She'd tried to convince herself many times that love at first sight was the construction of moviemakers and romance novelists, but ever since the day of their betrothal, she had yearned for him with a longing that went deep into the very fabric of her being. Was that love? She didn't know. It wasn't as if she'd had any stellar examples during her childhood.

"Well, even if he hadn't told me he was coming here, I'd certainly make time to see him if he was mine."

Mila forced herself to laugh and to make the kind of comment Sally would expect her to make. "Well, he's not yours, he's mine—and I'm not sharing."

As she expected, Sally joined in with her mirth. Mila kept her eyes glued to the screen for the duration of the segment about Prince Thierry—and tried to ignore the commentary about herself. The reporters were full of speculation as to her whereabouts, which had been kept strictly private for the past several years. Though she realized, if Sally had put two and two together as to who she was, what was to say others wouldn't, also?

She clung to the hope that no one would think to connect the ugly duckling of her engagement photo with the woman she had become. No longer was she the timid young woman with a mouth too large for her face and chubby cheeks and thighs. Somewhere between nineteen and twenty she'd begun a miraculous late-blooming transformation. The thirty extra pounds of puppy fat had long since melted from her body—her features and her figure fining down to what she was now, still curvy but no longer overweight. And her hair, thank goodness, had grown long and straight and thick. The dreadful cropped cut and frizzy perm she'd insisted on in a vain attempt to look sophisticated before meeting the prince was now nothing more than a humiliating memory. And she'd finally developed the poise that had been sadly lacking when she was just a teenager.

Would her soon-to-be husband find her attractive now?

She hated to think he'd be put off by her, especially given how incredibly drawn *she* was to *him*.

Sally had been one hundred percent right that Prince Thierry was hot. And all through the broadcast she saw evidence of that special brand of charisma that he unconsciously exuded. Mila watched the way people in the background stopped and stared at the prince—drawn to him as if he was a particularly strong magnet and they were nothing but metal filings inexorably pulled into his field. She knew how they felt. It was the same sensation that had struck her on the day of their betrothal—not to mention since, whenever she'd seen pictures of him or caught a news bulletin on television when she was home on vacation back in Erminia.

She'd return there in just a few weeks. It was time to retrieve the mantle of responsibility she'd so eagerly, even if only temporarily, shrugged off and reassume her position.

She should be looking forward to it. Not only because of the draw she felt toward the prince, but because of what the marriage would mean to both of their countries. The tentative peace between her native Erminia and Sylvain had been shattered many years ago when Prince Thierry's mother had been caught, *in flagrante delicto*, with an Erminian diplomat. When both she and her lover had died in a fiery car crash fingers had pointed to both governments in accusation. Military posturing along the borders of their countries ever since had created its own brand of unrest within the populations. She'd understood that her eventual marriage to Prince Thierry would, hopefully, bring all that turmoil to an end—but she wanted something more than a convenient marriage. Was it too much to hope that she could make the prince love her, too?

Mila reached for the remote and muted the sound, ready to turn her attention back to her work, but Sally wasn't finished on the subject yet.

"You should go to New York and meet him. Turn up at the door to his hotel suite and introduce yourself," Sally urged.

Mila laughed, but the sound lacked any humor. "Even if I could get away from Boston unchaperoned, I wouldn't get past his security, trust me. He's the Crown Prince of Sylvain, the sole heir to the throne. He's important."

Sally rolled her eyes. "So are you. You're his fiancée, for goodness' sake. Surely he'd make time for you. And, as to Bernadette and the bruiser boys," Sally said, referring to Mila's chaperone and round-the-clock bodyguards, "I think I could come up with a way to dodge them—if you were willing to commit to this, that is."

"I couldn't. Besides, what if my brother found out?"

Sally didn't know that Mila's brother was also the reigning king of Erminia, but she was aware that Rocco had been her guardian since they lost their parents many years ago.

"What could he do? Ground you?" Sally snorted. "C'mon, you're almost twenty-five years old and you've spent the last seven years in another country gaining valuable qualifications you'll probably never be allowed to use. You have a lifetime of incredibly boring state dinners and stuff like that to look forward to. I think you're entitled to a bit of fun, don't you?"

"You make a good point," Mila answered with a wry grin. As much as Sally's words pricked at her, her friend was right. "What do you suggest?"

"It's easy. Professor Winslow said that if we wanted he could get us tickets to the sustainability lecture stream during the summit. Why don't we take him up on it? The summit starts tomorrow and there's a lecture we could *attend*," she said the latter word with her fingers in the air, mimicking quotation marks, "the next day."

"Accommodation will be impossible to find at this short notice."

"My family keeps a suite close to where they said the prince is staying. We could fly to New York by late afternoon tomorrow—Daddy will let me use his jet, I'm sure, especially if I tell him it's for my studies. Then we check into the hotel and you could suddenly *feel ill*." Sally hooked her fingers into mimed quotation marks again. "Bernie and the boys wouldn't need to be with you if you were tucked up in bed with a migraine, would they? We'll take a blond wig so you can look more like me. After a couple of hours, I'll pretend I'm going out but instead I'll go to your room and go to bed and pull the covers right up so if she checks on you she'll think you're out for the count. We'll swap clothes and you, looking like me, can just slip out for the evening. What do you say?"

"They'll never fall for it."

"It wouldn't hurt to try, though, would it? Otherwise when are you going to get a chance to see the prince again? At your wedding? C'mon, what's the worst that could happen?"

What was the worst that could happen? They'd get caught. And then what? More reminders of her station and her duty to her country. Growing up in Erminia constant lectures about her duty and reputation had been all she'd known, after all. But after living and attending college in the States for the past few years, Mila had enjoyed a taste—albeit a severely curtailed one—of the kind of freedom she hadn't even known she craved.

She weighed the idea in her mind. Sally's plan was so simple and uncomplicated it might just work. Bernadette was always crazy busy—even more so since she'd begun making plans for Mila's return to Erminia. A side jaunt to New York would throw her schedule completely out—if she even agreed to allowing it. But Mila still had the email from the professor saying how valuable attending the lecture would be. Mila knew she could put some emotional pressure on the chaperone who'd become more like a mother-figure to her and convince her to let her go.

"What's it going to be, Mila?" Sally prompted.

Mila reached her decision. "I'll do it."

She couldn't believe she'd said the words even as they came from her mouth, but every cell in her body flooded with a sense of anticipation. She was going to meet Prince Thierry. Or, at least, try to meet him.

"Great," Sally said, rubbing her hands together like the nefarious co-conspirator she was at heart. "Let's make some plans. This is going to be fun!"

Two

Dead.

The king was dead. Long live the king.

Oblivious to the panoramic twilight view of New York City as it sparkled below him, Thierry paced in front of the windows of his hotel suite in a state of disbelief.

He was now the King of Sylvain and all its domains—automatically assuming the crown as soon as his father had breathed his last breath.

A flutter of rage beat at the periphery of his thoughts. Rage that his father had slipped away now, rather than after Thierry had returned to his homeland. But it was typical of the man to make things awkward for his son. After all, hadn't he made a lifetime hobby of it? Even before this trip, knowing he was dying, his father had sent Thierry away. Perhaps he'd known all along that his only son would not be able to return before his demise. He'd never been a fan of emotional displays.

Not that Thierry would likely become emotional. The

king had always been a distant person in Thierry's life. Their interactions had been peppered with reminders of Thierry's duty to his country and his people and reprimands for the slightest transgression whether real or imagined. Yet, through the frustration and rage that flickered inside him, Thierry felt a swell of grief. Perhaps more for the relationship he had never had with his father, he realized, than the difficult one they'd shared.

"Sire?"

The form of address struck him anew. Sire—not Your Royal Highness or sir.

His aide continued, "Is there anything—?"

"No." Thierry cut off his aide before he could ask again what he could do.

Since the news had been delivered, his staff had closed around him—all too wary that they were now responsible for not the Crown Prince any longer, but the King of Sylvain. He could feel the walls closing in around him even as he paced. He had to get out. Get some air. Enjoy some space before the news hit worldwide headlines which, no doubt, it would within the next few hours.

Thierry turned to his aide. "I apologize for my rudeness. The news...even though we were expecting it..."

"Yes, sire, it has come as a shock to everyone. We all hoped he would rally again."

Thierry nodded abruptly. "I'm going out."

A look of horror passed across the man's features. "But, sire!"

"Pasquale, I need tonight. Before it all changes," Thierry said by way of explanation even though no explanation was necessary.

The reality of his new life was already crushing. He'd been trained for this from the cradle and yet it still felt as though he had suddenly become Atlas with the weight of the world on his shoulders.

"You will take your security detail with you."

Thierry nodded. That much, he knew, was non-negotiable, but he also knew they'd be discreet. Aside from the film crew that had caught him arriving at his hotel yesterday, his visit to the United States had largely gone untrumpeted. He was a comparatively small fry compared to the other heads of state from around the world who had converged on the city for the summit. That would all change by morning, of course, when news of his father's death made headlines. He hoped, by then, to be airborne and on his way home.

Thierry strode to his bedroom and ripped the tie from his neck before it strangled him. His elderly valet, Nico, scurried forward.

"Nico, a pair of jeans and a fresh shirt, please."

"Certainly, sire."

There it was again. That word. That one word that had created a gulf of distance between himself and his staff and, no doubt, the rest of the world with it. For the briefest moment, Thierry wished he could rage and snarl at the life he'd been dealt, but, as always, he capped the emotions that threatened to overwhelm him. He was nothing if not controlled.

A few moments later, after a brief shower, Thierry was dressed and waiting in his suite's vestibule for his security detail—all ready to go.

"It's cool out this evening, sire. You'll be needing these," Nico said.

The older man's hands trembled as he helped Thierry into a finely woven casual jacket and passed him a beanie and dark glasses. At the visible sign of his valet's distress, Thierry once again felt that sense of being crushed by the change to his life. Now, he was faced not only with his own emotions at the news of his father's death, but with those of his people. So far, his staff had only expressed their condolences to him. It was time he returned that consideration. He turned and allowed his gaze to encompass both Pasquale and Nico.

"Gentlemen, thank you for all your support. I know you, too, have suffered a great loss with the death of my father. You have been in service to my family for longer than I can remember and I am grateful to you. Should you need time to grieve, please know it is yours once we return home."

Both men spluttered their protestations as they assured him that they would take no leave. That it was their honor to serve him. It was as he'd expected, but that didn't mean they wouldn't carry a sense of loss deep inside.

"I mean it," he affirmed. "Nico, will you see to the packing? I believe our plane will be ready by 8 a.m."

The head of his security, Armaund, entered the suite with three of his team.

"Sire, when you're ready."

With a nod of thanks to Pasquale and Nico, Thierry headed for the door. Three security guards fell in formation around him as one went ahead to the private elevator that serviced this floor.

"We thought the side entrance would be best, sire. We can avoid the lobby that way and hotel security have swept for paparazzi already."

"Thank you, that's fine."

He felt like little more than a sheep with a herd of sheep dogs as they exited the elevator downstairs.

"Some space, please, gentlemen," Thierry said firmly as he picked up his pace and struck out ahead of his team.

He could sense they didn't like it, but as long as he didn't look as if he was surrounded by guards, he was relying on the fact that in a big city such as New York he'd soon become just another person on the crowded sidewalk. It was the team who would likely draw attention to him rather than his own position in the world.

Thierry rounded the corner and headed for the exit. Not far now and maybe he could breathe, really breathe for the first time since he'd heard the news.

"'Fun,' she said," Mila muttered under her breath as she walked the block outside the hotel for the sixth time that evening.

Once she'd overcome the sheer terror that had gripped her as she'd escaped Sally's family's hotel suite, anticipation had buoyed her all the way here. But she'd yet to feel that sense of fun that Sally had mentioned. Leaving the suite had been nerve-racking. She'd been sure that Bernadette or one of the guards would have seen past the blond wig she wore and realized that it wasn't Sally leaving the suite, but they'd only given her a cursory glance.

The walk to the prince's hotel hadn't been too bad, but it had given her too much time to think about what on earth she was doing here. And far too much time to begin to regret it—hence the circuits around the block. Any minute now she'd be arrested, she was sure of it. She'd already started getting sideways glances from more than one person.

She took a sip from the coffee she'd bought to steady her nerves and ducked into a doorway at the side of the hotel just as the skies opened with a sudden spring shower of rain. Great, she thought, as she watched the rain fall, making the streets slick and dark and seeming to emphasize just how alone she was at this exact moment, even with the tens of thousands of people who swirled and swelled around her. One of those people jostled her from behind, making her lurch and sending her coffee cup flying to the pavement. She cried out in dismay as some of the scalding liquid splashed on her hand.

"Watch it!" she growled, shaking the residue from her

stinging skin and brushing down the front of her—no, she corrected herself, Sally's—jacket.

So much for making a good impression, she thought. Wet, bewigged and now coffee-stained—she may as well quit and go home. This had been a ridiculous idea from start to finish and there'd be hell to pay if she got caught out.

"My apologies."

The man's voice came from behind her. It was rich and deep and sent a tingle thrilling down her spine. She wheeled around, almost bumping into him again as she realized he was closer to her than she'd anticipated.

"I'm sor—" she began and then she looked up.

The man stood in front of her, an apologetic smile curving sinfully beautiful lips. A dark beanie covered the top of his head, hiding the color of his hair, and he wore sunglasses. Odd, given the late hour but, after all, this was New York. But then he hooked his glasses with one long tanned finger and slid them down his nose, exposing thick black brows and eyes the color of slate. Everything—all thought, all logic, all sense—fled her mind.

All she could focus on was him.

Prince Thierry.

Right there.

In the flesh.

Mila had often wondered if people were exaggerating when they talked about the power of immediate physical attraction. She'd convinced herself that her own initial reaction to the prince years ago had been largely due to nerves and a hefty dose of overactive teenage hormones. Now, however, she had her answer. What she'd felt for him then was no exaggeration, since she felt exactly the same way now. Her mouth dried, her heart pounded, her legs trembled and her eyes widened in shock. Even though she had come here with the express purpose of meeting him, the reality was harder to come to terms with than she'd anticipated.

Sally had said he was hot. It had been a gross understatement. The man was incendiary.

Mila lowered her eyes to the base of his throat, exposed by an open collar. A pulse beat there and she found herself mesmerized by the proof he was completely and utterly human. A shiver of yearning trembled through her.

"I'll get you another coffee."

"N-no, it-it's okay," she answered, tripping over her tongue.

Think! she commanded herself. *Introduce yourself. Do something. Anything.* But then she looked up again and met his gaze, and she was lost.

His eyes were still as she remembered, but what had faded from her memory was that they were no ordinary gray. They reminded her of the color of the mountain faces that were mined for their pale slate in the north west of her country, and the north east of his. She'd always thought the color to be mundane, but how wrong she had been. It was startling, piercing, as if he could see to the depths of her soul when he looked at her. His irises were rimmed with black and lighter striations of silver shone like starlight within them. And his lashes were so dark they created the perfect frame for his eyes.

Mila realized she was staring and dropped her gaze again, but it did little to slow the rapid beat of her heart or to increase her lung capacity when she most needed a deep and filling breath.

"Si—?"

A man loomed beside them and angled his body between the prince and herself. One muttered phrase from the prince in his home language stopped the man mid-speech and he slipped back again. Security, obviously, and none too happy about their prince mixing with the natives.

Except she wasn't native, was she? And, she realized with a shock, he didn't seem to recognize who she was.

The prince turned his attention back to her and spoke again, his voice laced with concern. "Are you sure you're okay? Look, your hand is burned."

Mila started as he took her hand in his and held it so he could examine the pinkness left by the hot coffee. Her breathing hitched a little as his thumb softly traced around the edges of the tender skin. His fingers were gentle and even though he held her loosely—so she could tug herself free at any time—they sent a sizzle of awareness across the surface of her skin that had nothing to do with hot coffee and everything to do with this incredibly hot man.

"It's nothing, really," she said, knowing she should pull her hand loose but finding herself apparently unable to do so.

Nothing? It was everything. This was the magnetism she'd seen in action on TV earlier today. She was as helpless against it as everyone else had been.

"Please," he said, letting go of her and gesturing down the sidewalk. "Allow me to buy you another coffee."

His simple request was her undoing and she searched his face, seeking any sign that he knew who she was, and fighting back the disappointment that rose within her when he didn't. Of course he wouldn't expect to find himself face-to-face with a princess on the streets of New York, let alone *his* princess, she rationalized. But in spite of herself, Mila felt annoyance quickly take disappointment's place. Was he so disinterested in her and their eventual union that she wasn't on his mind at all?

But perhaps she could use this to her advantage. The plan she'd made with Sally had been for her to reintroduce herself to the prince, but what if she didn't? What if she let herself just be another anonymous person on the streets of New York? Without the weight of their betrothal making them formal or awkward with each other, she could use this chance to get to know him better. To see for herself who this man was, while he was emotionally unguarded and not on show, and to gauge for herself what kind of man she would be marrying.

"Thank you," she said, quelling her irritation and drawing on every gram of serenity and inner strength that had been instilled in her since her birth. "I would like that."

His lip quirked up at the corner and, just like that, she found herself mesmerized once again. His eyes gleamed in satisfaction, the faintest of lines appearing at their corners. She forced herself to look away, to the street, to the rain, to basically anything but the man who guided her to walk at his side.

Ahead of them, one of his security team had already scoped out the same small coffee shop where she'd bought her cup earlier, and discreetly gestured an all-clear. It was done so subtly that if she hadn't been so used to looking for it for herself, she wouldn't even have noticed.

They entered and went to the counter to order. Mila was struck by how surreal this all felt. He was acting as if he did everyday things like walk down the street for coffee all the time, when she knew he certainly did not. His security team were dotted around the premises, two by the door and one near a table to which the prince guided her once they had their orders.

"Friends of yours?" Mila commented, nodding in the direction of his shadow team.

He made a sound that was something between a snort and a laugh. "Something like that," he acknowledged. "Do they bother you? I can ask them to leave."

"Oh, no, don't worry. They're fine."

She settled in her chair and looked at the tray Prince Thierry placed on the table, noticing he'd also ordered a small bowl of ice. She watched in bemusement as he took a pristine white monogrammed handkerchief from his pocket and wrapped some of the ice inside it.

"Give me your hand," he commanded.

"Really, it's not that sore," Mila protested.

"Your hand?" he repeated, pinning her with that steely gaze and Mila found herself doing as he'd bidden.

He cradled her hand in his while gently applying the makeshift ice pack. Mila tried to ignore the race of her pulse as she watched him in action. Tried and failed.

"I apologize again for my clumsiness," he continued. "I wasn't looking where I was going."

"Seriously, it's okay," she answered with a smile.

"Let me be the judge of that," he said firmly, smiling to take the edge off his words.

Clearly he was a man used to being in command. The idea sent another thrill of excitement coursing through Mila's veins. Would he take command in all things? She pressed her thighs together on a wave of need that startled her with its intensity.

He looked up. "I'm Hawk, and you are?"

"A-Angel," Mila answered, defaulting to the diminutive of the name she was known by here in the United States. If he could use a moniker, then why shouldn't she also? Why shouldn't they just be two strangers meeting on the street just like anybody else?

"Are you in New York on business?" she asked, even though she knew full well why he was here.

"Yes, but I return home in the morning," he replied.

She was surprised. The summit was scheduled to last for four days and only started tomorrow. He had just arrived here yesterday and now he was already returning to Sylvain? She wanted to ask why but knew she couldn't. Not when he was supposed to simply be a stranger she'd just met on the street.

He lifted the makeshift ice pack from her hand and gave a small nod of satisfaction. "That's looking better."

"Thank you."

The prince let go of her hand and Mila felt an irrational sense of loss. His touch had been thrilling and without it she felt as though she'd been cast adrift.

"And you?" he asked.

Mila looked up and stared at him. "Me, what?"

"Are you in New York on business or do you live here?"

The skin around his eyes crinkled again. He was laughing at her, she was sure of it, but not in an unkind way. For a moment she was struck by the awful and overwhelming sense of ineptitude that had marked her first meeting with the prince. She recalled how embarrassed she'd felt back then. How she'd found herself so unworthy of this incredibly striking, self-assured man.

She wasn't that girl anymore, Mila told herself firmly. And tonight, incognito, she could be anyone she wanted to be. Even someone who could charm a man like Prince Thierry of Sylvain. The thought empowered her and bolstered her courage. She could do this.

"Oh, sorry," she laughed, injecting a note of lightheartedness to her voice. "You lost me there for a moment."

"But I have you now," he countered.

Warmth flooded her as his words sank in.

"Yes," she said softly. "You do."

Three

The air thickened between them—conversation forgotten for the moment as they stared into one another's eyes.

Thierry found himself willingly drawn into her gaze. Her brows were perfect dark arches, framing unusual amber eyes fringed by thick dark lashes. Their coloring seemed at odds with her long blond hair, but she was no less beautiful for it. If anything, it made her even more striking. Her cheekbones were high and gently sculpted, her nose short and straight. But it was her lips to which his eyes were most often drawn. They were full and lush and as she parted them on an indrawn breath he felt a deeply responsive punch to his gut. Arousal teased at his groin. It was as if he was in a spell of some kind. A spell from which he had no desire to break free.

It was only as someone walked past their table, bumping it and spilling some of her coffee, that the enchantment between them was broken.

Angel laughed and sopped up the mess with a paper

napkin. "Seems I'm destined not to finish my coffee this evening. And in answer to your question, no, I live in Boston. I'm only visiting the city."

"I didn't think your accent was from around here," Thierry commented.

With elegant fingers, she balled the napkin and picked up her cup to take a sip of what was left of her drink. He found himself captivated by her every movement. Enthralled by the flick of her tongue across her lip to taste a remnant of the topping of chocolate and milk foam that lingered there. Thierry swallowed against the sudden obstruction in his throat. It was as if his heart had lodged there, hammering wildly.

He shouldn't be here with this woman. He was engaged to another—someone he barely knew, even though he would be married to her by the end of the month. And yet, not in all his years of bachelorhood had he felt a compulsion to be with someone as he did with the enchanting female sitting opposite him. It was almost as if he knew her already, or felt as if he should. Whatever the sensation was that he felt, he wanted more of it. Hell, he wanted more of her.

Angel put her cup back down. "Actually, I'm in New York to attend a lecture on sustainability initiatives."

Thierry felt his interest in her sharpen. "You are? I was scheduled to attend that lecture tomorrow myself."

"And you can't delay your return home?"

The dark pull of reality crept through him and with it the reminder of what tomorrow would entail. Eight and a half hours by air to Sylvain's main airport, then another twenty minutes in his private helicopter to the palace. All of which to be followed by meetings with his household and the heads of government. His time wouldn't be his own until after his father was buried in the family vault near the palace. Maybe not even then.

"Hawk?" Angel prompted him.

He snapped out of his train of thought and gave her his full attention. "No, I must return home. An urgent matter. But enough of that. Tell me, what takes a beautiful young woman like yourself to a dusty old lecture hall?"

She looked affronted by his question. "That's a little sexist, don't you think?"

"Forgive me," he said quickly. "I did not mean to undermine your intelligence, or to sound quite so chauvinistic."

He was disappointed in himself. It seemed the apple hadn't fallen far from the tree, after all. Thierry's father had been nothing but old-fashioned in his view that women were for the begetting of heirs and to be a faithful and adoring ornament by his side. His consort had failed miserably at the second part. Instead of considering that he might have made a mistake in his treatment of her, the king had clung more fiercely to his opinions about a woman's role in the monarchy and it was obvious in palace appointments that his chauvinism guided his choices.

Thierry had recently begun to wonder if part of the reason for his mother's infidelity had been a lack of self-worth caused by her husband's condescending treatment. Maybe his actions had meant that she'd desperately sought meaning for her life anywhere but within her marriage. But that mattered little now. She and her lover had died in a fiery car wreck many years ago. The resulting scandal had almost brought two nations to war and it was one of the reasons Thierry had vowed to remain chaste until marriage and then, after he was wed, to remain faithful to his spouse. He also rightly expected the same in return. While he wouldn't marry for love, his marriage would last. It had to. He had to turn the tide of generations of marital failure and unhappiness. How hard could it be?

Across the table, Angel inclined her head in acknowledgment of his apology. "I'm glad to hear it. I get quite enough of that from my brother." She softened her words with another smile. "In answer to your question, my professor recommended the lecture."

For the next hour they discussed her studies, particularly her interest in developing sustainable living solutions, equal opportunities for all people and renewable energy initiatives. He found her fascinating. Her enthusiasm for her causes made her quite animated and he relished the pinkish tinge of excitement that colored her cheeks. The subjects they discussed were dear to his heart as well, and topics he wished to pursue further with his government. His father had seen little point in breaking away from the methods that had been tried and true in Sylvain for centuries, but Thierry was acutely aware of the need for long-term planning to ensure that future generations would continue to benefit from and enjoy his country's many resources—rather than plunder them all into oblivion. Their discussion was exhilarating and left him feeling mentally stimulated in a way he hadn't anticipated.

The clientele of the coffee shop had thinned considerably during their talk and Thierry became aware that the members of his security team were beginning to shift uncomfortably at their tables. Angel appeared to notice it, too.

"Oh, I'm sorry to have taken so much of your time. When I get on my pet subjects I can be a little over-excited," she apologized.

"Not at all. I enjoyed it. I don't often get to exchange or argue concepts with someone as articulate and well-versed as you are."

She looked at her watch, its strap a delicate cuff of platinum and, if he wasn't wrong, diamonds. The subtle but obvious sign of wealth made him even more intrigued about her background.

"It's getting late. I guess I'd better head back to my

hotel," she said with obvious reluctance. "This has been really nice. Thank you."

No. Every cell in his body objected to the prospect of saying goodbye. He wasn't ready to relinquish her company yet. He reached out and took Angel's hand.

"Don't go, not yet." The words surprised him as much as they appeared to surprise her. "Unless you have to, of course."

Damn. He hadn't meant to sound so needy. But in the face of the news he'd received tonight, Angel was a delightful distraction in what was soon to be a turbulent sea of chaos. He looked deep into her eyes, struck again by the beauty of their unusual whiskey-colored hue. He'd seen that color before, he realized, but he couldn't quite remember where. Thierry looked down to where their hands were joined. She hadn't pulled away. That had to be a good sign, right? He certainly hoped so. He wasn't ready yet to relinquish her company.

"No, I don't have to, exactly…" Her voice trailed away and she looked at her watch again before she said more firmly. "No. I don't have to go."

"No boyfriend waiting for you at home?" he probed shamelessly, running his thumb over her bare fingers.

Angel chuckled and his heart warmed at the sound.

"No, no boyfriend."

"Good. Shall we walk together?" he suggested.

"I'd like that."

She rose with a fluid grace that mesmerized him, and gathered up her coat and bag. He reached for her coat and helped her into it, his fingertips brushing the nape of her neck. He'd felt a shock of awareness when he'd touched her hand, but that was nothing compared to the jolt that struck him now. It was wrong, he knew, to feel such an overpowering attraction to Angel when he was engaged to another woman. Was he no different than his mother, who had been incapable of observing the boundaries of married life?

Thierry pulled his hands away and, balling them into fists, he shoved them deep into his pockets. A sense of shame filled him. This was madness. In a few weeks' time he'd be marrying Princess Mila and here he was, in New York, desperate to spend more time with someone whose first name was almost the only thing he knew about her. Well, that and her keen intelligence about topics dear to his heart. Even so, it didn't justify this behavior, he argued silently.

And then she turned to look at him and smiled, and he knew that whatever else was to come in his life, he had to grasp hold of this moment, this night, and make the most of the oasis of peace she unwittingly offered him.

They headed out of the coffee shop and turned toward Seventh Avenue. His security detail melted into the people around them. There, ever vigilant, but not completely visible. The rain had stopped and Thierry began to feel his spirits lift again. This felt so normal, so unscripted. It was a vast departure from his usual daily life.

"Tell me about yourself," he prompted his silent companion. "Any family?"

"I have a brother. He's in Europe right now," Angel said lightly, but he saw the way she pressed her delectable full lips together as if she was holding something back. "How about you?" she asked, almost as if her question was an afterthought.

"An only child."

"Was it lonely, growing up?"

"Sometimes, although I always had plenty of people around me."

Angel gestured to the guard in front and the others nearby. "People like them?" she asked.

"And others," he admitted.

They stopped at a set of lights and she lifted her chin and stared straight ahead. "Sometimes you can be at your most lonely when you're surrounded by people."

Her words struck a chord with him. There was something about the way she'd made her statement that made him think she spoke from personal experience. The thought made something tug inside him. He wished he could remove the haunted, empty tone from her voice and fill it with warmth. *And what else*, a voice inside him asked. He pushed the thought aside. There could be nothing else. Come morning he would be a different man to the rest of the world. A king. This interlude of normality would be nothing but a memory. One, he realized, he would treasure for a long time to come.

"So what do you do?" Angel asked him after they'd crossed the street.

"Do?"

"Yes, for a living. I assume you do work?"

Yes, he worked, but not in the sense she was probably expecting. "I'm in management," he said, skirting the truth.

"That's a very broad statement," she teased, looking up at him with a glimmer of mischief in her tawny eyes.

"I have a very broad range of responsibilities. And you, what do you plan to do once you have completed your studies?"

Her expression changed in an instant—the humor of before replaced with a look of seriousness. Then she blinked and the solemnity was gone.

"Oh, this and that," she said airily.

"And you accused me of being vague?" he taunted, enjoying their verbal sparring.

"Well, since you asked—I want to go home and make a difference. I want people to listen to me, to really listen, and to take what I have to say on board—not just dismiss me out of hand because I'm female."

He raised his brows. "Does that happen a lot?"

"You did it to me," she challenged.

"Yes, I did, and I apologize again for my prejudice. I hope you get your wish." He drew to a halt beside a food truck. "Have you eaten this evening?"

"No, but you don't have to—"

"I'm told you haven't been to New York until you try one of these rib eye sandwiches."

She inhaled deeply. "They do smell divine, don't they?"

"I'll take that as a yes."

He turned to the head of his security and gave an order in Sylvano. The man grinned in response and lined up at the food-truck window.

They continued to walk as they ate, laughing in between bites as they struggled to contain their food without spilling it.

"I should have taken you to a restaurant," Thierry said as Angel made a noise of disgust at the mess she had left on her hands when they'd finished.

"Oh, heavens no! Not at all. This is fun...just messy." She laughed and gingerly extracted a small packet of tissues from her bag so she could wipe her fingers.

Thierry felt his lips pull into a smile again as they had so many times since he'd met her. What was it about her that felt so right when everything else around him felt so wrong?

"I can't get over this city," Angel exclaimed. "There's never a quiet moment. It's exhilarating."

"It is," he agreed and then looked over at her. "Do you dance?"

"Are you asking me if I'm capable of it, or if I want to?" Angel laughed in response.

Thierry shrugged. "Both. Either." He didn't care. He suddenly had the urge to hold her in his arms and he figured this would be the only way he could decently do so without compromising his own values.

"I'm not exactly dressed for it," Angel said doubtfully.

"You look beautiful. I've heard of a quiet place not far from here. It's not big and brash like a lot of the clubs. More intimate, I suppose, and you can dance or talk or just sit and watch the other patrons if that's all you want to do."

"It sounds perfect."

"So, shall we?"

She grinned back. "Okay, I'd like that."

"Good." He took her hand in his, again struck by the delicacy of her fingers and the fine texture of her skin.

What would it feel like if she touched him intimately? Would her fingers be firm or soft like a feather? Would she trace the contours of his body with a tantalizing subtlety, or would her touch be more definite, more demanding? He slammed the door on his wayward thoughts. It seemed he had more of his mother in him than he'd suspected. Still, there was nothing wrong with dancing with a woman other than his betrothed, was there? He had to do it at state functions all the time.

He tugged her in the direction of a club he'd visited on his last trip to New York and sent Armaund ahead to ensure they'd gain entry. The night was still young and he wasn't ready for it to end yet.

Drawing her into his arms on the dance floor was everything he'd hoped for and more. The only problem was that it made him *want* more—and that was something he'd forbidden himself until marriage. He was determined to hold sacred the act of love and making love. It was something he would share with his wife and his wife alone. He hadn't remained celibate purely for the hell of it. Sometimes it had been sheer torment refusing to acknowledge the demands of his flesh. But he'd promised himself from a very young age that he would not be that person. He would not allow physical need to cloud all else. Over the centuries his family had almost lost everything several times over because of a lack of physical control.

He'd always believed his forebears' susceptibility to fleshly pursuits to be a mark of weakness, and nothing had happened in his thirty-one years to change his mind. Except perhaps the young woman dancing with him right now. Even so, he denied himself any more than the sensation of her in his arms—the brush of her breasts against his chest as he held her close, the skim of her warm breath on his throat—they were torments and teases he could overcome. When he boarded the plane a few short hours from now, to return to Sylvain, he would do so with the full knowledge that he had honored his vow to both himself and to the woman he was to marry.

But until then, he'd enjoy this stolen night as much as his duty and honor would allow.

The night had been magical—something even her wildest imagination could never have dreamed up. In fact, Mila doubted even Sally, with all her romantic ideas, could have come up with something like the night she'd just had. She felt like Cinderella, except in her fairy tale the prince was seeing her home and it was well past midnight. As the limousine, which had been waiting outside the club when they'd left it, pulled up outside her hotel she turned in her seat to face the prince. Tonight, she'd seen a side of him she'd never anticipated—and she was utterly captivated by him.

Maybe it was the champagne they'd drunk at the club, or maybe it was simply the knowledge that at month's end she'd be standing next to him beneath the ancient vaulted ceilings of the Sylvano palace cathedral and pledging her life to him, but right now she felt as if she was floating on air.

At least now she knew what Thierry was like away from the pomp and ceremony that was attached to his position in the world. Once they were married and had the chance to spend time together alone, without all the trappings and formality of their official lives, she believed that they could become important to one another beyond what their marriage would gain for their respective nations. Tonight she'd had a chance to get to know the man beneath the crown. The man who would be her husband—who would share her days and her nights. And, given the fierce attraction between them, she looked forward to getting to know him even better. In every way.

He'd been the consummate gentleman tonight and, for the first time in her life, she'd *felt* like a desirable woman—one who could be confident that she would be able to make him happy in their marriage, too.

She turned to face him in the seat of the limo. "Thank you, Hawk. Tonight was incredible. I will never forget it."

He took her hand and lifted it to his lips, brushing them across her knuckles in a caress that sent a bolt of longing straight to her center.

"Nor I."

Thierry leaned forward, his intention to kiss her cheek obvious, but at the last minute Mila turned her head, allowing their lips to brush one another. It was the merest touch, sweet and innocent, and yet in that moment she felt something expand in her chest and threaten to consume her. It shook Mila to her core.

Words failed her and she pulled away, blindly reaching for the door handle and stumbling slightly as she left the private cavern of the vehicle. She didn't look back. She couldn't. If she did she might ask for more and it wasn't the time or the place to do that.

She moved swiftly through the hotel lobby and to the elevator and swiped her key card to head for the penthouse.

In the elevator car she reached up and tugged the blond wig loose and locked her gaze with her reflection in the mirrored walls. She'd been a stranger to Thierry tonight and he'd enjoyed her company. But would he enjoy it quite so much when he met the real Angel, or would he remember the gauche and chubby girl for whom he'd shown a moment of disdain? Only time would tell.

Four

"Of all the stupid, irresponsible, brainless things to do! What if the media catches wind of this? Did you even stop to think about that? You'll be crucified and all of Sylvania will reject you before you even cross their border."

Mila sat back in her chair waiting for her brother's tirade to subside. It didn't look as if it would be soon, though. He was working up another head of steam as he paced the priceless Persian carpet on his office floor. She kept her head bowed, her tongue still in her mouth. It was no easy task when she'd become used to offering her opinion—and having it respected.

"You were raised to behave better than this. What made you sneak out like nothing more than a common tramp? Was this idea concocted by that friend of yours in America? Sally what's-her-name?" Anger and disgust pervaded his tone.

That got her riled. "Now wait a minute—!" she protested, but Rocco cut her off with a glare.

"You are a princess of Erminia. Princesses do not sneak out of hotel rooms in the dead of night and stay out until dawn with strangers."

Unless you live in a fairy tale, Mila amended silently, remembering her favorite bedtime story about the twelve dancing princesses. But this, her life, was no fairy tale. Besides, Prince—no, *King*, she reminded herself—Thierry wasn't a stranger to her anymore. At least, not completely. But she'd endure Rocco's lecture. For now, it suited her not to tell her brother whom she'd spent her night with. The secret was hers to hold safely in her heart. She didn't want to share it with her brother who would no doubt worry about the political ramifications of her and Thierry's impromptu date. Ramifications that would sully her memory of that wonderful, magical night.

Rocco strode to the large arched window set deep into the palace wall, which offered a view of the countryside beyond it. Mila looked past him to the outside—to freedom. A freedom she'd never truly taste again. The anonymity of life in the United States had been a blessing, but now that she was back home for good she was expected to kowtow to protocol—and that meant doing whatever it was her brother decreed. She began to wonder if perhaps it might not have been better not to have known the freedom she'd experienced after all. The comparison made coming home this time so very much harder.

"So, Rocco, what are you going to do? Throw me in the dungeons?"

Her brother turned and she was struck by how much he'd aged since she'd last seen him a year ago. As if stress and worry had become his constant companions, leaving lines of strain on his face and threads of gray at his temples. And some of that strain, and no doubt several of those gray hairs, were due to her, she acknowledged with a pang. She loved her brother dearly, and had no desire to hurt him or cause him distress, but she just wished he'd listen to her once in a while—really listen as if she and what she had to say had value.

"Don't think I won't do it," he growled. "Such flippancy is probably all I can expect from you after allowing you so much leeway these past seven years. I should never have been so lenient. Our advisers recommended that you marry the prince immediately when you turned eighteen but no, I had to allow you to persuade me to send you away—for an education, not so you could bring our family name into disrepute." He pinched the bridge of his aquiline nose and drew in a deep breath before continuing. "I felt sorry for you back then, Mila. You were no more than a schoolgirl, entering into an engagement with an older man—someone you had barely met, yet alone knew. I understood that you felt stifled by that and, I hazard to say, somewhat terrified at the prospect of what came next. You were so much younger than your years, so innocent."

He sighed and turned away for a moment. Mila bristled at his description of her. Innocent? Yes, of course she'd been innocent. Given her strict and restrictive upbringing there had been little opportunity to learn anything of the ways of the world and the people within it. It was part of why she'd begged her brother for the chance to study abroad. What kind of ruler could she be if she couldn't understand her people and the struggles and challenges they lived with every day? Rocco continued to speak.

"And so I agreed when you asked me for time until your twenty-fifth birthday. I thought it was the best thing to do for you and that it might help to make your eventual union a happier one. I should have known it would come to this—that the lack of structure in your life overseas would corrupt you and deviate you from your true path."

Lack of structure? Mila bit her tongue to keep herself from saying the words out loud. While her life in Boston had not been like her life here in the castle, how on earth did Rocco think she'd attained the measure of academic recognition she'd achieved without structure? And even aside from her scholastic successes—won through hard work and discipline—she'd also dealt with the social restrictions of a team of bodyguards, not to mention a chaperone who vetoed nearly every opportunity to relax or try to make friends. She had barely even socialized with any of the other students on campus.

But her brother was on a roll now. If she tried to explain, he would not listen, and she knew it. To say anything while he was still so angry with her would be a complete waste of time. Instead, she let his words flow over her, like the water that, during a heavy downpour, spouted from the gargoyles positioned around the castle gutters.

"Even I cannot turn back time. You are home now and you will prepare for your marriage. Your wedding takes place four weeks from today. And there will not be one wrong move, one misstep, or one breath of scandal from you. Do you understand me? Too much rides on this, Mila. The stability of our entire nation depends on your ability to do the job you were raised to do."

The job she was raised to do. There it was—the millstone around her neck. The surety that she had no value as a human being beyond that of being a suitable wife for a powerful man.

"And the late king's funeral this week? Am I not to attend that with you as a mark of respect?"

"No. You will stay here."

She wanted to argue, to say she had every right to be there at her fiancé's side as he bid a final farewell to his father, but she knew the plea would fall on deaf ears. Mila shifted her gaze to look her brother straight in the eyes. She hated seeing him like this—so angry and distraught—so she said the words he was expecting to hear.

"I understand you, brother. I will do as you ask."

But he hadn't asked, had he? He'd ordered it from her. Not once, at any stage during this audience with him—for it couldn't be deemed anything else—had Mila felt as if he was pleased to welcome his baby sister home. Instead she'd felt like nothing more than a disappointment. A burden to be off-loaded. A problem to be corrected.

There hadn't been a single word of congratulations on her achievements while she'd been away. No mention of her honors degree or the publication of her treatise on Equal Opportunity and Sustainable Development in European Nations. Her only value was in her ability to play the role of a proper fiancée and wife. She was merely a pawn on her brother's chessboard.

She kept her eyes fixed on Rocco and she saw the minute the tension that held his body began to ease from his shoulders. His eyes, amber like her own, but several shades deeper, softened.

"Thank you. You understand, don't you? I don't ask you to do this for myself, but for our people. And for your sake as well, since I couldn't bear to see you do anything to jeopardize your chance at winning your husband's trust and respect."

And there it was. The glimpse of the brother she'd grown up loving more than life itself—the brother who had been her protector and defender all throughout her childhood. But that was all she was permitted to see because the veil of command he perpetually bore took up residence once again on his visage.

"I understand," she answered with an inclination of her head.

And she did. Even though, inside, her emotions spun in turmoil. It was entirely clear that her value—to her brother and her future husband—came from her chastity and unimpeachable honor. Her knowledge, her insight, her plans to better society and improve conditions for her people, and even the grace, poise and confidence she had gained in her years abroad mattered little to their society compared to her reputation.

Nothing had changed in all the time she'd been away. She didn't even know why she would have expected it to. Erminia was still locked in the old days where a woman's place was not beside, but behind her husband, or her father or brother or whichever male figure led her household—her thoughts and ideas to be tolerated but not celebrated or given any respect.

Even in the Erminian parliament women were a rare breed. Mila wanted to see that change, and for their government to acknowledge women's intelligence and their value as vital members of the very fabric of Erminian society as a whole. But she knew that change would be very slow to come…if it came at all.

"You don't sound excited about your wedding," Rocco prompted. "I thought you would be full of chatter about it."

Mila sighed. "Rocco, I'm not a little girl about to go to a tea party in her favorite dress. I am a full-grown woman with a mind and thoughts of her own, about to enter into a marriage with a man I barely know."

He stepped closer to her and placed a finger under her chin, lifting her face up to his. "You've changed."

"Of course I've changed. I've grown up."

"No, it's more than that." A frown furrowed his brow and his eyes narrowed. "Are you still…? Did you…?"

Mila held on to her temper by a thread. "What? You're actually asking me if I've kept myself chaste? Do you really think I'd compromise the crown by throwing my virginity away on a one-night stand?"

Her brother paled. "You will not speak to me in that tone. I might be your brother but, first and foremost, I am your king."

Mila swept down into a curtsey. "Sire, I beg your forgiveness."

"Mila, don't mock me."

She rose again but did not look directly in his eyes. "I do not mock you, Your Majesty. I am well aware of my position in this world. I will do my duty and you can rest assured that by my wedding day no man will have touched me, with even so much as a kiss, before my future husband does. But, just in case you don't believe me, please feel free to have the royal physician examine me to ensure that I am indeed a woman of my word."

"Mila—"

"I believe I have an appointment for a dress fitting now. If you'll excuse me?" she said, turning before his reaching hand could touch her.

She knew that, deep down, he probably hated the exchange they'd just shared even more than she did. But duty drove him now, and that meant the needs of the country always came first. He couldn't be the doting older brother who had sheltered her for so many of her younger years. Ten years her senior, Rocco had been forced to prematurely take the crown after their father's assassination when Rocco had been only nineteen. Mila could barely remember a time since when his shoulders hadn't borne the weight of responsibility that had descended with the crown. Almost overnight, he'd gone from the teasing and protective older brother she'd adored, to the domineering sovereign she knew today. The man who showed no signs of weakness, no chink in the armor that shrouded his emotions.

As she let herself out of his office and barely held herself back from storming down the ornately decorated corridor of the castle to her suite of rooms, a part of her still mourned the boy he'd been while another continued to rail internally at how he'd spoken to her just now. He still saw her as a silly, empty-headed child; that much was clear. And no matter what she did or said, that would probably never change. She had to learn to accept it as she'd had to learn to accept so much about her life. But maybe, just maybe, she would be in a position to effect change once she was married.

Later, as she fidgeted under the weight of the elegant silk-dupion-and-lace gown that was being fitted to her gentle curves she couldn't help but think back to that moment when she and Thierry had kissed good-night—or perhaps it had been good morning, she thought. She couldn't hold back a smile as she remembered the exquisitely gentle pressure of his lips upon hers. If she closed her eyes and concentrated she could almost feel him again, smell the subtle scent of his cologne—a blend of wood and spice that had done crazy things to her inside—and sense the yearning that there could be more. A tiny thrill of excitement rippled through her—a ripple that was rapidly chased away by the sensation of a pin in her thigh.

"I'm so sorry, Your Highness, but if you'd just keep still for me a moment longer..." The couturier's frustration was evident in her tone.

"No, it is I who should apologize," Mila hastily assured the woman. "I wasn't concentrating. It is not your fault."

She focused on a corner of a picture frame on the wall and kept her body still, turning or lifting and dropping her arms when asked—like a marionette. And that, essentially, was all she was to her brother, she realized with a pang. A puppet to be manipulated for the benefit of all of Erminia. There wouldn't have been such pressure on her if he had married by now himself. But, when faced with a royal proposal, the girl he'd loved through his late teens and early twenties had decided royal life was not for her, and since then he'd steered clear of romantic entanglements.

Rocco's crown might sit heavily on his dark curls, Mila

thought with a sad sigh, but hers was equally burdensome. But, there was a silver lining, she reminded herself. Her night with Thierry showed they were intellectual equals and he had at least appeared to respect her opinion during their discussions.

If he could give a total stranger his ear, why wouldn't he extend the same courtesy to his wife?

It was 2:00 a.m. and Mila was still wide awake. Never a good traveler, she struggled to adjust to the change in time zones. While most of the good people of Erminia would be fast asleep in their beds about now, Mila's body was on Boston time and for her it was only seven in the evening. Granted, it had been an exhausting day with the hours of travel followed by that awful meeting with her brother. Given how she always suffered severe motion sickness, which left her physically wrung out, logically she should be more than ready to sleep. Sadly, logic was lacking tonight, she accepted with a sigh as she pushed back the covers on her pedestal bed and reached for the light robe she'd cast over the end of her mattress before retiring.

Maybe some warm milk, the way Cookie used to make it for her back when she was a child, would help. After donning her robe, Mila headed for the servants' stairs toward the back of the castle. Sure, she knew that all she had to do was press a button and someone would bring the milk to her, but a part of her craved the inviting warmth and aromas that permeated the castle kitchens and that were such an intrinsic part of her happier childhood memories.

Her slippers barely made a sound on the old stone stairs and, as opposed to the usual daily busyness that made the castle hum with activity during normal waking hours, the air was still and serene. She could do with some of that serenity right now.

To her surprise, the sound of voices traveled up the

corridor toward her. Obviously some staff was on duty around the clock, but it was unusual for the senior household steward to still be afoot at this time of night. Mila recognized Gregor's voice as it rumbled along the ancient stone walls. For a second she was prepared to ignore it, and the younger female voice she could barely hear murmuring in response, but her ears pricked up when she caught Thierry's name mentioned.

Mila slowed her steps as she approached the open door of the steward's office and listened carefully.

"And you're certain of this?" the steward asked.

Mila was surprised Gregor's voice sounded so stern. While the man held a position of extreme responsibility, he was well-known for his warm heart and caring nature—it was part of why the royal household ran so smoothly. His brusque tone right now seemed at odds with the person she remembered.

"Yes, sir. My second cousin assists the king of Sylvain's private secretary. He saw the document soliciting the woman's—" the young woman hesitated a bit before continuing "—services."

"What does your cousin plan to do with this information he so willingly shared with you?"

"Oh, sir, he didn't do so willingly. I mean, it wasn't meant as gossip."

"Then what did he mean by it?"

Mila heard the younger woman make a sound, as if holding back tears. "Oh, please, sir. I don't want him to get into any trouble. It troubled him that the king would seek the services of a courtesan so close to his marriage, especially when it is known within the Sylvano palace that the prince is—was—saving himself for marriage."

A courtesan? Mila's ears buzzed, blocking out any other sound as the word reverberated in her skull. Her stomach lurched uncomfortably and she fought the nausea that swirled with a vicious and sudden twist.

A sound from the steward's office alerted her to the movement of the people inside. She couldn't be caught here, not like this. Mila turned back down the corridor and slipped into another office, this one dark and unoccupied. With her arms bound tight around her middle, she stared at the closed door framed by a limning of light. Her mind whirled.

Thierry had procured a professional mistress? Why would he even do such a thing? How had she misjudged him so badly? Their time together that night in New York had been wonderful, magical—and entirely chaste, without the slightest hint that he was seeking physical intimacy. It had thrilled her to think that he was staying untouched for her, just as she had done for him. None of what she'd learned about him in the hours they'd spent together made sense against what she'd just overheard.

Mila stiffened as she heard a light pair of footsteps walk briskly down the hallway—the maid, leaving Gregor's office by the sound of it. She waited, wondering if she'd hear Gregor leaving the same way, and as she waited her mind spun again. What should she do now she had this knowledge? She couldn't refuse to marry Thierry. That would cause upheaval on both sides of the border. And she didn't want to, not really. But how could she consider a future with a man who was already in the process of installing a mistress in a home they were meant to share? She had toiled long and hard to make herself into a worthy wife for the man she thought he was. Had she been wrong about him all along? Was he just another ruler who treated marriage as nothing more than a facade—like so many royal marriages that had taken place in the past? Had he already given up on the idea that Mila could possibly make him happy?

Was their marriage really to be nothing more than a peace treaty between neighboring nations? Were they not to share the communion of two adults with shared hopes and dreams for the future? Tears burned her eyes, but she blinked them back furiously. She would not succumb to weakness in this. There had to be a way to stop him from taking a mistress, a way to somehow circumvent this. *Think!* she commanded herself. Here she was, well educated, astute about women's issues and keen to do something about them, and yet, when faced with a problem all she could do was hide and then fight back tears? How clichéd, she scolded silently. Mila loosened her arms and let them drop to her sides and lifted her chin. She was a princess, it was about time she started to think and act like one.

An idea sprang into her mind. An idea so preposterous and far-fetched it almost took her breath away with its audacity. Even Sally would be proud. But could she do it? Thinking about it was one thing, undertaking it quite another—and it would involve far more people than just herself.

Just how important was a happy marriage to her? Was she prepared to accept a union in which she was merely a figurehead and lead her own separate life, or did she want Thierry as her husband in every way, emotionally and physically? The answer was resoundingly simple. She wanted it—*him*—all.

Mila reached for the door handle and entered the corridor and resolutely trod toward Gregor's office.

Five

"But, Your Royal Highness!" Gregor protested. "What you're suggesting…it borders on criminal. In fact, kidnapping *is* criminal."

She'd expected resistance and she'd hoped it wouldn't have to come to this. Mila had long believed the pledge of absolute obedience made by staff to the royal household to be archaic and, frankly, ridiculous. Who in their right mind would vow to serve their royal family *unquestioningly* in this day and age—especially if it meant doing something illegal? But tradition still formed the foundation of everything in Erminia and, in this case, the end justified the means. It had to. Her happiness and that of any children she might bear depended on it. She couldn't allow Thierry to begin their marriage with a professional courtesan already in place as his mistress—not without making every effort to win his love for herself, first.

"Gregor, it is your princess who asks this of you," she said imperiously. She hated herself for having to act with such superiority. She'd never been that person—never had to be. In fact, she'd never believed she could be, but, it seemed, when pushed hard enough she was no different from her forebears. "I have no desire to take another woman's leavings when I meet my groom at the altar," she said, taking the bull directly by the horns.

Before her, Gregor blushed. One didn't discuss that sort of thing in front of a member of the royal family—especially not a princess. He looked as if he was about to protest once more, but Mila held her ground, staring directly into his eyes. The man never faltered. He held her gaze as if he could change her mind by doing so but then it appeared that he realized she was set on her course of action—whether he helped her, or not.

"I understand, ma'am."

And he did. She could see it in his eyes. No one who lived and worked within these walls understood her dilemma better. In his position he'd seen one generation after another form marital alliances that had been alternately mediocre and miserable—which, Mila guessed, was only to be expected when people were picked for their pedigree alone and not their compatibility. Thierry's family had been little different, even though his parents purportedly married for love—and look how that had ended. Deep in her heart she knew that she and Thierry could have better than that. They deserved it.

"Then you'll assist me?" she pressed.

"Your safety is paramount, ma'am. If at any time you are under threat—"

"There will be no risk of that," Mila interrupted. "First, however, we must find out who this *courtesan*—" she said the word with a twist of distaste on her lips "—is, and what her travel plans are. Everything hinges on that."

"It won't be easy, ma'am."

"Nothing worthwhile ever is," Mila said with a twinge deep down inside. "And, Gregor, thank you."

"Your wish is my command, ma'am," Gregor said with a deep bow. "Your people only wish for your happiness."

Her happiness. Would she be happy, she wondered? She'd darn well better be if this plan to kidnap the courtesan and take her place worked. If not, well, the outcome did not bode well for any of them.

Thierry ripped the ceremonial sword belt from his hip and cast the scabbard onto his bed with a disrespectful clatter.

"Nico!" he commanded. "Assist me out of this getup immediately, would you?"

His valet scurried from the dressing room and helped Thierry from the formal military uniform he'd worn to his father's funeral this afternoon. The weight of the serge and brass and loops of braid was suffocating and Thierry wanted nothing more than to divest himself of it and all it signaled for his life to come.

The day had been interminable. First the lengthy procession from the palace to the cathedral, following his father's coffin on foot through streets lined with loyal, and some not so loyal, subjects crowding the pavements. One step in front of another. It had gotten him through the ghastly parade of pomp and ceremony and through the endless service at the cathedral and finally through the gloomy private interment in the royal tomb back here at the palace. The entire event had been sobering and a reminder of the years of restrictive duty that stretched before him and what was expected.

It was nothing more than he had been brought up to do, and nothing more than his children would be brought up to do after him, God willing. Children. He'd never stopped to think about what it might be like to be a parent. He only remembered his own dysfunctional childhood where his parents had been distant characters to whom he was always expected to show the utmost respect and reverence. Even to his mother, who'd thrown her position and her responsibilities to the wind long before she'd embarked on her final, fatal affair.

"Is there anything else you require, sire?" Nico asked, as he took the last of the heavy raiments on his arm.

"Not this evening, thank you, Nico. I'm sorry I was so short with you just now."

"No need to apologize. It's been a trying day for you."

Trying. *Yes, that was one word for it*, Thierry thought as he stalked in his underwear toward the massive marble bathroom off his bedroom. He stripped off his boxer briefs and turned on the multiheaded shower in the oversize stall and set the jets to pulse. He had a meeting scheduled with King Rocco of Erminia in an hour. An appointment dictated by duty, although if they could shed their various hangers-on, one that could prove fruitful as they both wished for the same outcome. Peace between their countries and an opening of the border, which was slated to improve both their economies.

Of course, there were still plenty of the old-school holdouts in their respective governments who wished to maintain the status quo. Trust no one, was their motto—and Thierry could see how that motto had been earned. But that era needed to end and it was time their nations grew with positive change rather than remain forever entrenched in the old ways.

Water pounded against the tension in his neck and shoulders, slowly loosening the knots. Thierry wished he could escape to his hunting lodge in the mountains tonight, but he had to abide by the protocols set by others before him. The meeting with King Rocco needed to be a productive one. After all, the man was set to become his brother-in-law in only three weeks' time.

Later, in his library, Thierry lifted the heavy crystal

stopper from a decanter and looked across to the power-fully built dark-haired man who lounged comfortably in one of the armchairs by the window.

"Brandy?" he asked.

"Actually, I'd kill for a beer," his guest, the King of Erminia, said with a dazzling smile that lifted the darkness of his expression.

Thierry replied with a smile of his own. "Glass or bottle?"

"The bottle is made of glass, isn't it?" Rocco replied.

A man after his own heart, Thierry decided as he opened the fridge door, disguised as a fourteenth century cupboard, and snagged two longnecks from the shelf. No doubt their respective protocol advisers would have a fit if they could see them now. Well, let them. Thierry twisted off the tops and handed Rocco a bottle. They drank simultaneously, sighing their satisfaction after that first long pull.

"A local brew?" Rocco asked.

Thierry nodded.

"I don't believe we carry it in Erminia. We might need to do something about that, among other things."

And there they were, at the crux of their meeting. His forthcoming marriage to Rocco's sister. Thierry tried to summon the interest he knew the subject was due—it was his duty after all—but it had been a long time since his first meeting with Princess Mila and it had not gone well at all. Though he supposed, it had gone better than if she'd thrown up on his shoes, and from the look he'd seen on her face, that had certainly been a possibility.

No, he castigated himself. He wasn't being fair to her. She'd been a child still, brought up in a sheltered environment, nervous at meeting her future husband for the first time. What else had he expected? A beautiful woman of the world? Someone he could converse with at length on topics near and dear to his heart?

For a moment he was caught by a flash of memory of

a woman who'd been exactly that. That brief moment in time with Angel was less than a week ago, but it felt as if an entire lifetime had passed since then. He pushed the memory from his mind but he couldn't hold back his body's response. Just a thought of Angel and excitement rippled through his veins. For the briefest instant he wished he could have been an ordinary man. One who might have been permitted to pursue, to court, to bed his Angel. But he shoved the thought unceremoniously from his mind. His was no ordinary life. He was no ordinary man. And, he was soon to marry a princess.

And just like that the thrill that had coursed through him was gone. Thierry took another slug of his beer and turned to his guest.

"How is Mila? Did she enjoy her time in the United States?"

And, pow, there it was again. The memory of his own time in the United States, with Angel. The scent of her skin as he held her while they slow-danced. The sweet, *sweet* taste of her lips as they bade one another farewell.

He realized that Rocco had spoken and was awaiting a response. "I'm sorry," he apologized swiftly. "Could you repeat that?"

"Daydreaming about your bride already," Rocco said with a tight smile. "A promising start to your forthcoming nuptials. I said that she has returned both well-educated and well-polished. Provided you look after her, she will make a most suitable consort for you, I'm sure."

There was a thread of protectiveness in Rocco's tone that was unmistakable. Rocco could rest assured that Thierry had no intention of harming his new bride. In fact he was taking steps to ensure that she was well-satisfied in their union, both in bed and out of it. But that wasn't the kind of thing one shared with the brother of your fi-

ancée, Thierry thought as he schooled himself to make a
suitable response to Rocco's comment.

Before long they turned their discussion to broader topics relating to their two nations, and how they hoped to
mend the rifts between them. By the time Rocco withdrew from their talks three hours later, they'd reached an
accord—one underpinned by an implicit understanding
that while Rocco's sister's happiness was of the utmost importance, of equal magnitude was the well-being of both of
their countries, starting with reconciliation and moving on
toward growth and prosperity. In fact, if pushed, Thierry
wasn't certain if Rocco did not give the latter even more
weight and consequence than his sister. Perhaps the two
went hand in hand, he reasoned as he saw his guest from
the room. One thing had been made adamantly clear, however. If relations between him and his new bride failed, the
uneasy peace between their nations would shatter, causing
a return to the economic instability that currently gripped
his country and possibly even early stages of war. It was a
sobering thought.

As the door closed behind his visitor, Thierry reached
for the brandy decanter and poured himself a measure.
Taking it over to one of the deep-set windows, he looked
out toward Erminia. What was his bride doing now?
Brushing up on Sylvano protocol, perhaps?

He hoped she was well prepared for the life she would
soon face. There was only so much sheltering he could do
for his new wife. She had duties already diarized for when
they returned from their honeymoon and he wouldn't be
able to continue to protect her from the glaring lens of
the media as she had been to date. Still, he considered,
as he took a sip of the brandy and allowed it to roll on his
tongue, he had excellent staff who would assist her in her
transformation from princess to queen consort if that was
necessary. Perhaps he needed to focus less upon Princess

Mila and what she needed to do and more upon himself and what he needed to do to keep her happy.

His upbringing had made one thing absolutely clear to him—if the royal couple were not united in everything, the entire country suffered. And so he had taken steps to ensure his education in the delights of the marital bed. Before his wedding day, he would learn how to keep his wife satisfied—and those lessons would be undertaken well away from any media spotlight. He looked forward to it. Of course, his personal vows meant that the instruction would be strictly hands off, with no actual physical intimacy between himself and his instructor. But even without direct demonstration, he knew there was still so much he could learn that would help him start his marriage on the right foot. He wanted to know exactly what it was that a woman needed to be seduced—not only physically, but emotionally and spiritually as well—into remaining committed to her union with him.

Neither the example his parents had left him, nor several generations of grandparents before them, was conducive to the kind of future he sought to achieve with his wife. He wanted to be happy and stable in his marriage, and he wanted his children to know the same happiness and stability. Was that too much to ask? He didn't believe so. It wouldn't necessarily be easy to achieve, since he and his bride would be entering marriage as strangers, but that was where his lessons would help.

Thus, his employment of the services of a discreet courtesan. Who else could educate him on the subtleties of what gave a woman the ultimate in pleasure? Being prepared had always been vital to him. He hated surprises. He would go into this marriage educated and ready, and he would take any steps necessary to make his wife love him enough to offer him the same commitment and fidelity that he was prepared to offer her.

He would do what he had to do.

Six

"This is beyond preposterous! I'm traveling on diplomatic papers. Why have I been brought in here?"

From the room where she was hiding, Mila could hear the woman arguing with the Erminian border official in a back office. She looked up as Gregor hastened through a side door.

"You have her documents?" Mila asked, rising to her feet.

"I do." He started to hand her the papers but then hesitated. "Are you certain you wish to go through with this, ma'am? The risks—"

"Are outweighed by necessity," Mila said firmly.

She held out her hand for the papers and took a moment to check the woman's passport. Long dark hair like her own, similar shape to her face. As long as no one looked too closely at eye color or height she would get away with this. An advance scouting party had already informed her of the clothing the woman had been wearing and Mila was dressed identically, right down to the large-lensed sunglasses she held in her hand and the Hermès scarf already tied over her hair. It was a relief to know that the documentation that had been confiscated from Ottavia Romolo ensured direct passage through the border crossing into Sylvain. Mila supposed that it was unlikely the prince would want his newly procured mistress to be delayed.

Nerves knotted in her stomach and she slipped on her sunglasses. Hopefully the Sylvano driver was more focused on the officials examining the contents of the trunk of his car than on the exact identity of the passenger who was about to enter the rear compartment of the limousine.

"Wish me luck, Gregor."

"Good luck, ma'am," he responded automatically, but the expression on his face was woeful.

Mila shot him a smile. "Don't worry so much, Gregor. I'm not going into enemy territory under live fire."

"You may not be under fire, ma'am, but rest assured I most certainly will be if your brother discovers what you've done and my part in it."

"Then we must make sure that doesn't happen. You have the hotel suite and security team organized for Ms. Romolo?"

"We do. She will be quite comfortable while you're away."

"Right," Mila said and straightened her shoulders. "Let's do this."

"As we discussed, I will stand on your left as we go through the outer office. Hopefully everyone will be too busy outside to pay us much attention."

"You are certain the border official is fully compliant with this?" Mila checked.

"He is, ma'am."

"Good." Mila nodded. "Let's go."

Their passage through the outer office went smoothly until they reached the main door. Someone coming through from outside bumped into Mila hard enough to knock the sunglasses from her face. She caught them in her hand before they fell far and immediately slid them back into place, briefly acknowledging the apology of the elderly gentleman who had just entered. She was so busy concentrating on getting out the door without further mishap that she didn't notice when the man did a double take before bowing deeply in her direction—his movement attracting the attention of the woman still arguing at the counter.

Outside the air was cool and redolent with the crisp scent of pine. Mila inhaled deeply and walked with confidence toward the waiting limousine. Beside her, Gregor gave a nod to the official overseeing the examination of the vehicle and he barked an order in Erminian to the border guards who promptly stepped away from the car and instructed the driver to resume his journey. Mila sank onto the wide leather seat and fastened her seat belt, surprised to find her fingers were quite steady. A minor miracle considering how fast her heart was beating, she thought. She looked up to Gregor with a smile and removed her sunglasses for a moment.

"Thank you, Gregor. I won't forget this," she said softly.

He gave her a brief nod of acknowledgment and then closed the door.

"I apologize for the waste of time, Ms. Romolo," the driver said through the intercom. "You can never trust these Erminians. Rest assured that heads will roll over this."

Mila stifled her reflexive desire to defend her people and merely murmured, "Oh, I hope not."

"I will attempt to make up the time lost through the rest of our journey. We should reach our final destination by seven-thirty this evening."

"Thank you. I think I will try to rest now."

"Certainly, Ms. Romolo. I will let you know when we are nearer the lodge."

In the last few days Mila had done her best to discover where Thierry's lodge was, but its location remained a well-kept secret. Which only served her purpose even better, of course, since it was highly unlikely they would be interrupted. But it was just a little worrying that no one who was in on this escapade with her would know exactly where she was. Her personal staff had been sworn to secrecy about her mission and her brother was still away from the palace and not expected back for another week, at least. Still, what did it matter that nobody would be able to find her? As she'd said to Gregor, it wasn't as if she was going into enemy territory.

Although, the chauffeur's comment did raise a question. He'd been very clear about how he felt about the people of her country. Was that indicative of how most Sylvanos felt? If that was the case, it would make her role as Thierry's wife that much more demanding. Not only did she have to win over her husband and his people, she would have to do so on behalf of all of the people of the land she would be leaving behind. There was a weight of responsibility on her shoulders. Maybe she should not have stayed so long in America. Not only had she distanced herself somewhat from her own people, but she'd missed the opportunity to build a rapport with Thierry's.

Mila bit pensively on her lower lip and stared out the window at the passing countryside. She'd been so determined to better herself—to become the person she thought she should be for her future husband—that she'd lost sight of other, equally important, matters. While she'd thought she was being so mindful of her duty, she'd also been terribly remiss. But it was too late to change any of that now. All she could do was try to make wise decisions going forward. But was this current plan truly wise?

She wanted to build a strong marriage with Thierry, and surely that would have to start by making herself the only woman her husband would want in his bed. Still, she'd taken a massive risk doing this. If she'd made a mistake, there was no going back now. She simply had to make this work. She had to be the courtesan Thierry was expecting and she had to make him fall in love with her so that he would never look outside of their relationship again. She was unwavering in her determination not to become a casualty of the past.

But did that mean she'd become a casualty of the future?

They'd been driving beside a massive stone wall for some time now, the road narrow and winding as it crept higher and higher into the mountains. Mila had napped on and off, but for the last half hour she'd been wide awake—too nervous to close her eyes even though weariness and anxiety pulled at her every nerve. Her mouth was dry and her head had begun to throb. Tension, that's all it was. Once she saw Thierry again she knew she'd be all right. Wouldn't she?

Of course she would, she told herself firmly. She was there to do his bidding. What man would turn that away? Her body warmed as she thought about the intensive cramming she'd done since making her decision to kidnap the courtesan and take her place. Things like, what on earth did a courtesan do?

A surge of longing swept through her body at the thought of some of the duties, making her clench her legs on the unexpected spear of need. Inside her French lace bra her breasts swelled, exerting a gentle pressure against the delicate cobwebs of fabric that barely restrained her and which teased her hardened nipples to sensitive points. She ached to feel pressure against them—the pressure of large, strong fingers or a hard, naked male chest perhaps?

Heat flooded her cheeks. Clearly her research had been quite thorough if she could react like this only based on thinking about what she'd learned. Books—both fiction and not—romantic films and even those less romantic and more blatantly erotic, had filled her days—and her nights. She'd tried to approach the information as she would any research project she'd been assigned, but she hadn't factored in her own response, or the sheer physical frustration the research engendered. While she was no stranger to her body, to say that imagining herself and Thierry engaged in the acts she'd seen had left her painfully unfulfilled would be an understatement. Right now she felt like a crate of nitroglycerin used to blow tunnels through mountains—fragile, unstable and ready to blow at the least provocation.

The car began to slow down while at the same time her pulse rate increased. Before them stood iron gates that were at least twelve feet high. Twin guard boxes stood at each side. One guard, in a Sylvano army uniform, came to the car. Mila shrank back in her seat. The driver opened his car window, said but a few words and the gates began to slowly open. They were through within seconds and, as they began to ascend the steep, winding driveway, she looked back. The gates clanged shut and a tremor passed through her body. Fear, she wondered, or anticipation of what was to come? Slowly, she turned around and faced forward. Hopefully facing her future and not failure.

Thierry stirred from the deep leather button-back chair in his study as Pasquale materialized beside him and cleared his throat.

"Sire, the guard at the gate has alerted us that Ms. Romolo's car is about twenty minutes away."

"Thank you, Pasquale, that will be all."

Thierry stared into the flames set in the ancient stone fireplace a moment longer, then rose to his feet.

"Pasquale, one more thing," he called to his departing assistant. "Please see to it that we are not disturbed this evening. In fact, please dismiss the staff until further notice."

"All the staff, sire?"

"All of them—yourself included."

"But your meals?"

"I think I can survive seeing to my own needs for a week or two," Thierry replied, with a hint of a smile on his lips. "We are well provisioned, are we not?"

"Whatever you say, sire," Pasquale said. "But I must insist that the security staff remain on the perimeter and throughout the grounds."

Thierry nodded. "Of course. And, Pasquale?"

"Yes, sire?"

His assistant gave him a look that almost begged Thierry not to make any additional scandalous requests. Thierry summoned a smile and chose his words carefully, knowing that Pasquale would not be pleased with what he had to say next.

"Please see to it that all forms of communication within the lodge are disabled. There is to be no internet, no radio, no television. In short, no distractions."

Pasquale visibly paled. "And the telephones, sire?"

"And the telephones. Obviously, for security, the radios can continue to be used."

"I must advise you against this, sire. It is foolish to leave yourself so vulnerable."

"Vulnerable? No, I don't believe so. As we just discussed, the royal guards will still be on duty. But the fewer eyes and ears that are party to this, the better. As for myself, I wish to be completely off the grid, as they say. I want no communications coming in here, or going out. Privacy, through the next week, is paramount. If necessary, you can make a statement on my behalf that I have sequestered myself in mourning for my father."

Pasquale's shoulders dropped. "Whatever you say, sire."

"Thank you, that is all. Enjoy your time off."

His assistant looked as if the man would rather suffer a root canal without pain relief than take time away from his king, but he merely gave Thierry a short bow and left the room.

Thierry walked to the mullioned windows at the end of the study and looked out over the drive. It was already busy below. Even though he'd had just a skeleton staff here since his arrival, their leaving caused a momentary upheaval as they exited the property. He watched as the last car pulled away, Pasquale's censorious expression still visible even from this, the second floor, as he was driven away.

Silence reigned. Thierry took in a deep breath and absorbed the reality of being alone. It was such a rare commodity in his life and felt strange, at odds with the norm. It excited him, along with the knowledge that shortly his guest would be here. His education would begin, in absolute privacy—only the two of them and nothing and no one else to observe.

He turned from the window, strode to the door and headed downstairs so he could wait near the front entrance for her arrival. The driver had already been instructed to leave his passenger and her luggage at the door. Thierry would welcome her and see to her things himself. He fought back a grin. This was becoming quite the adventure.

Downstairs, he waited in the great hall. In the massive fireplace, logs crackled and burned bright and warm. Even though it was spring, the air still held a bite to it up here in the mountains, and he was warmly dressed in a cream merino wool sweater and jeans. He held his hands to the heat of the flickering flames and was startled to find his fingers shook a little. Anticipation, or trepidation, he wondered. Probably a little of both.

Expectancy rolled through him like a wave. These next

days would make all the difference to the rest of his life. No wonder he was a bit nervous.

He heard the faint sound of tires on the graveled turning bay in front of the lodge. Thierry listened to the slam of a car door and the crunch of footsteps on the gravel before another door slammed closed. There was a shuffle of movement up the wide stone stairs that led to the front porch, then the sound of footsteps moving away, followed by a car door again and then the sound of the vehicle being driven away.

This was it. He straightened and moved toward the door as he heard the heavy knocker fall against the centuries-old wood. He reached for the handle and swung the door open, for a moment blinded by the low slant of evening light as it silhouetted a feminine form standing in the entrance. Every nerve in his body sprang to full alert, his blood rushing through his body as if he was preparing for battle.

His vision adjusted as the woman lifted her head and looked him in the eyes. Shock rendered him temporarily speechless as he recognized her.

"Angel?"

Seven

Thierry's pulse throbbed as his eyes raked over her. It had only been a matter of days since he'd seen her last, yet it had felt like an eternity. He hadn't expected ever to see her again, let alone here at his hunting lodge—a location so zealously guarded that no one could enter unless it was at his specific invitation. He barely believed his eyes, and yet, there she stood.

He swallowed against the questions that rose immediately in his throat, the need to know who she really was. Was she the Angel he'd met in New York or the courtesan whose services he'd contracted for the next week? Of all the people…

He realized that Angel had not yet spoken, in fact, she looked anxious, unsure of herself. Did he have it wrong? Was she not the woman he'd already met in a city so distant from the country they were now in? He began to notice the differences—the hair that was black instead of blond, the clothing she wore so vastly different from what she'd worn that evening in New York. Even the way she held herself was different—more confident and assured, although the innocence on her face was at complete odds with the way she was dressed in a figure hugging garment that both concealed and revealed at the same time. A dress designed, no doubt, to entice and intrigue a man. And the four-inch spikes she wore on her feet aided in defining the lines of her calves and making her slender legs look incredibly long and alluring.

Then she lifted a delicate hand to her face and removed her sunglasses, exposing the deep-set amber eyes that had so intrigued him. It was her. Positive recognition flooded his mind and his body. He knew her. He wanted to know her better.

This wasn't what he'd bargained for at all. He'd requested a courtesan to educate him, believing he could separate his emotions from the tutelage. That he wouldn't even think about breaching his own vow of chastity until he was with his wife for their first time together. But judging by the sensation coursing through his body, the hunger clawing with demand at the very basis of his being at the mere sight of his Angel, this was not going to be a series of easy lessons.

Thierry stepped forward and offered a hand to his guest. "Welcome to my lodge. I hope you will be comfortable here."

The formality of his words was at complete odds with the chaos of his emotions. Angel. He still couldn't believe she was here.

"Thank you, Your Majesty. I have looked forward to this time," she replied, dipping into a curtsy.

As she rose to her full height again, he realized he still held her fingers in his.

"Come inside," he said, dropping her hand and standing aside to let her pass.

As she did he caught a whiff of fragrance and felt a

moment of disillusion. The heady spicy scent was not the same as the lighter, enticing fragrance she'd worn in New York. This one spoke of experience, of sultry nights and even hotter days. It suited her, and yet, did not. It was as if his Angel was two different women. And, dammit, he was painfully attracted to both.

Why did she make him feel so intensely? Why her? He'd met hundreds, possibly thousands, of attractive women over the years. Women of aristocratic and royal birth as well as those from the people. Many had attempted to entice him into bed. But never had he felt like this. It was confusing and disturbing at the same time.

"M-my bags—shall I bring them in?" Angel asked, bending to grab the handle of a large case.

"I'll see to them myself in a moment. They will be safe there."

"Y-yourself?"

Again, that slight stutter. Could it be his courtesan was nervous? The idea fascinated him. Why would a woman like her be nervous? Surely she was used to such situations—meeting a client for the first time. Did he dare hope that her response to him left her as unsettled as he felt at the sight of her?

He smiled and gestured for her to precede him into the great hall. "I am quite strong. I think I can manage a few cases."

His words were teasing, but he saw the way her body tightened in apprehension. This wasn't how he had imagined his first meeting with a courtesan to be going at all. She was dressed like a siren, smelled like sin and seduction and yet her expression still hinted at naïveté. Perhaps that was her stock in trade, he realized. In her line of business she could be no innocent. But the appearance of it would be a highly prized commodity. He closed the door behind her and noticed her flinch at the resounding thud it made.

Discontent plucked at him, making his voice harsh when he spoke. "Why did you say nothing of this when we met in New York?"

"I—I was not engaged for your service that evening. When I am not working, I prefer to maintain discretion about my particular career. And if you recall, you were the one who bumped into me and began our conversation. I didn't seek out your company. We were simply strangers enjoying a visit to a foreign city, nothing more. I'm sorry if it disturbs you to see me again," she said in a voice so soft he wasn't even certain she'd spoken.

Her eyes were on the floor beneath her exquisitely shod feet, her hair a dark fall that almost curtained her face. He stepped closer and lifted her chin with a thumb and forefinger.

"Disturb me? No, you don't disturb me," he lied.

Hell, she disturbed him on every level but he wouldn't tell her that. Not now and probably not ever. She couldn't know quite how deeply she affected him. He was King of Sylvain and he was about to be married. He would not yield so much as a gram of his power to another. Weakness was always exploited by others less honorable. He would not give anyone the satisfaction of providing them with an "in" or a point of leverage that might lead to even wider cracks in a monarchy he was determined to preserve and to rebuild its long-lost glory. He would not be played for a fool.

"It's a good thing, isn't it? That I don't disturb you," she said, looking up beneath her lashes.

"That quite depends on whether we met by accident last week, or by design. If the latter, I should probably have my security team escort you from here immediately."

Shock slammed into Mila's chest and stole her breath away. Be taken away? Already? No. She couldn't allow that to happen. She *had* met Thierry by design, but not in the manner he thought. What was another lie on top of the gigantic one she perpetrated already? She lifted her head and straightened her shoulders, staring him directly in the eyes.

"I had no idea that I would meet you in New York," she said as boldly, and as honestly, as she could.

"But you recognized me, didn't you?" When she nodded, he added, "And you didn't see fit to introduce yourself as who you really are?"

"I did not. Meeting you like that was a bonus. A chance to see you unguarded. To understand the man behind the title, if you will."

It wasn't a lie—she meant every single word of what she'd just said. She'd treasured every second of the time they'd spent together that night. The chance to know Thierry as a man, not a prince or a king.

"And, Angel? Why go by that name?"

"It's a name I'm known by from time to time."

Again, not a lie.

Thierry studied her and she fought not to shift uncomfortably under that steely gaze. Mila allowed her gaze to take in the beauty of the man standing before her. From the second he'd opened the front door he'd taken her breath away.

Even though he was dressed casually, she couldn't help noticing the lean but powerful build of his shoulders beneath the knitted sweater. The cream wool offset the olive tone of his skin to perfection and highlighted the stubble on his jaw, making him seem dark and dangerous. A wolf in sheep's clothing? She almost laughed out loud at the irony. His jeans sat snugly on his hips, with well-worn creases at his groin that made her mind boggle on the idea of what hid beneath the fabric.

A piercing streak of need plunged to her core. Physical awareness warred with a combination of apprehension and a desire for the discovery of what making love would be like with this man. How she kept her body and her voice calm was a testament to her years of training in decorum. She wanted nothing more than to step forward. To inhale the scent of his skin at the hollow of his throat. To feel the rasp of his stubble on the tender skin of her neck, her breast, her thighs.

She had to stop this or she'd be melting into a puddle of craving helplessness. For a second she silently cursed the reading and viewing she'd done—for the want it aroused within her. But then she remembered why she was here, what she planned to do and what was at stake. Summoning every thread of control tightly to her she focused her eyes on his once more. Calming the clamor of body and forcing herself to become the worldly woman she was here representing herself to be.

Thierry appeared to come to a decision and gave her a brief sharp nod of his head.

"It seems I will have to trust you on what you say."

He hesitated as if waiting for her to say something, but Mila held her silence. One thing she had learned from a very young age was that it was often better to say nothing at all than to open your mouth and step straight into a minefield. You learned a lot more in silence than by making a noise.

Apparently silence was the right choice. Thierry continued, "You must be tired after your journey. Would you like to freshen up before having an evening meal?"

She inclined her head. "Thank you. That would be lovely."

"I'll show you to your rooms."

Her rooms? A moment of confusion assailed her. She'd expected to be staying in *his* rooms, in his bed. Was that not what he'd summoned a courtesan for? As she ascended the wide wooden staircase beside him her thoughts whirled in confusion. Perhaps he preferred to keep his own rooms and to visit his courtesan in hers. Either way, it wasn't exactly what she'd expected.

Mila reminded herself it was thc cnd goal in sight that was paramount. She'd travel whatever route it took to get there. After all, hadn't most of her life been one act or another?

Thierry led her down a long, wide wood-paneled corridor, the darkness of the walls broken here and there with paintings or hunting trophies. She shuddered as they passed one of the latter, the points of the antlers on the deer head intimidating and imposing at the same time.

"You're not a fan of hunting?" Thierry remarked as they reached the end of the corridor.

"Not especially. Not when it's for trophies alone."

"Is that a note of censure I hear in your voice?"

She stiffened, unsure of what to say next. She didn't want to criticize or to alienate. Not when she'd only just arrived. "Not censure, Your Majesty. Never that."

"Don't!" he said, the word sharp in the air between them.

"Your pardon—" she began.

"No, don't do that. Here, I am Thierry, not Your Majesty. I am simply a man."

"I beg to differ. You are not simply a man. In fact, I doubt you're *simply* anything."

He pierced her with another of those looks. But she held her ground. And then he smiled, the expression on his face easing as mirth crept into his gaze and softened the imperiousness of his stare.

"You're probably right, Ms. Romolo. However, I would prefer that you not use my title while we are within the walls of this estate. If you will not use my first name, perhaps you will continue to call me Hawk, as you did in America?"

"If you will continue to call me Angel," Mila suggested.

"Angel," he repeated, lifting his hand and stroking the curve of her cheek with the back of his index finger. "Yes, it suits you better than Ottavia."

She was glad he thought so, since she didn't think she could stand to hear him call her by another woman's name when they were intimately engaged. "Then we are agreed?"

"Yes." She offered him her hand. "It's a deal."

He took her hand in his and she felt the heat of his palm against her own. The sensation made her catch her breath, her imagination already working overtime imagining that dry heat on other, more sensitive, parts of her body.

Thierry let her hand drop and turned to open the door before them. They entered a tastefully furnished ladies' sitting room. It looked as if it had barely changed in the past hundred years.

"It's beautiful," she said, walking toward the deep-set window and looking out over the lawn and gardens. As far as she could tell the outlook here was the only manicured part of the property, the rest had been left in its natural forested state. The lush foliage now appearing on the trees afforded the lodge its own special brand of privacy, locked as it was in a wooded cocoon. They could almost be the only two people in the world. "You must love it here. It's so isolated."

"I do," Thierry answered. He crossed the sitting room and opened another door. "This is your bedchamber."

She smiled at the old-fashioned term, but as she stepped through the doorway she acknowledged that the phrase far better fit the opulence and beauty of the furnishings than the term "bedroom."

"And you call this a hunting lodge?" Mila commented as she reached to touch the lovely, feminine silk drapes that hung at the window. "I thought hunting lodges were generally a male domain?"

"This suite has always been reserved for the mistress of the house."

Was it her imagination or did his lips curl somewhat over the term mistress? And did he mean mistress as in the female head of the household, or as another word for a temporary paramour, such as she was pretending to be?

"It's lovely. Thank you. I shall be very comfortable here."

"Fine, I shall get your bags. Your bathroom is through there. Please, take your time and come downstairs to the great hall when you're ready."

He was gone in an instant. For a big man he moved with both elegance and stealth, she realized. Mila rolled her shoulders and forced herself to relax a little now that she was alone. She'd take a shower, she decided, and change into something fresh—provided he brought her bags up as he'd promised. Strange that so far she'd seen no staff at the lodge. Why would he fetch and carry for her himself, when he should have a full complement of staff to complete his every wish?

She stepped through to the bathroom and began to disrobe, deciding that she would find out all that, and no doubt more, about him in due course. While the guest sitting room and bedroom were exquisite examples of old-world elegance and femininity, the bathroom was a tribute to unabashed luxury. Gold-veined cream marble surfaces abounded and the heated tiled floor was warm beneath her bare feet. The shower was a large glassed-in area with multiple showerheads and settings. She chuckled to herself as she figured out how to do the basics and lathered up beneath the generous spray of hot water, luxuriating in the sense of feeling fresh and clean again after her journey.

After her shower she dried herself off with a thick soft towel and shrugged into the pristine white robe that hung on the back of the bathroom door. If Thierry hadn't brought her bags up yet, she would have to attend their supper together dressed just as she was. Or maybe that had been his intention all along? A frisson of nervousness prickled across her nape. Was she well enough prepared for this charade? Could she be convincing enough? She had to be, she told herself as she tightened the sash around her waist. That was all there was to it.

In the bedroom she found her luggage—well, Ottavia Romolo's luggage. She felt like little more than a trespasser as she opened a case and began to sort through its contents. It really didn't sit comfortably with her, touching the other woman's personal things this way, but Mila steeled herself to do it. She couldn't have switched out the woman's luggage for her own without alerting the driver. The end had to justify the means. She uttered a silent thank-you to Gregor, who had suggested she pack her voluminous handbag with her own specially-purchased intimate apparel—undergarments that were far racier and far more enticing than what she would usually wear—because, while she was virtually slipping into another woman's skin, she absolutely drew the line at using her underwear.

Mila put the lace confections that were Ottavia's lingerie to one side and concentrated on unpacking the rest of the garments from the large cases. Looking at the variety of clothing, she wondered just how many changes per day the courtesan had planned for the short duration of her stay. Several, by the looks of things—or perhaps Ottavia was just the kind of woman who preferred to have multiple choices at hand.

She held up a pair of wide-legged pants in amethyst purple and a matching tunic that was deeply embroidered and beaded around the neckline and at the ends of the three-quarter-length sleeves. This outfit would do for this evening, she decided. She dressed quickly and shivered a little as the silk trousers skimmed the surface of her buttocks. She was unused to wearing such scant underwear as the G-string she'd pulled on, but she had to admit the sensation of the finely woven fabric against her skin was a sensuous pleasure in its own right. She quickly finished unpacking and shoved the cases away in the small box room she discovered off the sitting room.

Once dressed, Mila reapplied her makeup, darkening her eyes with thick black eyeliner and a charcoal-colored shadow and applying a sultry ruby-red gloss to her lips. She brushed out her hair, leaving it to swing loose over her shoulders and slid her feet into a pair of black sandals with a delicate heel. Thank goodness she and the courtesan shared the same shoe size.

She took a final glance in the mirror to ensure she was quite ready—and a stranger looked back at her. If anything, looking at this altered version of herself gave her a sense of strength. She could be whatever she needed to be, whomever she needed to be—and do what needed to be done. A wave of desire rolled slowly through her as she contemplated the night ahead. Would they make love tonight? Would it all begin here and now? Her eyes glittered and her cheeks flushed in anticipation.

She was ready for him—oh, so very ready.

Eight

Mila tried to steel herself for what lay ahead as she descended the stairs. As she reminded herself, nothing ventured nothing gained. But how much did she stand to lose if this went wrong? Her fingers tightened on the shiny wooden balustrade. In a word, everything. Which is exactly why she had to make it work, she told herself as she reached the bottom of the staircase and entered the great hall.

Thierry stood by the fire, apparently mesmerized by the dance of flames across the massive log of wood set deep in the wide stone fireplace. She took a minute to simply take in the sight of him. Tall and upright, dressed casually still in his jeans and sweater, and yet still with that incredible air of regal command sitting so comfortably on his broad shoulders. Again she felt a pull of attraction and wondered how she would initiate their first encounter. And, what he expected of it. If, as rumor had it, he was as chaste as she, it should be a breathtaking experience for them both.

Mila focused on her surroundings. Rich, jewel-bright, hand-knotted carpets scattered across the flagstone floor, lending warmth to the hall. Comfortable furniture stood in groupings, creating nooks for conversation or privacy or simply somewhere to curl up and read a book. And then there was the massive fireplace that dominated the room. In front of it sat a long, low coffee table while comfortably worn leather couches stood in a horseshoe shape around the table, facing the fire. It looked inviting—even more so because of the man standing there with his back to her.

She drew in a breath and stepped forward. Thierry turned as her sandals made a sound on a bare patch of flagstone floor.

"You found your way back here all right," he said with a smile. "Good. Are you hungry?"

Her stomach growled in response to his question, the sound echoing in the large room and making them both laugh. "I think you can take that as a yes," she said.

A flush of embarrassment heated her cheeks. She was ravenous. She'd been far too nervous to eat breakfast this morning, or lunch. Now, she was almost light-headed with hunger. Or perhaps it was more her reaction to the nearness of her future husband that made her feel this way—as if every nerve in her body was hypersensitive and attuned to his every movement and every expression.

"I have a platter of antipasto here," Thierry said, gesturing to the coffee table. He pulled several cushions down off the leather couches and piled them on the floor by the table. "Will this do to get started?"

"It looks delicious," Mila answered and slipped off her sandals before lowering herself to the cushions as gracefully as she could. "This feels like a picnic of sorts."

"You'd prefer to sit on the sofa?" he asked, settling down beside her.

"Oh, no! I like this. It's very relaxed."

"Good," Thierry replied with a firm nod. "I want you to feel relaxed."

Mila looked at him and raised a brow in surprise. "Shouldn't I be the one making you feel that way?"

For a second Thierry looked startled and then he let loose a laugh that came from deep inside. When he settled again he gave her a piercing look. "Humor. I like that in a woman."

Mila held her tongue. She had no idea what to say in response to that. As it turned out, speech wasn't necessary. Thierry handed her a small white plate and indicated to her to help herself to the platter.

"Please, eat," he instructed.

"What do you like best?" she asked, her hand hesitating over the selection of cold meats, cheese and vegetables.

"This isn't about me," he said, a quizzical expression on his face.

"Isn't it?" she replied, looking him square in the eye. "I beg to differ. Our lessons may as well begin with this. Have you ever been fed by someone before?"

"Not since infancy," he countered.

"There's a great deal of intimacy in the act of feeding another person, don't you think? And it speaks volumes as to the give and take required in a relationship—the learning and the understanding of what pleases your partner."

She selected some slivers of artichoke heart and finely sliced salami. Wrapping the salami around the artichoke, she held it to him, silently inviting him to taste. He hesitated, then leaned forward, his lips parting. Mila's heart hammered in her chest so hard she wondered if he could hear it, and when his mouth closed around the morsel she offered—his lips brushing against the tips of her fingers—she forgot to breathe.

The sensation was electric and sent a buzz of excitement through her, making her tremble ever so slightly. He noticed and caught her with one hand, his fingers curling around her slender wrist with a gentle touch.

"I see what you mean," he said, looking at her from below hooded eyes. "It appears to affect you also. Are you okay? You don't need to be nervous with me. I'm not a king here. I'm simply…Hawk."

The man wasn't *simply* anything, Mila decided. He was *everything*, and right now that everything was just a little too much. She tugged free of his hold and inclined her head in acknowledgment.

Seeking distraction from her racing pulse and erratic breathing, she scooped up a little hummus on a slice of roasted red pepper and offered it to him. He smiled in response, just a sweet curve of his lips, before opening his mouth to take the morsel. He nodded and made a sound of approval at the combination of flavors before reaching for some food, which he then offered to her. Mila found it disconcerting to be on the receiving end of his attentions, but as the piquant flavor of the tomato relish on the sliver of garlic bread he'd chosen for her burst on her tongue she gave herself over to the delight of flavor and texture even as she tried to distance herself mentally from the man in front of her.

Tried, and failed.

"What would you like to drink?" Thierry asked. "Do you prefer red wine, or white? Or, perhaps, you'd prefer champagne to celebrate our coming together?"

There was something in the way he'd said those last two words that made Mila's inner muscles squeeze hard on a piercing hunger that had nothing to do with food and everything to do with him.

"Champagne, I think," she said.

He rose to his feet. "I'll be right back."

Why did he not summon a staff member to pour for

them, she wondered. Her question must have registered on her face because Thierry hesitated a moment.

"Is there something wrong?"

"No, not at all. I was just wondering, where is your staff? They seem to be absent tonight?"

"They are absent altogether."

"I beg your pardon?"

"I have dismissed my staff for the duration of your stay. I'm sure you understand. I had no desire for an audience, or for distractions, during our time together."

They were completely alone? The idea both thrilled and terrified her.

"I believe I can make my own bed," she said with a small laugh, then realized that she'd brought their conversation immediately to her sleeping arrangements.

"I'm sure you are as resourceful as you are beautiful. Now, I'll get that champagne."

He was gone in an instant and Mila leaned back against the sofa behind her wondering what to make of it all. Of course he wouldn't want witnesses to their liaison, why hadn't she considered that before? Not so much for her protection as for his, she understood, but in its own way it worked out even better for her. There was less chance that someone might recognize her—not that she expected anyone to. She'd been overseas for such a long time and during her childhood she had all but melted into obscurity as the awkward, unattractive younger sister of the Erminian king. Looking back she barely recognized herself sometimes. And yet, deep inside, there still remained the girl who simply wanted to please and to know she was loved. Would Thierry fall in love with her?

She could tell he was definitely attracted to her. The warmth in his gaze when it drifted over her body was clearly the interest of a man toward a woman. The knowledge gave her a sense of power and she wondered again when they would begin to put her research to practice. He did not seem to be in any hurry to take her to bed. And as for her, she knew she wanted him, but she wanted all of him, not just physically. How would she be able to ensure that?

"You look deep in thought," Thierry said, returning to the hall with an ice bucket in one hand and two crystal champagne flutes in the other.

"I was," she admitted, shifting a little on the bed of cushions. "To be honest, I was wondering what it is you expect of me. After all, I am here to please you, am I not?"

Thierry halted halfway through removing the foil from the bottle of one of France's finest vineyards.

"You are, and I believe your brief was made clear to you in our correspondence."

Damn, Mila thought. Of course there would have been correspondence between Thierry and the courtesan. Why had she not thought this through further? She pulled her scattered thoughts in order and smiled back at him before speaking.

"I would like to hear, in your own words, exactly what you expect of me."

"You are to instruct me in the art of seduction. It is important to me that my future wife be well satisfied in the bedroom," he said, pouring the champagne adeptly.

Mila felt her eyes open as wide as saucers. That wasn't what she had been expecting. He was doing this for *her*?

"That is very noble of you, Hawk," she said, accepting one of the flutes and holding it up in a toast. "Perhaps we should make a pledge, to each strive to do our best to ensure you have a very long and a very happy marriage."

Thierry lifted his glass and clinked it against hers. "To my long and happy marriage," he repeated.

The bubbles fizzed over the surface of her tongue in much the same way that anticipation now sparkled through her veins. A new thought occurred to her, and she voiced it without filtering the words in her head.

"And what about when you're out of the bedroom? Do you plan to keep your wife satisfied in all things?"

Thierry took a long drink of his champagne before nodding. "If I can. I want you to know that the success of my marriage is paramount in my mind. I do not want to be the object of pity or gossips or to repeat any of the mistakes of the past that my parents and theirs before them perpetuated."

His words came through loud and clear. There was no mistaking the emotion or the intent behind them. It was something Mila had not expected. It seemed that they both wished for the same in their marriage.

"I understand."

He turned to her. "Do you? I wonder. I imagine for a woman such as yourself that it is hard to understand that a man should want a happy marriage."

"Not so impossible," Mila countered. "I would like to believe that deep down it is every man's desire—and every woman's also. It's my greatest wish to have a happy and fulfilling union with my husband one day."

Thierry did not reply, simply looked toward the fire, and Mila watched as the reflection of the flames etched sharper lines on his face. She leaned forward and placed a hand on his forearm.

"You speak of giving your wife satisfaction. Tell me, Hawk, exactly what you mean. Right here, right now, what you expect of me to achieve this?"

"I want you to tell me what will make my wife happy. I want to know how to understand everything about her— her moods, her needs, her desires. All of it."

"Don't you think you would have been better served to have talked to *her* about those things?"

He shook his head. "It has been impossible. She has

lived overseas for the past seven years and she was such a frightened rabbit the first time I met her I doubt she would have welcomed any overtures from me in the interim. I am afraid that she will consider our marriage to be a duty, and nothing more."

"But the two of you *are* marrying for duty, are you not?"

It felt weird to be talking about herself to him like this, as if she were another person.

"Yes, we are. But our marriage need not be entirely based on duty."

"So, you want to take your relationship with her slowly?"

He barked a cynical laugh. "That will be impossible when we are to be married at the end of the month."

"And you cannot court her once you are her husband?"

He shook his head. "There will be…expectations put upon us from the start. It will be difficult to court her with the eyes of every man, woman and child in both Sylvain and Erminia upon us."

She understood, perfectly. Since she'd been home she had struggled with the knowledge that there were eyes upon her all the time. It had made it difficult to disappear on this quest but, thankfully, not impossible. With her brother away on official business she'd only had to inform his immediate staff that she would be taking some time to herself and retiring for some privacy before the pomp and ceremony of her wedding.

Thankfully, no one had questioned it and with the vow of deference to her will that her staff had taken, they basically had no choice but to accede to her commands and go through the motions of transporting her to the royal family's summer lake house. It still sat uncomfortably on her shoulders that she'd had to go to such lengths, but being here with Thierry like this, she knew she'd done the right thing. When else would she have had the opportunity to get to know him like this?

"So, as you see, I need to fast-track our courtship," Thierry commented, selecting another morsel from the platter and offering it to her. "Let's begin with foreplay, hmm?"

Mila shook her head. As hungry as she'd been before, she could barely think about eating now. Her mind was in overdrive. She'd totally underestimated Thierry—taking on face value alone the idea behind him requesting the services of a courtesan. Not for a moment had she considered that he had done so for her benefit. There still remained the ugly stain of jealousy, though, that he had not planned to come to his marriage as virginal as she, that he had chosen to learn seduction from a stranger rather than seeking to learn together with her, as husband and wife. Getting to understand him, even in the tiny slice of time they'd had together today, she knew she wanted to be the only one to give him pleasure. To show him the kind of physical love that melded hearts together forever.

"I think it is safe to say that a woman wants to be made to feel special all the time. Not just when you're going to bed."

Thierry cocked his head at her and feigned a look of complete shock. "Really?" he said, as if she'd just disclosed a secret of monumental importance.

Mila reached over and gave him a playful shove. "Yes, really. Are you prepared to listen to me, or not?"

"Of course I am prepared to listen to you," he said, stretching lazily in front of the fire.

Mila couldn't help but watch him. Not for the first time she was reminded of a jungle cat. Long and lithe and powerful. Seductive by virtue of its leashed power and strength alone, but when combined with its beauty a woman could become totally and irrevocably lost. And she was. Lost in him. She ached to tell him the truth about who she was but she couldn't. Not yet, not until she felt certain that he cared for her the way she did for him.

Cared? The word was an insipid descriptor for the way her emotions churned in a constant roil of awareness in his presence.

She snapped her attention back to their discussion.

"It is not enough to simply smile lasciviously at your wife at bed time and tell her how sexy she looks."

"That is something I should not do?"

"No, you misunderstand me. Or, perhaps, I misrepresent what I'm trying to say." She sighed and tried to get her thoughts in order. Not an easy task when he lay on display in front of her, looking sinfully appealing. Mila cleared her throat and directed her gaze beyond him, to the flames that flickered and danced over the log in the grate. "What I mean is that you can find opportunities to seduce your wife every single day. From first waking until you go to sleep at night. You need to season her day with expressions of love, with touches that show her you're thinking of her."

"I'm to grope her at every occasion?" Thierry smiled with a glint of mischief in his eyes.

"Even you should know that's not appropriate. Sure, a gentle brush of her buttocks or her breast from time to time occurs in a natural day, but it's the other touches. The smoothing of a strand of hair, the tangle of fingers as you walk together. Intimacy grows in the little things. Something as simple as making eye contact when you both witness something that you each know the other will find amusing. Or something more concrete, like the note you leave on her pillow or the text you send when you're apart to say you're thinking of her, or the picture you take and message to her because you know she would appreciate it. It is all the things like that which show you care."

"Involving her in my day-to-day moments, you mean. And when she physically shares those with me, I should show her I'm glad she is with me. That sort of thing?"

Mila smiled in approval. "Yes, exactly that sort of thing.

Seduction—particularly when your goal is to win over her heart as well as her body—is a constant thing, not just a something to use when you want to get into a woman's pants."

"Even if I do?"

"I guess there's a time and a place for that. I just know that for many women, myself included, I can't simply turn my libido on and off with a switch. We generally don't compartmentalize like that. Our thoughts and responsibilities are a nest of interconnected strands. I would respond best to my senses being wooed throughout the day, with repeated reminders that I am valued and desired. To small indications that someone is thinking of me and, if I'm not with them, that they wish I was."

"So, first I need to seduce my bride's mind?"

"Basically. It is a shame that the two of you have not had any contact since your betrothal."

Thierry got up and stretched before settling on the deep leather chair opposite hers. "What would be the point? Our marriage has been preordained. It's not as if I need to convince her to accept my proposal."

"But you say you want a happy marriage. Don't you think your bride deserves to get to know you—to understand you?"

"She doesn't seem to think so. I have had nothing but a series of stilted correspondences from her. No photos, no calls. Getting better acquainted is a two-way street, is it not?"

Mila felt the color drain from her cheeks. Of course he was right. It was unfair of her to expect him to do all the work, to make all the effort. It seemed that in matters of the heart she was as immature as she was in matters of the body. If she'd ever doubted her decision to undertake this crazy mission, she could cast such thoughts aside. This was an education, all right. For them both.

"It most definitely is, which brings me to another question. How can your bride court you? What things can you do so she knows you welcome her into your life and your daily affairs?"

Thierry chuckled. It was a warm sound that made Mila feel happy inside and it coaxed a smile from her.

"Are you planning to spend some time educating my fiancée as well?" he asked, then laughed again at the ridiculousness of the idea.

"Would that I could," Mila murmured and avoided making eye contact. "Do you think it would work in terms of couples counseling?"

"Oh, yes, definitely." His smile died and his face grew serious again. "But the princess and I are no ordinary couple, are we? We are two strangers who will be making a life together under the strain of uniting two countries at the same time."

Mila played with the stem of her wineglass. That fact had not escaped her. So much hinged on the successful outcome of their marriage. The reopening of trade between the countries, the relaxation of military positions along the border, the widening of educational opportunities, not to mention what they could achieve in matters of ecological significance through the pooling of resources. It was true that not every couple faced the same hurdles and some would say that their hurdles were taller than most. But they could be overcome. They could be tackled if they were unified as husband and wife in more than just ceremony. Which was why it was so important that she get this right.

"Your fiancée, she is well educated, isn't she?" she asked, going through the motions of pretending to not fully understand who his fiancée was.

"Indeed. Her brother very proudly informed me of her achievements at our recent meeting, before warning me not to hurt her feelings."

Mila fought back a grin of sheer delight. Her brother had done that? She would never have believed it of him. Not the stern man she'd met with when she'd arrived home.

"And do you think you two will be compatible, mentally?"

"Of course, why wouldn't we be?"

"So what is it that worries you most? Why do you fear you will not be able to truly bond as man and wife? Is she not attractive enough?"

"Looks are not the key issue here."

"Is it the physical side of your relationship that concerns you?" Mila pressed curiously.

"Only in that I wish to learn how to please her. She will be my consort, the mother of my children. My partner, I hope, for a lifetime. I want to be able to hold her interest. To share respect for one another. To share dreams for our future. Nothing too outstanding, I suppose, but these things, they are important to me."

As they were to her also. "Then why are you so worried? Don't you think she'll want the same from your marriage?"

"I don't know. I barely know her. In fact, I barely know anything of her. I need to know how to seduce my wife— not just physically, but emotionally, too. I never want to see loathing in her eyes when she looks at me, as my mother did so often when looking at my father. And I never wish to treat her with the disdain my father showed to my mother. They could barely tolerate one another toward the end. I will not have a marriage like that."

A vein pulsed at the side of Thierry's brow, and while his voice had remained level, Mila could see the strain in his eyes as he turned to face her again.

"These are the reasons why I have employed you. I want you to teach me how to make my wife fall in love with me so deeply she will never look to another man for her fulfillment. Can you do this?"

Nine

Thierry stared into the glowing amber of Angel's eyes and willed her to give him the answer he craved.

"Let me get this clear," she said softly. "You want me to teach you to seduce your fiancée's mind and her senses, and then her body?"

"I do."

She looked surprised for a moment, but then her face cleared and her eyes shone bright as she smiled.

"Your demand is not quite what I expected but I will do what you ask."

"How do we begin this?" he asked.

"Well, when seeking to win someone over, it is customary to ask a person about the kinds of things they like, and to look for common ground amongst those things. For example, what do you like to do in your spare time?"

"Spare time? Perhaps it would be better if I understood more fully what spare time was."

Angel laughed and the sound made him feel lighter inside for the first time in days.

"Perfect!"

Thierry tried to hide his confusion. "Perfect?"

"Yes, humor is a wonderful icebreaker when you're trying to get to know someone."

Except he wasn't trying to be funny. His time was always filled with something—other than when he was here, up in the mountains. This was where he recharged for the year ahead, where he learned to calm his mind and prepared it for the demands that would be made upon him the next time he surfaced. Thierry inclined his head.

"I see. So, shall we try this? Pretend we've never met before? What if I get it wrong?"

Angel shifted on the cushions, angling herself to face him fully, and rested one elbow up on the seat of the sofa behind her. "Hawk, this is no different from when we met in New York. You did not seem to suffer from any fear of failure then."

"I was not speaking to my betrothed then," he said bluntly and was surprised to see her expression change to one of shock.

Or maybe he imagined it. Her eyelids fluttered down and when she looked up again her expression was composed once more.

"I see. Let's pretend, then, that I am your fiancée. What is it that you want to know about me?"

For a few seconds Thierry was flustered, wondering where to begin. Angel let go of that enticing laugh again and leaned forward to give him a gentle shove with one hand.

"Oh, come on! It's not that hard. What's wrong? Are you scared of her? Is she such a dragon?"

"No, of course not." Dammit, but he sounded like just the kind of stuffed prig he hated talking to. How could he expect his courtesan, let alone his bride, to enjoy talking with him and learning about him when he could barely stand the sound of his own voice right now?

"Then relax, Hawk. She probably won't bite you."

Thierry stared back at Angel, at the smile currently on her exquisitely beautiful face. At her straight white teeth. And he wondered what it would be like to feel those teeth upon his skin. Desire clawed at him, shocking him after his years of carefully honed restraint.

This had been a crazy and foolish idea. He wanted to learn how to know and understand Princess Mila, not feel hopelessly drawn to another woman. This wasn't the first time he'd experienced desire, but this was the first time he'd truly been tempted to act on it. He pushed himself upright and took a few steps closer to the fireplace. He reached for the mantel and gripped the rough-hewn wood as if his life depended on its stability, as if he could anchor himself somehow to the fact it had remained here for several hundred years. Battered and scarred but still whole and strong. The way he needed to be.

"I find it impossible to relax tonight," he announced. "Perhaps it would be best if we started anew in the morning. When we're both fresh."

He heard a rustle of movement behind him, then felt her move up close. Her scent was sultry, but subtle, and stole its way past the barriers he was trying so hard to maintain.

"I'm sorry, Hawk. I didn't mean to—" Her voice trailed off before she finished her sentence.

"No, it's not you. I expected too much from tonight. I have so little time and—"

She interrupted, "And I can see how important this is to you. It's okay, I understand. I will see you in the morning."

She moved away and he fought the urge to try and stop her, reminding himself he needed some time and space to shore up his strength against the enticement she presented.

"Yes, the morning. Do you ride?" he asked abruptly and spun around to face her.

"It has been a while but, yes, I am capable of riding."

"We'll ride before breakfast, then. Meet me in the stables out back when you wake."

"I'm an early riser," she said, cocking her head to one side. "Are you?"

He couldn't help it. He sensed innuendo in every word that fell from those lush and inviting lips, and God help him but he wanted to act on it. Only half a dozen steps would take him from where he was now to where she stood. Six strides and he could have her in his arms. Could press his mouth to hers and taste again the nectar that he'd tasted all too briefly when they had kissed in New York. He felt his body begin to move, took one step, then stopped himself from going any further.

"Yes," he bit out. "I am awake with the birds most mornings."

She inclined her head gracefully, her hair falling forward to expose the gentle curve of her neck. His fingers itched to caress that fall of hair. His lips tingled in anticipation of placing a kiss, just there on that exposed section of skin. Thierry shoved his hands into the front pockets of his jeans to stop himself from reaching for her.

He watched as she ascended the stairs, her sandals dangling from her fingers. The fabric of her tunic drifted over her body in places he should not be looking. But he looked. And he craved.

With a muttered epithet Thierry spun on his heel and made for the front door and, flinging it wide open, he strode outside into the evening. He made a sharp left and headed for the woods. He would work this out of his system somehow.

* * *

The moon's silvered light filtered across the edges of the mountains as he made his way back to the lodge. Even the birds had ceased their chatter and had settled down for the night. There were few lights on at the lodge as he approached, a stark reminder that he had dismissed his staff and that inside only one person remained. A person he had summoned here without realizing how alluring she would be.

How stupid could a man be? Calling upon the services of a courtesan without realizing that he would be lured into her web of temptation.

It was simple, he'd decided on his tramp through the woods. He would send her on her way in the morning. Forget the horse riding. Forget the education. Forget everything. He had made up his mind.

Right up until he stepped inside the lodge. Thirsty after his walk, he made his way into the expansive kitchen at the rear of the building. There, perched on a chair at the kitchen table was the woman who had unwittingly become his Achilles' heel. Dressed in a diaphanous robe which barely concealed the slip of satin and lace beneath it, she was biting into a chunk of bread, layered with what looked like cheese and cold meat, as if she hadn't seen a meal in a week.

She looked up, startled, as he burst into the kitchen, and fought to swallow the bite of food in her mouth. He looked at her in surprise, but then understanding dawned.

"Forgive me. I knew you were hungry and I didn't see to your needs. I am a terrible host."

She shook her head. "It's okay. I'm a big girl. I am quite capable of looking after myself."

"Do you have enough there?"

He gestured to the antipasto platter which she'd obviously brought through from the hall.

"Yes, do you want some? You must be hungry, too."

He had an appetite all right. But not for food. He shook his head in reply to her question and grabbed a glass from the cupboard and filled it with icy cold water from the kitchen faucet.

"The water here is from a mountain spring," he said, trying his best not to watch her mouth as she took another bite of her open sandwich. "Would you like a glass?"

Angel shook her head again and gestured to the glass of milk she had before her. He found a smile tugging at his lips. She was such a study in contrasts, dressed in gossamer-fine silk and eating a meal with the vigor of a farm hand after a hard morning in the fields. Earlier, she'd sipped her champagne with elegant nonchalance, but now she drank down her milk with the enthusiasm of a child. Her face was clean of makeup and she looked younger than she had before. He liked this side of her better, he decided, although he'd prefer her to be in less of a state of undress even if only for his own barely constrained sensibilities.

"Did you enjoy your walk?" she asked when her mouth was once again empty.

Enjoy it? He'd been too angry at himself to enjoy anything. The time had been utilized to rid himself of the overwhelming need to touch the woman who now sat so innocently in his kitchen. And while he had been successful in repressing his feelings for that moment in time, it seemed he only needed to be within a meter or two of her to be reduced to the same state of neediness once again.

"The woods are always lovely this time of year."

She tipped her head and studied him carefully. "You're avoiding the question. Do you do that a lot in conversation?"

"Perhaps. It is often easier than giving a straight and honest response," he admitted grudgingly.

"And do you plan to be evasive with your new wife also?"

"No," he said emphatically. "I wish to be able to be honest with her in all things. Deception is a seed of discontent. I won't have that between us."

Angel nodded slowly and selected an olive from the platter, then studied it carefully as if it was the most important thing in the room right now. She popped it in her mouth and chewed it thoughtfully before answering him.

"I'm pleased to hear it," she said simply. "So I'll ask you again. Did you enjoy your walk in the woods?"

He sighed a huff of frustration. "No. I barely noticed the woods. I went out angry and I didn't stop to enjoy the beauty that should've calmed me and now I'm angry at myself for that, too."

Angel laughed gently. "Well done. I applaud your honesty. There, now. That wasn't so hard, was it?"

"It was hell," he admitted, then unexpectedly found himself laughing with her.

"Clearly we need to work on that, hmm?" she said, slipping from her chair and picking up her plate.

He watched as she took it across to the dishwasher and put it inside before going to clear the rest of the table. Every movement silhouetted the lines of her body—the fullness of her breasts as they swayed gently with her actions, the curve of her hips and buttocks, the length of her thighs. Honesty wasn't the only thing he needed to work on. He turned and poured himself another glass of cold water. Self-control was definitely very high on that list, too, he acknowledged as his jeans became more uncomfortable by the second.

"Leave the mess. I'll clean up. It's the least I can do as your host," he said gruffly after downing the cool clear liquid in his glass. If only it was as quenching to the fire deep within him as it was to his thirst.

"Okay, I will," she said with a cheeky grin. "I'm always better at making a mess than clearing it."

"Somehow that doesn't surprise me."

Her smile widened. "Well, I think I'm quite safe in saying that I doubt you have to clean up after yourself on most occasions, hmm? After all, why would you when you normally have a bevy of staff at your beck and call."

"It's not always everything it's cracked up to be. I have little privacy."

"I can quite believe it," Angel said, solemnity replacing the fun on her face. "Well, I'll leave you to it and see you in the morning."

"Sleep well, Angel."

"Thank you. You, too, Hawk. Sweet dreams."

She turned and left the kitchen and once again, for the third time since he'd met her, he realized, he watched her walk away from him. His gut twisted and something deep in his chest pulled tight. He didn't want her to leave. It was ridiculous. He barely knew the woman. One night in New York, a brief time together tonight, and he was smitten.

Perhaps his personal vow of chastity hadn't been the right thing to do for all these years. Perhaps, if he'd been a little more free with his wants and needs, this desperate hunger would be less consuming.

She was a courtesan, he reminded himself. Her job was to entice, to be alluring. To make a man feel important and wanted and needed and desired. Clearly, she was *very* good at her job. The reminder should have been sobering—should, at the very least, have dampened the fire that simmered and glowered beneath his facade of normality. It wasn't and didn't.

Thierry turned his attention to the platter left on the table and decided to finish off the remnants. Not that there was much left. It seemed his courtesan had quite the appetite. Did that appetite for food extend to everything else she did? He groaned out loud. Damn, there he went again. Letting his mind travel along pathways that were forbidden to him.

He'd always believed himself to be a patient man. One who'd made restraint an art form. Now, it seemed, he was to test that restraint to the very edge of its limits. Somehow he had to get through the next seven days without breaking.

Ten

Mila sprang from her bed before 6 a.m. and raced through her shower. She hadn't expected to sleep well after the turmoil of last night, but the moment her head had hit the pillow she'd been lost in a deep sleep. Now, however, she was fully revitalized and ready to go.

The discussions with Thierry last night had been a complete eye-opener for her. Even now she could scarcely believe his intentions toward the courtesan—toward her. A cheery grin wreathed her face as she played his words over in her mind yet again. He was doing this all for her—the princess. It was as astounding as it was unbelievable…and it had raised one big question in her mind. Why was he so committed to doing this for her?

Maybe today she'd get to discover his reasons for his decision.

After dressing and tying her hair back in a tight ponytail, Mila riffled through the drawers, wishing she remembered better exactly where she had put everything.

She knew she'd seen a pair of riding pants amongst Ottavia Romolo's things—ah yes, here they were. She eased
into them and drew on a snug T-shirt and a sweater, then
grabbed the riding boots that had been packed. Ms. Romolo had been exceedingly well prepared, Mila conceded.
She had something for every possible eventuality, which
made Mila wonder whether the woman might have been
equally as surprised as she was upon discovering that
Thierry was more concerned with learning about how to
seduce his future wife's mind than her body.

She shoved all thoughts of the other woman from her
head. She didn't want to think, or to worry about her right
now. It was enough to know her staff would be taking very
good care of her. Surely it would make little difference to
Ms. Romolo to be paid to have a luxurious holiday rather
than to be with a client?

Mila headed downstairs in bare feet, gasping as her
soles hit the flagstone floor at the foot of the stairs. She
plonked her butt down on the bottom step and quickly
pulled on a pair of woolen socks, then the boots, huffing
a little as she did so. Man, she was out of condition if pulling on a pair of fitted boots made her breathless. Or maybe
it was just the idea of seeing Thierry again so soon that
made her heart skip and her lungs constrict.

She went through to the kitchen, grabbed an apple from
the fruit bowl on the tabletop and crunched into its juicy
sweetness as she found a corridor that led to a door at the
rear of the lodge. Outside, the morning air was crisp and
cool, but the sun had begun its ascent in the clear blue sky
and the day promised to be warm.

She crossed a wide courtyard and walked toward a large
stone barn. Inside she could hear the nicker of horses and
the sound of hooves shifting on the barn floor. It was warm
in the building and the scents of horses, hay and leather all
combined to make one of her favorite aromas. She paused

a moment in the doorway and simply inhaled, a wide smile spreading on her face. She loved this environment. It was one of the things she'd missed most while in America. Of course there had been plenty of riding stables available, but it wasn't the same as being in her own place with her own animals. Neither was this, she reminded herself. But it would be, once she and Thierry were married. And then, she'd have her own horses here, too.

"Good morning. You weren't kidding about being an early riser," Thierry said, coming out of a room at the side of the stables carrying a saddle.

He wore riding pants and boots with a fitted polo shirt. His skin was tanned and his bare arms strong and beautifully muscled. Not too much, and definitely not too little. He hefted the saddle onto a waiting tall bay gelding as if it weighed no more than the saddle blanket that already lay on the horse's back.

"Why waste a beautiful day like this in bed?" she answered.

She hadn't meant a double entendre, but it hung in the air between them as thick and as potent as a promise. Oh, she could spend a day in bed with him and not consider it wasted in the slightest, she realized. Hot color suffused her cheeks and her throat and she turned away from his direct gaze, searching for something to do or say that would distract him from her discomfort.

"Can I help you get the horses ready?" she squeaked through a constricted throat.

"I'm almost done," he replied, turning away from her and focusing his attention on cinching the girth strap and checking the stirrups. "I thought you might like to take a ride on Henri, here. He's big, but he's gentle with women."

Like you? she almost asked, but instead she stepped forward and reached out to stroke the blaze on the gelding's forehead.

"That's good," she answered, offering Henri the remains of her apple. "As I said last night, it's been a few years since I've ridden."

"He'll take good care of you, don't worry," Thierry said, dropping his hand to the horse's rump and giving him a gentle slap.

Was it Thierry's turn for double entendre now, she wondered? Would *he* take good care of her also? Before she could ask, Thierry unhooked the reins from the hitching post and began to lead Henri outside through the other end of the barn. There, another horse—this one a majestic gray stallion—waited, already saddled up.

"Oh, he's beautiful," Mila exclaimed.

"Don't tell him that, he'll get too big for his shoes," Thierry said with a laugh.

But even so, he patted the horse's neck and leaned in to whisper something to the animal that only it could hear. The horse whickered softly in response. The sight warmed her and Mila felt Thierry ease just that little bit deeper under her skin and into her heart as she observed the relationship between man and beast. Oh, he was so easy to love, especially when he was sweet and relaxed like this. He straightened and turned to face her.

"What's his name?" she asked.

"Sleipnir, it's—"

"Norse, I know. What a noble name for a noble steed. Have you had him long?"

Thierry looked taken aback at the fact she knew the origin of his horse's name. "About five years. I raised him from a colt."

"He suits you," she said, saying exactly what was on her mind.

She had no doubt the two of them would make a formidable sight paired together.

"Shall we get on our way? Perhaps I can help you mount?"

"Thank you. I wouldn't normally ask, but it's been a while."

"No problem," Thierry answered without further preamble. "Let me give you a hand."

He came around to the side of her horse and bent down, cupping his hands for her to step one foot into. His shirt stretched tight across the breadth of his shoulders and the bow of his back. Her fingers itched to reach and touch him, to stroke those long muscles along his back, to trace the line of his spine down to its base. Thierry turned his head.

"Are you ready?"

She flushed again at being caught staring at him—woolgathering and wasting time while he patiently waited for her.

"Yes, thank you," she said and hastily placed her foot in his cupped hands.

He gave her a boost and she flung her leg over the saddle to seat herself comfortably, her feet finding the stirrups and her hands gathering the reins up so she was ready to go.

"That length okay for you?" Thierry asked, one hand on her thigh as he once more checked the girth strap and the stirrups.

"Y-yes," she answered, barely able to concentrate on his question with the warmth of his hand resting so casually on her leg.

Just a few more inches inward and upward, she thought—no! She slammed the door on the wayward idea before it could bloom in her mind and get her into even more trouble.

"Yes," she said more firmly and urged Henri forward. "This is perfect, thank you."

Thierry made a grunt of assent, then swung up onto his own mount and drew up alongside her. "I thought we could take a path through the woods at first and then let the horses have their heads through the meadows on the other side. Are you up for that?"

"It sounds great. I'm up for whatever you want to do."

He gave her another of those penetrating looks and Mila wondered if she was going to have to filter every word from her mouth from now on. She hadn't meant that to come out quite the way it had…or had she? She didn't even seem to know her own mind right now. Instead, she dropped her head and stared at Henri's ears and then urged him to follow as Thierry and Sleipnir led the way out of the courtyard and toward the woods.

Birdcalls filtered around them as they entered on the bridle path. It looked well used and Mila wondered how often Thierry had the time to come up here to this private hideaway. The tranquility that surrounded them seemed worlds away from the life of a ruler she knew Thierry now lived. She'd seen firsthand what her brother's life was like—how his time was not his own. How it had changed him when he'd ascended to the throne. Would that be Thierry's fate also now that he was King of Sylvain? She hoped not. Thierry would, at least, have her by his side. Someone to share the weight of his crown when he was out of the public glare.

They rode through the woods in silence, the horses happy to simply amble along, and Mila relaxed in her saddle. No doubt she'd be a little stiff from the ride tomorrow, but for now she was loving every creak of the leathers, every scent of the woods and every sound of the awakening forest.

After about twenty minutes, the trees began to thin.

"You can give Henri his head now if you want," Thierry called from a few meters ahead of her and then did just that with his horse.

Mila and Henri were hard on their heels as they burst from the woods and into an idyllic hillside meadow, the grass interspersed with dots of color from wildflowers beginning to bloom. Mila laughed out loud as she and her mount began to gain on Thierry and Sleipnir, but it was soon apparent they were outclassed. When she eventually caught up with him, he'd dismounted beside a brook—the scene so picture-perfect it was almost cliché.

She said as much as she dismounted from Henri. Thierry came swiftly up behind her, his hands at her waist before her feet could even touch the ground.

"You think I'm cliché?" he asked with one eyebrow cocked.

She shook her head. "No, not you, just...this!" Mila spread her arms wide. "It's all so impossibly beautiful. How on earth do you stand going back to the city?"

Thierry was silent for a moment. "It's my favorite place on earth and knowing it's still here waiting for me is what makes me able to stand it."

She put a hand on his chest and stared him straight in the eyes. "Is it so hard, being royal?"

"It's my life. I don't know any different."

The words were simplistic, but there was a wealth of unspoken emotion behind them. Mila let her hand drop again and opted to attempt to lighten the mood a little.

"So it's not all tea parties and banquets?"

The corner of Thierry's mouth kicked up and she ached to kiss him, just there.

"No, it is not. Which is for the best. If it were, I would be the size of a house."

"True," she said with a considering glance his way. She poked him in the belly, her finger finding no give against his rock-hard abdomen. "You're getting a little soft there, Your Majesty."

He grabbed her hand. "Hawk. Here I am Hawk and nobody else."

She nodded, all mirth leaving her as she studied the serious expression on his face.

"Do you ever wish all of Sylvain could just be like this spot here?" she asked as they walked over to the brook to allow the horses a drink.

"Yes and no. Obviously industry is required for our country to continue to move forward and for our economy to support our people. But I am encouraging our government to always consider sustainable practices when they discuss lawmaking and our constitution. Regrettably, my direction often falls on deaf ears. It isn't always easy to persuade people to change, especially when additional cost is involved."

"I think we stand a better chance to effect change if we start at school level, so all children grow up with the idea that sustainable development is the right way—the only way—to move forward. With education and understanding, things will become easier."

"But will it happen soon enough?" Thierry mused, his gaze locked on a distant mountain peak. "Up here everything is so simple, so clean and pure. And yet, past those mountains, you can already begin to see the haze of civilization as it hangs in the air."

"I'm not convinced you'll ever see great change in our lifetime, but essentially you're not effecting change simply for change's sake, are you? You're doing it for the future, for your grandchildren and their grandchildren."

"Grandchildren," he repeated. "Now there's a daunting thought when I'm not yet married."

"They are a natural progression, are they not?" she probed.

Mila knew that she wanted children, three or four at least. She had grown up as one of a pigeon pair with an age gap that had meant she and her brother had never had as close a relationship as she would have liked. Thierry had been an only child.

"Yes, they are. To be honest, I hadn't considered children as being a part of my marriage just yet. I know I have a responsibility to my position to ensure the continuation of the line, but I want to know my wife—truly know her—before we take that step."

"Those are honorable words."

"I mean every one of them. I look at the world my forebears have created and sometimes I ask myself if I should even marry—if I should have children—or whether I should simply let the monarchy die with me."

"No! Don't say that!" Mila protested.

"Let's be honest. Monarchy is an outdated concept in this day and age."

"But you still have a role to play. You remain a figurehead for your people. A guiding light. Look at your work so far on the Sylvano waterways, how you've spearheaded campaigns to ensure clean, safe water throughout your country," she argued passionately.

"It's a step in the right direction," Thierry conceded.

"It's more than a step. You are seen to be doing the things that matter to you. You don't just pay lip service to them. You lead from the front. You give your people someone to look up to and aspire to emulate. You can't throw that away."

"And I will not. I will continue the royal line, as is my duty. I am promised to Princess Mila and I honor my promises. We will marry."

There was a note in his voice that dragged a question from deep inside her. "And if you were not already promised to her? Would you still marry the princess?"

Thierry remained silent for several seconds before answering. "I don't know."

"Well, that's honest at least," Mila muttered.

"Ah, Angel, you sound so disappointed. Have I shown to you I have feet of clay?"

"No, you've shown me you're a man. Like any man.

With the same weaknesses and worries, but with strengths, too." She paused for a moment before continuing. "I am glad you are an honorable man and that you will marry the princess, whether you think you want to or not."

And she was. Because the more she got to know the complex man who was soon to be her husband, the more she knew she would spend the rest of her life loving him.

If only she could help him to love her, too.

Eleven

"Whether I think I want to, or not?" Thierry repeated.

It was an odd way for her to phrase such a sentence, he thought as he studied her.

"Yes, although I think you probably do your princess a disservice."

"How so?"

"Perhaps her feelings are not so distant from your own. Perhaps she, too, is mindful of her duty to her king and her country—and your country, as well—and, perhaps, all she wants to do is find a common ground between you so that you can have a full and happy life together."

He felt his lips pull into a smile. Angel's speech on behalf of an unknown woman was supportive and compassionate. He really liked that about her. In his experience, the women in his circles were never invested in each other's well-being in the way that Angel apparently was for Princess Mila. It showed another side to her that pulled strongly at him. If only he had the luxury of marrying a wife of his own choosing, he would definitely have chosen a woman such as Angel. But then again, he rationalized, if he wasn't who he was with an arranged marriage ahead of him, he would never have had cause to meet his courtesan beyond their stolen evening in New York, would he?

He looked at her, really looked this time. In the early morning light she appeared fresh and invigorated. Eager to seize the day they had ahead of them and all that it offered. Her long dark hair was drawn tightly off her face in a ponytail, exposing delicate cheekbones and a jaw that was made for a line of sensual kisses that would lead a man directly to those invitingly full lips. If he wasn't mistaken, she didn't wear so much as a slick of lipgloss this morning. Her naked face was even more beautiful than the visage of the seductress who'd joined him for antipasto yesterday evening.

The simmering sense of awareness that sizzled through his veins whenever he was near her burned a little brighter and his body stirred with longing.

"You make an interesting point," he eventually conceded, dragging his gaze from her face and looking long into the distance as if that could erase the growing need for her that unfurled inside him.

"Of course I do. I'm a woman. I know what I'm talking about," Angel said lightly, then punctuated her words with a small shove at his shoulder. "You should listen to me."

He laughed. "I'm listening. Now, tell me more about how I am to seduce my bride's mind."

"Be interested in her, genuinely interested."

Thierry was taken aback. "It's that simple?"

Angel groaned in response. "Of course it is. What do women do when they meet someone?"

He looked at her blankly. How was he supposed to know that?

"They ask questions," Angel said, a thread of irritation

evident in her voice. "They show an interest. Like this for example. Your horses are beautiful, do you buy them yourself or does your stable master do that for you?"

"The horses here at the lodge are all handpicked by me or bred through the breeding program I have established at the palace stables."

"See? It's as easy as that. With my question and your answer, we've opened up a dialogue that could keep us in conversation, discovering similar interests, for some time. And it branches off from that. For example, did you get that scar beside your right eyebrow while riding? It's so faint as to barely be noticeable but—" she lifted her hand and caught his jaw with her fingers, turning his head slightly to one side "—when the light catches you just so, it's visible."

Thierry tried to ignore the sensation of her fingers on his jaw. He hadn't shaved this morning and the rasp of her skin across his stubble sent a tingle through him. If he moved bare millimeters, he would catch her fingertips with his lips. He slammed the door on those thoughts before he could act on them. A lifetime of analyzing his every thought and action gave him the strength he needed right now to bear her touch without showing her how it affected him. He drew in a breath, waited for her to release him and let the breath go in a long steady rush of air as she did so.

His voice was calm when he answered, "Very observant of you. Yes, I wasn't paying attention one day when out riding. My mount was a rascal, prone to dropping riders whenever he felt like it. I was so busy talking to my companions as we rode that I didn't notice a low-lying branch. It collected me and dumped me quite unceremoniously on my royal behind. Of course, there was a major panic when everyone saw the blood, but, despite the scar it left, the wound was minimal and the experience taught me to be more aware of my surroundings at all times."

"How old were you when it happened?"

"I was eight years old. My father scolded me soundly for being so careless even while my mother fussed over me as if I had a life-threatening injury."

"I'm sorry."

"Sorry? Why?"

"The contrast in the ways they treated you tells me that you were probably left very confused afterward."

Confused? Yes, he had been confused and sore. But how had she known that? Most people asked him how many stitches he'd had or joked about him making a royal decree to have the tree chopped down or, worse, have the pony destroyed. No one had ever come to the conclusion Angel had just now. Something in his chest tightened as her care and understanding worked its way past his defenses.

Angel lifted her hand again, one finger tracing the silvered line that ran from his eyebrow to his hairline. Her eyes were fixed on the path of her fingertip, her expression one of concern and compassion, but all of a sudden her expression changed and she let her hand drop once more. This time her fingers curled into a fist before she crossed her arms firmly around her, almost as if she couldn't trust herself not to touch him again. The thought intrigued him and made him step forward a little, closing the distance between them to almost nothing.

"And you?" he asked. "Do you have any interesting tales to tell about any scars you might have hidden upon your body?"

Angel lifted her chin, her lips parted on a breath. "I…"

Suddenly she stepped away and walked over to where Henri was now grazing and gathered up the reins.

"You're getting the hang of it," she said.

"The hang of it?" He was momentarily confused.

"Getting to know someone. Shall we carry on? We can talk while we ride."

Why was she creating distance between them all of a

sudden? he wondered. It was she who had suggested he ask questions and probe his conversational partner to discover more about her. And yet, when he asked one simple thing she backed away as if she was afraid to answer. The thought intrigued him and he stowed it away to explore further another time.

"Certainly, if that's what you want. We can head back to the lodge for breakfast."

"That sounds like a good idea."

He drew close beside her and squatted down to offer her a boost onto the horse. This time he couldn't help but notice how the fabric of her riding pants clung to her thighs and buttocks as she bent her leg and put her foot in his hand. She sprang up into the saddle and gently guided Henri away from him, as if she was determined to create some distance between them.

Thierry wasted no time in mounting Sleipnir. "We'll take a different path back," he called to Angel, leading the way again.

Back at the lodge she dismounted quickly and led Henri into the barn and began to undo the girth strap of his saddle. Thierry hastened to her side and put his hands at her waist to gently pull her aside.

"Leave that. It will be taken care of."

"I'm not a delicate flower, you know. I can help."

"Fine," he replied, letting her go before he did something stupid like give in to the urge to pull her hard against his body and rediscover what it would feel like to hold her in his arms. He nodded toward the tack room. "Get the brushes while I remove the saddles."

She did as he asked and he took the opportunity to watch her walk away. She held herself straight and tall and moved with an elegance that was at odds with her attire. He tore his gaze away from the ravishing picture she made and put his attention back toward the horses.

* * *

In the tack room Mila took a moment to steady herself. Being with Thierry was proving insightful and immensely difficult at the same time. She ached to tell him the truth about who she was and remove the veils of subterfuge she'd wreathed between them, but she couldn't. She doubted he'd take too kindly to being tricked like this but she wished—oh, how she wished—she could be herself with him. There'd be time enough for that once they were married, she reminded herself, and looked around the room for the brushes he'd sent her to find.

Grabbing two, she went back out into the barn. Together they finished tidying up and grooming the horses before returning them to their stalls. Once they were done, Mila dusted her hands off on her pants. The atmosphere between them had been easy enough while they attended to the horses, but right now she felt awkward.

"Shall I go and see what I can put together for breakfast?" she asked.

"You don't trust me to cook?" Thierry lifted one eyebrow, as if punctuating his question. Her heart did a little flip-flop in her chest.

"It's not that," she protested.

"It's okay. I am man enough to take advantage of your offer. I'll go and shower while you do your thing in the kitchen."

Mila narrowed her eyes at him. "Are you being sexist again?"

"Again?"

"Like you were in New York."

He snorted a laugh. "Not at all, at least I didn't mean it to come across that way. To make up for any offense I may have caused, I'll provide the rest of our meals today. Is that punishment enough for my apparent lapse of manners?"

She couldn't help it—she smiled in return and inclined her head in acceptance. "Thank you. That would be lovely."

"And that is the perfect example of how I should have responded," he commented.

"You're a quick study," she teased, feeling herself relax again.

"I'll need to be if I'm to ace all my lessons with you."

And in an instant, there it was again. The sensual tension that drew as tight as an overstretched bow between them. Mila felt as if every cell in her body urged her to move toward him. Did he step closer to her? Or she to him? Whether it was either or both of them, somehow they ended up face-to-face. She felt his hands at her waist again, hers suddenly rested on his chest. Beneath her palms she felt the raggedness of his breathing, the pounding of his heart. And when he bent his head and pressed his lips to hers, she felt her body melt into him as if this was what they should have been doing all along.

No more skirting around the subject of getting to know a person. Simply a man responding to a woman. And what a response. She flexed her body against his, relishing the hard muscles of his chest and abdomen against her softness, purring a sigh of pure feminine satisfaction when she felt the hardness at his groin. The concrete evidence that he found her attractive.

All the years of feeling as though she'd never be anything to him but the gauche teenager she'd been all those years before fell away as if they were nothing.

His hands were at her back, pressing her more firmly to him. Her breasts were pressed against his chest and she welcomed the pressure, felt her nipples harden into painfully tight points that begged for more of his touch. The restrictions of her bra and clothing were too much, and too little at the same time.

Thierry's lips were firm against hers, coaxing. She opened her mouth and gave a shudder of delight as he gently sucked her lower lip against his tongue. The heat of his mouth against that oh-so-tender skin made her fingers curl against his chest, her nails digging into the fabric of his shirt as if she needed to anchor herself to him, to anything that would stop her from floating away on the tide of responsiveness that coursed through her.

And then, in an instant, there was nothing but air in front of her. Mila almost lost her balance as she opened her eyes and realized Thierry had thrust her from him and taken several long steps away.

"H-Hawk?" she asked, reaching out a hand.

"Don't!" he snapped in return and wiped a shaking hand across his face. "Don't touch me. I should not have done that. I apologize for my actions."

"But…why not? What is wrong? I'm here as your courtesan, am I not?"

Confusion swirled through Mila's mind as she fought to understand.

"I must remain faithful to my promise. I cannot touch you like that again. This was a mistake. Being here with you, of all people—it's making me weak."

There was genuine pain in his voice. Pain laced with disgust. At himself, she recognized, not her.

"Your promise to marry the princess?" she probed, seeking more clarity.

"Yes, my promise to her. And my promise to myself."

"Tell me of your promise to yourself," she asked softly.

"I can't—not right now. Please, go inside the lodge. I just need some time to recompose myself." He looked at her, his eyes as stormy as a mountain lake on a cloudy, windswept day.

But she didn't want to let it go. Not when her entire body still hummed with the effect of his kiss.

"No, tell me now. I'm here to help you. How can I do that

if you shut me out?" She walked toward him and caught him by the hand. "Hawk, let me understand you. Please?"

She watched the muscles in his throat work as he swallowed. He held himself so rigid, so controlled, that she feared he would reject her overture. But then, millimeter by scant millimeter she began to feel him relax. He drew in a deep breath and then slowly let it go again. His voice, when he spoke, was raw, as if his throat hurt to let go of the words.

"Fidelity is everything to me."

"As it should be," she said softly.

"No, you don't understand." He shook his head.

"Then tell me. Explain it to me," Mila urged.

"I grew up watching my parents live side by side but I never saw them as a couple, not in the true sense of the word. By the time I was old enough to notice, they barely even liked one another, but they couldn't live apart because of their position. They spent years barely tolerating one another, with my father putting every other obligation and concern ahead of his wife's happiness until my mother could no longer put up with it. She followed her heart into a relationship with someone who she believed would love her—and it destroyed her. I will not put my wife through anything like that."

"And yourself? What about what you want?"

"I just want to be the best I can be, at everything, and ensure that no harm comes to my people...including my wife."

"Hawk, that is admirable, but you have to realize that you can't control *everything*."

He pulled away. "I can. I am King of Sylvain. If I cannot control the things within my sphere of influence, what use am I? I won't be my father. I won't just stand by and allow my inadequacies as a person to lead to others' misfortune. I will have a successful marriage and my wife will love me."

"And will you love your wife equally in return?"

Twelve

Thierry felt her words as if they were a physical assault.

"I will respect her and honor her as my consort and I will do everything in my power to make sure she is happy. Isn't that enough?"

Angel looked at him with pity in her eyes. "What do you think, Hawk? If you loved someone and respect and honor was all you could expect from them for the rest of your life, do you think that would be enough for you? Isn't that no more than your father offered your mother?"

Thierry snorted. "He did not respect her nor did he give a damn for her happiness. She was a vessel for his heir—no more, no less—and when she refused him and wouldn't share his bed he found others more accommodating."

She looked shocked. Clearly she had not heard the rumors about his father's many affairs. None of them proven, of course, but Thierry knew they had happened. Discreetly and very much behind closed doors. Where else had the idea of a courtesan come from but his father? Hell, the man had even offered to arrange one for Thierry. He studied Angel carefully.

"I would never treat my wife so cruelly," he assured her. "I will ensure that she is always treated with the dignity due to a princess."

"But you want more than that from her," she argued. "You want her to love you. Yet you won't offer her love in return?"

"I…cannot promise her that," he choked out.

The shock had faded from her face, but now it was replaced with disappointment.

"Then I am sorry for your bride," she said eventually, her voice hollow. "Because I could not live without love."

She turned and went inside the lodge and he watched her every step feeling as if, piece by piece, slices of his heart were being torn from him. She could not live without love? He didn't even know what love was. He'd never experienced it firsthand. But he did understand attraction and how it could lead to trouble.

He turned and walked away from the lodge and headed back into the woods, stopping only when he could no longer feel the pull that urged him to follow her. To apologize for the things he'd said and to tell her that—

That what?

That he loved *her*? The idea was ridiculous. He was drawn to her, but that was all.

He should have stuck with his decision last night and sent her away. This whole exercise was a waste of time. He was not achieving his objectives, only complicating matters. With the thought firming in his mind, he returned to the lodge. The words telling her that her services were no longer required hovered on his tongue until she turned to face him and he could see she'd been crying.

Pain shafted him like an arrow straight to his heart and

he crossed the floor to gather her into his arms. She resisted a little, at first, then gave in to his embrace.

"I am sorry," he murmured as he pressed his lips to the
top of her head. "I didn't mean to upset you."

"Y-you didn't," she hiccupped on a sob. "It was me and
my stupid ideals."

"It isn't stupid to want to be loved," he countered.

As he said the words, he realized that he meant them.
That they weren't the hollow uttering of a man so jaded
by his parents and so many of the people in his sphere that
he'd lost all belief in love. When he was with Angel, he
wanted to believe that love was possible. But he couldn't
even begin to contemplate such a thing with her. She was
his courtesan, not his princess. Which begged the question, why did she feel so right in his arms and why did
every particle in his body urge him to simply follow his
instincts and to revel in all she could offer?

Angel pulled loose from his arms and stepped back.

"It isn't the role of a courtesan to be loved," she said
bleakly. "But I do think you should at least be open to loving your wife if you expect to have a long and happy marriage. You seem to have this idea that you must keep her
happy, which is admirable. But should she not also provide
that same service to you?"

Her question raised an interesting point. "I hadn't considered that necessary until now," Thierry conceded.

"So now you believe it is necessary?"

He nodded. "I do. You have a lot to teach me, Angel.
I'm glad you're here."

She hesitated before speaking. Her eyes raking his
face—to see, perhaps, if he was telling her the truth. He
would not have thought it possible, but every word he'd
told her had been truthful. And now, having begun to understand how he felt, he realized just how much he wanted

what she had suggested. Could he hope to achieve that with Princess Mila?

He cast his mind back and tried to assimilate how he felt now with the young woman he remembered. Try as he might, the ideas of love and intimacy did not spring immediately to mind. And yet, when he turned his attention back to Angel, he had no difficulty at all.

"So you're not going to send me away?" Angel asked, lifting that softly rounded chin of hers in a challenge.

"How did you—?"

"It was only natural you would consider it. You are a king. I opposed your thinking, contested what you said. You could do with me whatever you wanted."

Thierry felt a flush of shame color his cheeks. "It crossed my mind," he admitted ruefully. "I would like to think that I am man enough to withstand a bit of criticism, but it seems that I am a little different from everyone else when it comes to that."

"Your wife may not always agree with you, but she will still be your wife. How do you plan to cope with that? You can't exactly throw her down an oubliette these days, or banish her to a convent."

There was a thread of humor in Angel's voice, but beneath it he detected a genuine concern for the woman he was intending to marry.

"I hadn't considered my marriage in those terms. But you can rest assured that I will neither imprison nor banish my queen consort."

"Well, that's reassuring," she commented with a touch of acerbity. "She has much to look forward to then, doesn't she?"

"I will do my best," Thierry said firmly. "And you will help me to deliver that, won't you?"

Again there was that hesitation, as if she was turning over his request in her mind before reaching her conclusion.

"Yes. I will," she promised.

Angel crossed the kitchen to the massive double refrigerator that hummed energetically.

"Eggs and bacon?" she asked over her shoulder after giving the contents a cursory glance.

"Sure. What can I do to help?" he offered.

"Nothing. Just leave it to me."

"Leave the cleanup to me, then. If you don't mind I'll go and shower."

She smiled, but it didn't reach her eyes. "That's fine."

Thierry started to leave the kitchen and hesitated a second in the doorway. He was burning to ask her why their earlier encounter had made her cry. The memory of seeing her tears sent another shock of pain through him, reminding him that he was allowing himself to become too emotionally attached to this woman.

He resolutely continued on his way upstairs, determined not to think about Angel and how she had so easily inveigled her way beneath his barriers. Somehow he had to find a way to keep her in her place—to keep things simple and straightforward between them. Teacher—to—pupil—and that was all.

It had been several days since that first ride in the woods, and she and Thierry had settled into a pattern, of sorts. They spent their early mornings riding or walking in the woods. Together they had covered a wide variety of conversational topics and Mila took every opportunity to encourage him to do so—hoping that he would continue to seek her opinion once they were married. It began to weigh upon her that he would probably not be too thrilled when he discovered her deception, but she rationalized that with his own desire to know how to please her. Who better to instruct him than herself?

Their evenings, on the other hand, were a lesson in

torture. After that first day, Thierry had begun to ask her advice about the physical side of a man and a woman's relationship. About the gentle touches that a couple might enjoy together in a nonsexual way to reinforce their togetherness. It had seemed only natural for Mila to steer their conversation toward more intimate and sensual matters and last night, by the time she ascended the stairs to her rooms, every nerve in her body had been screaming for release. Satisfying her frustration in the deep spa bath in her en suite bathroom had left her feeling physically gratified but emotionally empty and strung out. Judging by Thierry's bear-headedness this morning, he had been left feeling much the same way.

When she'd told him she would not be riding with him this morning, but planned instead to take advantage of the beautiful library, with its floor-to-ceiling shelves, on the ground floor of the lodge, he'd been short with her to the point of rudeness. She'd let him go without comment, even though his words and manner had left her feeling as if she'd done ten rounds with an angry wasp's nest. The skies had opened shortly after he'd left on Sleipnir and he hadn't returned for several hours.

It was hard to concentrate on the book she'd selected from the shelves as she waited for him to return. She'd lit the fire set in the grate and the library was warm and cozy, a wonderful retreat on what had rapidly turned into an unpleasant day. Mila had totally given up on reading by the time she heard the clatter of hooves on the courtyard outside. She looked out the window and saw Thierry dismount and lead Sleipnir into the barn. It was half an hour before he came inside the lodge and went straight upstairs.

She put the book she'd taken back on its shelf and composed herself in a chair in front of the fire—keeping her focus on the dancing flames and wondering what type of mood Thierry would be in for the balance of the day. She would need to be able to recognize and handle them all, she reminded herself, even though she had shrunk from attempting to appease him this morning. And why should she appease him, she asked herself. A man was entitled to his moods as much as she was. And she'd certainly been in a terrible mood this morning. Had he tried to appease her? Not at all, in fact he'd done his level best to exacerbate her frustration. It seemed they both had a lot to learn about living with one another, she reflected with the benefit of hindsight.

The door to the library flung open and, even though she had expected Thierry, she started in surprise.

"Oh, you're back," she said, forcing nonchalance into her voice as if she hadn't been counting every tick on the centuries-old clock that hung on the library wall. "Did you have a nice ride?"

"I did not," he answered in clipped tones.

She quieted the sense of unease that built in her stomach. If he was going to be in a mood all day then it might be best if they didn't spend any more time together just yet. She watched him as he stalked to the fireplace and spread his hands in front of him, absorbing the heat as if he was chilled to the bone.

"I'm sorry to hear it," she said as lightly as she could, and rose from her seat. "Would you like me to leave you alone?"

Thierry whirled around and grabbed her hand, jerking her around to face him as she began to walk away. "No, I would not."

She wasn't certain exactly what happened next, but within seconds she was pulled up against the hardness of his body and his lips had descended upon hers. This kiss was vastly different from the one they'd shared in New York, and equally so from the one after their first morning ride. This embrace was about him dominating her, using the kiss to express his anger and frustration. She knew it would be impossible to pull away when he held her so tightly, so she did the opposite. She became unresponsive in his arms—her hands still by her side, her mouth unmoving as he attempted to plunder her lips.

She wanted nothing more than to wrench herself from his embrace and to leave this room, leave him to his wrath, but within seconds she felt a change begin to come over him. In an instant his arms loosened around her, allowing her the freedom to pull free, and his mouth lifted from hers. Instead of stepping away, however, she held her ground.

"Do you feel better now?" she asked in as level a voice as she could muster.

Somehow it seemed more important to her to face up to him than to walk away. They needed to do this, to face the demons that had raised his ire and to deal with them.

Shame filled his face and Mila felt a wave of compassion sweep over her. He was a man in so very many ways and yet, when it came to his emotions, he was as untutored as a child.

"I should not have done that. Angel, I'm sorry. If you wish to leave I won't stand in your way. I'll arrange for a car immediately."

"That won't be necessary. You contracted me to do a job, and I won't leave until I have finished my contract. However—" she allowed a small smile to pull at her lips "—it seems I have been remiss in my duties if that is the best you can do."

She watched his eyes as disgrace at his behavior warred with the pride of a sovereign born. Eventually both were replaced with something else, humility.

"Again, I apologize. Perhaps you would afford me another opportunity to show you how much I have learned."

She didn't have time to speak before he drew her more

gently against him. One hand lifted to her chin and tilted her face upward so her eyes met his and nothing else existed between them.

"Angel? May I kiss you?" he asked.

She nodded ever so slightly, but it was all the encouragement he needed. This time, as his lips claimed hers he did so with infinite care, coaxing a response from her that made her blood sing along her veins while her body unfurled with desire and heat. He traced the seam of her lips with the tip of his tongue, making her open her mouth on a sigh of longing that went soul deep.

This was what she wanted from him. A sharing of connection that opened them both up to one another—that stripped everything bare and left them each vulnerable and exposed and yet safe in the knowledge that they each had only the other's best interests at heart.

Mila cupped his face with her hands and deepened their kiss, her tongue sweeping into his mouth and stroking the inside of his lips, his tongue, until her senses were filled with the texture and taste of him. Thierry groaned into her mouth, the sound giving her a sense of power and yet making her recognize his susceptibility toward her was a gift beyond measure.

Thierry's hands swept beneath the sweater she'd pulled on this morning, his fingertips touching her bare skin and leaving a trail of fire in their wake as he stroked the line of her spine then splayed his fingers across her rib cage as if he couldn't get enough of her. His mouth left hers and he peppered the edge of her jaw with tiny kisses that tracked toward the curve of her throat. Mila shivered as he kissed the hollow at her earlobe then followed the line of her throat to the curve of her shoulder and down the deep *V* of her sweater.

Her breasts ached for his touch, for the tug of his lips at the taut, sensitive peaks. And then his hands were cupping her, the clasp of her bra undone without her even realizing it and the coarse strength of his fingers gently kneaded at her fullness. The pads of his thumbs brushed across her nipples so sweetly and gently she couldn't hold back the moan of longing that had built from deep within her core.

Mila's legs shook and she felt a combination of heat and moisture at the juncture of her thighs, intermingled with an ache that she knew only Thierry could assuage. She flexed her hips against him, felt the hard evidence of his arousal pressing back in return.

She drifted her hands down his strong neck, over those broad shoulders and down, down, down until she could pull at the hem of his shirt and tug it from his jeans—could finally feel the satin smoothness of his skin as she stroked him, her fingertips tingling as she encountered the smattering of hair on his belly, just above the waistband of his jeans. Her fingers were clumsy as she reached for his belt, guided by instinct and desire over expertise.

And then his hands were at her wrists, tugging them away from their task, lifting them upward to his mouth where he kissed first one wrist then another before letting her go. She was speechless and shaking with need, unable to speak to voice any objection when he reached under her sweater and refastened the clasp at her back. When it was refastened, he drew her back into his arms in a hold that, in its innocence, defied all logic of the passion they'd just shared.

Beneath her ear she could hear his heart beat in rapid staccato and his breath came in short, sharp bursts—much the same as her own. She felt the pressure of his lips on the top of her head and then his arms loosed her again and he stepped away.

For endless seconds they could only stare at one another. She had no idea what he expected of her now. What he thought she might say. She only knew that their embrace had ended all too swiftly and that the physical hunger that clawed at her was nothing compared to the way he'd beguiled his way into her heart. That kiss had been an exhibition of what their relationship could have been, had it been given the chance to be nurtured and grow in a normal manner. Instead, they faced one another with untruths between them—her untruths, her manipulation, her lies.

How could she ever come back from this and expect him to trust her? She'd believed that the end justified the means, but how wrong had she been? He'd said that fidelity was everything to him. Wasn't honesty a part of that? Hadn't he kissed her just now with his soul laid bare? A sob rose in her throat but she forced it back down. Reminded herself she was not Princess Mila right here and right now. She was a courtesan—a woman experienced in joys of the heart and pleasures of the body.

Her mind scrambled for the right words, the right level of insouciance that might lessen some of the awful tension that gripped her. She settled for a shaky smile and drew in a long breath.

"If you plan to kiss your wife like that, I'm sure you will find no complaint coming from her quarter. That was—"

"That was dangerous," Thierry interrupted, releasing her and shoving a shaking hand through his short cropped hair. "When I am near you I am incapable of restraint. I didn't expect this. I can't want this and yet I do."

"You are a man of great passions. I saw that already in New York when we spoke together that night. It only makes sense that your physical passions should be equally as strong as your intellectual ones." She rested a hand on his chest and let the radiant heat of his body soak up through her palm. "Hawk, do not worry. Everything will be all right."

But even as she said the words she wondered, would it? Could it, when what lay between them was a thick web of lies?

Thirteen

Thierry had prowled the lodge like a restless tiger for the balance of the day, unable to settle into anything. Following their encounter in the library he could hardly blame Angel for steering out of his way. Something had to give, but what?

Angel had kept herself scarce, although he'd smelled the scent of baking coming from the kitchen at one stage during the afternoon. He'd been tempted to see what it was that she was making, but the thought of seeing her in such an environment would just make him want more of what he couldn't have.

He'd learned from a young age not to want the things that were out of his reach. A cynical smile twisted his lips at the thought of how people would react if he ever said such a thing. As if anyone would ever believe that anything was truly out of reach for a young prince. But there were many things that money and influence couldn't buy. Things that, despite so many years of schooling himself to quell the yearning, he still craved, though he kept his desires buried beneath the surface.

So, no, he had refused the urge to go to the kitchen, to sit at the table and to watch Angel move about in a cloud of domesticity. It was hardly likely that Princess Mila would be the kind of woman who would do such a thing, and Thierry had no wish to deepen his desire for something he could never have. He was not a normal man living a normal life, even though he craved such an indulgence.

Now it was evening and he was seated here in the great hall, staring at the fireplace and trying to rein in his temper, which felt even more out of sorts than it had been this morning. He rolled his shoulders and groaned as the tightness in his muscles made a protest. He heard Angel walk from the kitchen toward the hall.

"Hawk, are you ready for dinner? I reheated a casserole that I found in the freezer and warmed some bread."

"Quite the domestic princess, aren't you," Thierry responded, then instantly wished the words unsaid as he saw hurt flicker briefly in Angel's tawny eyes. She had not deserved that and he was quick to apologize. "I'm sorry, that was uncalled for. I am grateful for your expertise in the kitchen. We may have starved if you were not so capable."

Angel laughed but it was a small and empty sound. "I had some experience while attending university in America. It gave me the opportunity to do many things I had never tried before."

He could well imagine. Was that where she had gained her experience in matters of the flesh? Had she worked her way through her degree by conducting the oldest known profession? A bitter taste invaded his mouth at the thought and he discovered he had come to hate the idea of Angel with another man. He wanted her to himself, for himself—but even that idea was impossible. He would not be his father. He would not promise himself in marriage to his princess while he sought fulfillment in another woman's arms.

Thierry shook the thoughts from his mind and followed Angel to the kitchen, where they'd been taking their evening meals—both agreeing that the formal dining room with its table large enough to seat twenty-four was less intimate than either of them liked. Even though they ate a simple meal, he noticed she continued to make the small arrangements of fresh spring flowers from the woods and the garden, and set the table with fine linen placemats and napkins and placed fresh candles in a three-branch silver candelabra.

Yet despite the pleasant atmosphere she'd worked hard to create, conversation was strained between them throughout the meal, the tension of the morning still hanging between them like a palpable barrier. After they'd finished eating, Angel began to clear the table.

"Leave that," Thierry commanded.

Angel stopped stacking their plates and looked at him with a question in her eyes. "And who will tidy up after us?" she asked, with one eyebrow cocked.

He looked at her, taking in the sultry ruby-red gown she wore this evening and noting the way it caressed her curves. From the front, it was cut to conceal, yet with every movement it teased and hinted at the feminine delights behind the silky weave of fabric. And when she turned around the tantalizing line of her back was exposed to him, making him ache to trace a line of kisses down her spine. Every evening Angel had made the effort to change for him, to entertain him by word and deed—to be the courtesan he'd contracted. And every night he looked his fill while his body clamored for more. She was strikingly beautiful, fiercely intelligent and exhibited a warm humor that touched him on an emotional level in ways he hadn't expected.

He *wanted* her—was entitled to her since he had bought her services—and yet he continued to deny himself the privilege. Some would say he was crazy—hell, sometimes even he thought he was mad as he twisted in his sheets at night, his body craving the indulgence of physical pleasure he knew would exceed his expectations. But he had kept his discipline all these years. He could not loosen the reins now, no matter how much he wanted to.

"Hawk?" Angel prompted him, making him realize he'd been staring at her and had yet to answer her question.

"I will, in the morning. Come with me now. I have something to show you."

He held out his hand and felt a surge of masculine protectiveness as, without question, she put her smaller hand in his. Thierry led Angel back through the ground floor of the lodge and across the great hall to a corridor on the other side.

"Where are you taking me?" she asked, looking around her at the ancient tapestries that lined the walls.

"To my sanctuary within my sanctuary," he said enigmatically.

"That sounds intriguing."

"Very few people ever set foot in there and never without my express permission. It is a place I go when I want to be completely alone."

"And yet, you're taking me?"

"It seems appropriate," he conceded.

He took a key chain from his pocket and, selecting the correct key, he unlocked a massive wooden door at the end of the corridor. The door opened inward onto a small landing and light from the hall filtered down a descending curved stone staircase.

"You're not leading me to your dungeon, are you?" Angel said, half jokingly.

"No, I like to think of it more as a hidden treasure."

He reached out to flip a switch on the wall and small discreet pockets of light illuminated the grotto beneath. Thierry led the way down the stairs and smiled as he heard Angel's gasp of delight when she saw the massive natural pool gleaming in the semidarkness. He lit a taper and moved about the cavern, lighting the many candles scattered here and there.

Angel moved closer to the edge of the pool and bent to dip her hand in the inky water.

"It's warm!" she exclaimed. "How on earth did you build a heated underground pool?"

"Nature's grand architect provided it," he answered simply. "The pool is fed by a thermal underground spring and has been here for centuries. At some time, centuries past, I believe it may have been used as an area of worship or congregation, perhaps even healing. I know I always feel better after I have been in the water here."

Angel looked around her at the shadows cast by the subdued lighting and the flickering of the candles. She closed her eyes and breathed in deeply before letting the breath go on a long sigh of relaxation. "I see what you mean. There's an—" She broke off and wrinkled her brow, searching for the right words. "I don't know, maybe an *energy* about it, isn't there? You can feel the longevity and peacefulness of the place simply hanging here in the air. Almost hear the echo of voices long gone."

She laughed as if embarrassed by the fancifulness of her thoughts, but he knew what she meant. He felt it himself.

He nodded. "I thought you might enjoy the pool. It's a great way to unwind, especially when it's been a demanding day."

"Demanding, yes, you could say that. And I would love to swim here. I'll just go upstairs to get a swimsuit—"

"No need, I will let you enjoy the pool in privacy."

Angel looked at him from under hooded eyes, her head

cocked slightly to one side. "But what about you? Hasn't today been equally demanding for you also?"

In the half light it was difficult to see whether she was serious or if, once again, she was teasing him as she had so often these past few days. He settled on the latter, choosing it by preference because in his memory no one had ever had the cheek to mock him to his face before. He found her boldness tantalizing and infuriating in equal measure. And, even more strangely, he found he really liked that.

"You would like me to swim with you?" he asked, seeking clarification.

She nodded. "I think it would be an interesting lesson, don't you?"

In torment, perhaps. "And what would this lesson achieve?"

In response, Angel reached up to unfasten the top button at the back of her gown.

"It would enhance your appreciation of sensual delights. Of the combination of visual stimulation paired with the physical sensation of the water caressing your body. We need not touch, Hawk. You set the boundaries. I will respect them."

Would she? Could *he*? Right now he hated those boundaries, every last one. He watched as she slid her zipper down and eased her dress off her shoulders, exposing a delicate filament of lace, strapless and backless, masquerading as a bra. He was hard in an instant. This had been a stupid idea. He should leave her to her swim, but it was as if his limbs had taken root in the ancient stone floor beneath his feet. And all he could do was watch as she let the dress slither over the rest of her body to drop in a crimson pool at her feet.

His mouth dried as he followed the curves of her body, the shape of her rib cage, the nip of her waist and the lush roundness of her hips and thighs. Hers was a body made for love, for pleasure. A safe haven in a world of harshness. And he dare not touch her because if he did he would be lost, well and truly and very possibly forever.

She reached up behind her and unfastened her bra, allowing her full breasts to fall free. He swallowed at the sight of deep pink nipples and watched as, under his heated gaze, they grew tight—their tips rigid points. Thierry's hands curled into tight balls, every muscle from his forearms to his biceps taut with restraint.

Heat poured through his body. He should leave now, but arousal urged him to move forward—to touch, to taste. He fought the compulsion with every ounce of strength he had, but even he could not hold back the sound of longing that escaped him as she hooked her thumbs in the sides of her lacy panties and slid them down her legs.

"Are you just going to stand there?" Angel asked.

Her voice was husky, sensual—but the soft tremor behind her words belied a nervousness that caught him by surprise. She was a woman no doubt well used to the lasciviousness of male eyes, and yet she blushed before him.

"For now," he said through a throat constricted with need.

"Suit yourself," she answered with a brief curl of her lips.

She turned and he found himself captivated by the length of her spine, the dimples at the small of her back and the shape of her buttocks. Was there any part of this woman that didn't peel away his long-established layers of protocol and decorum and expose, instead, raw hunger in its purest form? It seemed not.

He watched as Angel found the steps that led into the pool and, captivated, saw her sink deeper and deeper into its warmth. He knew all too well the sensation of the warm, silky water against bare skin. How it teased and caressed the parts of your body that were normally hidden from view. Did she enjoy it—the freedom, that soft caress as it licked centimeter by centimeter up the smooth muscled length of her legs and higher to the soft curve of her inner thighs?

This was beyond torment, he realized as the muscles holding him rigid with tension screamed for release. But it didn't stop him from imagining how she felt right now as the water lapped gently at her belly, then higher to stroke the curve of her breasts until she sank right down, obscuring all but the gentle sweep of her shoulders from his view.

"This is divine," Angel commented as she did a smooth breast stroke from one end of the pool to the other, leaving a ripple of wake on the water behind her.

The paleness of her skin shone with an almost iridescent glow beneath the surface of the pool, distorting her image and making her appear intriguingly otherworldly. She turned and dipped her head until she was completely submerged, then rose again and swam toward the edge furthest from him—her long dark hair a black river down her back.

Burning need battled with disciplined restraint, just as they had done since he'd opened the door of the lodge to see his Angel standing before him. But now, for the first time in his life, need won.

Somehow, sometime, he made a decision, but he was not consciously aware of it. His clothes had melted from his body. The distance between the edge of the pool and where he stood had disappeared. He entered the water in a smooth slide of muscle and movement, gliding toward Angel as she sat on the ledge on the side of the pool, her legs still dangling in the water like some earth-bound mermaid.

She was a goddess here in this grotto. Her skin shimmering with the moisture that clung to her skin and which refracted light from the candles around them as if each one was a jewel.

Thierry pulled himself up between her legs, reaching for her as if he had every right to take her, every right to draw her beautiful body to his and every right to take her lips in a kiss that spoke volumes as to his hunger for her.

He was lost in a maelstrom of impressions that chased through his mind—of her acquiescence as she flowed against him, of her mouth responding to his kiss, of the sounds of pleasure from her throat, of the gentle drift of her fingertips across the top of his shoulders.

He kissed her and probed the soft recesses of her mouth with his tongue, tasting her and knowing that one taste would never be enough. His hands went to her breasts, cupping the full warm flesh with his fingers, kneading them gently and teasing the hard points of her arousal. She moaned and strained against him, her body slick and wet and warm and driving him crazy in the best way imaginable.

He bent his head to take one nipple in his mouth, rolling his tongue around the distended tip before gently grazing it with his teeth. A shudder ran through her body and he felt an answering response in his own. How had he managed to deny himself these pleasures for so very long? And how was he to stop now he'd allowed the floodgates of desire to open? The question was fleeting and all thoughts of bringing this to a halt were swiftly quelled as her fingers raked through his hair—her hands holding him to her as he licked and nipped and suckled at her.

Her hips undulated against him, her heated core brushing against the hardened length of his shaft. He wouldn't have believed it possible but he swelled even more under her gentle assault on his body.

Thierry let his hands drift down over her rib cage, past the sweep of her waist and the curve of her hip and then around to the fullness of her buttocks. Gripping her he pulled her firmly against him and groaned at the sweet shaft of pleasure that pieced him. But he still didn't feel close enough.

"You are a torment to man, a seductress simply by your existence," he murmured against her throat before gently nipping at her skin.

"And you are everything I have ever wanted," Angel sighed in response.

Her words, so simple yet so disingenuous, struck him to his heart and he gave himself over to the joy they engendered. At this moment she was the foundation of his existence. Here, in this natural grotto, in the heated spring water that felt like silk and seduction against a man's skin, they were locked in a world apart from the reality that lingered outside.

"And you, my sweet Angel," he said, kissing her once again and drawing her lower lips gently between his teeth before releasing it again. "You are so much more than I could imagine wanting. Ever."

His hands were still at her buttocks and he edged her slightly farther forward until the tip of his penis brushed against her entrance. All Thierry could think about was the woman in his arms, the need that pulsed and demanded as if it was the most fundamental part of his existence. She tipped her pelvis and he slid just inside her. They both gasped at the contact and Thierry reveled in the sensation of her.

He couldn't stop himself. His entire body shook as demand overtook him, his senses filled with the feel of her in his arms, the soft sounds of her ragged breathing and the incredible heat that generated where their bodies joined together. He thrust forward, but instead of sliding fully into her body he met with resistance. It didn't immediately make sense to him, but then again, right now, nothing did but the driving need to push past that barrier and find the fulfillment his body craved.

Confusion clouded his mind, pushed past the roar of desire that had driven him to this point, until the confusion suddenly cleared and realization dawned.

His Angel was a virgin.

Fourteen

"Please, don't stop now," Mila urged him.

Her fingers curled into his shoulders, her nails biting into his skin as ripples of pleasure surpassed the burning fullness of his penetration and cascaded through her body. But instead he withdrew.

"What's wrong?" she asked.

"You…you're a virgin," he said as if he could scarcely believe the words.

"As are you, are you not?"

She searched his eyes for some response but all she could see was shock reflected back at her. Eventually he nodded.

"Does it not make this sweeter?" she asked, sliding her hands down his body and slipping them around his waist, pulling him back against her.

She felt her body ease to accommodate his length and fullness and she wanted to move against him, to welcome him deeper into her body. She lifted her face to Thierry's and kissed him, sliding her tongue between his lips in a simulation of what she wanted him to continue.

"Touch me," she whispered against his lips. "Touch me, there, with your fingers. Feel yourself inside me."

He did as she asked and she saw his pupils dilate even more as his fingers touched that special place where they joined. She gasped as his knuckles brushed her clitoris.

"Yes," she urged, "and there, too."

"Like this?" he asked, repeating the movement.

"Yes, oh yes."

The ripples that had begun with his possession of her intensified with each stroke and she moved her hips in tiny circles, urging him to follow her movements with his hand. He was a quick study and, as pleasure suffused her, her inner muscles began to clench and release, to encourage him to push deeper, to conquer the barrier between them.

And then that barrier was gone, and so was she—on a wave of passion so intense it took her breath completely away as paroxysms of pleasure coiled and released over and over, spreading from her core to her extremities and making her arch her throat and shout his name so that it echoed back to them from the cavernous ceiling.

Thierry's hips pumped with increasing speed, water lapping all around them, until he, too, reached his peak, the muscles on his back taut with tension and his entire body straining as he surged and surged yet again.

"Ah, my Angel, I love you!" he groaned against her throat as with one final push he came deep inside her.

It was sometime later when he moved again and Mila finally became aware of the pressure of the smooth stones at her back. She shifted to ease her weight off the uncomfortable surface and reached for Thierry as he began to pull away.

"In a hurry to leave me now?" she asked, trying to inject a note of playful banter into her voice.

It was, perhaps, an impossible goal to attempt to keep the atmosphere light between them. They'd just been passionately intimate with one another and, judging by the look on Thierry's face, he was already beginning to regret it.

"Hawk?" she asked, prompting him again. "Is everything all right?"

"No," he said fiercely pulling free of her touch and pushing back in the water to where she could not reach him. "Everything is not all right. We shouldn't have done this. I gave in to weakness even though I'm promised to another woman. I've destroyed forever the one thing I wished to hold sacred between her and myself."

There was a wealth of self-loathing in his voice and she couldn't bear to hear it. "But—" she started.

"There are no buts," he said firmly, cutting her off. The self-loathing was now tinged with a bitterness that brought tears to Mila's eyes. "Don't you understand? By making love to you, I have become the man I least wanted to be. How can I go ahead with my marriage to the woman I have been promised to for the past seven years when I love you? It would make everything I believe in, everything I am, a lie."

Mila remained where she was, stunned into total silence as his words, riddled with pain and torment, echoed into obscurity in the air around them. Thierry finished crossing the pool and rose from the water. Rivulets cascaded down his back and over his firm buttocks and even now, in this awful atmosphere of disillusion and self-loathing, her body responded with desire at the sight of him.

"Hawk! Stop. Wait, please?" she begged, moving to follow. She staggered up the steps that led to the edge and reached for him, but her fingers found nothing but air. "Hawk, please. Listen to me. I love you, too."

He shook his head. "That only makes it worse. I am a

king. I cannot love you or accept your love—the entire situation is impossible. Knowing how I felt about you I should have sent you away the moment you arrived, but I didn't. In another lifetime, another world, perhaps we could have been more to one another, but we live here and now."

Thierry made a sound of disgust and reached for a towel from inside a discreetly hidden cupboard. He threw one to her and grabbed another for himself.

"Tomorrow you will leave. I will not see you off."

Mila's mind whirled. This was going all wrong. She'd achieved what she'd set out to do—he loved her. Yet now everything was falling apart. But then, he didn't know who she really was.

"We need to talk," she started again, desperate to get him to listen to her.

"No, the time for talking is done. We have nothing further to say to one another. The blame for what has transpired between us falls directly on my shoulders. I recruited your services. I kept you here even though I knew it could lead to trouble."

"Trouble? You're calling our love for one another trouble? That's not right, Hawk. Love is a gift."

"A gift? I thought so, but now I realize it is a burden. Tell me, how am I to face my bride and pledge myself to her, knowing my heart belongs to you?"

"But I am—"

He cut her off again. "No more!" he bellowed. "I've made a liar of myself. A mockery of everything that I told myself was important. Now I have to live with what I've done. I've made my decision. Your car will be here first thing tomorrow."

He stalked away from her up the staircase and was gone before she could work out what to say. What did he mean—live with what he'd done? Did he plan to call off the wedding? She had to find him, to tell him who she really was. To explain to him why she'd tricked him.

Mila dried herself quickly and dragged her dress on over her head. Her wet hair clung to her back but she barely noticed as she gathered up her other things and moved quickly toward the stairs. It was as she reached the second floor that she began to slow down, her heart hammering in her chest, her thoughts a whirl.

Thierry had been angry. Not at her, but at himself. Was now the best time to confront him with her duplicity? Yes, he'd just admitted he loved her, and she knew—after getting to know him better this past week—that he could not have made love to her if he didn't. The thought filled her with hope for their future but at the same time he loved a woman who, technically, didn't exist. *His Angel*, he'd called her. And she wanted so much to be that woman for him. But would he still love her when she revealed her true identity?

She came to a halt in the hallway at the intersection of the corridor to Thierry's rooms. Her heart pounded as she considered what to do next. Was it too late to explain to him, to make him see the truth? Had she ruined everything?

Understanding his past and his family, as she did now, she could see why it was so important for him to keep himself only for her. In this day and age his idea would be considered by most people to be ridiculously outdated, but to her it showed exactly how seriously committed he was to their marriage. Far from being the distant man she'd met so long ago, she'd learned he was multifaceted. Sure, he was powerful and handsome and had a higher IQ than many—not to mention the wherewithal to use that power and IQ for the good of the people who looked to him for leadership. And he had a good store of arrogance hiding under that handsome exterior, as well. But beneath all that he was vulnerable and caring and he'd wedged himself into her heart in such a way she knew that no one else would ever be able to dislodge him.

She loved him because she knew him, appreciated and valued everything about him. That was how she knew his honor was everything to him—and that she'd abused it with her deceit. He wouldn't look upon her actions lightly. She made him cross a personal boundary with her behavior tonight. It had been selfish of her, knowing how he felt, to tempt him into breaking his self-imposed chastity.

But as guilty as she felt for the torment he was experiencing now, she still couldn't completely regret their lovemaking. Their joining had been everything she'd ever imagined it could be. The pleasure had been far more intense and the act of lovemaking so intimate that she felt as though she was joined to him forever already. Marriage would simply be a ceremony to appease the rest of the world as to their intentions toward one another, but in her soul Mila was married to Thierry, her Hawk, already.

But what would Thierry say when she stopped hiding behind the veil of another woman's identity?

Thierry paced the floor of the library. He had been unable to settle in his room. Even his own bed appeared to mock him in the gloom of night with the way he couldn't help but picture Angel's naked form spread across its broad expanse of white sheets. His body told him he was all kinds of fool. Instead of abandoning her in the grotto, he should have simply brought Angel to his bed, used the bounty her body so freely offered. Whispered sweet nothings into the night until they were both so exhausted they could do nothing but sleep—until they woke and reached for one another again. He could not bring back his lost chastity, so why waste time mourning it when he could be enjoying his new sexual freedom?

If he was any other kind of man that is exactly what he'd have done. Hell, he'd have probably bedded her on the very first night she'd arrived. But, he thought looking up to the portrait of his late parents where it hung above the fireplace, he wasn't his father. Nor was he yet his mother— a woman who'd entered into marriage with all good intentions and yet found herself adrift and alone and desperate for the attention and love of a man.

He turned away from the portrait and went to stand over by the window. The clock chimed the half hour. Soon the sun would begin to rise and a new day would dawn, and he was no closer to making his decision about what to do next.

At the forefront of his mind was the long standing betrothal to marry Princess Mila. He knew if he went through with it, he'd end up inflicting the same kind of pain upon her as his father had upon his mother. No, he wouldn't neglect her or disrespect her the way his father had his mother. But even as he took his marriage vows, he would know that he would never be able to love her the way she deserved. Not when another woman had already taken possession of his heart.

But how could there be peace between their countries if their marriage did not go ahead? And on the other hand, could he imagine being married to one woman while longing with every cell in his body for another?

In the endless night just gone, he'd even asked himself if he could be like his father—maintain the facade of a marriage while continuing to keep a mistress. But how could he even think about doing that to Angel, let alone his new bride? He'd always vowed he'd be different to the other men who had been in his family—be a better man, period.

Perhaps his family was forever cursed to be unhappy in marriage—to be forever disappointed in love.

Half an hour later he began to hear movement about the house. He'd sent word to Pasquale for a skeleton staff to return, even though he had no wish for company right now. A car swept into the turning bay of the drive and parked at the front door—Angel's ride out of here, away from him, forever. The thought struck a searing pain deep into his heart. Having to send her away was unarguably the hardest thing he'd ever had to do. But do it, he must.

A sound at the door behind him made him wheel around. Angel. His chest constricted on a new wave of pain, even as his body heated in response to her arrival. She looked as if she'd slept as little as he had. There were dark circles beneath her eyes and shadows lurked in the amber depths.

"The car is here," he said in lieu of a greeting.

"Hawk, I need to speak with you. There is something important I need to say before I go."

Even her voice was flat and weary. He wished he could ease the sorrow he saw reflected back at him in her gaze. Perhaps he could give her just this opportunity to say her piece. Goodness knew he could offer her little else. He inclined his head.

"Please speak freely," he said.

She drew in a short breath and began to step closer to him, but then appeared to think the better of it. He was glad. He was strung so tight right now it was all he could do to maintain a facade of calm. If she touched him he'd weaken. He'd once again become the man he despised.

"I know you are undergoing a major battle with yourself over what we did last night," she started. "But I want you to know that everything will be all right."

"All right?" he barked an incredulous laugh. "How can you say that? I have betrayed everything I stand for. Nothing will be all right again."

She clasped her hands together, squeezing them so tightly he saw her fingertips lose all color. "I love you, Hawk. You have to believe that."

A prickle of emotion burned at the back of his eyes but he furiously refused to allow it to take purchase. To allow the sentiment to swamp the rationality he so desperately needed right now. "It makes no difference," he said harshly. "You are a courtesan. I am a king. Worse, I am a king betrothed to another."

"I know that, and you must not let what we have done stop your marriage to your princess. You must go through with the wedding."

"I must? Who are you to tell me what to do?" he demanded, taking refuge in the anger that continued to grow inside him at the situation he'd created through his own weakness.

For a second he caught a glimpse of hurt in her eyes but then she seemed to change. Her expression became less vulnerable, as if she'd assumed a mask upon her exquisitely beautiful face. Her shoulders and neck straightened and she lifted her chin ever so slightly, almost regally.

"I am Princess Mila Angelina of Erminia."

Shock slammed into him with the force of an avalanche. "Be very careful, Angel. There are strict laws governing imposters," he growled when sense returned.

She licked her lips and, damn him, he couldn't help but remember what the tip of that tongue had felt like as it delved delicately inside his mouth. He willed his body not to respond but, as with this entire situation, it refused to submit to his control.

"I am not lying to you. Not anymore."

"You had better explain."

"I was at school in Boston when I saw the news report on your visit to New York. I hadn't seen you in seven years, and with our wedding only weeks away, I couldn't resist the chance to try to contact you. When I met you in New York I had gone to your hotel with the intention of visiting you in your suite. I had planned to introduce myself—to see, somehow, if I could get to know you a little before our wedding. But my courage failed me. I was just on the verge of giving up on seeing you when you bumped into me."

"But you don't look…" He let his voice trail off. How did you tell a woman she looked nothing like her unattractive teenaged self?

She was quick to hear the words he'd left unspoken.

"I don't look like I did at eighteen? No, I don't. When you didn't recognize me in New York, it hurt me at first. But then I thought it might be a bit of fun—a good opportunity to get to know the real you."

"When I dropped you off, why didn't you tell me who you were?"

"I—I don't know," she admitted with her eyes downcast. "I guess I was enjoying the way you looked at me when I was just Angel. I didn't want you to lose that look when you connected me with the girl you met when we got engaged."

Thierry felt a flush of shame. Yes, he'd been taken aback when he'd met the princess that first time. But even then he'd committed to her fully—right up until last night when he'd done the unthinkable with a woman who he'd believed was a courtesan. Which brought them straight back to where they were now. The realization flamed the fire of his fury.

"You took a terrible risk doing what you have done," he bit out.

"Not so much in New York, but here, yes."

"And what of Ottavia Romolo? Is she in on your scheme also? Am I to expect to be blackmailed by her for her part in all of this?"

"No! Not that."

"Then what?" he demanded.

"She, um. She has been detained in Erminia."

"Detained?" Thierry gripped his hands into fists. "What

exactly do you mean by that? Are you holding her some-where against her will?"

The princess hung her head, not answering. But he could see the truth in every line of her body.

"Why? Why would you risk so much—with your repu-tation, with mine? What made you go to such lengths and lie to me like that? Don't you realize what will happen when the truth comes out?"

"I felt great lengths were required when I overheard that my betrothed had contracted a courtesan just a few weeks before our wedding!" she snapped back, a flash of temper sparking in her beautiful eyes. "All these years, I'd worked so hard to try to become someone you could value and de-sire. And then to hear that you'd invited another woman to be your lover..." She turned her face away, dropping her gaze to the floor. "I couldn't bear the thought of it. I had to take her place."

She lifted her head to face him again and he could see tears swimming in her gaze. "I just wanted you to love me."

Something twisted in his gut at the pain in her voice, on her face, in her eyes. Love? She'd done all this for love? He closed his eyes for a moment, took a steadying breath. He knew love didn't last, not for people like him. Even-tually he sighed.

"I am at a complete loss, Princess."

"Why? Shouldn't this make everything okay? You love me, you said so yourself, and I love you, too. You can let go of your guilt. I'm your princess, you haven't betrayed me. We can move forward from this, knowing we were meant for one another," she implored.

"Really?"

A part of him wished their lives could be as simple as she'd just said. But he knew they couldn't. Theirs were not normal lives. Instead they were a confluence of expectations and protocols over which they had no control. And there was still the matter of her duplicity.

He continued, "I have to ask myself, if you were prepared to undertake such a deception as you have perpetrated since our meeting in New York, why should I believe a single word you say? Don't you think it would be more appropriate for me to question everything you say and do? What else would you be prepared to lie about to me? Your profession of love? Your promise, at our wedding, to love and honor me as your husband? I have to ask myself—how can I trust you?" He steeled himself to say the next words. "And the answer is that I can't."

Her shoulders sagged and he could see hope fracture and disappear in her eyes as the tears she'd been holding back began to fall. He wanted to step forward, to take her in his arms and assure her that everything would be okay. But how could it be? He'd told her how he felt. Had said on more than one occasion how important honesty was to him. And still she'd continued to lie.

"Leave me now," he commanded.

"No! Hawk—!"

The princess stepped forward, thrusting out both hands, imploring him with her body, the expression on her face, the raw plea in her voice, not to send her away.

It was the most difficult and painful thing he had ever done, but he turned his back on her. He didn't move when he heard her footsteps drag across the library floor, not when he heard the door close behind her. Out the window he saw her move outside and onto the driveway, hesitating just a moment at the car door that had been opened for her. He watched, telling himself over and over that he had done the right thing. That her lies had been a betrayal of everything he stood for. But as the car disappeared from view he sank to his knees and closed his eyes against the burning tears that threatened to fall.

* * *

All through that day and the night that followed he fought with his conscience—battled with the urge to follow his Angel and to bring her back to his side where she belonged. He'd made the decision by morning that he would contact her brother, request an audience with both Rocco and Mila to postpone the wedding, but that contact never eventuated as he read the newspaper left so neatly folded beside his breakfast in the dining room the next morning. The newspaper with the headline that shrieked that the virgin Prince of Sylvain had pre-empted his wedding vows with another woman. Paragraph after paragraph followed with endless speculation about the new Sylvano King's honor, or lack of it.

He felt sick to his stomach. Despite every precaution he'd taken, and there had been many, the news had still somehow been leaked. This was his worst nightmare. A scandal of monumental proportions. Grainy photographs taken with a long-distance lens from somewhere in the woods showed pictures of him with Angel—no, Princess Mila—as they rode together, picnicked together and kissed together. Every photo had its own lurid caption. Thierry left the table and made to leave the lodge—his sanctuary no longer.

The moment his people found out exactly who it was who was responsible, that person would pay for this invasion of his privacy and pay dearly.

Just before he got into the car that would return him to the harsh reality of his world, and no doubt the censure of his people, Pasquale arrived at his side with another newspaper that had just been delivered. Thierry's skin crawled as he read the headline, "Princess Mila Revealed as the King's Courtesan!"

Had she engineered all of this since last night in some kind of attempt to force him to go through with the wedding even though it went against everything he'd spent his lifetime trying to avoid? Did she think his fear of public disgrace would override his anger over her deception? If that was what she thought, she was wrong.

The scandal surrounding his mother's death had been an ongoing assault for years after her death. How on earth could Thierry think about loving or trusting a woman who had brought this back upon him, who had brought his carefully constructed world down around his ears? Worse, how could he ask his subjects to love or trust her, either? No amount of damage control would make a speck of difference. There was only one thing left that he could do.

He turned and marched back into the lodge and to his office where, on his secure line, he placed a call.

"King Rocco," he said as he was put through. "I regret to inform you that I can no longer marry your sister. The wedding is off."

Fifteen

Mila paced the floor of her bedroom. Back and forth like a caged animal. She'd known the minute she crossed the border and a palace guard had stepped out of the customs building, followed by her brother's head of palace security, that her ruse had been discovered. From the moment she'd been returned to the castle yesterday she'd been a virtual prisoner in her own rooms.

Not permitted to make or receive calls, her computer confiscated, her television disconnected—she was adrift from the rest of the world. Worse, she was actually locked in. She began to have a new appreciation for how Ottavia Romolo must have felt during her captivity. Although, it seemed, that the courtesan's incarceration had lasted only a matter of days. Somehow, the woman had managed to escape and warn Mila's brother of what she'd been up to—hence the welcoming committee when Mila returned across the border.

Mila hated waiting. Worse, she hated not knowing what

she could expect when she was eventually brought before her brother to face the music. And through it all was the fear and the worry that what she'd done had destroyed any chance of her and Thierry having their happy ending after all. She'd been a fool, going off half cocked and driven by emotion.

Hadn't she been raised to know better than that? Emotion couldn't be the main driving force in the life of a royal. Duty came before everything else. If she'd ever thought she knew that lesson before it was nothing on how she'd come to understand it now. She should have waited until her wedding. Allowed their relationship to grow and blossom the way it could have done under normal circumstances.

She should have trusted Thierry, even when she'd heard that he'd hired a courtesan. Should have believed he would never do anything to dishonor his commitment to her.

And there lay the crux of the problem. She hadn't trusted him. And in her insecurity, she'd set out to willfully deceive him. Her behavior had reaped the result she should have been doing everything she could to avoid. Whatever came next, she deserved it.

The aching hollow that had developed in her chest from the moment Thierry had sent her away grew even deeper. She doubted the pain of it would ever leave her.

There was a perfunctory knock at the door to her room which then opened, revealing General Andrej Novak, Rocco's head of the armed forces—the man who had escorted her home from the border yesterday.

"Your Royal Highness, please come with me."

So, Rocco had sent his top guy rather than one of the usual palace guards or even a general staff member. Clearly he wasn't taking any of this lightly at all. Unease knotted in her stomach as, wordlessly, she did as she'd been asked.

"He's furious with me, isn't he?" she asked the tall, forbidding-looking man at her side.

"It's not my place to say, ma'am."

She continued through the palace corridors until they arrived at her brother's office. The head of security tapped on the door and then opened it for her, gesturing for her to go inside. The sun beat in through the office windows, throwing the man seated in the chair at his desk into relief and putting Mila at a distinct disadvantage. If only she could see her brother's face, gauge his mood. Who was she kidding? Seeing his face wouldn't change a thing—he was undoubtedly furious with her, again. She sank into a curtsy. Her legs began to burn as she waited for his command to rise.

"Good of you to return home," her brother said in icy tones from behind his desk. He made a sound that sounded like a growl. "Get up, Mila, your subservience is too little, too late."

She rose and faced him, her eyes raking his face—searching for any sign of compassion. There was none. Banked fury lit his sherry-colored eyes and deep lines bracketed the sides of his mouth.

"Do you have the slightest idea what you've done?" he bit out. When she remained silent he continued, his voice lethally level and controlled. "Your impetuosity has destroyed any chance of a union between Erminia and Sylvain. King Thierry has called off the wedding."

"No!" Mila gasped in pain and shock. Her legs wobbled and she reached for the chair beside her to steady herself.

"Peace between our nations will now be impossible." Rocco rose from his chair and turned to face the windows, presenting her with his broad back.

"Surely not impossible. This is the twenty-first century, after all," she argued, futilely reaching for some thought or idea to present to her brother. "There must be something we can do."

"Do?" He turned to face her and shook his head. "You have driven open chasms in the very fabric of our security. I had hoped to avoid having to tell you this. Had hoped that your marriage to King Thierry would bring with it enough stability that this problem would become irrelevant, and you would have had no need to know."

"No need to know what?" she demanded. "What have you been hiding from me, and why?"

"Before your engagement I became aware of rumors of a threat against me. One that endangered you, too. We took steps to weed out the danger and we believed it under control, but before your return home the threat became a clear and present danger."

Mila's throat dried in fear. "What kind of threat?"

"At first we thought it might be a direct attack on my person, but it seems my position on the throne is the actual target."

"But how? You are the firstborn and only son of our father. Our lines of succession are quite specific."

"Firstborn and only *legitimate* son of our father."

"He had another son?"

Shocked, Mila couldn't remain standing another moment. She sank into a chair in an inelegant slump.

"Apparently."

"Who?"

"That's the problem. I don't know yet. But I will," Rocco said with grim determination.

"But even so, if he isn't our father's legitimate issue he has no claim on the throne."

Rocco made a noise that was between a laugh and a growl. "So we believed. However, it seems that there is an ancient law, still in force, that says that if I am not married by my thirty-fifth birthday *and* the father of legally recognized issue, I cannot remain king."

"But that's easy, isn't it? Marry. Have a baby! Or revoke the law."

"A list of potential brides is being prepared for me. But time is of the essence, so in the meantime, we are working with our parliament to see the law revoked. However that has opened a whole new set of problems. Some of our members apparently support the idea of a new king. It appears the flames of subversion have been subtly coaxed for some time."

"Oh, Rocco. What are you going to do?"

"Keep working to uncover who is behind this and keep trying to unravel the mystery before it's too late and we have a civil war on our hands. In the meantime, we need all the allies we can get, which is why I was counting on your now-canceled nuptials."

Mila began to shake.

"I…I…" Her voice trailed away. An apology seemed ridiculously insubstantial given the weight of what Rocco had said. "Sorry" just didn't cut it. "What can I do?"

Her brother came around the front of his desk and gave her look that she would never forget. He squatted down before her and took both her hands in his.

"I know that following orders has never been your strong suit, but I have one command for you now, little sister. Go back to Sylvain and change King Thierry's mind. Your marriage could be the only thing that saves Erminia from total destruction."

From the helicopter window Mila watched through the darkness as the lights at the border of Erminia disappeared behind her. Ahead lay Sylvain and what would unarguably be the most difficult task of her life. How did you convince a man who loved you but who no longer trusted you to go ahead with your marriage?

Flying had never been her favorite pastime and she usually survived long-haul flights with antianxiety medication that helped her sleep through most of it. That wasn't an option now, when she needed to stay alert, but taking a short flight in a helicopter had her heart racing and her nerves strung so tight she thought she might throw up if they didn't land soon.

As if he could read her mind the pilot made an announcement through the headset clamped to Mila's ears.

"We'll be landing at the palace grounds shortly, Your Royal Highness."

"Thank you," she responded. *And not a moment too soon*, she added silently as her stomach lurched in response to the change in altitude as they began to make their descent.

"Are you all right, ma'am?" the uniformed escort beside her asked.

She cast a look at him. In his late thirties, General Andrej Novak cut a dashing figure in his uniform and, as head of her brother's military, wielded an immense amount of power. But Mila felt there was always a hint of dissatisfaction hidden in the set of his mouth and the expression in his dark brown eyes. It made her wary of him, and served to increase her discomfort. She didn't understand why it had been so necessary for her brother to send him. It was hardly a high-profile visit. In fact, it was meant to be private and would, hopefully, remain so with just her and Thierry in the same room together.

Still, she reminded herself, appearances were everything to Rocco and he wanted to make it patently obvious that this visit to Sylvain was done above board and without a hint of scandal or subterfuge. Mila closed her eyes a moment and gripped the armrests of her chair as the skids of the chopper settled on the helipad set in the Sylvano palace's widespread and parklike grounds. A car waited nearby. The general exited the helicopter and turned to assist Mila to the ground. She was grateful for his steadying hand as she alighted and put her feet down on solid ground again.

A man got out of the car and walked toward them. He gave Mila a deep bow as he drew near.

"Your Royal Highness, Pasquale De Luca, aide to His Majesty King Thierry, at your service. Please come with me."

"Thank you, Mr. De Luca."

General Novak moved with her as Mila fell in step with Thierry's aide. The aide stopped abruptly.

"I'm sorry, General. But my instructions are clear. Only the princess is to come in the vehicle."

"And my instructions are equally clear," Andrej rumbled at Mila's side. "The princess is in my charge."

"King Thierry will see the princess, and no one else."

"It's okay, Andrej," Mila said, putting a hand on the general's arm. "I will be fine."

The man gave her a cold stare before making a short nod and taking a step back. "As you wish, ma'am."

She could tell by the way he'd bristled at her touch that he was none too happy about the situation, but she was grateful he'd given in, even if only temporarily.

"Take me to your king," she instructed Pasquale with as much decorum as she could muster.

Inside, her stomach roiled. Would Thierry listen to her plea? Could he forgive her the deception she'd wrought and the resulting flurry of scandal in the papers? Would he believe that she was not responsible for the leak? She had to believe that he would. That her love for him, and his for her, would help her overcome this awful situation.

As they reached the car, Pasquale opened the back door

and held it for her. Mila gave him a smile of thanks and got inside, but it wasn't until the door closed beside her and the vehicle began to move that she realized she wasn't alone in the back of the luxurious limousine.

"Thierry!" she said, startled by the sight of him.

"You asked to see me. I am here."

His voice was devoid of so much as a speck of warmth or humor and his eyes were as cold as steel.

"I expected to see you at the palace," she said nervously, her fingers pleating the fabric of her dress.

"You have no right to expect anything of me."

"You're right, of course." She forced herself to let go of her dress. "I'm sorry, Hawk, so very sorry for what I did."

"Do not call me Hawk."

She heard the underscore of pain in his voice and bowed her head in acknowledgment of her role in causing that pain. It made her heart sore that she had hurt him. That had never been her intention. She'd only wanted him to love her, as she loved him. Instead, she'd started their relationship on a series of lies. She'd abused his trust. It was no wonder he was still angry with her and looked at her now the way he did. She met his gaze—it was chillingly clinical, devoid of the passion and interest she'd come to take for granted.

"I apologize again. Can you ever forgive me? Can you please give me, us, another chance?"

Thierry shifted in his seat and turned his gaze to the privacy screen that shielded them from the car's driver.

"Another chance, you say?" He shook his head. "No, I don't believe in second chances."

"But I love you and I know you love me, too. You told me as much. Did you lie?"

He was silent for so long that Mila thought she might shatter into a thousand painful jagged fragments, but when he spoke, she knew the agony of waiting was infinitely preferable to the torment of hearing what he had to say.

"I didn't lie. I loved my Angel deeply, it's true. But love alone is not enough. I have seen what people do in the name of love, what they allow themselves to think is acceptable or permissible. You know from the confidences we shared what is important to me, don't you?"

Mila cleared her throat and tried to speak. The words came out rough and strained.

"Honesty and trust."

"Yes, honesty and trust. I trusted you, but were you honest with me?" He faced her again. "We both know you weren't, despite ample opportunity to be—both in New York and at my lodge."

She struggled with how to reply. Finally, she said, "Neither of us had an easy upbringing—in our positions, with our families, it was virtually impossible for us to learn about love. And yet we still prize love above all other things. I would do anything for true love, and I did. Right from when I first met you seven years ago I knew I could love you—but how could I have ever believed that you would love someone like me? I spent the next seven years trying to be the woman worthy of being by your side, of holding your heart. Even when I met you in New York that night, I knew I was more than half in love with you already. But then I heard that you had acquired Ms. Romolo's services, and I felt heartbroken. I had done so much, had worked so hard to make myself everything I thought you would need in a wife and partner, and yet you had chosen to turn to another woman instead. I know my actions were foolish. Reckless. Even dangerous. But I would have risked anything to find the intimacy and connection that we built together at the lodge."

She reached for his hand and held it firmly within her own.

"I wanted a real marriage—of hearts and minds and

bodies—not merely a facade to present to the people of our countries or to the world at large. I wanted a husband who would love me and stand by me as much as I want to love and stand by him. I came to the lodge in Ms. Romolo's place hoping we could build that together. I hate that I deceived you, but I'd be lying if I said I regretted those days we spent together. We can still have that relationship, that partnership based on love, if you'll just forgive me. I was wrong, I was stupid. I abused your trust, but I believed I was doing all of that for all the right reasons. I love you so much. You have my heart, my soul. You are my everything. Please…believe me."

For a moment she thought she might have broken through the shell of cold indifference that encased him, but then he pulled his hand free.

"I don't believe you. I can't. I can only regret that I misguidedly placed my trust in a woman who will do whatever it takes for whatever *she* wants and to hell with the consequences—just like my mother did."

Each word fell like a blow upon her soul and Mila felt paralyzed, unable to speak or move as her body suffused with the pain that filled her mind.

Thierry continued, "For the past seven years there was only one woman in my life. You. I didn't know you, but I planned to get to know you once we were married. I wanted to learn about what made you happy, what made you sad. What filled you with hope, what made you angry. What piqued your interest, what bored you rigid. I wanted to share your life, but I don't see how I can do that now. You destroyed our future with your lies. I simply can't marry a woman I can't trust."

He leaned forward and flicked a switch—to the intercom to the driver, Mila realized through the fog of grief that slowly engulfed her.

"Take us back to the helipad. The princess is ready to return to Erminia."

Her voice shook and she felt as if her heart had been absorbed by a gaping black hole of despair as she spoke once more. "Please, I beg of you—reconsider. We can delay the wedding—take as long as you need until you feel you can trust me again. Please give me another chance. I love you, Thierry. With all my heart. I will do everything in my power to make up to you for my foolishness."

"And what if *everything* is not enough?" he retorted as the car drew to a halt near the helipad. "There's nothing you can do to change my mind."

The car rolled to a halt.

Mila tried one more time to probe the seemingly impenetrable wall Thierry had erected between them. "Was it so very bad, loving me?"

Before he could respond, the door beside her opened. She barely acknowledged Pasquale as he offered her his hand to help her from the car. She waited for Thierry to respond to her question but he remained silent, his eyes forward. Her heart broke.

She had failed in her attempt to secure her happiness. Worse, she'd failed in her attempt to see to the security of her family, her people, her country. Even now, she didn't want to give up. Couldn't bring herself to accept that Thierry would never forgive her. Maybe it was too soon, perhaps she should have given him more time before making her approach. But time was a luxury they didn't have, not with the news Rocco had shared with her.

And even as she climbed back on board the helicopter and attempted to rationalize her thoughts, she knew that her mission would have failed, no matter what she'd said or how long she'd waited. Thierry was a guarded man. One who had shielded his love and emotions behind his duty and determination to live honorably. She had dishonored him, and herself, with her actions, and that was something he could not forgive.

Now she had to face her brother, the leader of her people, and tell him she had failed both him and them.

Flying in the dark was preferable to flying by daylight, Mila reasoned. At least this way you couldn't see how high you were or, conversely, how close to the ground that you were covering at unnatural speed. Even so, it seemed to her that they were descending far sooner than she'd expected. She looked across to the general who was again seated beside her.

"It feels like we are coming into land. Surely we're not in Erminia yet. Is there something wrong?"

"Perhaps it is a mechanical issue with the chopper," the general replied, looking unconcerned.

Mila looked out the window. Yes, they were very definitely being brought down to land, but where were they? In the dark it was impossible to make out any landmarks of distinction. The second they were down the pilot exited the chopper, and the general was quick to follow. Mila remained in her seat, wondering what on earth was going on. Through her window she watched as the two men began to talk.

Then, to her horror, she saw the pilot pull out a handgun and point it at the general.

A loud report followed and Mila screamed as the general fell to the ground in a crumpled heap. The pilot came to her door and yanked it open. "Come with me now," he demanded, waving the pistol toward her.

Horrified, she did as he told her. "What are you doing? Why—?"

"Silence!" the man shouted and grabbed her roughly by the shoulder, shoving her ahead of him. "Walk!"

Mila staggered but was pulled upright by the pilot.

"Don't try anything stupid, Your Royal Highness." He sneered as he used her title, as if it was an insult. "I will not hesitate to give you the same treatment I gave the general."

A large, black, all-terrain vehicle roared up out of the darkness and a group of men piled out before it was fully stationary. They all carried guns. She'd been frightened before, but now she was absolutely terrified. What on earth was going to happen to her?

Sixteen

"What do you mean the princess never returned to Erminia? We saw her helicopter take off with our own eyes."

Pasquale's features reflected his concern. "I know, sire, but it seems her transport was diverted before she reached the palace, and the princess was abducted. No one knows where she is."

"And the pilot and her escort? Where are they?"

"Her escort was the king's own general. He was shot but managed to escape, apparently. The report I received from inside the Erminian palace said he regained consciousness to find the princess gone and the helicopter abandoned. He flew it back to the palace himself."

Thierry shoved a hand through his hair and began to pace. This was his fault. He'd sent her away. If he'd only been more willing to listen, to give her that second chance she'd begged for—the chance they both deserved—then this would never have happened.

"What is Rocco doing?" he demanded.

"The king has dispatched troops to search for the princess. The general was vague about his whereabouts when he came to and it appears that the tracking on the helicopter had been disabled when it left here. He was battling to remain conscious during the flight, apparently, and has little recollection of the journey."

"And yet he made it to the palace?"

"It would appear so, sire."

Thierry sat back down at his desk and stared at the papers upon it as if they could shed some light on where the missing princess could be found. Something didn't feel right, but he couldn't put his finger on it.

"The general's injury, what was it?"

"A bullet wound, sire," Pasquale informed him. "He was shot at close range. He lost a considerable amount of blood and required transfusions and surgery to remove the bullet."

So the general couldn't have been party to the kidnapping, Thierry rationalized. No doubt Mila's brother would ensure the man was thoroughly questioned about the incident, but in the meantime Thierry wished there was something he could do. He'd been so full of fury since returning from the lodge he'd barely been able to see straight, let alone think or react rationally.

When Mila had requested an audience with him he'd agreed, but he hadn't been prepared to listen. He was so consumed with his anger all he'd wanted to do was make it clear to her that they stood no chance together. And yet, now, all he wanted to do was ensure her safety. The very idea that she was in danger sent an icy shaft of fear through him. But he couldn't show fear—he daren't. His focus now had to be on finding her, whatever it took.

Yes, that was what he needed to do. Find her, hold her and tell her he'd been a colossal fool to let her go. If he ever had the opportunity again he'd pull her in his arms and tell her he forgave her and he'd never let her go again. Certainly, he had been beyond angry when she'd revealed her identity. No man liked being taken for a fool. But he couldn't help but be moved by the way she had fought for their love. And when he considered the idea of his life without Mila in it, it stretched ahead of him like a barren desert.

He'd let his fury buoy him along these past days. Let it feed his outrage and disappointment in what she'd done. But how bad had it been, really? He'd opened his heart to her, shared his deepest fears and secrets with her—believing her to be a courtesan, rather than the woman he intended to spend the rest of his life with. How stupid could he have been? Those were the things he should have shared only with his wife, rather than a stranger.

What if Ms. Romolo really had come to the lodge—would he have come to regret sharing intimacies with her that should only be given to his princess? Instead, through Mila's machinations, he'd been sharing his thoughts and feelings with the right woman all along. He'd fallen in love with that woman. Shared the most intimate act of love with that woman.

And he'd reacted to her confession with an icy rage that far outweighed what she'd done. He'd been a fool. He didn't deserve her love. What she'd done, she'd done for them. For love. And he'd thrown that love away. He had to get her back.

"I must find her, Pasquale. Bring the tactical leader of our special forces team to me immediately."

A look of paternal approval wreathed Pasquale's face. "Certainly, sire. In fact, I believe the captain is already on his way here to your office."

Thierry looked at Pasquale in surprise. "Already?"

"I thought it best, sire, given how you feel about the princess."

"How is it that you know me better than I appear to know myself?"

The question went without answer when a sharp rap at the office door announced the arrival of the man Thierry needed most right now. As his aide let the captain in and made to leave, Thierry called out.

"Pasquale?"

"Yes, sire?"

"Thank you. From the bottom of my heart."

"Tell me thank you when you have her back, sire. Then we can all be grateful."

She'd been here five days already and the incarceration was driving her crazy. The room into which she'd been shown was austere and had the bare minimum of furnishings—just a bed and a straight-back wooden chair. The bed had nothing more than a mattress and a scratchy woolen blanket. She decided she should be grateful for small mercies. At least the rickety bed frame kept her off the cold stone floor.

From the familiar carved stone heraldic arms above the slit in the wall which served as a window, she realized that she was being held in an old abandoned fortress somewhere, probably inside the Erminian border. The border was peppered with these crumbling buildings that harked back to older, more dangerous and volatile times. Most of the structures were in a state of complete and utter disrepair. But judging by the hinges and locks on her door this one had been at least partially refurbished.

The irony of being kidnapped not long after she had done the very same to Ottavia Romolo was not lost on her, but at least she'd ensured the woman could enjoy some comfort, even luxury. This cell—it could be called nothing more than that—didn't even boast running water. It had galled her to be forced to use a chamber pot for a toilet and to have to hand it to a taciturn mercenary on guard outside her room when she was done. Once, she'd been tempted to simply throw it at the man and run for it when he opened the door, but where would she run? And who to? She had no idea where she was and her guards were no doubt well trained in how to use the guns they carried. She was certain they wouldn't hesitate to use them if it was necessary. No, she had to trust that Rocco would send his men to find her. And soon.

She'd had the briefest of audiences with one of her captors when she'd first been put in this room. He'd explained her purpose for being here, which had shocked her. He was a member of the movement that was determined to increase tensions between Erminia and Sylvain. Apparently the threat of potential war was big business and there were several players involved in this action—including the nameless and faceless pretender to Rocco's throne who had added his own demands. Mila was to be held until Rocco abdicated the throne voluntarily in favor of the illegitimate older brother. If Rocco refused, her captors would have no further use for her, which made it clear that her life was very much in danger.

She didn't want her brother to abdicate. Despite their differences she knew he was a good leader and a great man. It gave her no end of worry to know that she was now the cause of further unnecessary stress and trouble to her brother when he already had enough to deal with. And she didn't want to die, either.

Mila tried to distract herself by walking the perimeter of her room again, but she could already recite the number of blocks on each wall without even looking now and, besides, she felt as though she needed to conserve her depleting energy. It seemed that while a small portion of water was provided to her each day, her captors didn't think food was as important. The last time she'd eaten had been three days ago. Just thinking about the miserable serving of cold stew she'd been given made her stomach cramp on itself, but she tried to ignore the discomfort as she paused in front of the narrow opening to the world outside.

It was night and the cold dank air blowing through carried on it the promise of a coming storm. She hoped the thickness of the fortress walls would prevent any rain from entering her cell. It was bad enough to be tired and cold and hungry, but add wet to the equation and she had no doubt things would become infinitely worse.

Her thoughts turned to Thierry, to their last meeting together. She didn't want to die before seeing him again. She shook her head. She didn't want to die, period. Mila returned to the narrow bed and curled up beneath the thin blanket.

If she just closed her eyes she could turn her thoughts back to the idyllic week she'd shared with Thierry. To the long rides they'd taken most mornings, to the first time they'd properly kissed, to the night they'd made love before everything had imploded and she'd been sent home in disgrace.

Mila felt herself begin to drift off to sleep, her thoughts still firmly latched onto the man who held her heart in his hands whether he wanted it or not.

She was yanked from her dreams by the swoosh of her door being opened, followed by the murmur of a male voice.

"She's here."

"Mila! Are you all right? Wake up, my Angel," a familiar voice whispered fiercely in her ear.

Hawk? It couldn't be, she told herself as she shrank back under the covers. She had to be dreaming. Or maybe the days of little to eat and miserly rations of water had driven her over the edge into madness.

"Mila! Wake up!"

There it was again. That voice, this time accompanied by a strong hand on her shoulder giving her a solid shake. She opened her eyes. In the gloom it was almost impossible to see who it was. She could only make out the looming shape of a man, all in black, with his head and face covered by a dark balaclava. She drew in a breath to scream. Was this it? Was she going to be killed now?

The man put one hand over her mouth, muffling the cry that threatened to fill the air, and tore the mask from his head. Thierry! It was Thierry, he was here. He couldn't be real. She blinked her eyes as if doing so would clear her vision.

"Are you hurt?" the apparition demanded softly.

She shook her head and he took his hand from over her mouth before bending closer to take her lips in a kiss. If she'd doubted it was him before, the touch and taste of his lips on hers removed any lingering remnants of disbelief. His kiss was short and fierce, but exactly what she needed.

"Can you walk?" he asked in an undertone.

She nodded, wide awake now and fully aware of the need for silence.

"That's my girl." He smiled approvingly. "C'mon, let's get you out of here. Are you wearing shoes?"

"They took them off me."

He cursed softly and left her for a moment to speak to one of the men hovering in the doorway. One of them unslung a pack from his shoulders and pulled out several thick wads of dressing and rolls of bandages.

"These aren't ideal, but they'll protect your feet for a while," the man said as he bent to position the dressing on the soles of her feet before swiftly winding the bandages around her feet and ankles.

What happened next passed in a blur. All she was aware of was being flanked by a team of men carrying automatic weapons and wearing dark clothing, and the strength of

Thierry's arm around her waist as he silently hauled her along the passageway and finally, thankfully, outside.

The whole operation, from the fortress to the surrounding forest, couldn't have taken more than five minutes, and Mila was shaking with both fear and relief by the time they stopped running once they were deep in the forest. She couldn't understand it. No one had tried to stop them at any stage. There'd been no gunfire, no explosions. It had been nothing like what she'd seen in the movies that Sally had so loved watching back in America. Everything had been accomplished under a veil of stealth that had lent an even more surreal atmosphere to everything.

"Here," Thierry said, sliding out of the jacket he wore and helping her to put it on. "You're frozen."

"What now?" she asked through chattering teeth.

"Now I'm taking you home."

The call of a nocturnal bird bounced off the trees around them.

"That's our signal. Our transport is waiting a kilometer away. Can you make it just that bit further?" Thierry asked.

"Will you be with me?"

"Always."

"Then I can do anything," she said simply.

He looked as if he wanted to say something else, but one of the other men gestured to him that they needed to keep moving.

"We need to talk, but it will have to wait. First we get you to safety," he said grimly before wrapping his arm around her again.

It seemed to take forever, but eventually they broke out of the woods and piled into a pair of large armored vehicles. She was beyond exhausted, incapable of speech as Thierry lifted her into a seat.

"Radio ahead to the palace. Make sure a medical team is on standby and inform King Rocco we have her and we're bringing her home," Thierry informed the man standing nearest to him.

"N-no," Mila tried to protest.

She didn't want to go home. She wanted to be with Thierry. But, as Thierry climbed into the vehicle and pulled her onto his lap, the darkness fluttering around the periphery of her vision consumed her.

Seventeen

Thierry watched Mila as she slept in the castle infirmary. The grime of captivity still clung to her, but according to the doctor that had checked her over she was in good health considering what she'd been through. His eyes traced the tilt of her nose, the outline of her lips, the stubbornness of her jaw, and he felt his heart break a little as he realized he had almost sent her to her death. If he'd only been willing to forgive, none of this would have happened.

There was one thing that he knew without any doubt. He loved Princess Mila Angelina of Erminia with every breath in his body. He didn't want to face another minute, let alone another day, without knowing she'd be in his future.

"She's still sleeping?" Rocco's voice interrupted him.

"As you can see," Thierry answered, not taking his eyes off her for a minute.

"But she will be all right?"

"Yes."

Rocco settled on a chair on the other side of Mila's bed. "I can't begin to thank you—"

"Then don't. I did what was necessary. What you would have done yourself if you had reached her first." There had been several teams searching possible locations. It was just Rocco's bad luck that he hadn't been on the team that had been sent to the correct spot.

Rocco inclined his head. "I'm informed that the fortress was empty by the time my troops stormed the building. They must have left when they realized she'd been taken. Apparently there was an underground escape tunnel that wasn't on any plans."

"You're disappointed my men didn't detain Mila's kidnappers?"

"How can I be when an attempt to do so might have resulted in her being hurt…or worse? You did the right thing insisting on a stealth operation. We will catch the perpetrators eventually. They will be brought to justice."

Thierry nodded in agreement and the two men sat in silence, watching the woman they both loved as she rested. Eventually Rocco took his leave, pausing a moment to put his hand on Thierry's shoulder.

"Her heart is yours, my friend. Take care of it," he said carefully.

"For the rest of my life, if she'll let me," Thierry answered grimly.

Rocco made a sound of assent and then left, closing the door behind him quietly. On the bed, Mila began to stir and her eyes slowly opened. Her gaze searched for and found him. For a moment myriad emotions flashed across her open features—fear, relief, joy…and then they were hidden behind a schooled emptiness that scored Thierry's heart like a blade.

"You're awake," he said unnecessarily, and poured a

fresh glass of water for her. "Here, drink this. Doctor's orders."

She struggled to an upright position and took the glass from him. A wild flow of protectiveness shot through him when he saw her hand shake as she tipped the glass and drank deeply. He took the empty glass from her and refilled it.

"No, no more." She looked around, confusion evident on her face. "I'm back at home?" she asked, her voice husky and her eyes avoiding contact with his.

"Your brother felt it best."

Slowly, she looked up. "It wasn't a dream, was it? It was you at the fortress?"

"Together with my elite special forces team."

The explanation of how they came to be there, how his men had used every legal source available to them—and several that weren't—to track the helicopter to where it had landed, and then create a list of possible targets where she might have been held, could wait until another time.

She sank back against the pillows and closed her eyes again.

"Th-thank you," she said weakly.

"You don't owe me any thanks. I hold myself responsible for your capture. If I had been more of a man and less of an unreasonable, spoiled and angry child, it would never have happened."

Again that wave of fear and self-loathing coursed through him.

"No, don't blame yourself. You could have done nothing to stop them."

"If I hadn't let you go—"

Her eyes opened again. "Why are you here?"

"I'm here to ask your forgiveness."

"*My* forgiveness? For what?"

"For treating you so damnably. For not listening. For

not accepting your love when it was so freely given with such a pure heart. For painting you with the same brush that I had painted my mother and believing you were no different than her—that you were the kind of woman who cared for nothing but her own pleasure."

"Wow, that's quite a list," Mila answered. "But I still believe there is nothing for me to forgive. I'm the one who lied to you and cheated to get to you—I even arranged the detention of an innocent woman so I could achieve my goals. I am hardly a paragon of virtue. I wouldn't have blamed you if you'd left me to rot in that vile fortress."

"But your actions came from a place of love—from a determination to give the two of us the best possible chance to know and learn to love each other," he said calmly, earning a look of surprise from her.

"That doesn't excuse my choices."

"No, only I can do that."

"Will you? Will you forgive me?"

"I have already done so. When I heard you were missing I realized how stupid and proud I had been. How empty my life would be without you in it. How foolish I was, to spurn the one thing that I have craved all my life. Unquestionable, unconditional love." He took her hands with both of his and lifted them to his lips, pressing a dozen kisses to her knuckles. "I love you, my Angel. I hope you will give me another chance. I promise I will do my best by you, in all ways."

Tears filled her eyes and began to spill down her cheeks, leaving tracks on her skin. "You still love me?"

"I never stopped. And that made my anger all the harder to bear. I hated every second without you, but my pride was still wounded, and it kept me from trusting you— from trusting in *us*."

"I just wanted you to love me. To enter into our marriage together with the knowledge that ours would be a blessed union. That we wouldn't repeat the mistakes of my parents, or—" she hesitated and drew in a breath "—yours."

"We hardly had the best of examples, did we? Which is why it is going to be all the more important that we work hard together to make sure our children, and their children, know exactly what it is like to love and to be loved, don't you think?"

"Our children?"

"If you'll have me."

"Say it again, first. Say you forgive me."

"I forgive you without blame or conditions or recrimination. I love you, Princess Mila Angelina, and I want you to be my wife—to rule the kingdom of Sylvain at my side as my queen. Will you marry me, my Angel?"

"Thinking of a future without you was torture—an endless black hole of loneliness and despair. So, yes, I will marry you, my Hawk. Nothing would make me happier. I love you with every breath in my body, every thought in my mind and every beat of my heart. I promise I will always love you and I will raise our children with you with much joy and pride. They will always know they are loved and important each in their own right, but always you will be the most important thing in the world to me."

Mila alighted from the carriage, allowing her brother to assist her from the ornately gilded old-fashioned contraption and bestowing on him a smile that came straight from her heart.

"You look beautiful today, little sister."

"I feel beautiful. How could I not when I'm the happiest woman in the world today."

"As you should be," he murmured. He tucked her hand in the crook of his elbow and they traveled up the red carpet that lined the stairs leading to the massive Sylvano cathedral. All around them they heard the cheers and well wishes of the thousands of people that lined the roads on either side of the church. Flags from both Erminia and Sylvain dotted through the crowds. "You deserve to be," he added.

"As do you, brother." Mila gave him a look of concern.

"One day, maybe," he conceded.

There was more going on with him than he was prepared to admit, Mila thought. And hadn't that been the story of their lives since he'd become king? She wished with all her heart that he could know the same love that she and Thierry shared. Rocco needed to know that there would always be someone there for him, standing by his side.

Her brother cocked an eyebrow at her. "Having second thoughts?"

"Not at all, why?"

"Because we're dillydallying here on the carpet while your future husband awaits you inside."

"Well, we had better not keep him waiting a second longer," Mila answered with a swell of joy in her heart.

From the second they entered the doors to the cathedral her eyes were locked on Thierry. She felt a burst of pride that the tall and handsome man in his ceremonial garb was hers. Music billowed from the organ to fill the air to the rafters as she and her brother began their path down the carpet that led to what Mila knew would be the best of futures. All around her, people turned to stare and comments flew amongst them as she moved by in her gown, her long train sweeping along behind her.

She'd chosen not to have any attendants. She wanted to show Thierry she needed no one other than him for the rest of her life. As the ceremony began and Rocco gave her in marriage to the man standing by her side, Mila felt nothing but exhilaration in the moment. This man before her was her future. Her everything. And, reflected in his eyes, she could see he felt exactly the same way.

Sally stepped forward from the front pew to take Mila's bouquet and whispered, "I told you a fairy tale!"

"Every day for the rest of my life," Mila answered before turning back to Thierry and solemnly making the vows that would tie her to him for the rest of her life.

The rest of the day passed in a blur of pomp and ceremony, but despite her happiness at the celebrations, Mila wanted nothing more than to have Thierry to herself again. After the sumptuous formal reception and dancing she was only too happy when Sally drew her away so she could change for her departure. In the palace apartment that had been set aside for her, Mila hastened to disrobe from her gown.

"Slow down, you'll tear something if you're not careful," Sally chided playfully. "Besides, it won't hurt to make him wait just a little longer."

"It might not hurt him, but it's killing me!" Mila laughed as she shed the last petticoat and stepped free.

"I'm so happy for you, you know," Sally said as she helped Mila into a form-fitting gown designed by one of Erminia's newest up-and-coming designers. "You deserve your happy ever after."

"Thank you. I wish everyone could be as happy as I am right now."

And she was happy, incredibly so. The only potential fly in the ointment was the threat that still hung over Rocco's right to the throne, but she forced herself to put that from her mind. There was nothing she could do about it now.

A knock at the door sent the women scurrying to find Mila's shoes and bag.

"Just a minute," Sally called out when Mila was finally ready. "I'd wish you all the best but I can see you have it already," she said, giving Mila a warm hug.

"I do. I never thanked you enough for being my friend, or for suggesting that we take that trip to New York. Without that, I don't know if I'd be where I am right now."

Sally stepped back and gave her a smile. "Oh, I don't know. I like to think that fate has a hand in the very important things in life."

"Fate, friends—whatever it was. I'm grateful to you. Friends forever, right?"

"Forever."

Mila opened the door to discover Thierry waiting on the other side. He offered her his arm.

"Ready to come with me, my Angel?"

"Always," she answered.

* * * * *

"We'll be the only occupants at Cap du Mer," Mac added.

Rory swallowed at the low, sexy note in his voice. She'd be alone with Mac, on a Caribbean island with warm, clear water and white beaches and palm trees. Utterly and absolutely alone. She wasn't sure whether the appropriate response was to be thrilled or terrified. Or both.

Sex and business don't mix, she told herself. *He's your patient!*

Sun, sea, sexy island… sexy man.

Not liking the cocky look in his eyes, the glint that suggested that he knew exactly what she was thinking about, she lifted her nose. "Well, at least we won't disturb the neighbors with your screams of pain when we start physio."

"Or your screams of pleasure when I make you fall apart in my arms," Mac replied without a second's hesitation.

Rory's heart thumped in her chest but she kept her eyes locked on his, refusing to admit that he rattled her. That instead of making her furious, as it should, her entire body was humming in anticipation and was very on board with that idea.

Rory folded her arms and rocked on her heels. "I hate it when you say things like that."

"No, you don't. You hate it because it turns you on."

* * *

Trapped with the Maverick Millionaire
is part of the From Mavericks to Married series—
Three superfine hockey players
finally meet their matches!

TRAPPED WITH
THE MAVERICK
MILLIONAIRE

BY
JOSS WOOD

All rights reserved including the right of reproduction in whole or in part in any form. This edition is published by arrangement with Harlequin Books S.A.

This is a work of fiction. Names, characters, places, locations and incidents are purely fictional and bear no relationship to any real life individuals, living or dead, or to any actual places, business establishments, locations, events or incidents. Any resemblance is entirely coincidental.

This book is sold subject to the condition that it shall not, by way of trade or otherwise, be lent, resold, hired out or otherwise circulated without the prior consent of the publisher in any form of binding or cover other than that in which it is published and without a similar condition including this condition being imposed on the subsequent purchaser.

® and ™ are trademarks owned and used by the trademark owner and/or its licensee. Trademarks marked with ® are registered with the United Kingdom Patent Office and/or the Office for Harmonisation in the Internal Market and in other countries.

First Published in Great Britain 2016
By Mills & Boon, an imprint of HarperCollins*Publishers*
1 London Bridge Street, London, SE1 9GF

© 2016 Joss Wood

ISBN: 978-0-263-91865-6

51-0616

Our policy is to use papers that are natural, renewable and recyclable products and made from wood grown in sustainable forests. The logging and manufacturing processes conform to the legal environmental regulations of the country of origin.

Printed and bound in Spain
by CPI, Barcelona

Joss Wood's passion for putting black letters on a white screen is only matched by her love of books and travelling (especially to the wild places of southern Africa) and, possibly, by her hatred of ironing and making school lunches.

Joss has written over sixteen books for the Mills & Boon KISS, Mills & Boon Presents and, most recently, Mills & Boon Desire lines.

After a career in business lobbying and local economic development, Joss now writes full-time. She lives in KwaZulu-Natal, South Africa, with her husband and two teenage children, surrounded by family, friends, animals and a ridiculous amount of books.

Joss is a member of the RWA (Romance Writers of America) and ROSA (Romance Writers of South Africa).

To the "Book Sisters," Romy Sommers,
Rae Rivers and Rebecca Crowley. All are fantastic
authors but are also funny, supportive and kind.

Basically, you rock!

Prologue

Rory Kydd, dressed in a too-small T-shirt and battered pajama bottoms, walked into the kitchen of her sister's luxurious kitchen and looked at the dark screen of the TV sitting on the counter.

Her best friend, Troy, had texted to tell her the Vancouver Mavericks had won and there had been high drama during the post-game interview. She was tempted to turn on the TV to see what he was talking about but, because she had a paper due and exams looming—and because she was trying not to think about one Maverick player in particular—she decided to have a cup of coffee and go back to the books. But even if she didn't give in to temptation, it couldn't be denied, team newbies Kade Webb, Quinn Rayne and Mark "Mac" McCaskill were a handful both on and off the ice, and Vancouver had three new heroes.

Three young, unfairly talented and, it had to be said, stupidly good-looking heroes.

And the best-looking of the bunch, in her opinion, was dating her older sister Shay.

Rory poured herself a cup of coffee and leaned her butt against the counter. Shay and Mac made perfect sense, she told herself. Again. Shay was a model and a TV presenter. Mac was the supertalented, superfine center for the city's beloved hockey team. They were the perfect age, she was twenty-three and Mac a year older, and, according to the press, because they were both beautiful and successful, a perfect match.

It was all perfectly perfect.

Except that Rory wasn't convinced.

And that wasn't because Mac made her toes tingle and her stomach jump. It had nothing to do with her insane attraction to the man. No, she'd spent enough time around Shay and Mac to see the cracks in their relationship, to know the bloom was off the rose and Shay was acting like a loon. Judging by Mac's wary, closed-off expression whenever Rory saw them together, Shay had him on the Crazy Express.

Rory would bet her last dollar Shay was feeling desperate, calling and texting relentlessly whenever they were apart. Since they both had such demanding careers, they were apart *a lot*.

Rory knew why Shay was insecure, why she couldn't trust a man. Rory had grown up in the same house as Shay. The difference between them was that Shay kept hoping there was one man out there who could be faithful and monogamous.

Rory was pretty damn sure that, like unicorns and the yeti, such a creature didn't exist.

Rory scowled and wrapped her hands around her mug. Shay hadn't told Mac why she was acting crazy, Rory was pretty sure of that. To complicate matters further, Rory and Mac had somehow become friends. Sadly, that was all they could ever be. He was too good-looking, too much of a celebrity, too far out of her league. She was a college student. He was a successful player, both on and off the ice… Oh, and that other little thing—*he was her sister's boyfriend!*

Besides all that, Mac treated Rory as he would a younger sister. He teased her, argued with her and made her laugh. So she'd caught him watching her with a brooding look on that sexy face once or twice but she wasn't an idiot, she knew it didn't mean anything. He'd probably wanted to talk to her about Shay, wanted advice on how to deal with her volatility. Rory *never* wanted to have that conversation.

A couple of nights ago, he'd given her a lift home from work and she'd been surprised when he didn't mention Shay. Why he'd waited for Rory to finish her waitressing shift was still a mystery but sitting in his sports car, shoulder to shoulder, saying next to nothing, had been the best twenty minutes of her life.

He'd walked her to the door of her lousy apartment building—the same building that currently had no heat—and he'd stood there looking down at her. Something in his expression had heat swirling in her stomach; he'd looked like a man about to kiss a woman. But she knew that had to be her imagination working overtime. He was dating Shay, tall, slim, stunning.

But, just for a moment, she'd thought he'd wanted to kiss her, to taste her, to yank her into his arms… Rory sighed. It wasn't possible. He was dating her sister. He

was permanently off-limits; messing in Shay's relationship was a line she would not cross. Thinking about Mac,
like that, was a flight of fancy she had no right to take.
Enough of that now.

Rory heard the front door open and she waited for
Shay's yell that she was home. It didn't come, and Rory
heard heavy footsteps on the wooden floor, a tread that
couldn't possibly belong to her sister. The saliva in her
mouth dried up and her heart rolled; there was only one
other person who had a key to Shay's apartment and he
was the one person Rory didn't want to be alone with.

In her pajamas, with crazy hair, sans makeup and bra-
less.

Mac appeared in the doorway to the kitchen, scowled
at her and ran a hand over his tired face. He had a light
bruise on his jaw—he'd obviously traded blows on the
ice—and the beginnings of a black eye but his injuries
looked superficial. It was the emotion she saw in his dark
eyes that held her rooted to the spot; he looked frustrated
and wound up.

"Where's your sister?" he demanded, his deep, rough
voice rumbling over her skin.

"Hello to you too." Rory shrugged and his frown deepened at her response. "I have no idea where she is. Are
you okay?"

Mac let out a low, humorless laugh. "Hell, no, I'm
screwed." He scowled at her and placed his hands on his
hips. "Why are you here?"

"Heat's out in my apartment. Shay said I could sleep
here so I don't freeze."

"Just my friggin' luck," Mac muttered.

"Jeez, what's your problem?" Rory asked him as he
shrugged out of his expensive leather jacket and tossed

it onto the granite counter. A long-sleeved black T-shirt clung to his broad chest and fell, untucked, over well-fitting jeans. He looked hot and tired and so damn sexy she could jump him right now, right where he stood.

Sister's boyfriend, she reminded herself as he walked over to the fridge, pulled out a microbrewed beer and cracked the top. He took a long swallow, sighed and, closing his eyes, placed the bottle against his forehead.

"Bitching, horrible, freakin' revolting day."

She wouldn't have thought the big badass of the Mavericks could sound so melodramatic. "It couldn't have been that dire—you won the game."

Mac's ink-blue eyes lasered into hers. "Did you watch?" he asked, his question as pointed as a spear tip.

Rory shook her head. "Nah, had to study. Why?"

"Because I was wondering why my head was still attached to my neck."

Rory narrowed her eyes. "What did you do?"

Instead of answering, he gave her a long look. Then he placed his bottle on the center island and walked toward her. He gripped the counter, one hand on either side of her body. He was like a big human cage, she thought.

Up close and personal, she could see the slight tinge of auburn in his stubble, notice how long his eyelashes were, could see a faded scar on his top lip. And man, he smelled so good. She wanted to stand on her toes and kiss that scar, run her lips over that bruise on his jaw, kiss his eye better.

Sister's boyfriend, sister's boyfriend…she had no right to be standing this close to Mac, tasting his breath, feeling his heat. Playing with fire, coloring outside the lines was something her father did, his worst trait, yet despite that sobering thought she couldn't make herself move away, was unable to duck under Mac's arm. Even though Mac belonged to Shay, Rory wanted just one kiss from him. She wanted to know what he tasted like, how strong his arms felt around her, how it felt to be plastered against that solid wall of muscle. *Just one kiss*...

Gray eyes clashed with blue as his mouth hovered above hers. As she stood there, *so* close and *so* personal, she knew exactly what he'd do, how she'd feel...

His lips would slide across hers, cool, strong...smart. She'd open her mouth to protest, to say they couldn't do this—or to let him in, who knew—and he wouldn't hesitate. As his tongue slid into her mouth, his hand on her lower back would pull her into him and his other hand would delve beneath the elastic of her flannel bottoms to cup a butt cheek. His kiss would turn deeper and wetter and her hands would burrow under his loose T-shirt and explore the muscles of his back, his shoulders, his fabulously ripped stomach.

She'd think that it was wrong but she wouldn't be able to stop herself. Mac would, ever so slowly, pull her T-shirt up to expose her too-small breasts and she'd whimper into his mouth and push her hips against him, needing to rub herself against his hard, hard erection. He'd be what a man felt like, strong, hot, in control...

"I just saw our entire kiss in your eyes. God, that was so hot," Mac growled, and she tasted his sweet breath on her lips again.

"We can't, it's wrong." Rory pushed the words up her throat, past her teeth, through her lips. Four words and she felt like she'd run a marathon.

Mac's eyes stayed locked on hers and, in case she missed the desire blazing there, his erection nudging her knee let her know how much he wanted her. Mac wanted

her…he really did. Tall, built, smelling great, gorgeous…
how was she supposed to resist him?

Sister's boyfriend, sister's boyfriend…

Rory placed her hands on his pecs and pushed. Mac
stepped back but as he did, he lifted his hand to run his
knuckle over her cheek. That small, tender action nearly
shattered her resolve and she had to grab the edge of the
counter with both hands to keep from launching herself
into his arms, wrapping her legs around his hips and
feasting on that fallen-angel mouth.

So this was primal lust, crazy passion. She wasn't sure
she liked how out of control it made her feel. Squirmy,
hot, breathless…it was intensely tempting to throw cau-
tion to the wind and get lost in the moment. Did having
such a flammable reaction to Mac mean that she was
more like her dad than she thought? Ugh. This wasn't
going to happen, she decided. From this point on she
would not kiss, touch or think about her sister's boyfriend. This stopped. Now.

Rory held up a hand. "Back up."

Mac took two steps back and she could breathe. She
felt the craziness recede. He jammed his hands into the
pockets of his jeans and sent her a brooding look. "That
was…"

"Wrong? Crazy? A betrayal of my sister?"

Mac frowned. "Let's not get carried away here. We
didn't even kiss."

"We wanted to!"

"But we didn't so let's not get too caught up in the
melodrama." Mac picked up his beer, sipped and sighed.
His head snapped up and Rory heard the front door closing, heard her sister kicking off her heels. Rory tried to

keep her face blank but she felt like her brain and heart were on fire as guilt and shame pricked her skin.

We didn't actually kiss but I really, really wanted to...

"You're here." Shay tossed the words at Mac as she stepped into the kitchen. Rory frowned. Shay didn't walk up to Mac and kiss him. It was what she did, every single time she saw him, whether they'd been apart five minutes or five weeks.

Mac made no effort to touch Shay either. He just stood there wearing that inscrutable face Rory knew he used when he wanted to avoid a scene.

But a scene, she knew it like she knew her own signature, was what they were about to have. Why?

Rory turned her eyes to her sister's face. She recognized that expression, a mixture of betrayal, broken trust, hurt and humiliation. God, she looked devastated.

"What the hell, Mac?" Shay's shout bounced off the walls.

Rory's gaze jumped around the room. How could Shay know? Did she have cameras in the apartment? X-ray vision? A girlfriend's gut instinct?

Mac held his hands up. "I'm sorry, Shay, for all of it. I never meant to hurt you."

"Yet you're doing such a fine job of it." Shay wiped her eyes with the back of her wrist. "There were easier ways to get rid of me, Mac. You didn't have to humiliate me on national TV."

Rory looked at Mac and then at Shay. Okay, maybe this conversation had nothing to do with Rory and the almost-kiss. "What are you talking about? What did he do?"

Shay let out a laugh that held absolutely no amusement. "You haven't seen it?"

"Seen what?"

Shay's laugh was brittle. "Well, you're probably the only person in the city—the country—who hasn't!" She lunged for the remote on the counter and jabbed her finger on the buttons to get the TV to power up. While she flipped through channels, Rory snuck a look at Mac. He gripped the bridge of his nose with his finger and thumb and he looked utterly miserable.

Sad, sorry and, to be frank, at the end of his rope.

"And in today's sports news, Maverick's center Mac McCaskill was caught on an open mic commenting on sex, monogamy and hot women."

Rory snapped her head up and looked at the screen. Footage of the post-match news appeared on the screen. Quinn, Kade and Mac lounged behind a table draped with the Maverick's logo. Kade said something that was too low to hear and the three of them laughed.

"The blonde reporter in the third row is seriously hot." Quinn's voice was muffled and she could just hear his words.

"Did you see the redhead?" Kade demanded, his voice equally muted. "I have a thing for redheads."

"You have a thing for all women." Mac's voice was clear and loud; obviously his was the only microphone that was live. Oh…shoot.

"Like you do. When are you going to give up this relationship BS and start playing the field again?" Quinn demanded. "It's not like you're particularly happy with your ball and chain."

"I'm not and you're right, monogamy sucks," Mac said, looking past Quinn. Rory recognized that smile, the appreciation in his eyes. "Your blonde from the third row is very hot."

"Shay is also hot," Kade pointed out.

"Yeah but she's crazy. Besides, I'm bored with tall and built. I'm thinking that petite might be a nice change of pace— Why is Vernon gesturing to me to shut up?"

Then a rash of swear words was followed by: "My mic is on!"

Rory looked at Shay, who'd dropped into a chair at the kitchen table with a vacant look in her eyes. She'd stopped crying and she looked like she'd checked out, mentally and emotionally. Mac picked up his jacket from the counter and walked over to stand in front of Shay. He bent his knees so he could look directly into her face.

"I'm sorry I spoke behind your back and I'm so sorry that I hurt you, Shay. It wasn't my intention. I take full responsibility for running my mouth off. Not my finest moment and I *am* very sorry."

When Shay looked through him and didn't respond, he slowly stood up and placed his apartment key on the counter. Rory looked at her broken, desperately sad sister, grabbed Mac by the arm and pulled him into the hall, feeling as if her gray eyes must be full of angry lightning.

When their eyes met, he lifted one broad shoulder. "Told you I was screwed," he said.

"So you came over here to screw me?" she demanded, thinking about that almost-kiss, fury clogging her throat.

Mac's flashing eyes met hers. "Believe it or not, I'm not that much of a bastard. I didn't even know you would be here."

"What were you thinking, Mac?" she demanded, insanely angry. On behalf of her sister, but also because Rory had trusted him just as Shay had. "You've done so many interviews, you know how mics work."

"I wasn't thinking, dammit!"

Red dots appeared in front of Rory's eyes. "Did you plan this? Was the smack talk an easy way to get out of your relationship with Shay?"

"Contrary to the evidence, I am better than that."

Rory snorted. "You could've fooled me. First you insult my sister, then you almost kiss me? What was *that* about?"

Mac let out a harsh, angry breath. "I knew when I left that news conference that I was toast. I regret what I said. I came here to apologize to Shay but found you instead—"

"So you were angry and frustrated and I was there, a handy way to let off some steam!" Rory interrupted.

Mac's curses filled the small hallway.

Rory drilled a finger into his chest. "How many times have you cheated on Shay? Because that move with me was far too practiced to be your first time!" The red dots turned scarlet and her chest tightened.

Mac stepped back and anger sparked in his eyes. "I'm only going to say this once. I never cheated on your sister. And, babe, you wanted to kiss me as much as I wanted to kiss you! I'll take full responsibility for being a prick on national television but I *will not* take *all* the blame for what almost happened in there."

Guilt swamped her. She knew he was right and she hated it. She didn't want to shoulder *any* of the blame; it would be a lot easier if she could just blame him for everything: for being too sexy, for making her want something she had no right to want.

Mac raked his fingers through his hair. "Look, why don't we let this situation settle down and I'll call you? We can have coffee, chat. Sort this out?"

Pick up where we left off?

That wasn't going to happen. There was no way she could date someone who'd dated—*slept with*—her sister, who'd almost cheated on her. Someone who'd made Rory so crazy with lust that she'd almost betrayed her sister! He would've kissed her had she not stopped him. He would've cheated…of that she was categorically convinced.

She could never trust him.

Ever.

"Don't bother. I'm not interested." Rory walked around him, yanked open the front door and gestured for him to leave. "Go. You've created enough havoc for one evening, for one lifetime."

Mac, with a final inscrutable look, walked out of the Kydd sisters' lives. *Good riddance*, Rory thought. The last thing either of them needed was a cheating, backstabbing man in their lives.

Rory turned and saw her sister standing in the kitchen doorway. She'd heard every word of their conversation. So she'd stopped the kiss. That meant little. The truth remained: she wanted Shay's man, wanted him badly. They both knew she was more like their dirtbag father than either of them had thought possible. Shay was going to strip layers of skin off her and Rory deserved it.

"You two almost kissed? You had a moment?"

Facing her sister, she couldn't deny the truth. "Yes. I'm really sorry."

"Okay then. Thanks for getting rid of him," Shay told Rory in a cold and hard voice. "Now get the hell out of my apartment and my life."

One

Ten or so years later...

Rory made her way to a small table by the window in the crowded cafeteria of St. Catherine's Hospital, juggling a stack of files, her bag and a large blueberry smoothie. Dumping the files on the table, she took a berry-flavored hit before pulling out a chair and dropping into it. She'd been on the go since before seven, had missed lunch and was now running on fumes. She had two more patients to see. She might be able to get home before eight.

An early night. Bliss.

Her cell phone chimed and Rory squinted at the display, smiling when she saw her sister's name.

"Sorry, something just came up. I'll call you right back," Shay stated before disconnecting.

Rory smiled, grateful that she and Shay were really

close, a minor miracle after the McCaskill incident. Mac running his mouth off and his subsequent breakup with Shay had been the first major media storm involving one of the three most famous Mavericks. It had been the catalyst for the city's fascination with anything to do with Mac, Quinn and Kade.

Shay had been swept up into the madness; she'd been stalked and hassled by reporters and photographers for months. Her life had been a living hell. Unfortunately, because she refused to talk to Rory, Shay had weathered the media attention by herself. She'd lost weight and, as Rory had found out years later, she'd come close to a breakdown. Rory was so grateful the incident was solidly behind them; the man-slut captain of the Mavericks professional ice hockey team was not worth losing sleep, never mind a sister, over.

Except that she did, frequently, still lose sleep thinking about him. Rory sighed. He was her fantasy man, the man she always thought of when she was alone and well, she hated to admit it…horny. She wondered and she imagined and the fact that she did either—both— annoyed the pants off her.

The jerk.

Her cell rang again, Rory answered and Shay said a quick hello. "Sorry, as you picked up the delivery guy arrived."

"No worries, what's up?"

"Dane sent me two dozen red roses."

And, judging by Shay's frantic voice, this was a problem? "Okay, lucky you. Why are you freaking out?"

"Two dozen red roses? Who sends his wife of eight months two dozen red roses? He must be cheating on me."

Here we go again, Rory thought, exasperated. *I haven't*

had enough coffee to cope with Shay's insecurities.
Thanks again, Dad, for the incredible job you did mess-
ing up your daughters' love lives.

Rory sucked on her straw musing about the fact that
she and Shay had different approaches to life and love.
She was closed off to the idea of handing her heart over
to a man, yet Shay had never given up on love. She had
eventually, she was convinced, caught the last good
guy in the city. The fact that Dane was calm and strong
enough to deal with Shay's insecurities made Rory love
him more.

"He must be having an affair. Nobody can work as
much as he does," Shay fretted.

"Shay! Princess!" Rory interrupted her mumblings.
"Stop obsessing, you're getting yourself into a state.
You're a gorgeous blonde ex-model and you still look
like a million dollars. Dane married you and you promised to trust him."

Shay sighed. "I did, didn't I?"

"Look at your wedding photos. Look at how he's looking at you…like you're the moon and stars and everything
that's perfect." In spite of her cynicism when it came
to romance, Rory couldn't help feeling a little jealous
every time Dane looked at her sister, love blazing from
his eyes. What must it feel like to have someone love you
that much, someone so determined to make you happy?
Logically, she knew the risk wasn't worth it, but…damn,
seeing that look punched her in the heart every time.

"Dane is in the middle of a big case—some gang
shooting, remember? And he's the homicide detective
in charge—and sending you roses is his way of reminding you that he loves you."

"So, no affair?"

"No affair, Shay." And if there was—there wasn't!—but if there was then Rory would take Dane's own weapon and shoot him with it.

Rory said goodbye to her sister, shot off a text to Dane suggesting Shay might need a little extra attention—she and her brother-in-law worked as a team to keep Shay's insecurities from driving them both nuts—and looked down at the folders. She needed to make notes and read over the files of the two patients she was about to see.

She so wanted her own practice. Craydon's Physiotherapy patients were channeled through the system like cans on a conveyor line. There was little time for proper one-on-one care and she was providing patients with only enough treatment to see them through to the next session. Sometimes she wondered if she was doing any good at all.

If she had her own place, she'd slow it down, take more time, do some intensive therapy. But setting up a new practice required cash she didn't have, premises she couldn't afford. She'd just have to keep saving... Maybe one day.

She had barely looked over the first file when her cell rang again. This time it was a number she did not recognize. She answered the call with a cautious hello.

"Rory? Kade Webb, from the Vancouver Mavericks. We met a long time ago."

Kade Webb? Why on earth would he be calling her? "I remember...hi. What can I do for you?"

Kade didn't waste time beating around the bush. "I have a player in St. Catherine's, in The Annex Clinic, and I'd like you to take a look at his chart, assess his injury and tell me what you think."

Rory frowned, thinking fast. "Kade, the Mavericks

have a resident physiotherapist. I know because my bosses would kill for the Mavericks' contract. Why me?"

"Because you have an excellent track record in treating serious sports injuries," Kade replied. "Will you do it? Take a look and let me know what you think?"

"I—"

"Thanks. I'll call you back in a couple of hours."

Rory wanted to tell him that she had patients, that it was against company policy, but he was gone. Argh! She had questions, dammit! Who was the player? What room he was in? Did he know that she was coming? Had Kade spoken to her bosses about this?

Infuriating man, she thought as she stood up and gathered her possessions. It was said that Kade, like his two partners in crime, could charm the dew off roses and the panties off celibates. He hadn't bothered to use any of that charm on her, Rory thought with an annoyed toss of her head.

Not that she would've responded to it, but it would've been nice for him to try.

Mac McCaskill, you stupid idiot, Rory thought.

She'd had many variations of the thought over the past decade, some expressed in language a lot more colorful, but the sentiment was the same. However, this was the first time in nearly a decade that she wasn't mocking his tendency to jump from one gorgeous woman to another or shaking her head over the fact that he was, essentially, a man-slut.

As much as his social life irritated her, she felt sorry for him. He was an exceptionally talented player and as she looked at the notes on his chart, she realized his arm was, to use nontechnical terms, wrecked. For a player of his caliber that was a very scary situation.

"Rory, what are you doing in here?"

Rory, standing next to Mac's bed, flipped a glance over her shoulder and smiled, relieved, when she saw her best friend stepping into Mac's private room. If it had been someone other than Troy she would've had to explain herself.

This was all kinds of wrong, she thought. There were protocols around patient visits and she shouldn't be in Mac's room, looking at his chart, assessing his injury. She should've refused Kade's request, but here she was again, flouting the rules. What was it about McCaskill that made her do that?

"I need to get the mat on him, need to get his circulation restored as soon as possible," she said with urgency.

As a therapist, she wanted the best for him. Even if he was the man who'd hurt her sister. Even if her heart rate still kicked up from just looking at him.

"You're not authorized to treat him and if you're caught we'll both be fired." Troy closed the door behind him, his handsome face creased with worry.

"I'll take full responsibility," Rory retorted. "It's his *arm*, Troy. The arm he needs to slap those pucks into the net at ninety miles an hour."

"Mac usually reaches speeds of a hundred plus miles an hour," Troy, the sports fanatic, corrected her, as she'd counted on him doing.

"Exactly and the mat will start helping immediately," Rory retorted.

"Jobs, fired, on the streets," Troy muttered. Yet he didn't protest when she pulled a mat from her bag and placed the control box it was connected to on Mac's bedside table. When the lights brightened, she very gently wrapped the mat around Mac's injured arm. He didn't stir and Rory relaxed; he was solidly asleep and would be for a while.

Troy was right to worry. Earlier, she'd hesitated and had stood outside of his room, debating whether to go in. Partly because of that almost-kiss years ago, partly because she knew she shouldn't be there, despite Kade's request.

The bottom line was that Mac was a sportsman who needed her expertise and her mat. It was crucial to get his blood flowing through the damaged capillaries to start the healing process. The longer she delayed, the longer he would take to recover. Healing, helping, was what she did, who she was, and she'd fight the devil himself to give a patient what he needed, when he needed it.

Besides, there was little chance of her being discovered in Mac's room. The Annex Clinic was an expensive, private ward attached to St. Catherine's, the hospital situated in the exclusive Vancouver suburb of West Point Gray. Every patient admitted into The Annex had two things in common: they were ridiculously wealthy and they wanted total privacy. Each patient had their own private nurse, and Rory had lucked out because Troy was assigned to room 22.

Not only would he keep her interference a secret, but because he was in the room with her, Rory resisted the urge to run her hand through Mac's thick hair, over his strong jaw shaded with stubble.

He looked as good as he had years ago. Maybe better.

His beard was dark but when he grew it out, it glinted red in the sun. As did his dark brown hair. The corners of his eyes had creases that weren't there a decade ago. He looked, if she ignored his bandaged arm, stronger, fitter and more ripped than he had at twenty-four.

She was a professional, she reminded herself, and she shouldn't be mentally drooling over the man.

"How did you even know he was admitted?" Troy demanded.

"Are you sure he's asleep?" she asked Troy, ignoring his question.

"Morphine. He was in severe pain and it was prescribed." Troy looked at his watch. "Getting back to my point, he only came out of surgery two hours ago and was injured no more than six hours ago. How did you know he was here?"

Rory stood back from the bed and pushed her hands into her lower back as she stretched and explained that Kade, who'd taken on the CEO responsibilities and duties when the owner/manager of the Vancouver Mavericks died, had called and asked her to check on Mac and give her professional opinion.

Troy frowned, worried. "Which is?"

"It's bad, Troy."

Troy swore and Rory knew his disappointment and concern would be shared by most of the residents of Vancouver, Mavericks and Canucks fans alike. Mac was a hell of a player and respected for his leadership and skill. Maverick fans would be devastated to lose their captain for a couple of matches. To lose him for the season would be a disaster. Losing him forever would be a tragedy. But she'd treated enough sport stars to know the impact of his injury, both physical and emotional, would be tremendous.

"How did the surgery go?" Rory asked Troy.

"Good." Troy cleared his throat. "We really could get

fired, Rorks. Even though I know the voodoo blanket helps, it's still a form of treatment and you're not authorized. I like my job."

Rory knew he was right, but she still rolled her eyes at her best friend. "As I've explained to you a million times before, the blanket is not voodoo! It sends electromagnetic signals that stimulate the pumping of the smallest blood vessels. It will help normalize the circulation in this injured area. Kade asked me to be here. He'll work it out. It'll be okay, Troy."

When Troy narrowed his bright green eyes, Rory looked away. "This will run for the next thirty minutes," she said. "Why don't you go get some coffee?"

She needed to be alone with Mac, to get her thoughts—and her reaction to him—under control.

"Ok, I'll be back in thirty."

Troy sent her a worried smile and left the room. When the door closed behind him, she turned back to Mac and couldn't resist the impulse to place her hand on his chest, directly over his heart. Under the thin cotton of the hospital gown she felt the warmth of his skin.

She kept her hand there, trying not to wish she could run it over his hard stomach, down the thick biceps of his uninjured arm. He was so big, his body a testament to a lifetime dedicated to professional sports, to being the hardest, toughest, fastest player on the ice.

She glanced toward the end of the bed at his chart. Reading the chicken scrawl again wouldn't change a damn thing. Essentially, Mac had pulled a tendon partly off the bone and injured a ligament. The surgeons doubted he'd regain his former strength anytime soon, if ever.

That would kill him. Even in the short time they'd known each other, she'd understood that hockey was what

Mac did, who he was. He'd dedicated the last fourteen years to the Mavericks. He was their star player, their leader, the reason fans filled the arena week after week. He was their hope, their idol, the public face of the well-oiled machine Kade managed.

With his crooked smile, his aloof but charming manner and incredible prowess on the ice, he was the city's favorite, regularly appearing in the press, usually with a leggy blonde on his arm. Speculating about when one of the Mavericks Triumvirate—Mac, their captain, Kade as CEO and Quinn as Acting Coach (the youngest in the NHL but widely respected) were all hot and single—would fall in love and settle down was a citywide pastime.

A part of him belonged to the city but Rory doubted that anyone, besides his best friends, knew him. From that time so long ago she knew that Mac, for all his charm, was a closed book. Very little was known about his life before he was recruited to play for the Mavericks. Even Shay hadn't known more than what was public knowledge: he was raised by a single mother who died when he was nineteen, he was a scholarship kid and he didn't talk about his past.

They had that in common. Rory didn't talk about her past either.

Rory adjusted the settings on the control box and Mac shifted in his sleep, releasing a small pain-filled moan. He would hate to know that she'd heard him, she thought. Mac, she remembered, had loathed being sick. He'd played with a broken finger, flu, a sprained ankle, a hurt knee. He'd play through plagues of locusts and an asteroid strike.

Rory looked at his injured arm and sighed. He wouldn't

be able to play through this. How was she supposed to tell Kade that?

A big, hot hand touched her throat and a thumb stroked her jaw. Her brain shut down when he touched her and, just like she had in Shay's kitchen, she couldn't help responding. She allowed her head to snuggle into his hand as he slowly opened his eyes and focused on her face. His fabulous eyes, the deep, dark blue of old-fashioned bottled ink, met hers.

"Hey," he croaked.

"Hey back," Rory whispered, her fingers digging into the skin on his chest. She should remove herself but, once again, she stayed exactly where she was.

So nothing much had changed then. She hadn't grown up at all.

"They must have given me some powerful drugs because you seem so damn real."

Rory shuddered as his thumb brushed over her bottom lip. He thought he was imagining her, she realized.

"Helluva dream… God, you're so beautiful." Mac's hand drifted down her throat over her collarbone. His fingers trailed above the cotton of her tunic to rest on the slight swell of her breast. His eyes, confused and pain-filled, stayed on her face, tracing her features and drinking her in.

Then he heaved in a sigh and the blue deepened to midnight. "My arm is on fire."

"I know, Mac." Rory touched his hair, then his cheek, and her heart double-tapped when he turned his face into her palm, as if seeking comfort. She tried to pull her hand away but Mac slapped his hand on hers to keep her palm against his cheek. Everyone, even the big, bold

Mac, needed support, a human connection. At the moment she was his.

"It's bad, isn't it?"

What should she say? She didn't want to lie to him, but she had no right to talk to him about his injuries. She shouldn't even be here. "You'll be okay, Mac. No matter what, you'll be okay."

Pain—the deep, dark, emotional kind—jumped into his eyes. His hand moved to her wrist and he pulled her down until her chest rested on his. Her mouth was a quarter inch from his. God, this was so wrong. She shouldn't be doing this. Despite those thoughts ricocheting through her head she couldn't help the impulse to feel those lips under hers, to taste him.

Just once to see if the reality measured up to her imagination.

This would be the perfect time, *the only time*, to find out. She could stop wondering and move the hell past him, past the kiss they'd never shared.

There was no one in the room with them. Nobody would ever know.

His injured state hadn't affected his skills, Rory thought as he took control of the kiss, tipping her head to achieve the precise angle he wanted. His tongue licked its way into her mouth, nipping here, sliding there. Then their tongues met and electricity rocketed through her as she sank into him.

It was all she'd dreamed about. And a lot more.

Rory had no idea how long the kiss lasted. She was yanked back to the present when Mac hissed in pain. Stupid girl! He'd had surgery only hours before! He was in a world of hurt. Mac, she noticed, just lay there, his hand on her thigh and his eyes closed. He was so still. Had he fallen back to sleep? Rory looked down at his big tanned hand and licked her top lip, tasting him there.

It had been just two mouths meeting, tongues dancing, but his kisses could move mountains, part seas, redesign constellations. It had been that powerful. Kissing Mac was an out-of-body experience.

The universe knew what it was doing by keeping them apart. She wasn't looking for a man and she certainly wasn't looking for a man like Mac. Too big, too bold, too confident. A celebrity who had never heard of the word *monogamy*.

He was exactly what she didn't need. Unfaithful. She was perfectly content to fly solo, she reminded herself.

The machine beeped to tell her the program had ended, and Rory started to stand up. The hand squeezing her thigh kept her in place. When she looked at Mac, his eyes were still closed but the corners of his mouth kicked up into a cocky smile.

"Best dream ever," he said before slipping back into sleep.

Two

He'd been dreaming of Rory, something he hadn't done in years, Mac realized as he surfaced out of a pain-saturated sleep. She'd been sitting cross-legged on his bed, her silver-gray eyes dancing. Wide smile, firm breasts, golden-brown hair that was so long, he remembered, that it flirted with her butt…five foot three of petite perfection.

In his dream he'd been French-kissing her and it had felt…man…amazing! Slow, hot, sexy—what a kiss should really be. Okay, he'd had far too many drugs if he was obsessing about a girl he'd wanted to kiss a lifetime ago. Mac shoved his left hand through his hair before pushing himself up using the same hand, trying but failing to ignore the slamming pain in his other arm as he moved.

This was bad. This was very, very bad.

Half lying, half sitting, he closed his eyes and fought the nausea gathering in his throat. Dimly aware of people entering his private hospital room, he fought the pain, pushed down the nausea and concentrated on those silver eyes he'd seen in his dream. The way her soft lips felt under his…

He had been dreaming, right?

"Do you need something for the pain, Mr. McCaskill?"

Mac jerked fully awake and looked into the concerned face of a guy a few years younger than him.

"I'm Troy Hunter, your nurse," he said. "So, some meds? You're due."

"Hell yes," Mac muttered. He usually hated drugs but he slowly rolled onto his good side, presenting his butt to be jabbed as Kade and Quinn walked into the room. "Hey, guys."

Troy glanced at Mac's visitors with his mouth dropped open, looking like any other fan did when the three of them were together…awestruck.

Tall and rock solid, in both stature and personality, Mac wasn't surprised to see Kade and Quinn and so soon after his surgery. They were his friends, his one-time roommates, his colleagues…his family. They were, in every way that counted, his brothers.

After giving him the injection, Troy pulled up Mac's shorts and stood back to look at him, his face and tone utterly professional. "Let's get you sorted out. I need to do my boring nurse stuff and then I'll leave you to talk." He looked more closely at Mac. "You look uncomfortable."

Mac nodded. He was half lying and half sitting but the thought of moving made him break out in a cold sweat. "Yeah, I am."

"I can remedy that." Troy, with surprising ease and

gentleness for a man who was six-three and solid, maneuvered Mac into a position he could live with. While Troy wound a blood pressure cuff around Mac's arm, Kade sat down in the chair on the opposite side of the bed, his expression serious.

"We would appreciate your discretion as to Mac's condition," he told Troy. That voice, not often employed, usually had sponsors, players and random citizens scattering.

Troy, to his credit, didn't look intimidated. "I don't talk about my patients. Ever."

Kade stared at Troy for a long time before nodding once. "Thank you."

They waited in silence until Troy left the room and then Kade turned to him and let out a stream of profanity.

Here it comes, Mac thought, resigned.

"What were you thinking, trying to move that fridge yourself? One call and one of us would've been there to help you!"

Mac shrugged. "It wasn't that heavy. It started to fall and I tried to catch it."

"Why the hell can't you just ask for help?" Quinn demanded. "It's serious, Mac, career-ending serious."

Mac felt the blood in his face drain away. When he could speak, he pushed the words out between dry lips. "That bad, huh?"

Kade looked as white as Mac imagined himself to be. "That bad."

"Physiotherapy?" Mac demanded.

"An outside chance at best," Quinn answered him. He didn't sugarcoat his words, and Mac appreciated it. He needed the truth.

Kade spoke again. "We've found someone to work

with you. She's reputed to be the best at sports rehabilitation injuries."

Neither of his friends met his eyes, and his heart sank to his toes. He knew that look, knew that he wouldn't like what was coming next.

"Who? Nurse Ratched?" he joked.

"Rory Kydd," Kade told him, his face impassive.

"Rory? *What?*" he croaked, not liking the frantic note in his voice. It was bad enough seeing Rory in his dreams but being her patient would mean hitting the seventh level of hell.

There was a reason why he never thought of her, why he'd obliterated that day from his memory. He'd publicly humiliated himself and the world had seen him at his worst. Rory'd had a front-row seat to the behind-the-scenes action.

Saying what he had on that open mic had been bad enough but almost kissing his about-to-be ex's sister was unforgiveable. At the time he'd been thinking of Rory a lot, had been, strangely, attracted to Shay's petite but feisty younger sister. But he should never have caged her in, tempting them both. He knew better than to act on those kinds of feelings, even if his relationship with Shay had been sliding downhill.

His mother's many messy affairs had taught him to keep his own liaisons clean, to remove himself from one situation before jumping into another. He'd forgotten those lessons the moment Rory looked at him with her wide, lust-filled eyes. His big brain shut down as his little brain perked up...

In the months afterward he hadn't missed Shay—too needy, too insecure—but he had missed talking to, teasing, laughing with Rory. She'd been, before he mucked it up, his first real female friend.

That day he'd also unwittingly created a media superstorm and a public persona for himself. He'd been branded a player, a party-hard, commitment-phobic prick whose two objectives in life were to play with a puck and to chase skirts.

They had it half right…

Yes, he liked the occasional party and was commitment-phobic. Yes, he loved to play with a puck and yeah, he had sex, but not as much or with as many woman as was suggested in the tabloids. These days he was a great deal more discriminating about who he took into his bed, and it had been a couple of months since he'd been laid.

He looked down at his arm and scowled. It seemed like it would be a few more.

Quinn gripped the railing at the end of the bed with his massive hands. "Rory is the best and God knows you need the best. We need her because everything we've worked toward for the past five years is about to slip from our fingers because you were too pigheaded to ask for help!"

Kade frowned at their hotheaded friend. "Take it easy, Quinn. It wasn't like he did it on purpose."

No, but it was his fault. Mac tipped his head up to look at the ceiling. He'd failed again today, failed his team, his friends, his future.

And it looked like, once again, Rory would be there to witness it.

There had to be another option. "Find someone else! Anyone else!"

"Don't be a moron!" Quinn told him.

Kade, always the voice of reason, stepped between them before they started to yell. "You'll work with her while we do damage control on our end."

Mac rested his head on his pillow, feeling the sedative effects of whatever the nurse had stuck in him. Ignoring the approaching grogginess, he sucked in some deep breaths and forced his brain to work.

Dammit, why did Vernon Hasselback have to die before they'd concluded the deal they'd all been discussing for the past decade? It was a simple plan: when the time was right he and Kade and Quinn would buy the franchise from Vernon. They'd been working toward this since they were all rookie players and they'd hammered out a detailed plan to raise the cash, which included using their player fees and endorsement money to invest in business opportunities to fund their future purchase of the franchise. The strategy had worked well. Within a decade they had a rock-solid asset base and were, by anyone's standards, ridiculously wealthy. Money wasn't an issue. They could buy the franchise without breaking much of a sweat. But to take the team and its brand to the next level they needed a partner who brought certain skills to the table. Someone who had bigger and better connections in all facets of the media, who could open the doors to mega-sponsorship deals, who had merchandising experience.

Unfortunately, because Vernon died in the bed of his latest mistress, his widow and the beneficiary of his entire estate wasn't inclined to honor his wishes about passing the mantle on to the three of them. Myra wanted to sell the franchise to a Russian billionaire who'd acquired six sports teams in the past two years and was rebranding them to be generic, cardboard cutouts of the teams they once were and mouthpieces for his bland corporation. Kade had convinced Myra to give them some time but they knew she was impulsive and impatient. She would use any setback as an excuse to sell the franchise out from under them, and Mac's injury was a very big setback.

"No one can know how badly I'm injured."

Kade and Quinn nodded. "I'm very aware of that," Kade said. "I also have a potential investor on the hook. He's a loaded Mavericks fan, meets all our requirements and runs a massive media empire so nothing can jeopardize our negotiations. You are one of the reasons he wants to buy the team. He knows you only have a few more years left at this level and he wants you to spend that time mentoring the rookie talent."

So, no additional pressure then. Mac pushed the drowsiness away. "So I have to start playing with his team when the season opens."

"Essentially," Quinn replied, blowing air into his cheeks. "If not sooner."

Mac clenched his jaw in determination. It was the same attitude that had won the team the Stanley Cup two years ago, that had taken him from being just another rookie to one of the most exciting players of his generation. When he decided he was going to do something, achieve something, win something, nothing and nobody got in his way.

"Then I will be on the ice when the season opens."

If that meant working with Rory, so be it. Yes, he'd embarrassed himself a very long time ago. It happened and it was time to move the hell on. He refused to give in or give up—not while there was a chance of getting what he wanted.

"Set up the physio and let's get this party started."

Kade smiled. "You had surgery earlier today. How about getting some sleep first?"

"Are you convinced Rory is the best?" he asked with slightly slurred words.

Kade nodded. "Yeah, she is."

"Get her. Offer her what she needs so she can concentrate on me…" Stupid drugs, Mac thought, making him say the wrong thing. "On my arm. Not me."

Quinn placed a hand on Mac's good shoulder and squeezed. "Go to sleep, bud."

Mac managed a couple more words before slipping off into sleep. "Offer her whatever it takes…"

Rory paused outside the door to Mac's room the next day and hoisted her bag over her shoulder. She pushed her hand through her layered, choppy bob before smoothing out a crease that had appeared in her white and navy tunic, thinking that it had already been a weird day and it wasn't even mid-morning yet. Her day had started with Kade contacting her at the crack of dawn, demanding a meeting to discuss Mac and his injury. She'd told him she could only give Mac her assessment of his injuries and if Mac wanted Kade there, then that was his prerogative. Kade had seemed more amused than annoyed by her crisp tone and had followed up his demands by telling her he had a proposition for her…one that she'd want to hear.

That was intriguing enough to get her to meet with them during her morning break.

Just knock on the door and get this meeting over with, Rory told herself. *You are not nineteen anymore and desperately infatuated with your sister's boyfriend. You're a highly qualified professional who is in high demand. He's a patient like any other.*

Except none of her patients kissed her like he did, or flooded her system with take-me-quick hormones with one look from his navy eyes.

God, you are ridiculous, Rory thought, not amused.

Not allowing herself another minute to hesitate, she briskly knocked on the door, and when she heard his command to enter, she stepped inside. She ignored Mac's two friends standing on either side of his bed and her gaze immediately landed on his face. She told her libido to calm down and gave Mac a *professional* once-over. He was wearing a V-neck T-shirt and someone, probably Troy, had removed the right sleeve. His injured arm was bandaged from wrist to shoulder and was supported by a sling. Clear, annoyed and very wary eyes met hers.

Mac, she also noticed, was in pain but he was fighting his way through it.

Rory looked at his friends, good-looking guys, and smiled. "Hello, Kade. Quinn." Rory stepped toward the bed. "Mac. It's been a while."

Rory held her breath, waiting to see if he remembered the kiss they'd shared, whether he'd say anything about her being in his room the night before. His face remained inscrutable and the look in his eyes didn't change. Thank God, he didn't remember. That would make her life, and this experience, easier.

Or as easy as it could possibly be.

"Rory."

Her name on his lips, she'd never thought she'd hear it again. She desperately wished it wasn't under such circumstances. Rory gathered her wits and asked Quinn to move out of her way. When he did, she stepped up to the bed and pulled the smaller of the two blankets from her bag and placed the control box on the bedside table.

"What are you doing?" Mac demanded. "You're here to talk, not to fuss."

Rory looked him in the eye and didn't react to his growl. "And we will talk, after I set this up."

"What is it?" Kade demanded from his spot on the other side of the bed.

Rory explained how the blanket worked and gently tucked the mat around Mac's injured arm. She started the program, stepped back and folded her arms. "You need some pain meds," she told Mac.

"I'm fine," Mac muttered, his tone suggesting she back off. That wasn't going to happen. The sooner Mac learned that she wasn't easily intimidated, the better. The trick with difficult patients, and obstinate men, was to show no fear.

"You either take some meds or I walk out this door," Rory told him, her voice even. Her words left no doubt that she wasn't bluffing. She picked up the two pills that sat next to a glass of water and waited until Mac opened his hand to receive them. He sent her a dirty look, dry swallowed them and reluctantly chased them down with water from the glass she handed to him.

"You're not a martyr, nor a superhero, so take the meds on schedule," she told him in her best no-nonsense voice. Rory held his hot look and in his eyes she saw frustration morph into something deeper, darker, sexier.

Whoo boy! Internal temperature rising...

"You cut your hair," Mac said, tipping his head to the side.

"Quite a few times in the past decade," Rory replied, her voice tart. One of them had to get this conversation back on track and it looked like she'd been elected.

Fantastic kiss aside, Mac was a potential patient, nothing more, nothing less. She'd be professional if it killed her. She deliberately glanced at her watch and lifted her arched eyebrows. "I have another patient in thirty minutes…so let's skip the small talk and you can tell me why I'm really here."

"I need a physiotherapist."

"Obviously." Rory shrugged. "You're going to need a lot of therapy to get your arm working properly."

"I don't want it to work properly. I want it to be as good as new," Mac stated. "In two months' time."

"In your dreams." Okay, everyone knew Mac was determined but he wasn't stupid. "That's not going to happen. You know that's not possible."

Mac pulled on his stubborn expression. "It *is* going to happen and I'll be back on the ice with or without your help."

Rory sent Kade and Quinn a "help me" look but they just stood there. She was on her own, it seemed. "McCaskill, listen to me. You half ripped a tendon off the bone. It was surgically reattached. We don't know how much damage you've done to the nerves. This injury needs time to heal—"

"I don't have time," Mac told her. "I've got a couple of months and that's it."

Rory shoved her hands into her hair in sheer frustration. "You can sit out another couple of months—you are not indispensable!"

Dammit, her voice was rising. Not good. Do not let him rattle you!

"Two months and I need to be playing. That's it, Rory, that's all the time I've got," Mac insisted. "Now, either I get you to help me do that or I take my chances on someone else."

"Someone you will railroad into allowing you to do what you want, when you want, probably resulting in permanent damage." This was how he'd be in a relationship, she thought. All bossy and stubborn and determined to have his way.

After a lifetime of watching her father steamroll their mother, those weren't characteristics she'd ever tolerate.

"Maybe," was all Mac said.

Rory placed her hands on the bed and leaned forward, brows snapping together. "Why are you doing this, Mac? You have enough money, enough accolades to allow you to sit out a couple of months, a couple of seasons. This is not only unnecessary, it's downright idiotic!"

Mac pulled in a deep breath. For a split second she thought that he might explain, that he'd give her a genuine, responsible reason for his stance. Then his eyes turned inscrutable and she knew it wouldn't happen. "I play. That's what I do."

Rory shook her head, disappointed. He was still the same attention-seeking, hot-dogging, arrogant moron he'd been in his twenties. Did he really believe the hype that he was indispensable and indestructible?

"You're ridiculous, that's what you are," Rory said as she straightened. She sent his friends a blistering look. "You're supporting him in this?"

Kade and Quinn nodded, reluctantly, but they still nodded. Right, so it seemed like she was the only clear thinker in the room. She had to try one more time. "It's one season! You'd probably not even miss the entire season…"

Mac looked resolute. "I have to be there, Rory."

Mac had a will of iron. He was going to play, come hell or high water. She wouldn't be able to change his mind.

"It's my choice and I'll live with the consequences," Mac told her. "I'm not the type to create a storm and then bitch when it rains."

There was no doubting the sincerity in his words. Now, responsibility was something her father had never grasped, she thought. He'd been a serial adulterer and when he got caught—and he *always* got caught—there were a million reasons why it wasn't his fault. And, really, why was she thinking about her father? *Honestly, woman, concentrate!*

She might not agree with what Mac wanted to do, it was a colossal mistake in her professional opinion, but it seemed he was prepared to accept the consequences of his decisions. She had to respect that. But didn't have to be party to his madness.

She dropped her eyes from his face to look at the control box. "There's still twenty minutes to go. I'll ask Troy to disconnect the mat and pack it away. Have a nice life."

Rory turned around and walked toward the door, thinking that her bosses at Craydon's Physiotherapy would throw a hissy fit if they found out she'd turned down the opportunity to treat the great Mac McCaskill.

A part of her wanted to stay, to carry on trying to convince him—them—why this was the stupidest plan in history. *But you're not the jackass whisperer*, her brain informed her.

She had her hand on the door when Mac spoke again. "Rory, dammit…wait!"

Rory turned and saw the silent conversation taking place between the three friends. Kade nodded, Quinn looked frustrated but resigned and Mac looked annoyed.

Well, tough.

"Why can't anything ever be easy with you?" he muttered, and Rory lifted an eyebrow. This from the man who'd dissed Shay on national television and created a public scandal with her sister at the center? Who'd—sort of—made a move on Rory, thereby causing a riff between her and Shay that took many months to heal? Seriously?

"It isn't my job to make things easy for you," Rory retorted. "If there's nothing else…?"

"Hell yes, there's a big something else!" Mac snapped. "And if you repeat it I'll blow a gasket."

Rory just stared at him. The Kydd girls didn't blab. If they did they could've made themselves a nice chunk of change selling their Mac stories to the tabloids.

Mac rubbed the back of his neck with his good hand and proceeded to explain how his being hurt could materially affect the Mavericks. Rory listened, shocked, as Mac dissected the implications of his injury. "If Chenko buys the team, Kade will be replaced as CEO, Quinn's coaching contract won't be renewed and if I'm injured, I'm too old for them to give me another chance. The Mavericks will be turned into another corporate team—and I will *not* let that happen."

Rory took a moment to allow his words to make sense. When they did, her jaw tightened. The Mavericks were a Vancouver institution that had been owned by the Hasselbacks for generations and she knew—thanks to listening to Troy's rants on the subject over the years—that when corporate businesses took over sports teams, the magic dissipated. Traditions were lost; fans were disappointed; the players lost their individuality. It became soulless and clinical. She kept her eyes on Mac, pale-faced and stressed. "And if you do play?"

"Then we have a chance of saving the team."

"How?" Rory demanded.

"It's complicated, and confidential, but we need a particular type of partner, one who has the connections and skills in PR, merchandising, sponsorships. Even though we are retaining control, we are asking for a lot of money for a minor share and we have to accept that I am the face of the team and an essential part of the deal. I have to play." Mac rubbed his forehead with the tips of his fingers, his gesture indicating pain or frustration or exhaustion. Probably all three. "This isn't about me, not this time. Or, at least, it isn't all about me. If I could take the time off I would, I'm not that arrogant. But I need to get back on the ice and, apparently, you're my best bet."

Rory bit her bottom lip, knowing what he was asking was practically impossible. "The chance of you being able to play in two months' time is less than ten percent, Mac. Practically nonexistent."

"I can do it, Rory. You just need to show me how."

She nearly believed him. If anybody could do it then it would be him.

"Mac, you could do yourself some permanent damage."

Mac pressed his lips together. "Again, my choice, my consequences."

God, why did that have to resonate so deeply with her? Okay, so this wasn't *all* about him and his career. A part of it was, of course it was, but she knew how much the Mavericks meant to him. There had been many reports about the bond he shared with his mentor, the now dead owner of the team. The *cheating* dead owner of the Mavericks—dying in his mistress's bed.

Don't think about that, she told herself. With her history of a having a serial cheater for a father, it was a sure way to get her blood pressure spiking.

She had to disregard the emotion around this decision, try to forget he was attempting to save his team, his friends' jobs and the traditions of the Mavericks, which were an essential part of the city's identity. She had to look at his injury, his need and his right to treatment. If this were any other sportsman and not Mac, would she be trying to help him? Yeah, she would.

And really, if she didn't help Mac, Troy might never speak to her again.

She nodded reluctantly. "Okay. I'll help you, as much as I can."

Mac, to her surprise, didn't look jubilant or excited. He just looked relieved and wiped out. "Thank you," he quietly said.

Rory turned to Kade. "You need to contact my office, sign a formal contract with my employers."

Kade grimaced. "Yeah, that's the other thing…we'd like to cut out the middleman."

Rory lifted up her hands in frustration. Was nothing going to be simple today? "What does that mean?"

Kade jerked his head in Mac's direction and Rory saw that his head was back against his pillow and his eyes were closed. "Let's carry on this discussion outside and I'll fill you in."

"Why do I know that you're about to complicate my life even further?" Rory demanded when they were standing in the passage outside Mac's room.

"Because you are, obviously, a very smart woman," Kade said, placing a large hand on her shoulder. "Let's go get some coffee and we'll sort this mess out."

That sounded like an excellent idea since she desperately needed a cup of liquid sanity.

Three

Rory walked into the diner situated around the corner from St. Catherine's Hospital and scanned the tables, looking for her best friend. It had only been an hour since Kade had laid out his terms, and she needed Troy to talk her off the ledge…

Dressed in skinny jeans and a strappy white crop top, she ignored the compliments coming from a table of construction workers on her left. She waved at Troy and smiled at grumbles behind her when they saw her breakfast companion—huge, sexy and, not that they'd ever realize it, gay. With his blond hair, chiseled jaw and hot bod, he had guys—and girls—falling over him and had the social life of a boy band member.

Unlike her who, according to Mr. Popular, partied like a nun.

Troy stood up as she approached and she reached up

to place a kiss on his cheek. He'd changed out of his uniform into jeans and a T-shirt but he still looked stressed.

"Rough night? Is Mac being a pain in your backside?" she asked him.

"He's not a problem at all. I was at the home until late. My mom had a bad episode."

Rory sent him a sympathetic look. Troy's mom suffered from dementia and most of his cash went to funding the nursing home he'd put her into. Unfortunately the home wasn't great, but it was the best he could afford.

Rory had decided a long time ago that when she opened her clinic Troy would be her first hire, at a salary that would enable him to move his mom out of that place into a nicer home. Hopefully, if they did well, he could also move out of his horrible apartment and buy a decent car. "Sorry, honey."

Troy shrugged as they sat down on opposite sides of the table. "You look as frazzled as I do. What's up?"

"So much," Rory replied. "Let's order and I'll tell you a story." She pushed the folder she'd been carrying toward Troy. "Look at this."

After they ordered, Rory tapped the file with her index finger. "Read."

"Mark McCaskill?" Troy looked at the label. "Why do you have Open Mac's file?"

Rory pulled a face as the waitress poured them coffee. She'd always loathed that nickname since it was a play on the microphone incident from so long ago, something she didn't need to be constantly reminded of. Then again, his other nickname, PD—short for Panty Dropper—was even worse. "If you're not going to read it then fill me in on all the gossip about him."

Troy frowned. "Why?"

"I'll explain." She waved her hand. "Go. Center and captain of the Vancouver Mavericks hockey team. Incredible player, one of the very best. Dates a variety of women. What else?"

Troy rested his forearms on the table, his face pensive. "Well, he's spokesperson for various campaigns, epilepsy being one of them. He sits on the boards of a few charities, mostly relating to children. He's also, thanks to investing in bars, restaurants and food trucks, one of the wealthiest bachelors in town. He's also supremely *haawwwt*," Troy added. "And surprisingly nice, even though I know how stressed he must be wondering if this injury will keep him out for the season."

Mac—nice? Yeah, sure.

Troy flicked the file open and flipped through the pile of papers. "You're treating him?"

Rory nodded and Troy looked confused. "But this isn't a Craydon file," he added, referring to the distinctive yellow-and-blue patient files used at the physiotherapy practice she worked for. "What gives, Rorks?"

Rory folded her arms across her chest and tapped her foot, her big, silver-gray eyes tight with worry. How much to tell him? As much as she could, she decided, he was her best friend. She trusted him implicitly and valued his judgment. Still, sharing didn't come easily to her so she took a moment to work out what to say. "Mac and I have a...history."

Troy's snort was disbelieving. "Honey, you're not his type. He dates tall, stacked, exotic gazelles."

Rory scowled. She knew what type of woman Mac dated. She saw them every time she opened a newspaper or magazine. "I know that I am short, and flat-chested," Rory snapped. "You don't need to rub it in."

"I didn't mean it like that," Troy quietly stated. "Yeah, you're short but you have a great figure, you know that you do. And there's nothing wrong with your chest."

"Like you'd know," Rory muttered.

"I know that you desperately need some masculine hands on your boobs and on other more exciting parts of your body. It's been a year, eighteen months, since you've had some action?"

Actually it was closer to two years, but she'd rather die than admit that to Mr. Cool. "Can we concentrate on my McCaskill problem please?"

"He's a problem?"

"You've forgotten that Shay was dating him during the open-mic disaster."

Troy's mouth dropped open. "I *did* forget that. He said he was bored with her, that monogamy was for the birds."

"Yep. Obviously that's a position he still holds."

Troy leaned back so the waitress could put their food down. He frowned at Rory's sarcastic comment. "Honey, that was a long time ago and he was young. Shay's moved on...what's the problem?"

"He's a man-slut. It annoys me."

"It shouldn't. He didn't cheat on *you*," Troy pointed out, and Rory stared down at her plate.

No, he'd almost cheated on her sister with her. The intention had been there. He would've cheated if Rory hadn't stopped him. He was just like her father and exactly the last person in the world she should be attracted to.

It made absolutely no sense at all.

She'd never told Troy—or anyone—what had happened between her and Mac and she still couldn't. Hurting her sister hadn't been her finest moment.

"Okay, admittedly, Mac is not the poster boy for love and commitment so I kind of get your antipathy to him since you have such a huge issue with infidelity," Troy said after taking a sip of his coffee.

"Doesn't everyone?" Rory demanded. "Have issues with it?"

"No. And if they do, they don't take it to the nth degree like you do. Hell, Rorks, I recall you not accepting a date from a perfectly nice guy because you said he had a 'cheating face.'"

Rory ignored his air quotes and lifted her nose in the air. "Okay, maybe that was wrong of me."

"Wrong of you? It was properly ridiculous."

Troy tapped the folder before he attacked his eggs. "Tell me how this came about."

Rory filled him in and Troy listened, fascinated.

"So, they want you, widely regarded as the best sports rehab physio in the area, to work on Mac. Why didn't they just approach the clinic directly and hire you that way?"

She'd asked Kade the same question. "They are going to keep the extent of Mac's injury a secret from the public and the fans. They'll admit that he's pulled a muscle or something minor but they don't want it getting out that his injury is as bad as it is."

"Why the secrecy?"

"Sorry, I can't tell you that." Troy, to his credit, didn't push. "Kade asked me to take a leave of absence from the clinic to treat Mac."

Troy's eyebrows lifted. "Seriously?"

"Yeah."

"And you said yes, no, hell, no?"

"Thanks to the fact that I am a workaholic, I have

nearly two and a half months of vacation due to me that I have to either use or lose."

Troy just looked at her, waiting for her to continue.

"Kade offered me twenty grand for six weeks and another thirty if I get Mac back into condition by the time the season starts in two months."

"Fifty K?" Troy's mouth fell open. After a moment of amazed silence he spoke again. "With that sort of money you could open your own practice like you've been dreaming of doing."

And, more important, she could employ him. Rory nodded. "Yeah. I want to set up a clinic that isn't a conveyor belt of only treating the patient's pain—"

"No need to go on, I've been listening to you ramble on about your clinic for years." Troy's smile was full of love. "And Kade's offer will allow you to establish this clinic without having to take a loan or use the money you were saving for a house."

"Essentially."

"It sounds like a no-brainer, Rorks," Troy said quietly.

Rory sucked her bottom lip between her teeth. It did, didn't it? "Except for two rather major points."

"Which are?"

"First, I am stupidly, crazily attracted to Mac. Nobody makes my blood move like he does." She glared at Troy. "Don't you dare laugh! How am I supposed to treat him when all I want to do is crawl all over him?"

Troy hooted, vastly amused.

"Second, and more important, I don't think I can fix him, Troy, and especially not in two months." Troy stopped laughing and stared at her.

"I don't think he's got a hope in hell."

"Except that you are forgetting one thing…" Troy

cocked his head at her and slowly smiled. "When Mac McCaskill decides he wants something, he'll move hell and high water to get it. Everyone knows that if Mac says he is going to do something, he'll get it done. He doesn't know what *failure* means."

Yet he'd failed Shay and, in a roundabout way, failed her. He wasn't anywhere as perfect as Troy thought him to be.

The next morning Rory knocked on Mac's door and stuck her head inside after he told her to come in.

"I'm in the bathroom, I'll be with you in a sec," Mac called, so Rory sat down in the visitors' chair, her bag at her feet. Inside the folder that she placed on her knees was a signed contract to be Mac's physiotherapist for the next two months.

A little over two months...nine or so weeks. Rory felt panic bubble in her throat and she rubbed her hands over her face. She wasn't sure if she was scared, excited or horrified. A clinic, the last piece of a down payment for a house, a job for Troy, she reminded herself.

If she continued to save as she'd been doing, it would take another two years to gather what they were prepared to pay her in two months. This was a once-in-a-lifetime deal and she would be a moron to turn to it down. As she'd explained to Troy, there was just one little problem—she had to work with Mac, around Mac, *on* Mac. The chemistry between them hadn't changed. She was as attracted to him as she had been at nineteen, possibly even more. Young Mac had been charismatic and sexy and charming but Mac-ten-years-on was a potent mix of power, strength and determination that turned her to jelly. Kade might be the Mavericks' CEO, and Quinn was no pushover, but yesterday in this same room, Mac, despite his pain, was their undisputed leader. He had, thanks to his mental strength, pushed through pain and taken charge of the meeting.

Mac was determined and had a will to win that was second to none. He was also a rule breaker and a risk taker and utterly bullheaded.

Exactly the type of man she always avoided. They were fun and interesting and compelling, but they broke hearts left, right and center. Sometimes, as was the case with her father, they broke the same hearts over and over again.

She was too smart to let that happen to her.

Mac hated to take orders, but if she had any hope of fixing his arm, then he had to listen to her, do as she said when she said it. That would be a challenge. Mac, alpha male, was overly confident about his own abilities. She'd seen him in action; if he wanted to run a six-minute mile, he did it. If he wanted to improve the speed on his slap shot, he spent hours and hours on the ice until he was satisfied. If Mac wanted to fix his arm, he would work on it relentlessly. Except that muscles and injuries needed time to heal and, especially since his injury was so serious, he had to be careful. If he pushed the recovery process he could suffer irreversible damage and his career would be over. Permanently.

Yet if he wasn't healed in two months, the Mavericks, as Vancouver knew them, would be gone, and while she might have a brand-new shiny clinic, she might not have any clients if she couldn't fix the great Mac McCaskill.

Rock, meet hard place.

"Rory."

Rory snapped her head up to see Mac standing in the

doorway of the bathroom, wearing nothing more than a pair of designer denims and a deep scowl. His hair was wet and he'd wrapped a plastic bag around his arm to keep it dry. He hadn't managed the buttons on his jeans and through the open flaps she could see the white fabric of his, thank goodness, underwear. His chest was damp and a continent wide, lightly covered in brown hair in a perfect *T* that tapered into a fine trail of hair that crossed those fabulous washboard abs.

Sexy, almost-naked man in open blue jeans, Rory thought… *I could so jump you right now.*

Mac tried to button his jeans with one hand and swore creatively. Very creatively, Rory thought. She'd never before heard that combination of words strung together.

"Sorry," Mac muttered when he lifted aggravated eyes to meet hers. "But I am so damn frustrated I could punch something."

Rory placed the folder on the table next to her and slowly stood up. "Want some help?"

Mac looked at his watch and then scowled in the direction of the door. He looked as uncomfortable as she felt.

"Kade was supposed to come and help me get dressed and drive me home…"

"You've been discharged?"

"Yeah. The more time I spend here, the better the chances are of the press finding me." Mac lifted a muscled, tanned shoulder. "Besides, it's just my arm, the rest of me works just fine."

And looks pretty good too. Okay, get a grip, Kydd. You're a professional, remember? Try to act like one.

She rocked on her heels. "So, do you want some help?"

Mac looked at the door again and released a heavy sigh. "Yeah. Please."

Rory tried to keep her face blank as she reached for the flaps of his jeans. *Just get it done, fast*, she told herself, so she grabbed the first button and slotted it through its corresponding hole, brushing something that felt very masculine in the process, and not as soft as it should be. Keeping her head down, she moved on to button number two and repeated the action, very conscious of the growing bulge beneath her hands. She was flushed by the time she slotted in the last button, and she stepped back and pushed her hair out of her eyes.

She would not acknowledge his halfway-there erection. It was a conditioned response and something he couldn't help. Her hands were fiddling around his crotch; she could've been three hundred pounds with a mustache and he would've been turned on. It wasn't personal.

But damn, he was impressive… *Ignore, ignore, ignore.*

"Whoever packed for you was an idiot. Elasticized track pants or shorts would've been a better option," she stated, feeling hot from the inside out.

Mac ignored her comment and reached out to hold a strand of her hair. "I loved your long hair but this style works for you too."

"Uh…" Her brain needed oxygen. She couldn't think when he was so close, when she could smell the soap on his skin, could count every individual eyelash, see the different shades of dark blue in his eyes. What had he said? Something about her hair…

"Thanks."

Mac pushed her hair behind her ear and his fingers brushed her skin, and Rory couldn't help but shiver. This wasn't good, she thought, taking a huge step backward. He was dangerous, working with him was dangerous…

she shouldn't do this. It was a train wreck waiting to happen.

Clinic, house, practice, dream, her brain reminded her.

Shay, Mac cheating, men are inherently faithless, her soul argued. *Attraction leads to love and love leads to betrayal. Not happening.*

Rory jammed her hands into the back pockets of her jeans and nodded at Mac's bare feet. "Shoes?"

"Flip-flops," Mac replied, walking over to the bed and picking up a royal blue, V-necked T-shirt. He pulled the opening over his head and managed to slide his uninjured arm through the corresponding opening. Then he looked at his injured, immobile arm and cursed again.

"There's an art to dressing yourself when you're injured," she told him. Idiot that she was, she got up close and personal with him again, but this time she tried to avoid touching him as she pulled the shirt up and over his head. Shaking it out, she found the sleeve to his injured arm and gently slid the shirt up and over so that it bunched around his shoulder. He ducked his head through the opening, shoved his other arm through and the fabric fell down his chest.

It was wrong to hide such a work of art, Rory thought.

"Thanks."

Rory looked up at him, her head barely scraping his shoulder. God, he was big, six foot three of solid, sexy man. "Anything else?"

Mac shook his head. "No. I'm okay." He sat down on the edge of the bed and gestured to the chair she'd been sitting on earlier. "Take a seat, we need to talk."

Rory wasn't under any illusion that his quietly stated words were anything other than an order. Her spine straightened and her mouth tightened. Since there were, actually, a few things she had to say to him, she sat down and crossed her legs.

"You've had a little time to read over my chart, to assess the damage." Mac stretched out his long legs and sent her a hard look. "Thoughts?"

Rory pulled in a breath. "I presume you don't want me to sugarcoat it for you?"

"Hell, no."

Okay, then. "You ripped the lateral ulnar collateral ligament, luckily not completely from the bone, and it was surgically repaired. You also sprained the radial collateral ligament and the annular ligament."

"Which means?" Mac demanded, impatient.

"You're in a lot of pain and the injuries won't be easy to fix."

Mac's expression hardened. "Oh, they will be fixed. How much time does it normally take?"

She hated these types of questions; there were too many variables. Like bruised, broken and battered hearts, there was no time frame for recovery. "C'mon, Mac, you know better than to ask me that! Some people heal quicker, some never do. I can't answer that!"

"Can it be done in two months?" Mac pushed for an answer.

Rory tipped her head back to look at the ceiling. "I think you are asking for a miracle."

"Miracles happen," Mac calmly stated. "What can I do to jump-start the healing process?"

Rory thought for a minute. "My electromagnetic mat, for a start. We'll do treatments three or four times a day. It's noninvasive and will get the blood moving through the damaged capillaries. Anti-inflammatory drugs to take the swelling down.

"When *I* think it's time, we will start doing exercises," Rory added, and as she expected Mac's scowl deepened.

"I'm a professional player, I can take the pain," Mac said through gritted teeth. He wasn't listening to her, Rory realized. Did men like him ever listen to what they didn't want to hear?

"It's not about what you can endure, McCaskill!" Rory snapped. "It's about not making a very bad injury ten times worse! You will start exercising that arm when I say you can, with the exercises I approve, and not a minute before."

Mac glared at her and she kept her face impassive. "I'm not joking, Mac, this point is not up for negotiation."

Mac rubbed the back of his neck with his free hand. "Look, Rory, I'm not trying to be a jerk but a lot is riding on me being able to play in nine or so weeks."

"I understand that, but what you don't understand is that if you push, you might never play ever again! Is that a risk you are prepared to take?"

For a moment, Mac looked desolate, then his inscrutable expression fell back into place. He didn't respond to her question but she knew she'd made her point. "I don't want you to pussyfoot around me. You push me and you push me hard. As soon as you can."

He didn't allow for weakness, Rory thought, his body had to function how he wanted it to. She suspected he carried that trait into his relationships. His way or the highway...

Reason number fifty-four why they would never have managed to make a relationship work.

Going back to their actual conversation and pushing aside the craziness in her head, Rory realized that was the only concession he was prepared to make and she mentally declared their argument a draw. Good enough for her. She stood up to leave and gestured to the folder on the table. "I've signed your contract and I've been released from my job for ten weeks. We need to set up a schedule for when it's convenient for me to see you. To check on your mobility, to wrap your arm in the mat."

Mac shifted on the bed. "Where do you live?"

"I have an apartment in Eastside."

"I live in Kitsilano, not far from here actually. Commuting to my place three or four times a day is unnecessary. I have a spare room. You should move in."

Yeah, no way. Ever. That was far more temptation than she could handle. She needed to keep as much distance between them as she possibly could and if that meant trekking across town daily, or three or four times a day, then that was what she would do. She and Mac together in a house, alone, was asking for trouble. Trouble she needed like a hole in her heart.

Rory slowly shook her head.

"C'mon, Rory, it's not a big deal." Mac was obviously used to women moving in to his house on a regular basis but she wasn't going to follow those lemmings off a cliff. Nope, she'd deal with the devil if it meant the chance to run her own clinic, to treat her patients the way she wanted to, but she'd keep this particular devil at a safe distance.

"I'll live with the driving." She pulled her cell from her back pocket. "What's your address?"

Mac told her and also gave her his cell number, handing his phone to her so she could input hers into his state-of-the-art phone. When they were done, Rory looked at the door. She should leave. She picked up her bag and pulled it over her shoulder. "I'll see you later this evening. Around five?"

Mac nodded. She was almost at the door when Mac spoke again. "Are we not going to discuss it? At all? Pretend it didn't exist?"

Rory turned around slowly and lifted her hands. "What's the point? You insulted her on national television, we almost kissed, my sister heard us talking. She had to deal with a broken heart while she was stalked and hassled by the press. And she didn't talk to me for months."

Mac's jaw tightened and his lips thinned. "I'm sorry, I didn't think of that."

"You weren't thinking at all that day," Rory told him, her voice tart. "Admittedly, I wasn't either." Rory exhaled. "Look, it happened a long time ago and there's nothing to talk about."

Mac released a laugh that was heavy with derision and light on joy. "You're right. Nothing...except that the chemistry hasn't gone away. We're still attracted to each other."

She wished she could deny it but that would be a bald-faced lie, and she suspected Mac could still read her like a book. "I don't sleep with my patients."

Mac didn't look convinced. "You think we can resist each other? We'll be spending an enormous amount of time together and biology is biology."

"Unlike you, I can control myself," Rory told him primly.

Mac lifted an arrogant eyebrow. "Really? You think chemistry like ours just evaporates?" Mac snorted. "So if I kiss you, right here, right now...you can resist me?"

Rory rolled her eyes. "I know you find this hard to believe but there are women who can."

Mac smiled slowly. "You're not one of them."

Unfortunately he was probably right. Not that Rory would allow him to put his theory to the test. He'd already kissed her once and, despite the fact that he'd been as high as a kite, the kiss had blown her boots off. There was no way she would confirm his suspicions.

"Get over yourself, McCaskill. You're confusing me with those pretty, brainless bunnies that drop in and out of your life."

Mac took a step closer and his hurt arm brushed her chest. "Jealous?"

She wasn't even going to ask herself that question, mostly because she wasn't a hundred percent convinced that she wasn't jealous. Rory made an effort to look condescending. For good measure, she patted his cheek. "Bless your delusional little heart."

Mac's eyes darkened with fury, or lust, who knew, and he wrapped his good arm around her waist and pulled her up onto her toes, slamming his mouth against hers. No drugs affected his performance this time. This was Mac, pure and undiluted.

He didn't tease or tangle. The kiss was hard, demanding, harsh and urgent. *Hot.* On his lips she could taste her own bubblegum-flavored lip balm mixed with his toothpaste and the stringent tang of the mouthwash he must've used earlier. Rory felt his hand drop down her back to palm her butt, kneading her cheek until she was squirming, trying to get closer, needing to climb inside his mouth, his skin, to feel wrapped up within his heat...

Mac jerked back. "Dammithell." These words were followed by a string of others and it took Rory a minute to realize that his pale face and harsh breathing wasn't a result of the kiss, but from her bumping his injured arm.

She winced and lifted her hands to do something to help. When he took another step back she realized she'd done more than enough. Of everything.

Rory watched as Mac slowly straightened, as his breathing evened out. When she was sure he wasn't about to fall over, she slapped her hands on her hips. "That's not happening again. Ever."

One corner of Mac's mouth lifted to pull his lips up into a cocky smile. "Of course it won't," he replied, his voice oozing sarcasm. "Because we have no chemistry and you can resist me."

Lord give me patience. Rory yanked the door open and barreled into the passageway. *Because if You give me strength I'm going to need bail money, as well.*

Four

She'd had her hand on his crotch.

His life was currently a trash fire—messy and ugly—and all he could think about was how Rory's fingers felt brushing across his junk, how much he wanted her hand encircling his erection, how nobody had ever managed to set his blood on fire like that pint-size fairy who needed her attitude adjusted.

Mac glared at the half-open door, dropped into the chair and leaned his head back against the wall. He was not having a good day; it was just another day from hell in a series of hellish days in Hell City. He hadn't felt this crazy since that disaster ten years ago.

Wah, wah, wah... Admittedly, he sounded like a whiny ten-year-old, but wasn't he allowed to? Just this once? He hadn't been this unsure of his future since he'd hitched a ride out of his hometown fifteen years ago. And even then, he hadn't been that worried. He'd made excellent grades in school and a rare talent on the ice had translated into a full scholarship to college. He'd then been recruited to play for the Mavericks and earned serious money. By investing in companies and start-ups, he'd earned more. Considerably more. He was, by anyone's definition, a success. He was living the life, incredibly wealthy, popular, successful.

Despite his rocky upbringing, he believed he was, mostly, a functioning adult, fully committed to steering his own ship. He had an active social life; he genuinely liked women, and while he didn't "do" commitment, he wasn't the player everyone assumed him to be. Sure, he'd dated one or two crackpots but he'd managed to remain friends with most of the women he'd dated.

So, if he was a successful adult, why was he so insanely pissed off right now? Bad things happened to good people all the time...

He'd be handling this better if his fight with the fridge had only impacted his own life, his own career. Like that long ago incident with Shay, his actions had not only hurt himself but could hurt people he cared about too. He knew what it felt like to be collateral damage. He'd been the collateral damage of his mother's bad choices and perpetual negativity.

To this day, he could still hear her lack of enthusiasm for anything he said or did. His mother was the reason he had no intention of settling down. In his head commitment equaled approval and he'd be damned if he ever sought approval from a woman again. He didn't want it and he didn't need it...

Wanting approval was like waiting to catch a boat at an airport. Constantly hopeless. Endlessly disappointing.

It was far easier not to give people, a woman, the opportunity to disappoint him. Rory—funny, loyal, interesting—was a problem. He didn't care for the fact that he *liked* her, that this blast from his past excited him more than he thought possible.

You are overthinking this, idiot. This is just about sex, about lust, about attraction.

It had to be because he wouldn't allow it to be anything else.

That being said, he was playing with fire in more ways than one. Yes, Rory might be the best physiotherapist around and eminently qualified to treat him, but she was also his famous ex's sister. If the press found out about this new connection, they would salivate over the story. If they then found out he and Rory were attracted to each other they'd think they'd died and gone to press heaven.

There were many reasons to downplay his injury, but the thought of putting Rory through the same hell Shay experienced at the hands of those rabid wolves made him feel sick. *Not happening*, he decided.

Not again.

Thank God she'd refused his asinine suggestion to move in with him. Wasn't that a perfect example of how his brain shut down whenever she was around? If she moved in he'd give them, mmm, maybe five minutes before they were naked and panting.

He had no choice but to keep his attraction to her under control, keep his distance—emotionally and physically. He had to protect himself and protect her, and the only way to do both was to put her in the neutral zone— that mental zone he'd created for people, events, stuff that didn't, or shouldn't, impact him.

So he'd put her there, but he wasn't convinced, in any way, shape or form, that she'd actually remain there.

Rory stood on the pavement outside Mac's Kitsilano home, the key Mac had given her earlier in her hand. The house wasn't what she'd expected. She'd thought he'd have a blocky, masculine home with lots of concrete and steel. She hadn't expected the three-story with its A-pitched roof, painted the color of cool mist with dark gray accents. It looked more like a home and less like the den of sin she'd expected.

Rory walked up the steps to the front door, slid the key into the lock and entered the house, stopping to shove the key back into the front pocket of her jeans. There was good art on the wall, she noticed as she moved farther into the living area, and the leather furniture was oversize and of high quality. A massive flat-screen TV dominated one wall, and apart from a couple of photographs of the three Maverick-teers, there wasn't anything personal in the room. Mac had no hockey memorabilia on display, nothing to suggest he was the hottest property on ice. She'd expected his walls to be covered with framed jerseys and big self-portraits. Instead his taste ran to original art and black-and-white photographs.

"Rory?" Mac's voice drifted down the stairs. "Come on up. Top floor."

She walked back into the hallway and up the stairs. She reached the second floor, looked down the passage and wished she could explore. Instead she jogged up the short, second flight that ended at the entrance to an expansive bedroom. The high pitch of the roof formed the paneled ceiling. The room was dominated by a massive king-size messy but empty bed. Rory looked around and saw Mac sprawled on a long sofa on the far side of the room. His head rested against the arm and his eyes were closed. Pain had etched deep grooves next to his mouth. His normally tanned skin was pale and he was taking long, slow, measured breaths.

His eyes didn't open but his mouth did. "Hey, were there any press people outside when you let yourself in?"

"No, why?"

"Just asking."

Rory dropped her gaze and her eyebrows lifted at his unbuttoned white shirt, his unzipped gray suit pants and his bare feet. An aqua tie lay on the seat next to him, on top of what was obviously a matching suit jacket. Black shoes and socks sat on the wood coffee table in front of him.

Oh, hell, no! "Going somewhere?"

"Planning on it."

"The only place you are going is back to bed." Rory folded her arms against her chest. "You need a full-time nurse, McCaskill."

If she moved in then she could stop him from making stupid decisions. But would she be able to stop *herself* from making stupid decisions, like sleeping with him?

"I don't need a nurse, I need a morphine drip," Mac responded, finally opening his eyes and squinting at her.

"Would you care to explain why you are all dressed up when you should be in bed, resting that injury?" Rory demanded, annoyed. This was what she'd been worried about. Mac thought that he was a superhero, that the usual consequences of surgery and injury didn't apply to him.

Despite the fact that he was a very intelligent man, the wheel was turning but the hamster seemed to be dead.

"Don't give me grief, Rory," Mac said, sounding exhausted. "Trust me, there is no place I'd rather be than in bed but something came up."

"A wine auction? A ball? A poker game?" Rory asked, her eyebrows lifting. Mac was very active on the Vancouver social scene and he was, with the women who spun in and out of his life, invited to all the social events.

Mac, despite his pain, managed to send her an annoyed glance. "Myra Hasselback, current owner of the Mavericks, is holding an end-of-season cocktail party for the sponsors, management and staff. I can't miss it. As Captain, I am expected to be there."

"But…" Rory looked from him to his arm and back again. "Does she know that you are hurt?"

Mac's smile was grim. "Oh, she knows, but she doesn't know how bad it is. Kade told her it's a slight sprain, nothing for her to worry about. She told Kade to tell me she was looking forward to seeing me tonight. Besides, she knows I would move heaven and earth to be at the cocktail party. It's a tradition that was important to Vernon." Mac sat up slowly. "She'd suspect something if I wasn't there."

"Judging by your pale face and pain-filled eyes she's going to suspect something anyway." Rory sighed her frustration. "What do the other two Maverick-teers have to say on the subject?"

"They wanted me to fake a stomach bug or an allergic reaction to medication."

"Not a bad idea. Why not go with that?"

Mac looked uncomfortable. "I suppose I could but I don't want to give her an excuse to arrive on my doorstep after the party is over to check on me."

"She's done that before?" Rory asked.

Mac looked uncomfortable, and not from the pain. "Yeah, once or twice."

Rory turned his words over, recalling the thirty-year difference between Myra and her dead husband. Ah, the widow wanted naked comforting.

Rory wanted to ask if he'd slept with Myra but she mentally slapped her hand across her mouth. She had no right to ask that but... *But* nothing. She had no right to know.

"Anyway, about the party, I need to be there. The speculation will be endless if I don't attend. It would raise a lot of questions, questions I do not want to answer." Mac looked stubborn. "No, it's better for me to act like everything is normal as far as I possibly can. So, will you please help me finish getting dressed?"

"I'm not happy about this, Mac."

"I know. I'm not either."

But he'd go, Rory realized. He needed rest and time for that injury to heal but he would do what he always did. If this was his intended pace, they were in for some serious problems.

Rory walked across his bedroom to stand in front of the huge windows and watched a container ship navigate the sound. But her thoughts weren't on the gorgeous view, they were on that stubborn man who didn't know the meaning of the words *slow down, take it easy.* To heal, Mac needed rest and lots of it. It was that simple, that imperative.

That difficult.

Dammit, she was going to *have* to move in here. His arm, his career, the Mavericks were at risk and she was balking because he had the ability to melt the elastic on her panties. She was better, stronger, a great deal more professional than that.

She was a smart, independent, focused woman who could say no to what wasn't good for her. Who could, who *would*, keep their relationship strictly professional.

"Don't even think about it. You are not now, or ever, going to move in."

Dammit! Had he started reading her mind now? When? How? "But you suggested it earlier."

"I changed my mind. It would be a terrible idea. Moving on, are you going to help me or not?" Mac demanded, sounding irritable.

She wanted to be petty and tell him to go to hell but she knew he was stubborn enough to dress himself. *One fight at a time*, Rory thought.

"Yes. If you take some painkillers," Rory stated, her tone discouraging any arguments. "You look like a breath of wind could blow you over, Mac, and there is no way anyone will believe you have a slight sprain if you walk into that room looking like that. Painkillers…that's my demand."

"They make me feel like hell. Spacey and out of control," Mac muttered.

"I have some in my bag. They aren't as strong as yours but they'll take the edge off." Rory looked at her watch. "What time do you need to leave for this party?"

"Kade and Quinn should be here any moment." A door slammed below them and the corner of Mac's mouth kicked up. "Speaking of the devil and his sidekick…"

"Who is the devil and who is the sidekick?" Rory asked.

"Depends on the occasion. We all have our moments."

Now *that* she could believe. Rory jammed her hands

into the pockets of her jeans and rocked on her heels. "I'll run downstairs to get those painkillers and one of your sidekicks can come back up and help you dress."

"Aw, they aren't as pretty as you. Nor do they smell as good."

"I'm not so sure...they are both very pretty and they do smell good," she teased.

Mac sent her a narrow-eyed look. "Do not flirt with my friends."

He sounded jealous. But that was probably just her imagination running off again.

"Why on earth not?" Rory asked, deliberately ignoring the heat building between her legs and the thump-thump of her heartbeat.

"I wouldn't like it," Mac growled.

Rory forced herself to do a massive eye roll as she edged her way to the door. "I think you are confusing me with someone who might actually give a damn."

"Rory?"

When she turned, Mac did a slow perusal of her body. She felt like he'd plugged her into the electricity grid. "Seriously, no flirting."

"Seriously, you're an idiot." Rory made a big production of her sigh. "They really should invent a vaccine to prevent that."

The next morning Mac, dressed in a T-shirt and a pair of sweatpants, walked into his kitchen and, ignoring his two friends sitting at his table, headed straight for the coffeepot. Filling a cup to the brim, he gulped a sip, shuddered, swallowed another mouthful and prayed the caffeine would hit his system in the next thirty seconds. He felt like death warmed over. His arm was on fire, his head was pounding and he wanted to climb back into bed and sleep for a week. He supposed being out last night and pretending he was fine contributed to his less than stellar mood.

As did the drugs and the anesthetic, he realized. It always took time for drugs to work their way out of his system. He felt like a wet blanket was draped over his head. He'd work through it, as he always did.

He jerked his head at his friends and looked around the kitchen. "Where's Rory?"

"She went home," Quinn replied, taking a donut from the box on the table and biting into it.

"But…" Mac frowned, looking toward the front door. "I thought she was here earlier. She wrapped that mat thing around my arm."

"She was. Now she's gone," Quinn replied, stretching out his long legs. "Need anything? I can make eggs."

Mac shook his head, smiling internally. Quinn, their resident badass, was a nurturer at heart, intent on making the world around him better and brighter for the people he loved. There weren't many people he showed his softer side to. To the world he was an adrenaline-addicted bad boy, speed-freak player, but his family and close friends knew he would move heaven and earth for the people he loved.

"I'm good, thanks."

Kade pushed back his chair and pulled back the cuff of his shirt to look at his watch. It was new, Mac realized, and damn expensive. "I've got to get moving, my morning is crazy."

"Can you give me fifteen minutes?" Mac asked, picking up his coffee. "We need to talk."

He didn't want to do this. Frankly he was considering abdicating all his rights to adulthood at this point and going back to bed, but he leaned against the counter and held his cup in his good hand.

"What's up?" Quinn asked.

"This situation is a classic cluster…" Mac allowed his words to trail away and rubbed the back of his neck. He needed air. This kitchen was far too small for three six-foot-plus men.

"Let's go outside." Mac placed his cup on the table and grabbed a donut. Maybe a sugar rush would make him feel better. He took one bite, grimaced and tossed the donut back into the box.

Kade and Quinn exchanged a long, worried look, which made Mac grind his back teeth. He was about to knock some heads together—okay, he couldn't beat up a worm at the moment but the thought was there—when Kade stood up and walked over to the open doors that led to the small patio. Mac followed him out into the sunshine and Quinn lumbered to his feet to do the same.

They looked over the houses below them, across False Creek and toward the Lions Gate Bridge and the mountains beyond. God, he loved this city and its endless, changing views. He couldn't think of living anywhere else; this was home. He'd had offers from teams all over the continent but he'd never been willing to be traded, and Vernon had kept him, and Kade and Quinn. Unless they managed to buy the Mavericks, that would all change. Mac didn't mind change, as long it was the change *he* wanted.

"I'm really worried about the press finding out about my injury," Mac quietly stated.

Kade rested his forearms on the railing and cocked his head to look at Mac. "We put out a press release stating you have a minor injury and that you should be fine soon."

Not good enough, Mac decided. "There's too much at stake."

Quinn frowned. "But only the three of us and Rory know the truth. The doctors and nurses are bound by patient confidentiality. I think we'll be okay."

Mac rubbed his chin. "Until the press realizes I am spending an enormous amount of time with my ex-girlfriend's sister."

It took a minute for the implications of that scenario to register with his friends. When it did, they both looked uneasy. Kade rubbed his chin. "That was the incident that started their obsession with what we do, who we date."

Mac felt a spurt of guilt. "Yeah. And if they find out about Rory, how will we explain why we are spending time together?" He frowned. "I will not tell them we are seeing each other, in any capacity. God, that would open up a nasty can of worms, not only for Rory but for Shay, as well."

"And even if you told them she was your physio, that statement would raise questions as to why we aren't using our resident physios, why we need her to treat you," Kade said. "Especially since your injury is supposed to be a minor one."

"Bingo."

Quinn swore. "What's that saying about lies and tangles we weave?"

"Shut up, Shakespeare." Kade stood up, looking worried. So was Mac. He'd spent most of the night thinking about how they could avoid this very wide, imminent pitfall.

Quinn leaned his hip against the railing and narrowed

his eyes. "We've painted ourselves into a corner. We've downplayed your injury and said you'll be fine in a couple of weeks. When you are not fine in a week or two, how are we going to explain that?"

"I have a solution," Mac said. "I don't like it—in fact, I hate it. I need to be here, working with you on the deal to purchase the team. But it's all I can think of…"

"Well?" Quinn demanded, impatient.

"I need to get out of the city."

Kade tapped his finger against his chin. "Yeah, but any fool can see you are more badly injured than we say you are. We got away with lying once, only because the injury was brand-new, but we can't keep shoveling that story. Your eyes are dull, you can tell you are on hectic painkillers."

"I'll stop the drugs," Mac insisted.

"Now who is being stupid?" Quinn demanded.

"Last night you hadn't taken the proper pain meds and you looked like a walking corpse," Kade said. "The point is that people will notice and that will lead to complications. I think your instinct is right. It's best for you to leave. We can tell Myra, the press, anyone who cares that you are taking an extended vacation."

Mac swore. "I have no idea where to go. There's nowhere I *want* to go."

"The chalet in Vail?" Quinn suggested.

"No snow, and even if there was, I couldn't ski. Torture."

"An African safari?"

"Done that." God, didn't he sound like a spoiled brat?

"What about the Cap de Mar property?" Kade persisted.

He'd already considered Puerto Rico and he'd immediately dismissed that idea. Too hot, too isolated, too sexy…

"Are you nuts?" Mac rolled his eyes.

"No," Kade replied, his voice calm as he ticked off points on his fingers. "Not big on ice hockey so you'll be able to fly under the radar. Two, there's sun, sea and beaches…where's the problem? Three, you love it there. Four, Rory will go with you and she'll do her treatment there."

A vision of Rory dressed in nothing more than four triangles flipped onto the big screen of his brain and he shuddered with lust. This wasn't a good idea. The property was empty, the cove would be deserted, he and Rory would be alone and living together. Whenever he thought of Cap de Mar he thought about sunny days and sensual nights, warm, clear seas and sex…

"You have to go, Mac," Kade said, deeply serious.

Mac knew it was a reasonable option. Hell, he'd brought up the idea of leaving. But he couldn't help feeling like he had as a kid. Powerless over his situation.

"My life sucks," Mac grumbled.

"Yeah, poor baby. You're heading for a luxury house on a Caribbean island with a hot chick." Quinn mocked him by rubbing his eyes like a toddler. "Boo hoo."

Mac still had the use of his good arm. A well-placed punch to Quinn's throat would relieve a lot of his frustration.

Kade ignored Quinn. "I like the idea of you heading to the beach house for all the reasons I mentioned and one more."

"Uh-huh?"

"Nobody will know where you are so you'll be free of the media."

"Always a bonus," Mac agreed.

"And if something happens between you and Rory then they won't pick up on that either," Kade added.

Mac held Kade's mocking glare. Okay, yeah, of course that was a factor. He would try to resist her but his will-power where she was concerned wasn't a sure thing.

"It's not going to happen," he said, but he wasn't sure whether he was trying to convince his friends or himself.

Quinn laughed. "You're going to take one look at Rory in her bikini and be all 'let me show you the view from my room.'"

A punch to the throat would definitely shut Quinn up and would make Mac feel so much better, he mused.

Five

"Sorry, I'm late." Rory picked up her e-reader from her coffee table and shoved it into her tote bag.

"We've got time." Mac, standing by the window, looked at his watch. "Not a lot but some. And if the jet misses its time slot, we'll just request another."

Private jets and time slots. Rory tried not to look impressed. But she was. She was traveling to the Caribbean in *style*. Rory tried to think calmly. She'd done most of her packing last night but she'd thought she'd have time to finish up this morning. Thanks to Troy's mom going walkabout from her nursing home, that hadn't happened. She and Troy had spent three hours looking for her and had eventually tracked her down in a garden center sitting on a bench between two cherry trees. Rory was glad Troy's mom was okay but her temporary disappearance had put a serious dent in Rory's schedule.

"Passport and credit card," Mac told her. "You can buy anything else you need there."

So spoke the man with far too much disposable income, Rory thought. She held up her hand in a silent gesture for him to be quiet. She needed to think, and him standing in her little apartment, looking so hot, wasn't helping. All she could think about was that she was leaving the country with a sexy man who just had to breathe to turn her on.

Her eyes dropped to his arm, which rested in a black sling. He was injured, she reminded herself.

You could go on top...

Rory slapped her hand across her forehead.

"Tell me about Puerto Rico," Rory said, hoping the subject would distract her from thinking about straddling Mac, positioning herself so that...argh!

"It's an island in the Caribbean," Mac replied.

"Don't be a smart-ass. Tell me about the house where we're staying."

Mac leaned his shoulder into the wall and crossed his legs at the ankles. It was so wrong that he looked at home in her apartment, like he had a right to be there. "The house is situated about thirty-five minutes from San Juan, on a secluded cove near only two other houses. It's three stories, mostly open-plan and it has glass folding doors that open up so you feel like you are part of the beach and sea.

"The owners of the other two properties are off-island at the moment so we'll be the *only* people using the cove." Mac added.

Rory swallowed at the low, sexy note in his voice. She'd be alone with Mac, on a Caribbean island, with warm, clear water and white beaches and palm trees.

Utterly and absolutely alone. She wasn't sure whether the appropriate response was to be thrilled or terrified.

Or both.

Sex and business don't mix! He's your patient!

Sun, sea, sexy island…sexy man.

Get a grip, Kydd. Not liking the cocky look in his eyes, the glint that suggested he knew exactly what she was thinking, she lifted her nose. "Well, at least we won't disturb the neighbors with your screams of pain when we start physio."

"Or your screams of pleasure when I make you fall apart in my arms," Mac replied without a second's hesitation.

Rory's heart thumped in her chest but she kept her eyes locked on his, refusing to admit he rattled her. Instead of making her furious, as it should, his comments made her entire body hum in anticipation. Her body was very on board with that idea.

Rory folded her arms and rocked on her heels. "I hate it when you say things like that."

"No, you don't. You want to hate it because it turns you on." Mac looked up at the ceiling. When he looked back at her, his expression was rueful. "Ignore me, ignore that."

She couldn't do as he asked. They needed to address the pole dancing, come-and-get-me-baby elephant gyrating in the room. "Mac, I don't know what you think is going to happen in Puerto Rico, but us sleeping together can't happen, won't happen."

"I know why *I* think it shouldn't happen. I have a few solid reasons for thinking it would be a hell of a mistake, but I'm interested in hearing yours."

Rory bit the inside of her lip. God, she couldn't tell

him she thought he was just like her dad, unfaithful. That the fact he'd dated her sister bugged her. Or her personal favorite: that he drove her crazy.

Rory thought fast and latched onto the first reasonable excuse that popped into her head. "I'm on sticky ground here. I shouldn't treat you and sleep with you—that would be crossing some pretty big lines. I have to maintain professional boundaries with clients. I can't misuse or abuse my position of authority—"

"You have no position of authority over me," Mac scoffed.

"The point remains—" Rory gritted her teeth "—that if I engage in any nonprofessional behavior I can be pulled up before the board."

Mac stared at her, his face inscrutable. "Okay, for the sake of argument, may I point out that you'll be in a foreign country and nobody but us will know? And you're on holiday."

"I'd know," Rory said, her voice resolute. "You might be a rule breaker, Mac, but that's not a risk I'm willing to take."

"You're lying, Rory. Besides, last I checked, physiotherapists are allowed private lives." Mac shook his head. "Not buying it."

So much for using that as an excuse to keep some distance between them. Rory hated the fact that he could look past her cool, professional shell and see below the surface. And he was right. Nobody would believe she'd bullied Mac into having a relationship he didn't want to have. Yeah, sleeping with Mac wouldn't be professional but it wasn't a death sentence either.

She'd forgotten how damn complicated men could be.

"So what is your reason why we shouldn't scratch this particular itch?"

"God, I wish there was just one." Mac dropped a curse and rubbed the back of his neck. "But I can't remember any of them because I am too damn busy thinking about how you taste, how good you feel in my arms. I want to feel that, *feel you*, again. It's not smart, or sensible, but… to hell with being sensible and smart!"

"Mac—"

"Come here, Rorks."

She could say no, should say no, but she found herself walking toward him. Stopping when she was a foot from him, she tipped her head up to look at his face. His jaw held that sexy stubble, and the corners of his mouth suggested he was amused, but his eyes told her everything she needed to know. He was as turned on as she was.

Crazy chemistry.

Mac lifted his good hand, gripped the edge of her collar and pulled her toward him. Rising on her tiptoes, she kept her eyes locked on his, deciding whether she should kiss him or not. "I just want one kiss, Rory," Mac murmured, doing his mind reading thing again. "Stop thinking for a second and *be*."

He had a way of cutting to the heart of the problem. He was right; she was making far too big a deal of this. It didn't have to mean anything! Kissing him just made her feel good. Like chocolate or a foot rub.

"That's it, babe, stop thinking and kiss me."

Rory moved her head so her lips moved across his ear, under his short sideburns, through his surprisingly soft stubble, slowly, so slowly, making her way to his mouth. Mac's hand clenched her waist and she heard the low growl in the back of her throat as her tongue darted out to taste the skin on his jaw, to explore the space where his top and bottom lip met. She felt his erection against her hip and knew she had maybe five seconds before he exploded and all hell—possibly heaven—broke loose.

Rory moved her lips over his, her teeth gently scraping his upper lip, her hand grasping the back of his neck. She kept her tongue away, wondering how long he would wait before he took control of the kiss. Five seconds passed and then another ten. Rory sucked on his bottom lip.

He muttered something against her lips, something harsh and hot and sexy, and his big hand gripped her butt and lifted her up and into him. The time for playing, for teasing, was over. She'd never experienced a kiss so... sexual, Rory realized. This wasn't a prelude to sex. This was just another version of the act. His tongue pushed inside and retreated, swirled and sucked, and Rory felt her panties dampen as she unconsciously ground herself against his erection, frustrated by the layers of fabric between them.

She wanted to get naked. Now.

"Plane waiting. Puerto Rico," Mac muttered after wrenching his mouth off hers.

"You said you could get another time slot and the island isn't going anywhere." Rory snuck her hands under his shirt and scraped her nails across the skin covering the hard muscles of his abs.

"Rory..." Mac muttered a curse and slapped his good hand on hers to keep it from sliding lower. She looked up at him and half smiled at the seventy-shades-of-crazy look on his face. She'd put that look on his face, she thought, amazed. This sexy man looked like he couldn't go without her for one more heartbeat.

"We really should stop," Mac muttered. "We shouldn't take this any further."

"Why not?"

Mac looked rueful. "One reason would be because someone has been pounding on your door for the last minute. At least."

Rory jerked back, surprised. Really? She hadn't heard a damn thing. As the bells in her head stopped ringing she heard the *rat-tat-tat* on her doorjamb. Her heart dropped to the floor; there was only one person who used that particular combination on her door. As a child she'd considered it their secret code, as an adult—about to get lucky—it irritated the hell out of her.

"Problem?" Mac asked as she stepped away from him and pushed a hand into her hair.

"Yes, no...my father." Rory pulled a face. She lifted a hand, waved it toward her front door and grimaced. "Give me a sec, okay?"

Bad timing, Dad, she thought as she crossed the room to the door. Or maybe he'd arrived just in time to save her from making a very silly mistake. Either way, why was he here? She'd called her mother last night, told her that she'd be out of the country for the foreseeable future. Her parents lived in a suburb twenty minutes from here, and since they weren't close, Rory couldn't understand why her father had made the trek to see her.

Rory checked the peephole to make sure it was her father and opened the door. "Dad."

David Kydd had that sheepish look on his face that she was sure had charmed many a woman into his bed over the years. "There's my girl." He leaned forward to kiss her and Rory allowed him to brush her cheek. Since he wasn't one for spontaneous gestures of affection, Rory had to wonder what he was up to.

Okay, she was cynical, but being cynical protected her. She'd learned that if she had no expectations of him then she couldn't be disappointed by his behavior.

"Can I come in?" David asked.

Rory kept her body in the open space of the door so he couldn't look into the apartment and see Mac. Her father was a fan and she didn't want to spend the next hour listening to hockey talk. And, even if she begged him, she wasn't sure her Dad would keep quiet about seeing Mac at her place. Her Dad wasn't the soul of discretion at the best of times.

"It's not a good time. I told Mom last night that I was leaving the city for a while and I need to get to the airport."

"She told me." David gave her another of his sheepish grins. "I thought I'd make the offer to feed your animals or water your plants."

"I don't have pets or plants." As he was well aware. Rory narrowed her eyes at him. "Why are you really here?"

David dropped his eyes and shifted from foot to foot. Eventually he muttered an answer. "Your mother and I are going through a rough time."

Rory felt that familiar, piercing pain shoot through her heart. A rough time... How often had she heard that phrase over the years? *A rough time* meant her mother had caught him again—sexting, cheating, an internet relationship...who knew? He was a master at all of them.

Rory knew how it worked. Her parents would separate for a month or six weeks. Her dad would get bored with his latest conquest and beg her mother to take him back. She liked the begging, liked the attention, and they swore to make it work this time.

"Anyway, we thought that since you wouldn't be here for a while, I could move in to your place until you get back," David suggested, utterly blasé.

"No," Rory told him, her expression brittle. He needed to leave her, and her apartment, out of any games he was playing.

Rory stepped backward and rubbed her forehead with her fingertips. "I've got to go. I'm late as it is."

"Rory, come on," David pleaded.

"Sorry." Rory closed the door in his face and rested her forehead against the wood, trying to hold back the tears threatening to fall. She needed a minute to find her center, to process what had just happened.

She heard her father's footsteps as he walked away from her door. There went the reason why she found it difficult, impossible really, to trust that someone she allowed herself to love would not lie to her or abandon her. How could she put her faith in love after witnessing her parents' skewed perception of the emotion all her life? As a product of their twisted love, was she even worthy of being in a monogamous relationship? If such a thing even existed.

She was so damn confused about the meaning of love and marriage. Why did her parents stay together after all this drama? What did they get out of it? Their love, their marriage, their entire married life had been a sham, an illusion...

Love was a sham, an illusion...

"Rorks? You okay?"

Dammit. She'd temporarily forgotten Mac was in the room. He'd witnessed that silly conversation. She turned slowly. How could she explain this without going into the embarrassing details? She managed to find a smile, unaware that it didn't come anywhere near her eyes. "Sorry about that." She made herself laugh. "My folks, slightly touched."

Mac's skeptical look told her he didn't buy her breezy attitude. Yet there was something in his eyes that suggested sympathy, that made her want to confide in him, to tell him why her parents drove her batty. She had the strange idea that he might understand.

Rory bit the inside of her cheek, confused and feeling off-kilter. Since meeting Mac again, her life had done a one-eighty. She felt like she was standing in a fun house. The reflections didn't make sense…

"Excuse me a sec," Rory said before walking through her bedroom to the bathroom. Grabbing the counter in an iron-fisted grip, she stared at herself in the mirror.

What was she doing? Thinking? She simply wasn't sure and she wished she had more than five minutes to figure it out. This thing between her and Mac was getting out of hand, and she needed, more than anything, to control it, to understand it.

She was about to fly away with him and how was she going to resist him?

It was just sex, she told herself. Sex was physical. It wasn't a promise to hand over her heart. If she slept with Mac she would be sharing her body, not her soul, and she wouldn't be risking anything emotional. Could she be laid-back about such an intimate act? She would have to be, because love wasn't an option. She wasn't interested, and Mac wasn't the type of guy a girl should risk her heart on anyway.

But…

But it would be cleaner, smarter, less complicated if she didn't sleep with him. Passion and chemistry like theirs was crazy. Her libido was acting like a wild and uncontrollable genie. A genie who would be impossible to get back in the bottle if she popped the cork. It was far better to keep the situation, and her lust, contained.

Rory pointed her index finger at her reflection and scowled. "Do not let him pop your cork, Kydd."

In his seat, Mac scowled at his computer screen through his wire-rimmed glasses and wished he could concentrate. He needed to make sense of these balance sheets and read the profit and loss statements for a couple of sports bars they owned in Toronto. How was he supposed to do that when his mind was filled with Rory? He turned his head sideways to look at her and smiled when he saw she'd curled up in her seat and fallen asleep. He picked up a lock of hair that had fallen over her eyes and gently tucked it behind her ear.

So much more beautiful than she'd been at nineteen.

Mac pulled off his glasses and rubbed his eyes, conscious of the fiery throb in his arm. His head ached in sympathy. Truth be told, he was relieved to be leaving the city and to stop pretending he was fine. He could take the pain tablets, zone out and try not to worry about Myra and the investor and the fans and, God, whether the press would find out how serious his injury actually was and how much pain he was living with.

Rory let out a breathy sigh and he looked at her again, his stomach churning with the need to have her. That need worried him.

With her, he didn't feel in control and he hated that sensation. In his real life, he dated to get laid. He and the woman both had fun and then they moved on. He understood how much it hurt to have unmet expectations so he made no promises, offered no hope to the women who slept with him. In his world, sex didn't involve talking, sharing, caring. In that world, conversation took place horizontally; bodies spoke, not mouths.

He didn't confide in any of his lovers. He never shared his feelings, and the one guarantee his lovers had was that he'd always leave.

He never allowed anyone to get too close; he'd learned a long time ago to be his own champion, his own motivator. His mother hadn't believed in or supported him so he didn't expect anyone else to either.

Rory was different. She made him feel more, made him say more, want more. He was out of his depth with her and flailing...

Mac rubbed his temples with his fingertips. He was definitely losing it. *Flailing? Over a woman?* God, he sounded like a fool.

Irritated with himself and his introspection, he picked up his tablet computer and swiped his finger across the screen, immediately hitting the link for his favorite news site. Instead of focusing on the US elections or the migrant crisis in Europe, the headlines detailed the breakup of a famous Hollywood golden couple after ten years and fostering six kids.

Mac had been caught in the same type of media hype, on less of a global scale admittedly, and it had sucked.

Phoenix is currently being treated for depression and begs the media to give her some privacy, he read. He'd heard that Shay had suffered with depression during their breakup and the constant press attention had made the situation ten times worse. He couldn't do that to Rory, couldn't risk her like that. Yeah, it was Puerto Rico. Yes, they would be flying under the radar. But it just took one determined paparazzo, one photograph, and their world would implode.

Not happening. He had to keep his hands off her.

"You look like your brain is going to explode," Rory softly said.

Mac rolled his head on his shoulders and watched as she stretched. "It feels that way," he admitted, knowing he had to address this longing for her. Now or never, he thought.

You won't die if you don't have sex. You might think you are going to, but you won't.

Mac rubbed his temples again. "Look, Rory, I've been thinking."

Rory sent him an uncertain look. "Uh-huh?"

"Despite my smart comments about us sleeping together and that hot kiss, maybe it would be better if we didn't. Sleep together, that is."

He couldn't help noticing the immediate flash of relief in her eyes. So something had shifted in her after that bizarre conversation with her father. When she'd returned from the bathroom, sexy Rory had disappeared and had been replaced with enigmatic Rory. He still didn't know what to make of that.

"Want to clue me in on why you've had a change of heart?"

You scare the crap out of me? When I'm with you I feel like I am on shifting sand? I don't want to see you hurt or scared or feeling hunted?

Yeah, he couldn't admit to any of the above.

So he fudged the truth. "My arm is killing me. I'd like to get to the house and chill, take my meds and just zone out for a while. I want to relax and not have to worry about you or keeping you happy, in bed or out." Mac stared past her to look out the window. "I'd like us to play it cool, just be friends." Because he was a man and believed in keeping his options open, he tacked on a proviso. "For now?"

Rory didn't answer, her gray eyes contemplative. "Sure. Fine."

Mac watched her out of the corner of his eye and sighed. *Fine.* God, he hated that word, especially when a woman stated it in that hard-to-read way. What did it actually mean? Was she okay with waiting? Was she pissed? Did she actually want to say "Screw you"?

Sometimes, most times, women made no sense. At all.

Six

Rory loved the Cap de Mar beach house. Shortly after her arrival, she claimed one of the smaller guest rooms, partly because it had an excellent view of the U-shaped bay and mostly because it was a floor below and a long way from the massive master suite.

She pulled on a bikini, a pair of shorts and a T-shirt and, walking barefoot, she set out to explore the house. As Mac had said, the living areas, sitting and dining room and the kitchen were all open-plan, leading onto a massive balcony filled with comfortable chairs and day-beds either under the balcony roof or under umbrellas. Tucked into the corner of the balcony was a huge Jacuzzi and she could easily imagine sitting in that tub watching the sun go down.

It was mid-afternoon now, Rory thought, resting her elbows on the railing and looking down into the sparkling pool below her. In a perfect world she'd like to take a swim, lie in the sun and then sit on the beach with a glass of white wine in her hand and wait for the sun to paint the horizon in Day-Glo colors. That, she thought, would be a wonderful end to a rather difficult day...

Rory saw a movement out of the corner of her eye and saw Mac step out of his bedroom through the doors that led straight onto this balcony. He'd shucked his jeans and shirt and pulled on a pair of board shorts. He hadn't bothered with a shirt. Why should he? He had a torso to die for.

The rest of him was pretty spectacular too.

Rory huffed out a sigh. She had to corral her overexcited hormones. Speaking of hormones, she'd been caught flat-footed at Mac's suggestion they postpone sleeping together. She hadn't expected Mac would let his arm get in the way of pleasure, or that he was humble enough to admit he was in pain and needed some time.

Mac, barefoot, walked over and gestured to the cove. "Nice, isn't it?"

"Gorgeous," Rory agreed. "It almost feels like we are part of the beach."

Mac half smiled. "That was the intention when I designed it. I wanted to bring the outdoors in."

"You designed this?"

Mac sat down on a daybed and leaned back, placing his good hand under his head. His biceps bulged, his shoulder flexed and the rest of him rippled as he swung his legs up onto the cushions. "Yeah."

She remembered something about him and architecture, about studying it in college. When he was dating Shay, he'd just completed some business courses and Rory had been super impressed that he'd managed to study and still play for the Mavericks. He hadn't needed to study further; he was earning enough with his salary and endorsements that, if he invested it properly, he could live comfortably for a very long time.

This wasn't living comfortably, Rory thought, looking around. This was living large. An island home on a secluded beach translated into big-boy money. She recalled what Troy had said about him and his friends investing in property and businesses, and her curiosity had her asking, "How many properties do you own? How many businesses do you have?"

Mac looked at her from below half-closed eyes. "Enough." He yawned and dropped his arm to pick up a pillow and shove it behind his head. "You want a statement of my assets and liabilities, Rory?"

Rory flushed. Okay, admittedly, she had no right to ask him that; they weren't lovers. They weren't even friends. And she'd rather die than ask any of her other clients such a personal question.

"Kade, Quinn and I have our own projects but a lot of our assets are held together in a partnership, and all the assets we share have to generate an income, this house included. It's our rule. If it doesn't make money, we ditch it. That is why we get to use this property but, for the most part, it's rented out. Not so much during the summer months because it's so damn hot and it's hurricane season."

Rory darted a quick look toward the endlessly blue horizon. "Hurricanes?"

"They happen," Mac replied. "They aren't that bad. A lot of wind, a lot of rain."

"Super," Rory said drily.

Mac shifted in his seat and winced when he moved his injured arm, trying to find a more comfortable position.

"Did you take your painkillers and the anti-inflammatory pills?" Rory demanded.

"Yes, Mom, that's why I'm feeling so damn sleepy," Mac murmured. He waved a hand toward the house. "Food and drinks in the kitchen. I asked our rental agent to arrange for someone to stock the place. I've also arranged for someone to come and clean and do laundry a couple of times a week. Otherwise we're on our own."

On our own was a phrase she did not need to hear.

"Okay," Rory said, watching him fight sleep.

"Jeep in the garage. Keys in the kitchen. San Juan is thirty-five minutes away, north. Casinos, restaurants five minutes away, south." Mac yawned again. "Make yourself at home."

"Will do," Rory said, but she doubted he'd heard her because he'd drifted off to sleep. He still had a frown on his face as she moved an umbrella closer to him so he could sleep in the shade. Her thumb moved over the creases on his forehead and she wondered what was making him worry. Their deal to buy the Mavericks franchise, his injury, being alone with Rory in this house?

She might have her fair share of problems but Mac had his too.

He wasn't always who she expected him to be, Rory admitted. Sure, he could be overconfident about his abilities and about the effect he had on her, but he was also honest enough to admit that their attraction was a two-way street. She affected him just as badly. She didn't know Mac well, not yet, and because he was so damn reticent, she probably never would. But she did know he wasn't the arrogant jerk he'd been ten years ago. He was ambitious and determined, but he wasn't selfish. He was smart and loyal and, yes, infuriating.

It was a surprise to realize that she *liked* him. A lot. And that liking had nothing to do with his masculine face and sculpted muscles.

There was a great deal more to Mac McCaskill than his pretty packaging. Dammit.

With every conversation they shared he shattered another of her preconceptions. If they continued these conversations, she'd start to like him a little more than she should, and there was a possibility she would feel more for him than lust and attraction.

She couldn't let that happen. She would have to try to ignore him, try to avoid him. Because falling in lust with him was one thing, falling in *like* with him was another.

Falling in love with him would be intolerable.

So she simply wouldn't.

A week after landing in San Juan, Rory and Mac watched the sun go down in the small fishing village of Las Croabas. She was full to bursting from demolishing a massive bowl of crab seviche. She was relaxed and a little buzzy. The single glass of wine couldn't be blamed for that, she thought. No, it was a combination of the spectacular sunset—God was painting the sky with vivid purples and iridescent oranges—and the equally magnificent man who sat opposite her, hair ruffled by the balmy evening breeze.

A lovely sunset, a rustic restaurant, a really hot guy with a girl eating dinner…they could be an advertisement for romance, Rory thought. There would be no truth in that advertisement. Mac hadn't laid a finger on her since they'd arrived in Puerto Rico and he hadn't kissed

her again. Truthfully, she hadn't given him any opportunity to do either as she'd made a point of spending as
little time with him as she possibly could without shirk-
ing her duties.

But a girl had to eat, and over dinner she'd intercepted
a couple of intense looks from him, which made her think
he'd catch her if she decided to jump him.

Which she wouldn't. But the will-he-won't-he anticipation was, admittedly, very hot and incredibly sexy.

"There's something I have to tell you," Mac said.

That sounded ominous, Rory thought. "What is it?"

"There's a hurricane on the way." He lifted his seviche-
filled fork to his mouth.

"A big one?" she squawked, half lifting her butt off
her seat and whipping around to inspect the horizon. It
was still cloud-free. Shouldn't there be clouds?

Mac shrugged. "Big enough."

"How big is *big enough*?" Rory demanded. How could
he eat? A natural phenomena was about to smack them
in the face. "When will it arrive? Should we evacuate?
Are there bunkers?"

Mac sent her a puzzled glance. "It's a hurricane, not
a nuclear bomb, Rorks."

"You're not giving me any information!" Rory wailed.
She tried to recall what she'd read about preparing for a
hurricane and, unfortunately, it wasn't a lot. Or anything
at all. "Don't we need to put boards up or something?"

"I've arranged to have some guys come over tomorrow
to put the boards up. Stupid, because I could do them if
it wasn't for this arm!"

"I'm sure I can do it," Rory bravely suggested. She
didn't know if she could but she thought she should offer.

Mac smiled at her. "No offense, Rorks, but it'll take them a couple of hours and it would take you two weeks."

"Why do people always say 'no offense' and then go on to offend you?" Rory grumbled.

"How often have you wielded a hammer?"

Rory lifted her nose at his smirk. "I pound in my own hooks to hang pictures." Well, she had once and had lost a fingernail in the process. Troy then banned her from using tools. He'd fixed her cupboard door, replaced the broken tile in her shower, fixed the leaky pipe under her sink. Troy also changed the tires on her car, made a mean chicken parmesan and removed spiders. He'd be her perfect husband if he only liked girls. And if she was even marginally attracted to him.

"Liar," Mac said cheerfully.

His ability to see through her annoyed the pants off her. Actually, the way he looked, his deep voice, his laugh—all of it made her want to drop her pants, but that was another story entirely. "Tell me about the hurricane!"

Mac dug his fork into his salad. "I'm not sure what you want to know. There's a hurricane approaching. It'll probably hit land around midnight tomorrow night. There will be wind, rain. We'll be fine."

Rory scowled at him. "You are so annoying."

Mac's lips twitched. "I try." He dumped some wine into their glasses, picked hers up and handed it to her. "Drink. We might as well enjoy the gorgeous night before we die."

Rory rolled her eyes. "If you're going to be a smart-ass, there has to be some smart involved. Otherwise you just sound like an ass." She took the glass from his hand, looked into his amused eyes and sighed. "I'm overreacting, aren't I?"

Mac lifted his glass to his lips, sipped and swallowed. "Just a little." He sent her another quick, quirky smile. "We'll be fine. If I thought we were in danger, I'd be making arrangements to get you out of here."

Rory nodded and took a large sip of her wine. Okay, then. Maybe she could cope with the hurricane. She glanced at the sky. "Tomorrow night, huh?"

Mac lifted his hand and rubbed his thumb across her bottom lip. He lingered there, pressing the fullness before moving from her lip and drifting up and over her cheekbone. She watched as his eyes deepened, turned a blue-black in the early evening light. Rory tossed a look at the beach and wished she could jump up from the table and walk—run—away.

She'd been doing that for the last week, finding any excuse to avoid him. She left his presence when she felt the spit drying up in her mouth, when she felt the first throb between her legs. Because Mac spent most of his time shirtless, she'd spent a lot of time walking away from him. She'd run to the beach, run *on* the beach, had started canoeing and snorkeling again. She'd also taken a lot of cold showers.

She was *so* pathetic.

"You can't run off in the middle of a meal," Mac told her, his eyes dancing.

Rory lifted her nose and tried to look puzzled. "Sorry?"

"You've been avoiding me, running away every time something sparks between us," Mac said conversationally, dropping his hand from her face and popping an olive from his salad into his mouth.

"Uh—"

"You're not alone. Every time you do therapy on me,

I have to stop myself from grabbing you and kissing you senseless."

Rory groaned and dropped her chin to her chest.

Mac twisted his fingers in hers. "Your hands touch me and I inhale your scent—you smell so damn good—and my brain starts to shut down. It's not just you, Rory."

Rory picked up her glass and sipped, trying to get some moisture back into her mouth. "Ah... I'm not sure what to say."

"Avoiding each other makes it worse. It's driving me crazy. I barely sleep at night because I want you in my bed." Mac's voice raised goose bumps all over her skin. "What are we going to do about this...situation, Rory?"

Rory touched the top of her lip with the tip of her tongue and her eyelids dropped to half-mast. Couldn't he see the big fat take-me-now sign blazing from her forehead in flashing neon?

She blew out a breath and sent him a rueful shrug. Mac seemed to have a hard time taking his eyes off her mouth. He was enjoying the anticipation, too, she realized when his gaze slammed into hers, his eyes hot and filled with passion.

"How the hell am I supposed to resist you?" he demanded.

Rory rolled her shoulders and gripped his wrist.

"I don't do relationships," Mac growled.

"I don't either," Rory softly replied. "But I can't stop wondering whether we'll be as good together as all the kisses we've shared suggest."

Mac shot up and with one step he was standing in front of her and pulling her to her feet. Keeping his injured arm hanging at his side, he used his other arm to yank her into his hard chest. His mouth slammed against hers.

His tongue slid once, then twice over her lips, and she immediately opened her mouth and allowed him inside. He tasted of wine and sex and heat, and Rory pushed into him so she could feel her nipples touch his chest through the thin fabric of their cotton shirts. She sighed when his erection nudged her stomach, and she linked her hands at the back of his neck to stop herself from reaching down and encircling him. Kissing in a public place was one thing, but heavy petting was better done in a more private setting.

"You taste so damn good," Mac muttered against her lips, his hand sliding over her butt. "And you feel even better."

"Kiss me again," Rory demanded, tipping her head to the side so he could change the angle of the kiss, go deeper and wetter.

"If I kiss you again I don't know if I'm gonna be able to stop," Mac replied, resting his forehead on hers.

"Who asked you to?"

Mac half laughed and half groaned. "You're not helping, Rorks." He stepped back and pushed her hair, curly from the humidity, from her eyes. "Let's take a step back here, think about this a little more. Make damn sure it's what we want."

Rory glanced down, saw the evidence of his want and lifted an eyebrow. "We both want it, McCaskill."

"Yeah, but what we want is not always good for us," Mac said, suddenly somber. He picked up her hand and rubbed the ball of his thumb across her knuckles. "We're here for a little while longer, Rory. I don't want to muck this up. There are consequences."

"I'm on the pill and I expect you to use a condom."

"Noted. But those aren't the consequences I'm worrying about."

Rory cocked her head. "Okay, what are you talking about?"

"I don't want either of us to regret this in the morning, to feel awkward, to feel we've made a colossal mistake." Mac looked uncharacteristically unsure of himself as he tugged at the collar of his white linen button-down shirt. "Taking you to bed would be easy, Rory. Making love to you would be a pleasure. In the morning we're both still going to be here. You still need to treat me and we have to live together. I don't want it to get weird between us."

Those were all fair points. "Anything else?"

Mac looked around them, frowned and rocked on his heels. "We're flying under the radar here but if just one person sees us, snaps a photo—we're toast. If it gets out that you're my physio, or that we're sleeping together and you are my ex's sister, it'll be news."

She hauled in a sharp breath. Wow, she hadn't even considered that.

"The media will go nuts and you'll be at the center of it, like Shay was," Mac added.

The thought made her want to heave. She'd never felt comfortable in the limelight and couldn't think of anything worse than being meat for the media's grinder.

"They will wonder why you—the best physiotherapist around—are treating me and why are you doing it in secret. They'll dig until they find out the truth," Mac said.

Rory dropped her head to look at the floor.

"Are you prepared to risk all that, Rory? Can you deal with the consequences of the worst-case scenario?"

"It won't happen." Rory bit her bottom lip.

"Probably not, but what if it does? Can you deal?"

"Can you?" Rory demanded. "You have more to lose than I do."

"Yeah, don't think that I haven't realized that," Mac muttered, and pinched the bridge of his nose with his finger and thumb. When he opened his eyes, she saw the ruefulness, the touch of amusement, in his gaze.

"Yet I still want you. I'm really hoping to get over it," he added. His tone invited her to help him break the tension, to get over this awkward, emotion-tinged moment. He picked up his wineglass, drained the contents and looked at his empty glass. "See, you're driving me to drink."

Rory bumped her wineglass against his. "I feel your pain. You should try living inside my head."

Mac dropped a quick, hard kiss on her mouth. "Help me out and be sensible about this, Rorks. I'm relying on you to be the adult here because I have little or no sense when it comes to wanting you."

Well, that comment didn't help!

Seven

The next day Rory stood on the beach in front of the house and knew Mac was watching her from the balcony, his good hand gripping the railing, his expression brooding. She tilted her face up and looked for the sun, now hidden behind gloomy, dark clouds. She'd been, maybe obsessively, glued to the Weather Channel, and she knew the hurricane was about twelve hours away. It would slam into them later tonight.

The wind had already picked up and was whipping her hair around her head and pushing her sarong against her thighs. The sea, normally gentle, was choppy and rough, and foam whipped across the surface of the ocean. It looked nothing like the warm friend who had been sharing his delights and treasures with her on a daily basis.

Everything was changing, Rory thought. She picked a piece of seaweed off her ankle, tossed it and watched the wind whisk it away. Like she'd have to face the hurricane, she couldn't run away from Mac anymore. She couldn't hide. She couldn't avoid him or the passion he whipped up in her.

He was right, she had a choice to make…hell, she'd already made the choice. She knew it. He knew it… If she gave him the slightest hint, like breathing, he'd do her in a New York minute.

What she had to do now was stand strong and ride the winds, hoping she'd come out with as little damage as possible when it all ended. Her desire—no, her *need*—for him was too strong, too compelling. She just had to ride the crazy as best she could and hope she could stop the lines between lust and like—she absolutely refused to use any other *L* word—from smudging together.

She turned and looked back at the house and across the sand, across the shrubs that separated the beach from his house, their eyes met. Even at a distance she could see and feel his desire for her, knew that hers was in her heated eyes, on her face, in every gesture she made.

She couldn't run away anymore so she ran to him, into that other hurricane rapidly bearing down on her, one that was even scarier than the one approaching from the sea.

She couldn't wait another second, another minute. Her resistance had petered out. Her need for him was greater than her desire to protect herself. This was it, this was now…

Rory picked up the trailing ends of her sarong and pulled the fabric up above her knees and belted across the sand. The wind tossed her hair into her eyes and she grabbed the strands blowing in her face, holding them out of her eyes so she could watch Mac, watch for that moment when he realized she wasn't running away from

the storm but running to him, running into the tempest
she knew she'd find in his touch.

He wasn't an idiot so he caught on pretty quickly. She
knew it by the way he straightened, the way his apprecia-
tive glance became predatory, anticipatory. But he just
stood on the balcony, waiting for her to fly to him. She
knew he was waiting for her to change her mind, like
she'd been doing, to avoid the steps that led from the path
directly to where he was standing. He was expecting her
to veer off and enter the house, access her room via the
second set of stairs farther along.

She wanted to yell at him that she wouldn't change
her mind, that she wanted him intensely, crazily, without
thought. She hurtled up the steps and bolted onto the balcony, skidding to a stop when he leaned his hip against
the railing and jammed his hand into the pocket of his
expensive khaki shorts.

What if she'd read the situation wrong? What if he'd
changed his mind? Rory flushed with embarrassment
and dropped her gaze, looking at her cherry-red toes.
She'd picked the color because she thought it was vi-
brant, sexy, because she could imagine him taking her
baby toe, exquisitely sensitive and tipped with red, into
his hot mouth…

Rory let out a small moan and closed her eyes.

"You okay?" Mac asked, and when she heard the
amusement in his voice she flushed again. God, she must
look like an idiot. She *was* an idiot.

"Fine."

Mac's penetrating gaze met hers. "On the beach, you
made a decision."

She rocked on her heels. "Yep."

"You're sure?"

"Yep."

He didn't move toward her. Was he waiting for her to make the first move? Unsure, it had been so damn long since she'd danced this dance, she looked around for a temporary distraction because she had no idea what to do, to say. "Storm is on its way."

Mac's eyes didn't leave her face. "I know. Are you scared?"

Of this? Of liking you too much? Of making a mistake? Absolutely terrified.

"I'm a hurricane virgin," she admitted, trying for a light tone but hearing only her croaky voice.

"I have a plan to distract you," Mac softly stated, moving so he stood so close to her that his chest brushed her cotton shirt. He pushed his thigh between her legs as he placed his wineglass on the table next to him. "But in order for the distraction to work we have to practice, often."

Rory closed her eyes in relief and smiled. "Really? It'll have to be very good to distract me from the storm."

"That's why we have to practice." Mac placed his hand on her hip, sliding it under the fabric of her sarong, his hand making contact with the bare skin at her waist. Rory looked at his mouth and stood on her toes, reaching up so her lips met his. His mouth softened, his eyes closed and his long lashes became smudges on his cheeks. She felt him holding back, felt the tension as his mouth rested on hers, as if he were savoring the moment, taking stock. She placed her hand on his waist and flicked her tongue out to trace his lips, to encourage him to let go, to come out and play.

Mac exploded. His good arm went around her back and she was pulled flush against him as his mouth plundered hers in a kiss that was all heat and passion and pent-up frustration. His tongue twisted around hers and his hand pushed the fabric of her sarong down her hips. The knot in the fabric impeded his progress. He pulled back and hissed in frustration.

"You're going to have to help me, honey," he said, his voice rough and growly. He swore. "I want to rip everything off you but that's not gonna happen. Get naked, please?"

Rory, her hands now linked around his neck, dropped her head back so she could look into his frustrated face. Against her stomach she felt the hard, long line of his erection and she noticed the fine tremors skittering under his skin. He was half insane with wanting her and she liked him like that. Maybe she could drive him a little crazier...

It would be fun to try. "I think you need to get naked first," she said, stepping back.

"Uh, no." Mac gripped the hand that started to undo the buttons on his shirt. "If that happens then this is going to be over a lot sooner than we'd like."

Rory placed a kiss on the V just below his throat. "I'm not going to let that happen. I intend to go very, very slowly." She carried on with separating the buttons from their holes and then she pushed the sides of his shirt apart and placed her hands on his pecs, his flat nipples underneath her palms. Mac's hand reached between them to echo her movement by placing his hand on her breast.

"No bare skin," he complained.

Rory reached for her thin cotton shirt and pulled it over her head to reveal her strapless bikini top. Allowing him a moment to look, she pushed his shirt off his shoulder and gently maneuvered the shirt down his hurt arm, dropping kisses on the still-bruised skin. "You sure you can do this?" she murmured, her mouth against his biceps.

"My arm hurts, not the rest of me. Well, another part of me is aching, too, but in the best way possible." He tugged at the edge of her tangerine bikini top, looking impatient. "Take this off. Take it all off."

Rory reached behind her with one hand and undid the snap. The top fell forward and Mac pulled the fabric down, and she allowed it to drop to the ground as she watched him peruse her. His fingers drifted over her already puckered nipples and she sucked in a breath when he dropped his head so that his lips closed over her in a deep, seductive kiss.

She could feel her nipple on the roof of his mouth and shuddered as his tongue swept over her, once, twice. She was supposed to be making him crazy, she thought, yet he was the one pushing her. Dropping her head back, she threaded one hand into his hair to hold him in place as he put one knee on the daybed next to him to align his mouth perfectly with her chest. Moving away, he dropped a hot kiss onto her sternum before turning his mouth to the neglected nipple on her other breast. Rory pulled the knot of her sarong apart and pushed her bikini bottoms down her hips, forgetting about them as they fell to the floor.

She felt Mac stiffen as he looked down. What would he see? A flat stomach with a faded appendix scar, a narrow landing strip and short legs? She'd far prefer he touch rather than look.

"Mac," she groaned. God, she'd waited ten long years for him to touch her there yet he kept his forehead between her breasts, huffing like a freight train.

"Getting there," Mac muttered. "God, you're gorgeous. I could look at you forever."

"I'd prefer you use your hands and mouth," Rory told him, pushing his hand between her legs. She couldn't wait, she was burning with need.

Mac's hard, knowing fingers found her bud and had her arching her back. She felt the insistent throbbing that told her she was so very close to losing it. It took one sliding finger and she was exploding, bucking, sobbing and laughing, tumbling along that fantastically ferocious wave of pure, cosmic pleasure.

When her pleasure tapered off, leaving her lady parts still tingling, she realized she was half sitting on Mac's thighs, his mouth was on her breast and his erection was tenting his pants. Climbing off him, she helped him push his shorts over his hips so he was free to her touch. She wrapped her hands around him and smiled at his shudder and desperate groan.

He pulled her hands away one at a time and held her wrists behind her back with one hand. "I'm so close. If you squeeze me once…"

Rory shrugged. "Not a problem." Actually, she'd love to see him lose control.

"Hell, no," Mac said, dropping his lips to pull the skin beneath her ear. "I want to be inside you. I need to be inside you."

"Okay," Rory told him, her hand drifting across his eight-pack. "God, you have the most amazing body."

His erection jumped at her words and his mouth slammed onto hers. Pulling her down to the daybed, he lay on his back and Rory flung a leg over him, immediately settling her happy spot on his hard shaft. She was going to come again. Woo-hoo, lucky her.

"Condom," she gasped, needing him to slide on home.

Mac lifted his hips and pushed his hand under the cushion next to his thigh. He cursed when he came up empty.

"Try the other side," he huffed, and Rory leaned sideways to pat the space under the cushion. Feeling the cool foil packets, she pulled a condom loose, and instead of one, she held a four-pack in her hand. She looked down and then lifted an eyebrow in Mac's direction.

"Confident, aren't you?" she asked.

"Prepared. I have them stashed all over the house," Mac admitted, grabbing a condom and lifting the packet to his teeth to open it. He cursed at his clumsiness and Rory took it from him.

"So, when did you put the packet of condoms there, McCaskill?" she asked as she rolled the latex down his shaft.

Mac grinned. "Ten minutes after we arrived. Though, to be fair, I've had this fantasy about making love to you since the day we met."

Rory jerked at his words. Which time? Years ago or weeks ago? Then the questions disappeared as Mac pushed into her, stretching and filling and completing her.

She rose and fell, easily matching his rhythm. He filled her cold and empty spaces, she thought, as he speared up into her. She glanced down and saw him watching her, his eyes deep and dark and determined. "Come for me, baby."

Not able to refuse him, Rory shattered around him, and from a place far away she felt his last thrust, felt him pulse against her as her followed her over the cliff.

Rory collapsed against his chest. His good arm wrapped around her as she turned her face into his neck.

She inhaled the scents of the fragrant, perfumed air and sex, felt his thumping heart beneath hers, the rough texture of his chest hair beneath her cheek.

This place, here in his embrace, was the place she felt safest. Happiest. The place she most wanted to be.

Dammit.

Mac had always liked hurricanes. The power extreme weather contained was thrilling. He'd experienced two storms on the island before and neither had done much damage. He expected this storm would be more of the same.

He stood on the veranda and watched the sky darken. The wind was picking up and he mentally took inventory of his hurricane supplies. They had enough water and food for three days, adequate lighting for when the power went off and he had, and knew how to use, his extensive first-aid kit. They were ready for the storm; the boards were up courtesy of a couple of young guys from the village who'd made short work of the task. They'd also moved the outside furniture into the store rooms next to the garage and generally made themselves useful. They would be fine and if it was just him, he'd jump into bed with a good book and let the storm do its thing, but Rory was acting like it was the hour before the world ended. He turned his head and saw that she sat where he'd left her, in the corner of the couch, her arms clutching a pillow in a death grip, her eyes wide and scared.

"Relax, we'll be fine," he told her.

"We're on the edge of a beach with a hurricane approaching...which means big waves and big wind. I think I've got a right to panic," Rory retorted. "Will you please come inside?"

Mac lifted his face to the sky, enjoying the rain-tinged wind on his face. "I built this house to be, as much as possible, hurricane-proof."

"Don't you have a shelter?"

"That's for tornadoes, not hurricanes." Mac told her, walking back into the room. He lifted a bottle of wine and aimed the opening at her glass. "Have some wine, try to relax."

"Huh." Rory gulped from her glass and her anxious eyes darted to the rapidly darkening sky.

He needed to distract her or else she'd soon be a basket case. The wind howled and the lights flickered. Rory pushed herself farther into the corner of the couch. He sat down next to her, put his feet up onto the coffee table and placed his hand on her thigh beneath the edge of her shorts. More sex would be a great distraction, he thought, but Rory's white face and tense body suggested she might kick him if he proposed that. Besides, they'd done it three times since noon. She needed some time to recover.

And that meant talking. Dammit. Not his best talent. Maybe he'd get lucky and she'd start.

He was given a temporary reprieve when his cell phone buzzed. Picking it up, he saw a message from Quinn, checking whether they were okay, and he quickly replied. He picked up Rory's cell phone and tossed it into her lap. "I suggest you let your friends and family know there is a hurricane and you are safe. They tend to freak if you don't. And the cell towers sometimes go down during storms so we might lose our signal."

Rory nodded quickly and her fingers flew across the keypad. Within thirty seconds her phone buzzed and she was smiling at the message on the screen. "It's Shay, suggesting I climb under a bed with a bottle of vodka."

Shay…now there was a subject they'd been avoiding. He sipped his wine and rested his head on the back of the couch. "Did you take flak because we almost kissed?"

Rory tapped her finger against her glass. "You have no idea. She refused to talk to me for six months and it took us a while to find our groove again."

Mac frowned. "Look, I admit I wasn't exactly Prince Charming that night, I messed up in numerous ways but, God, we were young, and nothing happened!" Mac waited a beat. "Even if that open-mic incident hadn't happened, she knew we were on our way out—"

"She'd mentioned she thought she was approaching her expiry date," Rory interjected, her voice dry.

Mac winced. "Look, I can understand her thinking I'm a douche, but why couldn't she forgive you?"

Rory's eyes flicked to his face and went back to studying her wine. "The reason why Shay has such massive insecurities and the reason why I am not good at relationships is the same."

Wait. Why would she think that she wasn't good at relationships? She was open and friendly and funny and smart, who wouldn't want to be in a relationship with her? Well, he wouldn't…but he didn't want to be in a relationship with anyone so he didn't count. She had to be better at relationships than he was; then again, pretty much ninety percent of the world's population was. "How do you know that you are bad at relationships?"

Rory's laugh was brittle. She looked him in the eye and tried, unsuccessfully, to smile. "I can date, I can flirt, I can do light and fluffy, but I suck at commitment. I drive men crazy."

He couldn't imagine it. Here he was, the King of Easily Bored, and he was as entranced with Rory as he'd been from the beginning. "How?"

Rory waved his question away. "When I think things are getting hot or heavy or too much to deal with—when I get scared—I take the easy way out and I run. I just disappear."

There was a message in her statement and he was smart enough to hear it. When she thought their time was over she'd make like Casper and fade away. Good to know, he thought cynically. Thinking back, he remembered what she'd said earlier. "You said there was a reason why you and Shay act like you do. Will you tell me what it is?"

He was as surprised as she looked at his question. He hadn't intended to ask that. Did he really want to know the answer? It seemed he did, he reluctantly admitted. Rory was, when she let go, naturally warm and giving, and he wondered why she felt the need to protect herself.

"Well, that's a hell of a subject to discuss during a hurricane," Rory replied, tucking her feet under her. "Actually, it's a hell of a subject at any time."

"We can talk about something else, if you prefer." Mac backtracked to give her, and him, an out of the conversation. He stood and walked over to the open balcony doors, holding his flashlight in his hand. Unable to resist the power of the approaching storm, he stepped outside and let the rapidly increasing wind slam into him. He leaned forward, surprised that the wind could hold him upright as the rain smacked his face like icy bullets.

Hello, Hurricane Des, Mac thought as he stepped back into the house and closed and bolted the doors behind him. The lights flickered and he checked that the hurricane lamp and matches were on the coffee table. They would probably lose power sooner rather than later. Mac resumed his seat, linked his hands across his stomach and looked at Rory. "Want to talk about something else?"

Rory shrugged and pulled the tassels of the pillow through nervous fingers. He knew it wasn't only the crazy wind slamming into the house that made her nervous. The power dropped, surged and died.

"Perfect," Rory muttered.

Within a minute Mac had the hurricane lamps casting a gentle glow across the room and smiled at Rory's relieved sigh. "My parents are hugely dysfunctional..."

"Aren't they all?"

Rory cocked an eyebrow at his interruption but he gestured for her to continue. "When I was thirteen, I was in the attic looking for an old report card—I wanted to show Shay that I was better at math than she was." Rory tipped her head. "Strange that I remember that... Anyway, I was digging in an old trunk when I found photographs of my father with a series of attractive women." Rory pushed her hair back with one hand. Her eyes looked bleak. "It didn't take me long to realize those photos were the reason why my dad moved out of the house for months at a time."

Mac winced.

"He betrayed my mother with so many women," Rory continued. "I've always felt—and I know Shay does too—that he betrayed us, his family. He cheated on my mom and he cheated us of his time and his love, of being home when we needed him. He always put these other women before us, before me. Yet my mother took him back, still takes him back."

Okay, now a lot of Shay's crazy behavior made sense. "Hell, baby."

"He said one thing but his actions taught me the opposite."

"What do you mean?"

Rory shrugged. "He'd tell me that he was going on a work trip but a friend would tell me that she saw him at the mall with another woman. Or he'd say that he was going hunting or fishing but he never shot a damn thing. Or ever caught a fish.

"And my mother's misery was a pretty big clue that he was a-huntin' and a-fishin' for something outside the animal kingdom."

Underneath the bitterness he heard sadness and the echo of a little girl who'd lost her innocence at far too young an age.

"I thought the world of him, loved him dearly and a part of me still does. But the grown-up me doesn't like him much and, after a lifetime of lies, I can't believe a word he says. I question everything he does. As a result, trust is a difficult concept for me and has always been in short supply." Rory dredged up a smile.

Mac swallowed his rage and stopped himself from voicing his opinion about her father. Telling Rory that he thought her father was a waste of skin wouldn't make her feel better. Rory was bright and loving and giving and her father's selfishness had caused her to shrink in on herself, to limit herself to standing on the outside of love and life, looking in. She deserved to be loved and cherished and protected—by someone, not by Mac but by someone who would make her happy.

God, he wanted to thump the man for ripping that away from her.

"Tell me about your childhood, Mac," Rory softly asked, dropping her head to rest it against the back of the couch. "Dear God, that wind sounds like a banshee on crack."

"Ignore it. We're safe," Mac told her, slipping his hand between her knees. He never spoke about his blue-collar upbringing in that industrial, cold town at the back end of the world. It was firmly in his past.

But there was something about sitting in the semidark with Rory, safe from the wind and rain, that made him want to open up. "Low income, young, uneducated single mother. She had few of her own resources, either financial or emotional. She relied on a steady stream of men to provide both."

He waited to see disgust on Rory's face or, worse, pity. There was neither, she just looked at him and waited. Her lack of reaction gave him the courage to continue. "I was encouraged *not* to go to school, *not* to go to practice, not to aim for anything higher than a dead-end job at the canning factory or on one of the fishing boats. When I achieved anything, I was punished. And badly."

Rory sat up, and in the faint glow of the lamp, he could see her horrified expression. "What?"

Mac shrugged. "Crabs in a bucket."

"What are you talking about?" Rory demanded.

"You put a bunch of crabs in a bucket, one will try to climb out. The other crabs won't let that happen. They pull at the crab who's trying to escape until he falls back down. My mother was the perfect example of crab mentality. She refused to allow me to achieve anything more than what she achieved, which was pretty much nothing."

"How did you escape?"

"Stubbornness and orneriness…and my skill with a stick. I waited her out and as soon as I finished school I left. I simply refused to live her life. There was only one person in life I could rely on and that was myself. I was the only one who could make my dreams come true..."

"And you did."

Mac looked at her. Yeah, he had. The wind emitted a high, sustained shriek and Rory grabbed his hand and squeezed. He couldn't blame her; it sounded like a woman screaming for her life, and the house responded with creaks and groans.

Through the screaming wind he heard the thump of something large and he looked into the impenetrable darkness to see what had landed on the veranda. A tree branch? A plastic chair his guys had left behind? Maybe it wasn't such a good idea to stay in the living room next to the floor-to-ceiling windows, even though they were covered with boards. He stood up and hauled Rory to her feet.

It was also the perfect time to end this conversation... Looking back changed nothing and there was nothing there he wanted to remember.

"Where are we going?" she asked as he picked up the lamp.

"Bathroom."

"Why?"

"It's enclosed and probably the safest place to wait out the storm," Mac said, pulling her down the passage.

"Are we in danger?" Rory squeaked, gripping his uninjured biceps with both hands as they walked into the solidly dark house.

"No." At least, he didn't think so, but while he was prepared to take his chances with the storm, he wasn't prepared to risk Rory. Mac pulled a heavy comforter from the top shelf in the walk-in closet and handed Rory the pillows from the bed. In the bathroom, Rory helped him put a makeshift bed between the bathtub and the sink. He sat with his back to the tiled wall and Rory lay down, her head on his thigh. Touching her hair, he listened to the sounds of the storm.

Rory yawned and tipped her head back to look at him. "I'm so tired."

Mac touched her cheek with the tips of his fingers. "Go to sleep…if you can."

"Can I put my head on your shoulder?" Rory asked. "At least then, if the roof blows off, I'll have you to hold on to."

"The roof isn't going to lift, oh, dramatic one." But he shifted down, placed a pillow beneath his head and wrapped his good arm around her slim back when she placed her head on his shoulder. Her leg draped over his and her knee was achingly close to his happy place. It would be so easy, a touch here, a stroke there…

Mac kissed her forehead and pulled her closer to him. "Go to sleep, Rorks. You're safe with me."

"Tonight's conversation didn't seem that light and fluffy, Mac," Rory murmured in a sleepy voice.

It hadn't been, Mac admitted. They'd have to watch out for that. It was his last thought before exhaustion claimed him.

Eight

There was nothing like the aftermath of a hurricane to decimate a romantic atmosphere, Rory thought, standing on the debris-filled veranda and looking out toward the devastated cove. The sea had settled and broken tree branches covered the beach. A kayak had landed in the pool and there were broken chairs on the beach path. The fence surrounding the property was bent and buckled and the power lines sagged.

Mac had gone to town at first light to call someone about cleaning up the property and to check on how the small fishing village north of the cove had fared. Rory's cell phone wasn't working and she felt cut off from the world. Taking a sip from her bottle of water, she felt sweat roll down her back. It was barely 7:00 a.m. but it was very hot and horribly humid.

The scope of the damage was awful but Rory was glad

to have some time to herself, away from Mac. Yesterday had been a watershed day—the sex was explosively wonderful and the storm had scared her into opening up to Mac, and that frightened her more than the wind.

Why had she shared her past with him? She never did that! Had she been that seduced by their wonderful lovemaking? Was it the romantic atmosphere and him being all protective that prompted her to emotionally erupt? They'd agreed to keep it light but last night's conversation had been anything but! Deep and soulful conversations led to thoughts of permanence and commitment, and they'd agreed they weren't going there. She was an emotional scaredy-cat and he was incapable of commitment.

Mac, she reminded herself, didn't want a relationship anymore than she did. He'd taught himself to be his own champion and she admired the hell out of him. But he didn't need her. Anyone who could fight his way out of the enveloping negativity of Mac's childhood didn't need anyone. He'd learned to survive and then to flourish. He was emotionally self-sufficient, and a woman would never be more than an accessory and a convenience to him.

What did it matter, anyway? Rory gripped the plastic bottle so hard that it buckled in her hand, the water overflowing to trickle onto her wrist. Men always disappointed and love never lasted and the fairy tales the world fed women about happily-ever-afters were a load of hooey. No, she'd stay emotionally detached, and by doing that, she'd never feel hurt or as out of control as she had when she was a child.

Rory straightened her spine. Mac was a nice guy, a sexy guy, but he wasn't *her* guy. It would be sensible for her to remember that because if she didn't and she did something imbecilic, like fall in love with him, she was just asking for big, messy trouble.

Maybe she should stop sleeping with him…

But look at him, Rory thought, watching as Mac walked up the path from the beach. How was she supposed to resist? He was shirtless and wearing a ball cap and board shorts, his chest glistening with perspiration.

Rory leaned on the railing, and as if he sensed her watching him, he turned and looked up at her, pulling his sunglasses from his face. "Hey. You okay?"

"Fine," Rory replied. "Was the village damaged?"

"Not too bad. Trees, some missing tiles…it could've been worse. Is the power back on?"

Rory shook her head. "No. And it's so damn hot. I'm desperate for a shower."

Mac gestured to the sea behind him. "Big bathtub on our doorstep. Come on down, we'll have a swim."

Rory pulled her sticky shirt off her body. "Good idea. Do you want some water?"

Mac nodded. "And a couple of energy bars. I'm starving."

"Five minutes," Rory replied. Instead of heading inside she just stared down at him, unable to get her feet to move.

It would be so easy to love him, she thought. She was already halfway there.

Yeah, but she couldn't trust him. And what was love without trust? An empty shell that would shatter at the first knock.

Don't be stupid, Rory, she thought as she turned away. *Just don't.*

By sundown there was still no power. They gathered up a beach blanket, a lamp and a makeshift supper and headed for the beach. In the golden rays of the sunset, they cleared sticks and leaves from a patch of sand, spread out the blanket and looked at the docile sea and the sky free of all but a few small clouds.

"If it wasn't for the mess you'd think nothing had happened," Mac said, echoing her thoughts. It was scary how often he did that. Scary and a little nice.

"Fickle nature," Rory agreed, pulling her tank top over her head and dropping the shirt to the sand. She shimmied out of her shorts and stood in her plain black bikini, desperate to feel the water against her skin. She turned to Mac and found him looking at her with a strange expression on his face. "Are you okay?"

"Yeah...just thinking how gorgeous you look."

Rory flushed and lifted her hand in dismissal. "I'm already sleeping with you, McCaskill, there's no need to go overboard."

Rory turned away and walked toward the sea, foolishly hurt by his compliment. She wasn't stupid. She'd seen the pictures of him in the papers, normally accompanied by a skinny, long-legged giraffe who could grace any catwalk anywhere in the world. Shay had been his first supermodel-gorgeous girlfriend, and every girlfriend since had been slinky and sexy. Tall, dammit.

Mac's hand on her shoulder spun her around. She swallowed when she saw the irritation in his eyes. "Don't do that!"

She widened her eyes to look innocent. "Do what?"

"Dismiss me. I never say things I don't mean and if I say you look gorgeous then I mean to say that you look freakin' amazing and I can't wait to get my hands on you."

Warmth blossomed in her stomach at his backhanded compliment. Freaking amazing? Did he really think so?

"I see doubt on your face again." Mac cradled her cheek in his hand. "Why?"

Oh, jeez, he would think she was stupidly insecure and horribly lacking in confidence. Which she was, but she didn't want him to *know* that. "Uh—"

"Why, Rory?"

Rory kicked her bare foot into the sand. "Um, maybe because all the girls you normally...uh, date...are about a hundred feet tall and stacked and I'm a munchkin with a flat chest and a complex."

Mac stared at her before releasing a long, rolling laugh. Rory narrowed her eyes at him while he tried to control himself, wiping at the tears in his eyes.

"Glad I amuse you," she said, her tone frosty.

"Oh, you really do." Mac took her hand and pulled her to the sea. Thoroughly irritated with him she yanked her hand from his and dived into an oncoming wave. She started to swim, only to be jerked back by a hand on her ankle. She rolled onto her back and scowled as she tried to pull her ankle from Mac's grip.

"Let me go." She tried, unsuccessfully, to kick him.

"Pipe down...*shrimp*."

Oh, that was fighting talk. She swiped her arm down and sprayed a stream of water into his face. Mac dropped her ankle and she launched herself at him, throwing a punch at his uninjured arm. "You jerk!"

Mac easily captured both her wrists in one hand and held them behind her back. Then he inched up two fingers to pull the strings that held her bikini top closed. He let her wrists go so he could pull the triangles over her head and toss the top onto the sand behind them before stepping back to look down at her breasts.

Moving them back into the shallows until they were standing in ankle deep water Mac placed his hands on her hips, keeping an arm's length between them. His gaze traveled from the tips of her head to where her feet disappeared into the water. Rory bit her lip and looked at the beach behind him, but Mac's fingers on her chin brought her eyes back to his face.

"I refuse to let you spend one more second thinking you are second-rate." Mac's voice was low and imbued with honesty. His fingers drifted down her neck, across her collarbone and down the swell of her breast. His thumb rubbed across her nipple and it puckered under his touch. "Yeah, you're small but perfect. So responsive, so sweet."

He bent his head and sucked her nipple into his mouth, causing her to whimper and arch her back. He licked and nibbled and then moved on to the other breast before sinking to his knees, his hands on her hips. He looked up at her, the gold and oranges of the sunset in his hair and on his face. "You are small but perfect."

He repeated the words, his thumbs tunneling under the sides of her bikini bottoms. "I lose myself in your eyes, drown in your laugh and feel at peace in your arms." His thumb skimmed over her sex and she whimpered when he touched her sweet spot. "I find myself when I'm deep inside you."

"Mac." She whimpered, needing him to...to...do something. More. Touch her, taste her. Complete her.

Rory thought she heard Mac say something like, "You are the fulfillment of every fantasy I've ever had," but all her attention was focused on his fingers, now deep inside her. He could've been proposing and she wouldn't have cared as her bikini bottoms dropped to the sand and his hot, hot mouth enveloped her.

He licked and she screamed. He repeated the motion and her knees buckled. He sucked and she fell apart, her orgasm hot and spectacular. When she sank to her knees in front of him, he tipped her flushed face upward and dropped a hot, openmouthed kiss on her lips. "As I said, you are utterly perfect. Let's swim naked," he suggested, picking up her bikini bottoms and throwing them in the same direction as her top.

Impossible man, Rory thought when her brain cells started firing again. Sexy, crazy, *impossible* man.

In the same restaurant they'd visited two weeks ago—a pink-and-yellow sunset tonight and no hurricane on the way—Mac tucked his credit card back into his wallet and gave Rory a crooked grin. "Eaten enough?"

Rory leaned back and patted her stomach. "Sorry, I'm a real girl who eats real food." *Not like those models you normally date*, she silently added.

"You ate fish stew, two empanadas and you still had pumpkin pudding." Mac shook his head. "I know every slim inch of you and I have no idea where all that food goes."

Rory picked up her drink, put the vividly green straw between her lips and sucked up some piña colada. Instead of responding, she fluttered her eyebrows at Mac, who smiled. God, she loved it when he smiled. It made her heart smile every single time.

Mac stood up and held out his hand. Rory put her hand in his and allowed him to pull her up from her chair. "Oof. You weigh a ton."

Rory slapped his shoulder. "Jerk."

"Well, you're going to work that food off."

Oh, she couldn't wait. Making love with Mac was fun, fantastic, toe-curling and, yes, it was athletic. Win win.

"What I have in mind is a bit more adventurous... Are you game?"

"Maybe," Rory carefully replied, doubt in her voice. "If it's not too kinky or too weird..."

His laughter, spontaneous and deep, rumbled across her skin and she shivered. Mac had a great laugh and, like smiling, he definitely didn't do enough of it.

"It's a surprise. A surprise that you have to work for but I promise it will be amazing." Mac brushed his lips across the top of her head. Then his arm snaked around her waist and he kissed her properly, crazily, tongues going wild. She melted against him, into him, swept up in her desire for him.

As usual, Mac was the first to pull back. He jerked back, looked down the beach and back to her mouth.

"What?" Rory pushed her hair off her face.

"Deciding whether to scrap my plans and hurry you home." Rory huffed her frustration when he stepped back and distanced himself from her. "Nope, I really want you to see this."

Mac glanced at the sunset, then at his watch and Rory noticed it was nearly dark. "Okay, it's dark enough, let's go."

"Go where?" Rory asked as he took her hand and led her down the restaurant steps toward the beach. She kicked off her sandals and sighed when her feet dipped into the still-warm sand. She picked up her shoes, slid her hand back into Mac's and followed his leisurely pace down the beach. What was he up to? And really, did it matter? It was a stunning summer's evening on the island, the air was perfumed and Mac was holding her hand, occasionally looking at her with the promise of passion in his eyes...

They walked in silence for another five minutes and then Mac angled right, walking toward the ocean until they saw a kayak and a young, hot surfer guy holding life jackets over his arm. Mac called a greeting and Surfer Boy grinned. Rory felt like a spare wheel when he bounded over the sand to pump Mac's hand, ask him how his arm was, to thank him for some tickets Mac had procured for him. Surfer Boy was about to launch into a play-by-play description when Mac interrupted him. "Marty, this is Rory. Are we all set to go?"

Marty realized he'd all but ignored her and blushed. "Sorry, hi, I didn't mean to be rude." He smiled ruefully. "I'm hockey obsessed, as you can tell. My folks have a place here so I spend my time between Vancouver and the island and I'm a huge Mavericks fan."

Rory's lips twitched in amusement. "Hi." She looked past him to the kayak at the water's edge before lifting an eyebrow in Mac's direction. "Are we're going paddling? At night?"

Mac grinned. "Yep."

"Sorry to point out the obvious, but we're not going to see much because it's dark," Rory responded. "And you definitely can't paddle with that arm."

Mac scowled. "I know and I hate it. But that's why you're paddling and I'm riding shotgun."

Rory looked at him, tall and built and strong. "Uh, Mac? I'm half your size."

"It's as flat as a mirror and it's not far. You'll be fine."

"Okay...but why?"

Mac took her hand, lifted it to his mouth and placed a hot, openedmouthed kiss on her knuckles. It was an old-fashioned, sexy gesture and Rory felt her womb quiver. "Trust me," he murmured, his eyes as deep a blue and as mysterious as the ocean beyond them. "It'll be worth it."

It was an intense moment, and Rory heard that sensible voice in her head. *Whatever is between us is about sex, not romance. Don't fall for it. Don't expect hearts and flowers along with the heat. Disappointment always follows expectations.*

She wouldn't be seduced by the island and the sunset and the heat in Mac's eyes. She would take this minute by minute, experience by experience, and she was not going to ruin it by letting her mind be seduced along with her body.

"Earth to Rory…?"

Rory saw Mac looking at her quizzically, waiting for a reply. What had he said?

"There are one or two other things I could think of that I'd rather do in the dark—" she gave Mac a mischievous look "—but what the hell. Okay."

The corners of Mac's lips kicked up and a laugh rumbled in the back of his throat.

"Funny girl," he replied in his coated-with-sin voice as Marty pretended to ignore their banter. Dropping her hand, Mac took a step back and gestured to Marty. "Right. You'll be here when we get back?"

"I'll be here," Marty promised. "You need life jackets but put on bug repellent first. And lots of it."

Marty pulled out a container from his back pocket and handed it to Rory. "If you don't slap it on everywhere, the mosquitoes will carry you away."

Rory wrinkled her nose. Where on earth were they

going? Knowing she would just have to wait and see, she rubbed the cream on her face, over her arms and down her legs. Then she pulled on a life jacket, tightened the clasps and went over to the double kayak.

She kicked off her shoes and pushed the kayak into the water before hopping into the seat. While she waited for Mac to get ready, she pulled her hair back from her face and secured it into a ponytail with the band she'd found in the back pocket of her cotton shorts. The stars were magnificent, she thought, a trillion fairy lights starting at the horizon and continuing ad infinitum.

She trailed her hand through the warm water, now impatient to get wherever they were going. Mac took the front seat after helping Marty push the kayak into deeper water, still looking irritated that he wasn't paddling—the man hated relinquishing control. Within a couple of strokes Rory found her rhythm and she followed Mac's directions across the small fisherman's harbor to what seemed to be an entrance to a coastal reserve. Mac unerringly directed her toward a channel between huge mangrove trees. Only the light of his strong flashlight penetrated the darkness. It really was an easy paddle despite Mac's bulk. She listened to the sounds coming from deep within the forest, birds and frogs, she presumed, as she navigated the low-hanging branches of a tree.

"Not far now." Mac's deep voice drifted past her ear as they leaned backward to skim under another branch. "Are you okay?"

"Sure."

"Not scared?"

"Please." She snorted her disdain. "I survived a life-threatening hurricane. Though I wouldn't mind if I was the one lounging around while you did the work."

"I wish I was. I feel like I've surrendered my man card," Mac grumbled, but she heard the grin in his voice.

"I'll reinstate it later," Rory replied in her sultriest voice.

Mac laughed and she cursed as the bow of her kayak bounced off another branch. "Dammit. How far do we have left?"

"We're almost there," Mac replied as she moved backward and around the branch with the aid of the flashlight Mac held. Rory paddled for a minute more and then the channel opened and they entered a small bay. Mac told her to head for the middle of the bay.

When she stopped, she looked at the shadows of the mangrove forest that surrounded them. The moon hung heavy in the sky and the air caressed her skin. Gorgeous.

"Look at your oar, babe," Mac softly told her. Rory glanced down and gasped with delight. Every paddle stroke left a starburst in the water, a bright streak of bioluminescence that was breathtakingly beautiful.

"Oh, my God," Rory said, pulling her hand through the water, hoping to catch a star. "That's amazing. What is it?"

"Dinoflagellates," Mac replied. "Prehistoric one-celled organisms, half animal, half plant. When they are disturbed, they respond by glowing like fireflies."

"They are marvelous. So incredibly beautiful."

"Worth the effort?" Mac asked, lazily turning around to look at her.

Rory leaned forward to rest her temple on his shoulder. "So worth it. Thank you." A fish approached the kayak and darted underneath, leaving a blue streak to mark his route.

Mac reached for her hand. Their fingers linked but

cupped, they lowered them into the water. When they lifted them out it looked like they held sparkling glitter. The water dropped back into the lagoon, and when the initial glow subsided, the glitter still danced in the water.

"The mangroves feed the organisms, releasing vitamin B12 into the water. This, with sunlight, keeps them alive," Mac told her.

Her heart thumped erratically, her fingers, in his, trembled. With want. And need. With the sheer delight of being utterly alone with him in this bay, playing in Mother Nature's jewelry box. She wanted more experiences like this with Mac. She wanted to experience the big and small of life with him. The big, like seeing the bay sparkle, the small, like sharing a Sunday-morning cup of coffee.

She wanted more than she should. She wanted it all.

Rory dipped her paddle into the water and looked at the sparkling outline…spectacular. She knew Mac was watching her profile, his gaze all coiled grace and ferocious intent.

This was beautiful. He was beautiful, too, Rory thought. But like the bioluminescent streaks, he was fleeting.

She could enjoy him, marvel over him, admire him, but he was so very, very temporary.

Nine

There was too much resistance in his arm, Rory thought, frowning. On day twenty-one of physio, a month after his injury she stood behind Mac, gently massaging his bicep and trying to figure out why he was having a buildup of lactic acid in his muscle. The resistance exercises she'd given him shouldn't have made this much of an impact. She'd been very careful to keep the exercises low-key, making sure the muscle wasn't stressed more than it needed to be.

Unless…she stiffened as a thought slapped her. Hell, no, he couldn't be that stupid, could he?

Rory held his arm, her hand perfectly still as she turned that thought over in her mind. He wouldn't be sneaky enough to go behind her back and push himself, would he?

Oh, yeah, he would.

"Problem?" Mac tipped his head back and she looked into those gorgeous, inky eyes. Look at him, all innocent. Rory whipped around the bed and stood next to him, her hands gripping her hips and her mouth tight with anger.

"Did you really think I wouldn't notice?" she demanded, making an effort to keep her anger in control.

Mac sat up slowly, and she saw he was deciding whether to bluff his way out of the situation. It would be interesting to see which way he swung, Rory thought. Would he be a grown-up and come clean, or would he act like he had no idea what she was talking about?

"I knew that I could push a little harder," Mac replied in a cool, even tone.

Points to him that he didn't try to duck the subject. Or lie.

"Did you get a physiotherapy degree in the last month or so, smarty-pants?"

Mac ignored her sarcasm. "I know my body, Rory. I know what I can handle."

"And I have a master's degree in physiotherapy specializing in sports injuries, you moron! I know what can go wrong if you push too hard too fast!" Rory yelled, deeply angry. "Are you so arrogant you think you know better than I do? That my degrees mean nothing because you know your body?"

"I utterly respect what you do," Mac calmly stated, linking his hands on his stomach, "but you don't seem to understand that this body is my tool, my machine. I know it inside out and I need you to trust me to know how far I can push myself."

"You *need* to *trust* me to know what's best for you in this situation," Rory shouted. "This is a career-threatening injury, Mac!"

"I know that!" Mac raised his voice as well, swinging his legs over the edge of the bed. "Do you not think I don't lie awake every night wondering if I'm going to regain full movement, whether I'll be able to compete again? The scenarios run over and over in my head, but I've got to keep moving forward. That means working it."

"That means resting it," Rory retorted. "You're pushing too hard."

"You're not pushing me enough!" Mac yelled as he stood up. "I can do this, Rory."

Rory looked at him and shook her head. *Look at him, all muscle and hardheadedness*, she thought. Beautiful but so incredibly flawed. He had to go full tilt, had to push the envelope. But he refused to accept that this envelope was made of tissue paper and could rip at a moment's notice.

Would rip at a moment's notice.

She couldn't stop him, she realized. He'd ignore her advice and go his own way.

Rory lifted her hands, palms out. "I can't talk to you right now."

"Rorks—"

"I'm not discussing this right now." Rory walked toward the door.

Mac's arm shot out to block her way. When she tried to duck underneath it, he wrapped his arm around her waist and held her, far too easily, against his chest. "No, you're not just walking out. We're going to finish this argument. We're adults. That's what adults do."

"Let me go, Mac." Rory pushed against his arm. She struggled against him, desperate to get away.

"God, you smell so good." Mac dropped his mouth to her shoulder and nuzzled her. His teeth scraped over her skin and Rory shuddered, feeling heat pool low in her abdomen. She shouldn't be doing this, she thought. She should be walking away, but Mac's hand cupping her breast, his thumb gliding over her nipple, shoved that thought away.

Stupid, stupid, stupid, she thought as she arched her back and pushed her breast into his palm. Mac pulled her nipple through the cotton fabric as he pushed the straps of her shirt and bra down her shoulder with his teeth. His breath was warm on her skin and she reached back to place her hand on the hair-roughened skin of his thigh, just below the edge of his shorts. Hard muscle tensed beneath her hand and he groaned as he pushed his erection into her lower back.

Ooh, nice. Rory twisted her head up and back, and Mac met her lips with his, his tongue invading her mouth to tangle lazily with hers. Damn, he kissed like a dream. His kisses could charm birds from trees, move mountains, persuade a nun to drop her habit...

Persuade. The word lodged in her head and she couldn't jog it loose. She tensed in his arms as she pulled her head away from his. Persuade. Coax. Cajole.

Seduce.

Rory closed her eyes and slumped against him. God, she was such a sap, so damn stupid. Mac was distracting her from the argument, hoping she'd forget he'd gone behind her back. He used her attraction to him against her, thinking that if he gave her a good time, she'd forgive him for being a colossal jerk!

She pushed his arm and stumbled away from him, shoving her hair from her face with both hands. God, she finally understood how being in a man's arms could make you go against your principles.

This is how it would be with him; she'd object, he'd seduce her into changing her mind. I get it, Mom, I do. But unlike you, I'm going to listen to my head and not my hormones.

Rory locked her knees to keep herself upright and took a deep breath, looking for control. She pulled down the hem of her T-shirt, wishing she were in her tunic and track pants, her uniform. She'd feel far more in control, professional.

"Did you really think I'd fall for your little let's-seduce-her-to-get-me-out-of-trouble routine? I'm not that shallow or that stupid. And you're not that good." Rory slapped her fists on her hips, ignoring the flash of angry surprise she saw in his eyes. "You went behind my back to exercise your arm. That was devious and manipulative. I don't like dishonesty, Mac, in any form. Because of that and because you obviously don't trust me, I think it's best that I leave."

She could see from the expression on his face that he thought she was overreacting. Maybe she was, but he'd given her the perfect excuse to run. To get out of this quicksand relationship before she was in over her head and unable to leave.

"Our contract will become null and void," Mac said, his voice devoid of anger or any emotion at all.

"I don't care." Rory told him. She wanted her clinic, but not at the cost of living in quicksand. "I'm going upstairs to pack. I'll be out of your hair in a couple of hours."

Mac swore and swiped his hand across his face. "God, Rory...running away is not the solution!"

"No, the solution is you being honest with me, listening to me, but you won't do that, so we have nothing to talk about," Rory snapped before walking out the door. Yes, she was scared, but she couldn't forget that he'd been dishonest with her. That was unacceptable.

She'd forgotten, she thought as she ran up the stairs to her room. *You can't trust him; you can't trust anyone. Disappointment comes easily to those who expect too much. Don't expect. Don't trust.*

She wouldn't do it again. She wouldn't be that much of a fool. Mac would do his own thing, always had and always would. It was how he operated. He'd charm with his sincerity, his kisses. He'd say all the right things but nothing would change, not really.

The best predictor of future behavior was past behavior, she reminded herself.

"I'm sorry I went behind your back, but I was trying to avoid an argument," Mac said from the doorway to her bedroom.

"Well, you got one anyway." Rory picked up a pile of T-shirts and carefully placed them in her suitcase, her back to him.

Mac leaned his shoulder into the door frame and felt like he'd been catapulted back ten years. The argument was different but her method of dealing with conflict was exactly the same as her sister's.

The difference between the two sisters was that he *wanted* to apologize to Rory, *needed* to sort this out. He didn't want her to run.

"I didn't touch you to distract you or to get out of trouble. You're right, I'm not that good."

Rory's narrowed eyes told him he had a way to go before he dug himself out of this hole. But that particular point was an argument for another day. He sighed. "And yes, I should've been upfront with you about doing the exercises. Though, in my defense, it's been a very long time since I asked anybody for permission to do anything."

Like, never.

"The lie bothers me, but it's the insult to my intelligence that I find truly offensive. That you would think I wouldn't realize…"

Ouch. Mac winced. "Yeah, I get that."

Rory sighed. "That being said, I can't take lies, Mac. Or evasions or half-truths."

Rory tossed a pair of flip-flops onto the pile of shirts in her suitcase. Mac cursed himself for being an idiot. She'd told him about her father and his deceit, and if he'd thought about it, he would've realized keeping secrets from her was a very bad idea.

He sucked at relationships and that was why he avoided them. So if he was avoiding relationships, why the hell was he determined to get her to stay?

"Don't go, Rorks. It isn't necessary. I need you. I can't do this without you."

He could, but he didn't want to. A subtle but stunning difference.

He needed her. For something other than her skill as a physio and the way she made him feel in bed. It was more than that…his need for her went beyond the surface of sex and skill.

Dammit, he hated the concept of needing anyone for anything. It made him feel…weak. He was a grown man who'd worked damn hard to make sure he never felt that way again.

Yet he was prepared to beg if he had to. "Please? Stay."

Rory turned slowly. "Will you listen to me?"

"I'll try," he conceded, and lifted his hand at her

frown. He wasn't about to make promises he couldn't keep, not even for her. "Will you try to accept that I know my body, know what I can do with it?"

"It's such a huge risk, Mac." Rory bit her lip. "You're playing Russian roulette and you might not win."

"But what if I do?" Mac replied. "If I do, I place myself and my team and my friends in a lot stronger position than we are currently in. It's a risk I'm willing to take."

"I'm not sure that I am." Rory sat down on the edge of the bed. "I have a professional responsibility to do what's best for you, and this isn't it."

"I'll sign any waiver you want me to," Mac quickly said.

Rory waved his offer away. "It's more than playing a game of covering the legalities, McCaskill. This is your career, your livelihood at stake."

"But it's *my* career, *my* livelihood." Mac held her eye. "My decision, Rory, and I'm asking you this *one time* to trust me. I can't live with negativity, I just can't."

"I'm not being negative, I'm being realistic," Rory retorted.

"Your perception of reality isn't mine." Mac sat down next to her on the bed and looked down at the cotton rug below his feet. "I really believe that part of the reason why I've been successful at what I try is that I don't entertain negativity. At all. If I can think it, I can do it, and I don't allow doubt. I need you to think the same."

"Look, I believe in the power of the mind, but everything I've ever been taught tells me you need time, you need to nurse this… It will be a miracle if you regain full strength in that arm."

He couldn't force her to believe, Mac thought in frustration. He wished he could. He blew air into his cheeks and rolled his head to release the tension in his neck.

"Okay. But if you can't be positive then I need you to be quiet." She started to blast him with a retort but he spoke over her. "I'm asking you—on bended knee if I must—to stay and to trust me when I tell you that I know my body. I won't push myself beyond what I can do." Here came the compromise. It sucked but he knew he didn't have a chance of her staying without it. "I won't do anything behind your back and I will listen, and respect, your opinion. I still need your help, if only to keep my crazy in check."

Rory stared at the floor, considering his words, and he knew she was wavering.

"You told me about your clinic, how much having your own place means to you. Don't give up on your dreams for your own practice because I'm a stubborn ass who doesn't know the meaning of the word *quit*."

Rory lifted her head to glare at him. "Low blow, McCaskill, using my dreams to get me to do what you want me to do."

He shrugged as Rory glared at him. He didn't want her to leave and he would use any method he could to keep her on this island with him. He was that desperate.

"So, you'll stay?"

"For now." She pointed a finger at him. "You dodged a bullet, Mac. Don't make me shoot you for real next time."

On the private jet hired for the trip home, Rory watched as Mac stashed his laptop back in a storage space above his head. Looking at him, no one would realize Mac had gone through major surgery nearly eight weeks ago. She listened to him bantering with the flight attendant and couldn't help wondering if Mac was doing exercises on the side, working that arm in ways she didn't approve of.

Maybe. Possibly. His recovery was remarkable.

Rory thought back to their argument, still a little angry that he'd deceived her. Maybe it wasn't deliberate, maybe he'd just been thoughtless, but it had hurt. On the positive side, the argument had opened her eyes. It had been her wake-up call. From that moment on she'd stopped entertaining, even on the smallest scale, thoughts about a happy-ever-after with Mac.

He'd never be a hundred percent honest with her and she could never fully trust him.

There couldn't be love or any type of a relationship without trust, and she had to be able to trust a man with everything she had. She couldn't trust Mac so she couldn't love him. She'd decided that…hadn't she?

Okay, it was a work in progress.

The flight attendant moved away and Mac stretched out his legs, looking past Rory out the window by her head. Below them the island of Puerto Rico was a verdant dot in an aqua sea and their magical time together was over.

Back to reality.

Mac sipped his beer and placed his ankle on his knee. "This plane can't fly fast enough. Kade sounded stressed."

"He didn't say why he wanted you back in the city?" Rory asked. Mac had announced at breakfast that Kade needed him in Vancouver and by mid-morning they were on their way home.

Mac shook his head. "No, and that worries me." A frown pulled his eyebrows together and his eyes were bleak. He looked down at his injured arm and traced the red scar that was a memento of his operation. "What if it doesn't heal correctly? What will I do?"

She'd never heard that note in his voice before—part fear, part insecurity. "You go to plan B, Mac. There is always another plan to be made, isn't there?"

Mac picked up her hand and wound his fingers in hers. "But hockey is what I do, who I am. It's my dream, my destiny, the reason I get up in the morning."

Is that what he really thought? She stared down at his long, lean body. It was a revelation to realize she wasn't the only one in this plane with demons. She felt relieved, and sad, at the thought. "Yeah, you're a great hockey player, supposedly one of the best."

Mac mock-glared at her and she smiled. "Okay, you *are* the best...does that satisfy your monstrous ego?"

Mac's lips twitched but he lowered his face so she couldn't look into his eyes. That was okay. It would be easier to say this without the distraction of his fabulous eyes. "You aren't what you do, Mac. You're so much more than that."

"I play hockey, Rory, that's it."

Rory shook her head in disagreement. "You are an amazing businessperson, someone who has many business interests besides hockey. You are a spokesperson for various charities, you play golf and you do triathlons in the off-season. Hockey is not who you are or all that you do."

"But it's what I love best and if I can't do it...if I can't save the team by keeping it out of Chenko's clutches, I will have failed. It would be the biggest failure of my life." Mac sat up, pulled his hand from hers and gripped the armrests. *"I don't like to fail."*

"None of us do, Mac. You're not alone in that," Rory responded, her voice tart. "So, the future of the Mavericks is all resting on your shoulders? Kade and Quinn have no part to play?"

"Yes—no… I'm the one who was injured," Mac protested.

"Here's a news flash, dude, hockey players get hurt. They sustain injuries all the time. Kade and Quinn, if I remember correctly, are both out of the game because of their injuries. You getting injured was just a matter of time. You couldn't keep ducking that bullet forever! It's part of the deal and you can't whine about it."

"I am not whining!" Mac protested, his eyes hot.

Rory smiled. "Okay, you weren't whining. But your thinking is flawed. You are not a superhero and you are not invincible and you are not solely responsible for the future of the Mavericks. If you can't play again, you will find something else to do, and I have no doubt you will be successful at it. You are not a crab and there is no bucket."

Mac stared at her for a long time and eventually the smallest smile touched his lips, his eyes. He released a long sigh and sent her a frustrated look. "You might be perfectly gorgeous but you are also a perfect pain in my ass. Especially when you're being wise."

The mischievous grin that followed his words suggested their heart-to-heart was over. "Want to join the Mile High Club?"

Rory grinned. "What's that word I'm looking for? No? *No* would be it."

Mac turned in his seat and nuzzled her neck with his lips. "Bet I could change your mind."

"You're good, but not that good, McCaskill." Rory

tipped her head to allow him to kiss that sensitive spot under her ear. "But you're welcome to try."

Note to self: Mac McCaskill cannot walk away from a challenge.

Kade met them at the airport and kissed Rory's cheek before pulling Mac into that handshake/half hug they did so well. "Sorry to pull you back from the island sooner than expected, but I need you here."

Mac frowned. "What's happened?"

Kade looked around, saw that they were garnering attention and shook his head. "Not here. We'll get into it in the car. No, Rory, don't worry about your luggage, I've sent an intern to pick it up."

Nice, Rory thought. She could get used to this first-class life. She pulled her large tote bag over her shoulder, saw fans lifting their cell phones in their direction and wished she'd worn something other than a pair of faded jeans and a loose cotton shirt for the journey home. They'd both showered on the jet but Mac had changed from his cargo shorts and flip-flops into a pistachio-green jacket, a gray T-shirt and khaki pants. He looked like the celebrity he was and she looked like a backpacker.

Sigh.

Rory stepped away, distancing herself as fans approached Mac and Kade for their autographs. After signing a few, Mac jerked his head in her direction and the three of them started walking—Rory at a half jog. In the VIP parking lot, Kade finally stopped at a low silver sports car and opened the back door for Rory to slide in. Mac took the passenger seat next to Kade and within minutes they were on the highway heading back to the city.

"Talk." Mac half twisted in his seat to look at Kade, pulling his designer cap off his head and running his hand through his hair. "What's up? Why did we have to get home so quickly?"

Rory heard the note of irritation in Mac's voice. Funny, she would've thought he'd be happy to be returning home, to be getting back into the swing of things. Yet she couldn't deny they'd been enjoying the solitude of Cap de Mar, the long, lazy sun- and sea-filled days punctured by long, intense bouts of making love.

"How's your arm?" Kade replied.

"Fine."

Rory rolled her eyes. "Fine" was boy-speak for "I don't want to talk about it."

"Improving," Rory chimed in half a beat behind him. She ignored Mac's narrowed eyes and continued to speak. "It's a lot better but he's definitely not ready to play yet. If that's what you are thinking, then you can forget about it."

"I could play," Mac said, his tone resolute.

"Do it and die," Rory stated in a flat, don't-test-me voice. Hadn't they had this argument? Had he heard anything she'd said?

Kade swore, ducked around a pickup truck and a station wagon and floored the accelerator. Rory prayed they would arrive at their destination—wherever that was—in one piece.

Where was her destination? Mavericks' headquarters? Mac's house? Her apartment? She and Mac had been living together, sleeping together, for a little more than a month. But now they were back to normal and island rules didn't necessarily apply to Vancouver. Right, this was another reason why she avoided relationships; she hated walking through the minefield of what was socially acceptable.

"Slow down, bud. Not everyone craves your need for speed."

Kade slowed down from the speed of light to pretty damn fast. She'd take it, Rory decided, and loosened her hold on her seat belt.

"Right," Mac continued. "What's going on?"

Rory saw Kade's broad shoulder lift and drop, taut with tension. "God, so much. First, the press, especially the sports writers, are speculating that your injury is a lot worse than we've been admitting to and they are looking for the angles. Speculation has been running wild."

Rory saw a muscle jump in Mac's cheek and she wondered what it was like to live life under a microscope.

"Widow Hasselback is also asking how you are and I heard she met with the suits from the Chenko Corporation last week. She told me they've increased their offer."

Mac closed his eyes and gripped the bridge of his nose with his thumb and forefinger. His curse bounced around the car. "That's not all," he said.

"I wish it was," Kade agreed. "Bayliss, our new investor, would like to watch a practice match before making a commitment."

Mac frowned. "That wouldn't normally be a problem. We often have people coming to watch practice, but so many of the team are still on vacation."

"Between us, Quinn and I have reached them all. They understand what's at stake and they'll be there," Kade reassured him.

Mac pulled out his cell phone and swiped his thumb across the screen. "Scheduled for when?"

Kade's worried glance bounced off hers in the rear-view mirror. "The day after tomorrow. At four." He looked apologetic. "According to Bayliss, it's a take-it-or-leave-it deal."

The day. After. Tomorrow.

Rory shook her head. "Well, that's all fine and good but you can count Mac out of that match."

"I'm playing," Mac said, and she immediately recognized his don't-argue-with-me voice.

Well, this time she would out-stubborn him. Rory pulled in a breath and reminded herself to keep calm. Yelling at Mac would achieve nothing. If she wanted to win this argument she would have to sound reasonable and in control. And professional. "I admit that your arm is vastly improved and that no one, looking at you, would suspect how serious your injury actually is. But it's not mended, and one wrong move or twist would undo all the healing you've done and possibly, probably, aggravate the injury further."

"I'm fine, babe."

"You are not fine!" Rory heard her voice rise and she deliberately toned it down. "You are not fully recovered and you certainly don't have all your strength back. I strongly suggest, as your physiotherapist, that you sit this one out."

Mac ignored her to nod at Kade. "I'll be there."

"Did you hear anything I said?" Rory demanded from the backseat, her face flushed with anger. "Do you know what you are risking? One slap shot, one bump and that's it, career over, McCaskill!"

"Stop being dramatic, Rory," Mac said in a hard, flat voice. "I keep telling you that I know what I am capable of and you've got to trust me. I know what I'm doing."

"I know that you are being a friggin' idiot!" Rory shouted.

Mac turned around and looked her in the eye. His direct gaze locked on hers and she immediately realized that nothing she could say or do would change his mind. He was playing, nearly two months after surgery. He was risking his career, all the work they'd done... Rory felt like he was tossing away all her hard work too.

"I took my vacation time to help you heal. I've spent hours working on you, working on getting you to where you are right now. You play and you've wasted my time and your money," Rory said, her voice rising along with her anger.

"I don't have a choice, dammit! Why can't you understand that?" Mac yelled back. "This is about my family, my team, securing something that means more to me than anything else!"

Of course it did, Rory realized. To Mac, the Mavericks were everything. He wouldn't change his mind or see reason. Kade and Quinn and the team would always be his top priorities. Her opinion, as his lover or his physiotherapist, didn't really count.

She was done fighting him, done fighting this. Why did she care anyway? This was a temporary affair, a fling. He was a client. At the end of the day it was his choice whether to mess up his life or not; she had no say in it. It was his arm, his career, his future, his stupidity.

But she didn't have to be part of it. Rory sucked in air, found none and pushed the button to open her window a crack. Cool, rain-tinged air swirled around her head and she lifted her face to cool her temper. "You do this and I'm out of here. Professionally and personally."

"Are you serious?" Mac demanded, his tone hard and, maybe she was being a bit fanciful, tinged with hurt.

"Hell, Rory," Kade murmured.

"It's my professional opinion that your arm is insufficiently healed to play competitive hockey. I am not going to watch you undo all the hard work we've done and I am certainly not going to watch you injure yourself further."

Mac rubbed the back of his neck and he darted a scowl at Kade. "Pretend you're not here," he told him.

"Done," Kade promptly replied.

Mac turned his attention to her and she pushed her back into her seat, not sure what he was about to say. She just knew it would be important. "Rory, listen to me."

She dropped her gaze and closed her eyes. When he looked at her like that, all open and exposed, she found it hard to concentrate.

"No, look at me…"

Rory forced her eyes open.

"I know that asking you to trust me is difficult for you. It's not something you do easily. And I know I'm asking you to put aside your learning and your experience. You think that I believe I'm invincible or a superhero. I'm not. I know I'm not… I'm just someone who knows what he is capable of, what his body is capable of. This isn't just a practice match. It's the most important practice match of my life, of Kade's life, of Quinn's. If I sit it out I'm risking this team, my friends' futures, my brothers' futures. This isn't about me and my ego."

"It will be about you if you do more damage to your arm. Then neither you nor your team will have a future… or the future you want." Couldn't he see she was trying to protect him from himself? She was trying to be the voice of reason here?

"Trust me, Rory. Please, just this once. Trust me to know what I'm doing. Stand by me, support me. Do that by coming to the practice, make sure that my arm is taped correctly. It'll be fine. I'll be fine. Be positive."

"And if I don't?" Rory demanded.

Mac just shrugged before quietly telling her that he'd play anyway.

"So, really, this entire argument has been a waste of time." Rory turned away so he didn't see the burning tears in her eyes. With blurry vision she noticed that Kade was turning down Mac's street, and within a minute he stopped the car.

The silence was as heavy as the freighter that was making its way across the bay as Mac unclipped his seatbelt and opened his door.

"One of the interns will be along shortly with your luggage," Kade told him, giving him a fist bump. Mac gripped his shoulder and squeezed before leaving the car. In the open doorway Mac bent his knees to look over his seat at Rory. "You joining me, Rory?"

No. She wanted to go home, pull on her pajamas, grab a glass of wine and cry. "I don't think so."

Mac gave her a sharp nod and his lips tightened with annoyance. "As you wish. I'm certainly not going to beg."

"Like you would know how," Rory muttered, and his eyes flashed as he slammed the door shut on her words.

Rory folded her arms across her chest and hoped Kade didn't notice that her hands were shaking. "Can you take me home, Kade?"

"Yep. Can do. Come and sit up here with me."

Ten

Was she just being stubborn, Rory wondered as Kade capably, and silently, maneuvered his very fancy sports car through the city streets? She'd always been the type of therapist who encouraged her patients to listen to their bodies, to tune in to how they were feeling. She generally listened. If they said they felt better, she trusted they were telling the truth. Why couldn't she do that with Mac? Why was she balking?

Because there was so much at stake. This one decision could have far-reaching and potentially devastating consequences. Mac loved hockey above everything else and he was risking his entire career on a still fragile tendon and a practice match. She didn't want him to lose all that he'd worked for. He might be willing to risk it, but she wasn't prepared to sanction that risk. He was thinking of the team, she was thinking about him—only him.

There had to be another way. There was always another way. They just hadn't thought about it yet.

"Would it be such a bad idea to let this corporation buy the Mavericks?" she abruptly asked Kade.

Kade considered his response. "It would definitely be different. They have a history of clearing the deck and changing all the management, the leadership. That would mean Quinn, Mac and I would be figuratively on the streets."

"Other teams would snap you up," Rory argued.

Kade nodded as he stopped at a traffic light. "Sure, but we wouldn't be on the *same* team. We've been together for nearly fifteen years, Rory. We fight and argue and irritate each other to death but we know each other. We *trust* each other."

"There's that damn word again," Rory muttered.

"One you seem to have a problem with," Kade observed, sending her a smile. He really was a very good-looking man, Rory noticed. Not Mac hot, but still…phew!

"Am I being unreasonable?" she demanded, slapping her hand repeatedly against the dashboard. "The man has been injured! It was serious. I'm trying to protect him."

"Yeah. And he's asking you to trust him to know what he's doing," Kade responded, gently removing her hand from his dashboard and dropping it back into her lap. "It's too expensive a car to be used as a punching bag, honey."

Rory winced. "Sorry." She shoved her hands under her thighs to keep them from touching something she shouldn't and sighed heavily. "He makes me nuts."

Kade laughed. "I suspect he feels the same way about you." He tapped his finger against the steering wheel before turning his head to look at her. "Mac never asks anyone for anything."

Rory looked puzzled, not sure where he was going with this.

"He injured his arm because he tried to move a fridge on his own, something either Quinn or I or any of his teammates, coaching staff, support crew, maintenance guys or office staff would've helped him with…*had he asked*."

"Try living with him for nearly two months," Rory muttered, reminded of all the arguments she'd had with Mac. "I think it has something to do with the fact that his mother was emotionally, probably physically, neglectful of him. He learned not to ask because his needs were never met," she mused.

Kade switched lanes and sent her an astonished look. "He told you about his mother?"

"Not much. A little." Rory shrugged.

"Holy crap."

Rory shrugged again, brushing off his astonishment. "Not asking for help is stupid. Everyone needs someone at some time in their lives."

"I agree. I've been trying to tell him that for years," Kade said, turning into her street. He pulled up behind a battered pickup and switched off the growling engine. Pushing his sunglasses up into his hair, he half turned in his seat. "So, we agree that we are talking about a man who is ridiculously independent and stupidly self-sufficient and hates asking for a damn thing?"

"Precisely," Rory agreed, reaching for her bag, which sat on the floor by her feet. She dug around for her house keys and pulled out the bunch with a flourish. "Found them! Yay."

Kade's hand on her arm stopped her exit from the car. When she looked back at him, his expression was serious. "Interesting then that our self-sufficient, hate-to-ask-for-anything friend asked you to be there at the practice game, asked you to trust him. Practically begged you…"

Rory sucked in a breath and scowled at him. "Oh, you're good," she muttered as she stepped out of the car.

"So I'm frequently told," Kade smugly replied. Rory shook her head as she climbed out of the low seat, charmed and amused despite the fact that he'd backed her into a corner. She turned back to look at him and he grinned at her through her open window. "Frequently followed by…*can we do that again?*"

Rory slapped a hand across her eyes.

"I'll leave your name with security. Day after tomorrow. Four p.m."

Rory managed, using an enormous amount of self-control, not to kick his very expensive tires as he pulled away.

Mac couldn't help glancing around the empty arena as he hit the rink, as at home on the ice as he was on his own two feet. Stupid to hope that she'd be here. Intensely stupid to feel disappointed. There was nothing between them except some hot sex and a couple of conversations.

He was happy the way he was, happy to have the odd affair with a beautiful woman, happy with his lone-wolf lifestyle. Wasn't he?

Not so much.

Mac glanced at the empty seats and banged his stick on the ice in frustration. One thing. He'd asked her one damn thing and she'd refused. Talk about history repeating itself… It served him right for putting himself out there. He'd learned the lesson hard and he'd learned the lesson well that when it came to personal relationships, when he asked, he didn't always receive. With his mother he'd never received anything he needed.

His childhood was over, he reminded himself.

Besides, it didn't matter, he had an investor to impress, a team to save, Vernon's legacy to protect. Mac glanced over toward the coach's area and immediately saw Quinn and Kade standing, like two mammoth sentries, on either side of a slim woman and an elderly man who bore a vague resemblance to Yoda. The woman wore jeans and a felt hat and the older man was dressed in corduroy pants and a parka. These were their investors? Where were the suits, the heels, the briefcases?

Hope you have what we need, old man, Mac thought, as the rest of the team followed him onto the ice. Hellfire, his arm was already throbbing and he'd yet to smack a puck.

Maybe Rory was right and playing wasn't such a great idea. He swung his injured arm and only sheer force of will kept him from grimacing. The team physio had strapped his arm to give it extra support but the straps were misaligned and, he was afraid, doing more harm than good.

Crapdammithell!

"McCaskill!"

Mac spun on his skates and there she stood, a resigned look on her face. His heart bumped and settled as he skated toward her. She stood next to a large man who looked familiar, and it took Mac a minute to place him. His nurse from The Annex...what was his name? Troy? Unlike Rory, Troy was wearing a huge smile and his gaze bounced from player to player in the manner of a true fan.

Mac stopped at the boards in front of Rory and sent her a slow smile. Damn, he'd missed her.

"Thanks for coming," he said, wishing he could take her into his arms, kiss her senseless. He wanted, just for a moment, to step out of these skates, out of the arena and into the heat of her mouth, to feel her pliant, slim, sexy body beneath his hands. Huh. That had never happened before. Skating, hockey, the ice…nothing could normally top that.

Mac looked at Rory, arms folded across her chest, her expression disapproving. That didn't worry him; he'd learned to look for the emotion in her eyes. Those gray depths told him everything he needed to know about how she was feeling. Yeah, she was worried, but resigned. A little scared, but he could see that she was trying to trust him, trying to push aside her intellect to give him the benefit of the doubt.

Rory narrowed her amazing eyes at him. "I'm not for one moment condoning this, and if you do any more damage I will personally kick your ass."

Deeply moved—he understood how hard this was for her—he sent her a crooked grin, silently thanking her for taking this chance on him, on them.

Rory, stubborn as always, tried to look stern but her eyes lightened with self-deprecating humor. And, as always, there was a hint of desire. For the first time, he easily recognized tenderness in her steady gaze.

And concern. She was so damned worried about him. When last had someone cared this much? Never? Mac felt his heart thump, unaccustomed to feeling saturated with emotion.

"Noted," Mac gruffly said, needing a moment to regroup. Or ten. Pulling in a deep breath he pulled off his glove with his teeth and held out his hand for Troy to shake. "Good to see you."

Troy pumped his hand with an enthusiasm that had Mac holding back a wince. "You play?" he asked Troy.

Troy nodded. "College."

"When we're finished with the practice match, maybe you'd like to borrow some skates and join us on the ice?" Mac asked.

Troy looked delighted. "Awesome. My gear is in the car so I don't need to borrow a thing. Wow. Awe. Some."

Rory rolled her eyes and looked at Mac again. "You okay?"

"Pretty much. Better now that you are here." Mac looked over the ice to the other side of the rink, where Kade and Quinn were still in deep conversation with the investor. Quinn didn't look like he was about to call the team to order anytime soon. "Speaking of, can I borrow you for a sec?"

Rory nodded and he pushed open the hinge board and stepped off the ice. He sat on a chair and looked up at Troy. "It's great that you are so damn big, dude."

Troy grinned and made a production of fluttering his eyes at him. "I didn't think you noticed."

"Cut it out, Troy," Rory muttered.

Mac laughed and jerked his thumb toward Rory. "She's more my type. But I do need you to stand in front of me so Quinn and Kade, and especially that small old guy, can't see me."

Troy, smart guy, immediately moved into position. "Like this?"

"That works." Mac pulled off his jersey and leaned down and grabbed Rory's bag, holding it out to her. "I need you to re-tape my arm. The team physio did it but he's done something wrong, it's hurting like a bitch."

Rory looked like she was about to say "I told you so," and he appreciated her effort to swallow the words. While he ripped the stabilizing tape off his arm with his other hand, taking quite a bit of arm hair with it, Rory pulled out another roll of tape. He groaned when he saw that it was bright pink. "You're kidding me, right?"

"Consider it my silent protest," Rory said, a smile touching her mouth. She was still worried about him. He could see it in her eyes, in her tight smile. But she cut the tape into strips and carefully ran the tape over his biceps and elbow, her eyes narrowed in concentration.

"Quinn's getting ready to move," Troy told them.

"Nearly there," Rory muttered, smoothing the end of the last piece of tape across the other two. She nodded. "That should give you more support, especially when you extend."

Mac did a biceps curl and he sighed with relief. He took the jersey Rory held out to him and pulled it over his head. When he was dressed, he stood up and dropped a hot, openmouthed kiss on her lips. "You are brilliant."

"Do *not* hurt yourself."

"Don't nag." Mac kissed her again, still in awe that she was here, that she was helping him, standing by him, doing this. She'd shoved aside her training, had placed her trust in him, something she so rarely gave…

Quinn's impatient whistle broke into his thoughts and his voice drifted across the ice calling them to order. Mac turned back to Rory. "Kade has invited the team and some suits to a cocktail party tonight at Siba's. You know—the bar in the Forrester Hotel? Meet me there at seven?"

Rory scowled at him but her eyes were soft and still scared. "Maybe, if you're not back in the hospital."

Mac grinned at Troy. "Such a sarcastic little ray of sunshine. Thanks for your help. I'll see you in a bit."

"She'll be there," Troy told him.

"You'll damn well go," Mac heard Troy telling Rory as he skated, slowly it had to be said, away from them. "That man is nuts about you."

He really was, he reluctantly admitted.

"You are so in love with him," Troy crowed as he flung his hockey bag into the trunk of his battered SUV. Rory eyed his piece of rusty metal; she hated driving anywhere with Troy because she was quite certain her chances of, well, dying were increased a thousand percent whenever its tires met the road.

Rory, her hand on the passenger-door handle, looked down at the front wheel and sighed her relief. The tires had been changed and Troy had promised her it had just had its biyearly service. Rory had replied that it needed a funeral service but she'd eventually abandoned her idea of taking a taxi to the arena and allowed Troy to drive her in his chariot of death.

Rory tugged at the handle and cursed when it refused to open. Troy, already behind the wheel, reached across and thumped the panel and the door sprung open, just missing hitting Rory in the face. "I hate this car," she muttered, climbing in.

Troy nodded his head. "Yeah, me too. But it's paid for, thereby freeing up money for the nursing home."

Rory, grateful that they'd left the subject of Mac and her feelings, sent him a concerned look. "How is your mom? Any more walkabouts?"

Troy momentarily closed his eyes. "No, she's fine. Well, as fine as she can be." He stared at the luxury car parked next to them. "I've found a home just outside the city, a place that looks fantastic. They have space for her, could take her tomorrow, but I just can't afford it."

"I could…" She had to offer to loan him the money. He wouldn't take it, but she wished he would. He was her best friend, an almost-brother…why didn't he realize that she'd move mountains for him if she could?

Troy sighed. "I love you for offering but…no. I can't." Troy turned the key and the car spluttered and died. He cursed, cranked it again and Rory held her breath. It rumbled, jerked and eventually put-putted to life. "You wouldn't think that I'd just had it serviced, would you?"

"Nope. Then again, I think trying to service this car is like putting a Band-Aid on a slit throat."

"Nice," Troy said as they pulled out of the arena parking lot. "Let's get back to the interesting stuff. When did you fall in love with Mac?"

"Ten years ago," Rory replied without thinking. She jerked up and scowled at her friend. "I didn't just say that out loud, did I?"

Troy grinned. "You so did."

"Dammit." She didn't want to be in love with Mac. That meant she had to give him up, she'd have to retreat, do what she did best to protect herself and fade away. Loving Mac carried too many risks, too much potential heartache.

"So, are you going to keep Mac around or are you going to dump him when he gets too close?"

Lord, Troy knew her well. She had to make a token protest. "I don't do that."

Troy snorted. "Honey, you *always* do that. You meet a guy, you go on a couple of dates and when you think something might have a chance of developing, you find an excuse to dump him. You have massive trust issues."

"So does Mac. He also has abandonment issues!" she added.

"It's not a competition, Rory! Jeez," Troy snapped as they approached the first set of traffic lights. "Man, these brakes are soft. Didn't they check them?" They stopped and Troy looked at her. "Okay...continue."

Rory stared at the drops of rain running down the windshield. She might as well tell him, she thought, he knew everything else about her. "You know how Shay loves to tease me about stealing her boyfriends?"

"Yeah, and you get all huffy and defensive and embarrassed."

"She was dating Mac when she walked in on us...we were about to kiss," Rory quietly stated. "How would she feel if I started dating him, started a relationship with him?"

"I bet she'd be fine with it." Tory rolled his eyes, and without taking his eyes off the road instructed his cell phone to call Shay.

"What are you doing?" Rory demanded.

"Calling Shay," Troy replied, as if she were the biggest idiot in the world. Which she was, because she was talking to him about Mac.

"Troyks!" Shay's bubbly voice filled the car.

"Hey, oh gorgeous one. I'm in the car with Rory and we have a question for you."

"Shoot," Shay replied.

"It's not important—" Rory stated, leaning sideways to talk into the phone.

"Back off, sister." Troy growled. "Rory's using you as an excuse not to date Mac McCaskill. So how would you feel about them getting it on? You know, even though you're married to the hunkiest homicide detective in the city," Troy added, his tone wry.

"My Mac?" Shay asked.

Her Mac, Rory scowled. And didn't that just answer her question right away?

Shay was quiet for a minute. "Well, judging from the way they were eyeing each other way back when, I'd say it's about ten years overdue. A part of me is still slightly jealous that he never looked at me like that."

Like what? "Nothing happened!" Rory protested.

"Maybe, but you both wanted it to," Shay responded. "I think he'd be really good for you."

"He almost cheated on you, with me!" Rory half yelled. Okay, the straws she was grabbing were elusive but she was giving it her best shot.

"He was twenty-four, we were having problems and whenever the two of you were in the same room you created an electrical storm. Besides, as you said, nothing happened. It's not that big a deal."

Shay must've forgotten that being kissed by Mac was a very big deal.

"Go for it, Rorks."

Okay, who was this woman and what had she done with Rory's insecure, neurotic sister? "Are you high?" Rory demanded. "He's a commitment-phobic man-slut! He changes women like he changes socks!"

"I don't think that's true. Not so much and not any-more." Shay laughed. "I liked Mac. I still like Mac. He was a good egg and he put up with an enormous amount of drama from me. You should date him, Rorks, give this relationship thing a spin. Who knows, you might end up being... I don't know...*happy*?"

Troy looked triumphant and Rory placed her hands over her face. "You are high. It's the only explanation..."

"Or that my hot detective husband came home for lunch and, well, let's just say food wasn't a priority," Shay smugly stated.

Troy groaned and Rory let out a strangled *ewww*. Shay disconnected the call on a happy laugh. Rory stared out the window for a long time before turning to Troy. "Do you agree?" she quietly asked him. "Do you think I should take a chance, see where this goes?"

"Do you really love him?"

Rory thought about his question, not wanting to give a glib answer. "I'm worried that it's temporary craziness, that when the fire dies down, I'll run…or he'll run…and someone will get hurt. I'm scared to get hurt."

"Aren't we all?" Troy reached across the seats to grip her fingers in his. "Yeah, it might fail. It might burn out. You might get hurt."

"So encouraging," Rory murmured.

Troy sent her a sweet, sweet smile. "But, honey, what if it doesn't? What if this is the amazing love story you've been waiting for? What if he is the big *it*? What if it works?"

Rory looked at him and slumped in her seat. "Humpf."

Troy laughed, pulled his hand back and then his face turned serious. "Don't run, honey, not this time. Stand still and see what happens. Will you?"

Rory smiled at him and, liking the connection, reached across the seat to link her fingers back into his. "Yeah. I think I will. If—"

Troy groaned. "Oh, God."

Rory ignored his protest "—you will consider borrowing some money from me to move your mom into that home."

Troy sighed. "Diabolical."

Rory's smile was smug. "I try."

Eleven

Mac ran a hand through his hair and unbuttoned the jacket to his gray suit. He took a sip of his whiskey and looked at his watch; Rory was late but that was okay. He needed a moment to himself, to think, even if he had to take that moment while standing in a crowded cocktail bar, surrounded by his friends and colleagues. He sipped again and ignored the pain in his arm—thanks to his session on the ice—and the noise around him, ignored the insults, jokes and crude comments flying over his head. The pain wasn't as bad as he'd thought it would be but he definitely didn't have the power and strength in the limb that he was used to. His teammates had tried to cover for him and he was grateful for their efforts. Hopefully they'd done a good enough job to fool Bayliss.

On the plus side, Mac thought, Rory *had* arrived at the practice. He'd been surprised at the relief he felt, as-

tonished that as soon as he saw her, his heart rate accel-
erated but his soul settled down.

She was there. Everything was all right in his world.
When had that happened? When had she become so important to his emotional well-being that she could calm
him with one look, with one sarcastic comment?

*If you do any more damage I will personally kick your
ass.*

It wasn't an "I love you" or "I will support you no matter what," but it was Rory's version of "Okay, this one
time, I'll trust you." He could work with that.

God, he *wanted* to work through whatever this was
with her. Was it love? He didn't know, but he knew it was
something. Many women had caught his eye over the
years, and he'd slept with quite a few of them—probably
more than he should have—but Rory was still the only
person who'd come close to capturing his heart.

But…and, hell, there was always a *but*, Mac thought,
staring down at the floor between his feet. *But* he didn't
know if he could spend the rest of his life reassuring her
that he wouldn't cheat, that he wouldn't let her down.
He *wouldn't* cheat, but there would come a time when
he disappointed her, when he wouldn't be there for her,
when things went wrong. Would she bail at the first hint
of trouble or would she cut him some slack?

He was a man, one with little experience of this thing
called a relationship or how to be in it, and he knew, for
sure, that he'd mess up. When he did, and it was a *when*
and not an *if*, would she talk it out or would she walk? If
she walked, would he be able to stand it? The rational side
of him suggested it might be better not to take the chance,
to call it quits now before anyone—him—got hurt. That
would be the clever, the practical, the smart thing to do.

Except that would mean not having Rory in his life, and he didn't think he could go back to his empty life, hopping from one feminine bed to another. Nor did he think he could become a monk. Both options sucked. Mac scrubbed his hand over his face…

Relationships were so damn complicated and exhausting.

"Mac."

Quinn nudged his elbow into Mac's ribs and Mac turned to look down into the weathered face of Kade's investor. He'd changed into an ugly brown suit and combed his thin hair but he still didn't look like someone who could provide what they needed. *Don't judge a book by its cover*, Mac reminded himself. The granddaughter looked spectacular, Mac noticed, because he was a man and that was what men did. Her bright red hair was pulled back into a low ponytail and her wide eyes darted between him, Kade and Quinn.

Kade cleared his throat. "Mr. Bayliss, meet Mac McCaskill. Mac, Mr. Bayliss and his granddaughter, Wren."

Mac shook the man's hand with its surprisingly strong grip and made the appropriate comments. After they exchanged the usual pleasantries, Kade and Quinn drew Wren into another conversation and Mac tried not to squirm when Bayliss regarded him with a steady, penetrating look. "You've definitely lost power in your arm. Your slap shot was weak and ineffectual."

Hell, Mac had hoped he wouldn't notice. The old man was sharper than he looked. Mac pasted a nothing-to-worry-about expression on his face and shrugged. "I pulled a muscle a while back and this was my first practice. It'll be fine soon. I'm regaining power every day."

"We'll see. I'm not sure if you will ever regain your form."

Mac felt like the old man had sucker-punched him. "That's not something you need to worry about." He forced himself to keep his voice even. "I *will* be back to full strength soon and I *will* lead this team next season."

"We'll see," Bayliss repeated, and Mac wanted to scream. "Luckily, I see enough talent in this team to want to invest whether you are part of it or not, whether you play or not. It was nice meeting you, Mr. McCaskill. We'll talk again."

Mac stared at Bayliss's back as he and Kade walked away, then he forced himself to sip his drink, to look as though he hadn't been slapped.

Whether he played or not? Hell, if he didn't play, what could he do for the team? Kade was the management guy. Despite his youth, Quinn was a damn excellent coach… what did Mac bring to the party apart from his skill on the ice? If playing wasn't an option, there was no way he was going to float around the Mavericks on the outside looking in, making a nuisance of himself. He was either a full partner or not. A full contributor or not.

God, *not*. Was that a possibility?

"Want to dance, Mac?"

He blinked at the perfectly made-up face to his right and couldn't put a name to the gorgeous blonde. He looked toward the entrance, still didn't see Rory and decided what the hell. Dancing was better than standing there like an idiot freaking out over his future. He nodded, handed his glass to a passing waiter and allowed the blonde to lead him to the dance floor. When they reached the small circle, he placed his hands on her hips and wished she was Rory. He could talk to Rory about the bombshell he'd just experienced, about the fear holding him in its icy grip.

She'd help him make sense of it, Mac thought as his dance partner moved closer, her breasts brushing his chest. He felt nothing, no corresponding flash of desire and no interest down south. Huh, so if things didn't work out with Rory it looked like he'd be going the monk route.

He tried to put some distance between them but the dance floor was crowded and there was little room to move. Mac sighed when she laid her head on his shoulder. She didn't feel right, smell right; she was too tall, too buxom, too curvy...where the hell was Rory?

Over the heads of most of his fellow dancers he looked toward the door and there she was, dressed in a scarlet cocktail dress he wanted to rip off with his teeth. She had a small bag clutched under her arm and she was holding her cell phone... She was here, *finally*, and all was well with his world.

Then he lifted his eyes back up to hers and his heart plummeted at the expression on her face. Her eyes were huge and wide, her skin pale and she looked like she'd been slapped. Even from a distance he could tell her eyes were full of tears and her bottom lip trembled. *Oh, crap...*

He wanted to yell that her addition sucked. Two plus two did not equal seventeen! He was just dancing with the woman, not doing her on the dance floor. He hadn't given his dance partner one thought; in fact, he'd been desperately waiting for Rory to arrive to rescue him...

One dance and the accusations, as sure as sugar, were flying, silent and deadly. He could read her thoughts as clearly as if she'd bellowed them across the room. *I can't trust you. You've let me down. You've disappointed me.*

The voices in his head mocked him. Hell, even his mother's voice came to join the suck-fest.

You'll never be quite good enough. This is why you should keep your distance. This hurt is gonna be your constant companion for the rest of your life. You don't deserve normal and you sure as hell don't deserve love... She doesn't trust you. She never will. You always manage to mess it up...

The expression on Rory's face put it all into perspective. They'd been back together for a day, sort of, and with one dance with a complete stranger, he'd been unfairly fouled. And if that wasn't life telling him this would never work then he didn't know what was.

Rory looked down at her phone, lifted it to her ear and bit her lip. She sent him another look, one he couldn't quite interpret, spun on her heel and left the room. She was running as hard and as fast as she could. Mentally, emotionally and, dammit, literally.

That was that, Mac thought, walking off the dance floor toward the bar. He felt like he was carrying a fifty-pound anvil around in his chest instead of a heart. Since he wasn't about to have sex in the near future and he might be saying goodbye to his career with the Mavericks, he might as well have a drink.

Or many.

Rory sat next to Troy's bed, holding his hand and willing him to wake up. She'd been at his bedside for twelve hours straight and he was still unconscious. Rory looked at his medical chart at the end of his bed and told herself there was no point in reading it again, it wouldn't change the facts.

Troy, on his way to start his evening shift at The

Annex next door, had failed to stop at a traffic light and plowed his rust bucket into the side of a truck. He'd smacked his head on the steering wheel and had swelling on the brain. When the swelling subsided they would reevaluate his condition.

That damn car, Rory thought, placing her forehead on his cold wrist. Guess the car service hadn't included checking the brakes. The car was a write-off, Rory had been told by the paramedics; it was their opinion that he'd been lucky to escape alive.

Rory shuddered. Troy was her best friend and she couldn't imagine her life without him. And speaking of people who were important to her, where the hell was Mac? She'd risked using her cell in the ICU and left two brief, urgent, *desperate* messages on his cell for him to call her but he'd yet to respond. Why not? Why was he ignoring her? What had changed?

Sure she'd seen him dancing with that blonde but that didn't worry her. Anyone with a brain in her head would've noticed that it had been the blonde making all the moves. Mac had been supremely disinterested. In fact, despite the devastating news she'd just received about Troy—one of the nurses in the ER had texted her as soon as he was rushed in—she'd immediately noticed Mac looked distracted, worried. His eyes were bleak and that telltale muscle in his jaw was jumping.

Was this what their life would be like going forward, Rory wondered? Her being pushed down his priority list because there was something more important he needed to do, somewhere more interesting he needed to be? Could she cope with playing second fiddle to his career, his friends, his teammates? She'd done that with her father and she'd hated every moment.

She couldn't do that, not again. She loved Mac with everything she had but she wouldn't sacrifice herself for him, for any man. She didn't expect him to jump hurdles when she asked for any little thing, but Troy's critical condition was pretty mammoth. She had a right to ask Mac for his emotional support, to be there for her. At the very least, he could reply to her damn messages!

Damn, life had been so uncomplicated when she'd been unattached. Boring, but simple.

Mac, sitting on the couch in Kade's office, propped his feet onto the coffee table and stared at the massive photograph on Kade's wall. It was of the team, naturally, minutes after the final whistle of the Stanley Cup Final. He and Quinn and Kade had their arms around each other, all of them wearing face-splitting grins. Would he ever be that happy again, Mac wondered?

"How long are you going to sit over there and stare moodily at my wall?" Kade asked, replacing the handset of his desk phone into its cradle. "'Cause I've got to tell you, it's getting old."

Mac lifted a lazy middle finger and kept staring at the photograph. "That was a really good day at the office."

Kade's eyes flicked to the photograph. "It was. Now are you going to sit here and reminisce about the past or are you going to tell me what's got your lacy panties in a twist?"

Mac pulled a face. Over the past four days he'd been avoiding his friends to spend his days on his balcony staring out at the view, and he was, frankly, tired of himself and his woe-is-me attitude.

Rory and he were kaput. Admittedly, she had left two messages on his voice mail the night she bolted from the bar, which he'd ignored. Really, what was there to say? She either trusted him or she didn't, and it was clear that she didn't.

There was no point in discussing the issue.

Game over. Move on.

"Anymore news from the Bayliss camp?" Mac asked, dropping his feet to the floor and reaching for the bottle of water he'd placed on the coffee table.

Kade leaned back in his chair. "I'm expecting to see the first draft of an agreement today."

Even if Mac wasn't part of the day-to-day equation he'd be a part owner, and he was glad to see progress. At least with Kade and Quinn at the helm the Mavericks would have a good chance of keeping their identity. "That's good news."

Kade shrugged. "We'll see what the document contains. I know that Wren, the granddaughter and a PR specialist, has some strong ideas about what she wants to happen with the franchise."

Mac rubbed his jaw, thick with stubble. "Yeah, I don't think I'm part of those franchise plans."

Kade frowned at him. "What do you mean?"

"Didn't you hear what Bayliss said the other night?" When Kade shook his head, Mac explained, "He noticed that my arm was weak and expressed doubts as to whether I would still have a place on the Mavericks next season."

Kade narrowed his eyes. "That will never be his decision to make." His eyes radiated hot frustration even though his voice was calm. "He's providing marketing and merchandising opportunities, access to bigger sponsorship deals, connections. He will not be allowed to interfere with the team and its selection."

"Yeah, I don't think he got that memo," Mac replied in his driest voice. He took a deep breath and bit his lip. "If I, and my injury, become a point of contention, I'll back off. If it means keeping the team out of the clutches of that soul-sucking corporation then I'll be a silent partner."

Kade rolled his eyes. "Shut the hell up, McCaskill, you suck as a martyr. You will be back, at full strength, by the time the season starts or I will kick your ass. And I can still do it," Kade warned him.

"You can try." Mac stood up and crossed to the floor-to-ceiling windows. When he turned back to Kade his expression was serious. "We should think of a plan B, just in case I'm not."

"Rory told me you've made excellent progress."

Mac shrugged. He had, but it would take a lot more work, and he'd keep at it. He'd keep pushing himself but Rory wouldn't be there to monitor his progress, to keep him in check. The chances were high that he'd push himself too hard and do some serious damage. Or, because he was scared to make the situation worse, he wouldn't do enough.

Funny how he'd work his ass off for his arm but not for his heart.

Mac jerked at the thought and felt like a million lightbulbs had switched on in his head. Where had that thought come from? Did it really matter? The truth was the truth…and what he was thinking about his arm should apply to his life, as well. He and Rory had started something ten years ago, and because they were young, and dumb, they'd walked away from it not recognizing what it actually was.

A connection, a future, safety. She'd always been what he'd needed, what his soul needed.

Either way, without her, he was screwed. He was screwed anyway; his arm ached, his heart ached. He was thoroughly miserable. He wanted to see her. He needed to see her. He needed to see if she also thought they had something worthwhile, a connection worth working *on*. There was a good possibility she'd say no but he was willing to take the risk, to do the work. Nothing worth achieving came easy and if he failed, yeah it would suck but he refused to live with regret. He knew what he wanted and was prepared to work his ass off to get it.

He wanted Rory.

And if he failed to win her, he'd survive. He always did.

But he had no intention of failing. Because anything was better than this Rory-shaped emptiness inside him.

He belted toward the door, tossing a "Later" over his shoulder and ignoring the deeply sarcastic "Good chat" that drifted out of Kade's office.

Five days after his accident Troy finally opened his eyes. Three hours after that, when he started arguing with his nurse, Rory realized she could leave him. She could go home to her own bed and have a decent night's sleep. She could spend more than a couple of hours in her apartment, eat something other than fast food, cut down on her coffee.

Leaving Troy and the nurse to bicker, she walked out of his room. Once she was in the hallway, she placed her forearm against the nearest wall and buried her face in the crook of her elbow. Troy was going to be fine. She could stop worrying and start thinking about something other than planning his funeral. Rory felt the tears track down her face and thought how ridiculous it was that she was crying now, when he was finally out of danger, when it was all but over.

Intellectually she knew her reaction was because she could finally relax. She could stop the continuous praying, the bargaining with God. Stupid, but human nature, she thought. Saints alive, she was so tired.

Rory recognized the big hands on her hips and sighed when Mac gently turned her around. Through her tears she noticed his gentle, compassionate expression, the tenderness in his eyes. Even though she was mad at him—he'd certainly taken his time getting here!—she was still ridiculously glad to see him. Her throat tightened as the strength of her tears increased. She felt like she would shatter from the effort it took to not fling herself against his chest and burrow into his warmth.

He took the decision from her by sliding his big hand around the back of her neck and pulling her to his chest. Her arms, shaky with exhaustion, slid around his waist. His other arm held her as her knees buckled.

"It's okay, honey. I've got you," he said in her ear. "I've got you and I'm not letting you go."

She wished she could believe him but she was so fatigued, so emotionally drained she couldn't think. All she knew was that Mac was finally here and she could rest. So she did. Rory wasn't sure how long she stood in his arms. All she knew was that he was strong and solid and *there*. She wasn't alone.

When she'd regained some of her equilibrium, she stepped back, dashed a hand against her wet cheeks and stared at his hard chest. "How did you know I was here?" she asked in a brittle voice. Her tears, it seemed, were still very close to the surface.

Mac pushed her hair off her forehead. "Well, since

your phone has been off and you weren't at your apartment, I started to get worried. So I called Shay and asked about you."

"And she told you I was here?"

"Mmm, after coercing season tickets out of me," Mac said on a small smile that quickly died. "You should've told me about Troy. Why didn't you?"

Rory wasn't so tired that she couldn't react to that. "I thought my rushing from that bar was a good enough hint that something was drastically wrong! And you could've returned my messages!"

"I thought you were running from me because you saw me dancing with that blonde."

"She wasn't worth worrying about. No, I'd just heard about Troy."

Mac closed his eyes in obvious frustration. "I am such an idiot."

"No arguments from me," Rory said, stepping out of his reach. She gestured to Troy's door. "Troy had an accident. It was touch and go for a while."

"I know. Shay told me. She also told me you've spent every minute of the day with him since it happened."

Rory rubbed the back of her neck. "Not every minute. I went home to shower."

"He doesn't have any family?" Mac closed the distance between them.

"Only a mother who has dementia. That's why Troy was driving a crappy car, all his spare cash goes to her nursing home fees."

Mac's hand drew circles on her back and she had to restrain herself from purring like a cat. Rory, knowing how his touch could relax her and tempt her to forgive him too easily, snapped her spine straight. "Anyway, why are you here? I suppose you've been worried about your physio sessions." She tried to sound breezy but it didn't come out that way. "Sorry about that."

Mac's smile was one she'd never seen before, a combination of tenderness, protectiveness and love. It scared the hell out of her.

"Look, I'd appreciate it if you gave me a day to get some rest and then we can get back on track and schedule some sessions. Have you been doing your exercises?" she demanded.

Mac shook his head and bent his knees so they were eye to eye. "Rory?"

"Yes?"

"Shut up for a sec, okay?" Mac waited to see whether she would talk again, and when she didn't, he nodded his satisfaction. "So this is what is going to happen—I'm taking you back to my place and you're going to stand, or sit, in my shower until you are pink and boneless. Then you are going to eat something, soup maybe, and then we are going to climb into bed where you will sleep in my arms. Got it?"

"Uh..." She was beyond tired. She couldn't even find the energy to respond, let alone argue.

"Just say yes."

Rory nodded as tears welled again. "Excellent." Mac wound his arm around her shoulders and walked her down the passage toward the exit. "I like it when I get to boss you around," he teased.

Rory wasn't too tired to allow him to get away with that comment. "Don't get used to it, McCaskill. It's only because I'm exhausted."

Rory opened her lids and squinted in the bright sunlight stabbing her eyes. She placed her arm in front of her face to cut out the glare, looking out from under her arm across the pale floorboards to the partially open doors that led to a balcony.

A pair of very large sneakers were on the floor and a T-shirt, one she didn't recognize, was draped over the back of a black bucket chair. Through the open doors she saw a pair of bare feet up on a wrought-iron table, perilously close to a carafe of coffee.

Coffee. She'd kill for some. Rory sat up, looked down and couldn't help noticing she was naked. Casting her mind back, she remembered Mac carrying her up the stairs to his bedroom, stripping her down and pushing her into bed. She had a vague recollection of a warm body wrapped around hers as she fell asleep. Clasping the sheet to her chest, she sat up and pushed her hair out of her eyes, running her tongue over her teeth.

Coffee or a toothbrush? Either would do nicely right now.

"You look good in my bed."

Rory turned her head to see Mac standing in the doorway leading in from the balcony wearing a pair of straight-legged track pants and a black T-shirt. His hair was messed and his beard was about three days past stubble and she thought he was the sexiest creature she'd ever laid eyes on.

"Hi," she said, self-conscious.

"Hi back," Mac replied on a smile. "You're looking better, thank God. You scared me…you were totally out of it."

"I felt shell-shocked," Rory admitted, looking around. "Can you pass me something to wear?"

"Why? I rather like you naked," Mac replied, teasing. He picked up the black T-shirt that lay across his chair and held it up. "I did a load of laundry earlier and I tossed your clothes in too. Will this do?"

"You can do laundry?" Rory asked, amused as she caught the T-shirt he tossed her way.

"I can do lots of things," Mac replied, his voice quieter. "Would you like some coffee?"

Rory nodded and watched as he walked back out onto the balcony and returned with a cup of coffee, which he handed over. Rory took a sip and quickly realized it was barely warm but strong enough to put scales on her chest. Okay, so Mac wasn't as together as he sounded, she thought. Very good to know that she wasn't the only one in the room wondering what she was doing here.

What *was* she doing here?

Mac sat on the edge of the bed, his bended knee touching her thigh. He stared down at the floor, and when he spoke, his voice vibrated with emotion. "I once told you that hockey is everything to me, that it was the highest priority in my life."

"Mmm-hmm?"

"It has been my life for the past fifteen years. It's afforded me this amazing lifestyle and I've loved every moment I've spent on and off the ice."

Okay, he wasn't telling her anything new here.

"I love you more."

Rory's mouth fell open. Had he really said what she thought he'd said? She needed to make sure. "Say that again?"

"You are the highest priority in my life. You make it better, brighter and more fun." Mac sent her an uncertain look and his hand gripped her thigh covered by the sheet. "Look, I know I screwed up. I know you needed me, and I let my insecurities get the best of me. I hate that I let you down. I want to do better. I *will* do better. And I know you have trust issues too. You say you don't do relationships but I'd like us to try.

"Before you say no let me say this—I will never cheat on you, I promise. Actually, the closest I've ever come to cheating was that kiss we shared. I've never been involved with anyone deeply enough for this to be an issue but, in my defense, I've always ended one affair before I started another."

"Um…okay?"

"But you aren't an affair. You are the only person I can be real with. Someone I can really talk to… You are my best friend. I'm sorry I wasn't there for you. I want to make it up to you. I'll spend my whole life making it up to you, if you'll let me."

Rory placed her hand over her heart, her lower lip trembling as she listened to this innately masculine man humble himself before her.

"Give me a shot, Rory. Give *us* a shot," Mac pleaded, emotion radiating from his eyes.

"What if we fail, Mac?" she asked in a quiet voice.

"Aw, baby…" Mac blew out a breath and shrugged. "I don't fail and you're too important to me to let that happen. But if we do, then we'll go down knowing we gave it our best, knowing we loved rather than living a half-life, guarding our hearts and thoughts and emotions."

"You make it sound so easy," Rory whispered.

"It'll be anything but easy," Mac replied. "It'll be tough, and we'll fight and we'll sometimes wonder what the hell we were thinking. But through it all we'll love each other." Mac pushed an agitated hand through his hair. "We'll have to spend time apart when I'm on the road. But you'll have your own practice to keep you busy and we'll talk every night and text every hour. We'll spend every minute we can together and we'll work at it, dammit, because the one thing we are both good at is hard work, Rorks. If we work at loving each other as hard as we do at everything else, we can't do anything but succeed."

It was a compelling argument, Rory thought, wishing she could throw her fear aside and launch herself into his arms, into their future. "I'm scared, Mac."

"So am I." Mac leaned forward and rested his forehead against hers. "We can be scared together. Do you think you can love me, Rorks? Some day and at some stage?"

Rory pulled her head back, astounded at his comment. She placed a hand on his chest. "You think I don't love you?"

"Well, you haven't exactly uttered the words," Mac said conversationally, but she could feel his galloping heartbeat under her hand.

Rory linked her arms around his neck and looked into his eyes. "I do love you. I think I fell in love with you the first time you almost kissed me." Rory placed her forehead against his temple. "I thought I was going to be alone forever but I can't be. It's no longer who I am, who I've become by knowing you. Who I am now is someone who loves you—now, tomorrow, forever. I might have had a hand in rehabilitating your arm but you rehabilitated my heart."

Mac's hand on her neck tightened in response. "Oh, Rorks, you slay me. So, we agree that we love each other and this is it?"

"I so agree to that."

"Excellent." Mac grinned. "Now, let's move on to another important issue…"

Rory lifted her eyebrows as he pulled his T-shirt over his head. "I think we've covered the high points."

Mac dropped a hard, openmouthed kiss on her lips before lifting her shirt up and over her head. "Getting you naked is always going to be very high on my agenda."

Rory curled her hand around his neck as he pushed her back into the pillows. His eyes were soft as they connected with hers. He swallowed, started to speak, cleared his throat and tried again. "Everything that is most important to me is here, right now. I'm holding my world in my arms," Mac said, his tone low and soaked with tenderness. "It feels good."

"It feels amazing," Rory replied, her voice cracking with emotion. Blinking her tears away, she lifted her hips and wiggled. Her smile turned naughty as her hand drifted down his back to rest on one very fine butt cheek. "*You* feel amazing. So, McCaskill, are you going to kiss me or what?"

Mac grinned. "Oh, yeah. Anytime, anywhere—*everywhere*—for the rest of your life. Starting right now..."

* * * * *

MILLS & BOON®

Desire™

PASSIONATE AND DRAMATIC LOVE STORIES

A sneak peek at next month's titles...

In stores from 2nd June 2016:

The Baby Inheritance – Maureen Child *and*
Expecting the Rancher's Child – Sara Orwig

A Little Surprise for the Boss – Elizabeth Lane *and*
Saying Yes to the Boss – Andrea Laurence

His Stolen Bride – Barbara Dunlop *and*
The Renegade Returns – Dani Wade

Available at WHSmith, Tesco, Asda, Eason, Amazon and Apple

Just can't wait?
Buy our books online a month before they hit the shops!
visit www.millsandboon.co.uk

These books are also available in eBook format!

Lynne Graham has sold 35 million books!

To settle a debt, she'll have to become his mistress...

Nikolai Drakos is determined to have his revenge against the man who destroyed his sister. So stealing his enemy's intended fiancé seems like the perfect solution! Until Nikolai discovers that woman is Ella Davies...

Read on for a tantalising excerpt from Lynne Graham's 100th book,

BOUGHT FOR THE GREEK'S REVENGE

'Mistress,' Nikolai slotted in cool as ice.

Shock had welded Ella's tongue to the roof of her mouth because he was sexually propositioning her and nothing could have prepared her for that. She wasn't drop-dead gorgeous... *he* was! Male heads didn't swivel when Ella walked down the street because she had neither the length of leg nor the curves usually deemed necessary to attract such attention. Why on earth could he be making *her* such an offer?

'But we don't even know each other,' she framed dazedly. 'You're a stranger...'

'If you live with me I won't be a stranger for long,' Nikolai pointed out with monumental calm. And the very sound of that inhuman calm and cool forced her to flip round and settle distraught eyes on his lean darkly handsome face.

'You can't be serious about this!'

'I assure you that I am deadly serious. Move in and I'll forget your family's debts.'

'But it's a *crazy* idea!' she gasped.

'It's not crazy to me,' Nikolai asserted. 'When I want anything, I go after it hard and fast.'

Her lashes dipped. Did he want her like that? Enough to track her down, buy up her father's debts, and try and buy rights to her and her body along with those debts? The very idea of that made her dizzy and plunged her brain into even greater turmoil. 'It's immoral... it's blackmail.'

'It's definitely *not* blackmail. I'm giving you the benefit of a choice you didn't have before I came through that door,' Nikolai Drakos fielded with a glittering cool. 'That choice is yours to make.'

'Like hell it is!' Ella fired back. 'It's a complete cheat of a supposed offer!'

Nikolai sent her a gleaming sideways glance. 'No the real cheat was you kissing me the way you did last year and then saying no and acting as if I had grossly insulted you,' he murmured with lethal quietness.

'You *did* insult me!' Ella flung back, her cheeks hot as fire while she wondered if her refusal that night had started off his whole chain reaction. What else could possibly be driving him?

Nikolai straightened lazily as he opened the door. 'If you take offence that easily, maybe it's just as well that the answer is no.'

Visit **www.millsandboon.co.uk/lynnegraham**
to order yours!

MILLS & BOON®

MILLS & BOON®

The One Summer Collection!

2 free books!

Join these heroines on a relaxing
holiday escape, where a summer fling
could turn in to so much more!

Order yours at **www.millsandboon.co.uk/onesummer**

0616_MB523_OSA

MILLS & BOON®

Mills & Boon have been at the heart of romance since 1908... and while the fashions may have changed, one thing remains the same: from pulse-pounding passion to the gentlest caress, we're always known how to bring romance alive.

Now, we're delighted to present you with these irresistible illustrations, inspired by the vintage glamour of our covers. So indulge your wildest dreams and unleash your imagination as we present the most iconic Mills & Boon moments of the last century.

Visit **www.millsandboon.co.uk/ArtofRomance** to order yours!

AOR